WINDY CITY BILLIONAIRES SERIES
BOOK TWO

YINN QUIRÓS

CONTENTS

Content Warning

Trigger warnings include, but are not limited to: Sexual explicit content, talks about anxiety, panic attacks and domestic violence (not between characters).

Your mental health matters. Please stay safe.

"The most beautiful part is, I wasn't even looking when I found you."
—Autumn

*For those who've been strong for too long and
dream of someone to lean on—I hope you
find them, just like I did.*

*But until then... just flip the page—Lorenzo is
waiting for you.*

Playlist

Bed Chem | **Sabrina Carpenter**
Blank Space (Taylor's Version) | **Taylor Swift**
Daddy Issues (Remix) | **The Neighbourhood, Syd**
Dandelions | **Ruth B.**
Escápate Conmigo | **Wisin, Ozuna**
Family Line | **Conan Gray**
Fake Happy | **Paramore**
Heart Attack – Rock Version | **Demi Lovato**
Hunger | **Ross Copperman**
Intrusive Thoughts | **Natalie Jane**

Playlist

Look After You | The Fray
Maybe | James Arthur
MÁS DE UNA VEZ | Rauw Alejandro
Never Let Me Go | Florence + The Machine
Overdrive | Conan Gray
Poker Face | First to Eleven
Save My Life | Niall Horan
Somebody to Someone | Natalie Jane
Snow On The Beach | Taylor Swift, Lana Del Rey
Tenerife Sea | Ed Sheeran

One year ago...

Dizzy from the three orgasms I just had, I rest my head against the cold wall, its chill seeping into my skin. My chest heaves as I try to catch my breath, and my heart's rhythmic pounding starts to gradually slow as the post-orgasm high wears off.

I'm pretty sure I just had the best sex of my life.

No. I'm *absolutely* sure I did.

The only sound breaking our silence is the thumping music from outside this small cleaning closet. For most people, the after-sex haze is awkward, and while I'm not too fond of silence typically, I prefer it in this case. Small talk isn't what I'm after. All I'm looking for is release and the adrenaline that rushes through my body every time I do something thrilling. Like having sex in a cleaning closet at one of the most famous and busiest nightclubs in Downtown Chicago, for example.

Running my fingers through my hair, I do my best to smooth it out. There's no saving it at this point with how sweaty I am, but I'm not about to look like I'm doing the walk of shame. Holding onto one of the shelves where the cleaning supplies are kept, I adjust the spaghetti straps of my red double-slit minidress and look around for my black leather clutch. I know I had it when we came in here. But between the intense make out session and mind-blowing orgasms, I lost it.

I flip on the light switch, but the yellow glow barely illuminates the room. There are way too many things in this closet; I have no idea how I'm going to find it. I knew I should have brought a bigger bag. Or no bag at all.

Always no bag at all, Sophia. Seriously, have you learned nothing?

"Do you see my clutch anywhere?" I ask, squinting as I keep looking around.

"Your what?" he asks as he adjusts his belt.

I groan. "My small purse. I know I had it when we came in here."

He frowns, looking around, then crouches and picks it up. "Here."

"Thanks."

As I'm grabbing it, our fingers graze, and the same electric charge I felt when he placed his hands on my hips before we started dancing passes between us again, making my body shiver.

"Listen," he starts.

I raise my hand to stop him from speaking. "Save it. I don't want your number, and you certainly don't want mine."

He takes a step back in this ridiculously small room, hitting the shelf with his back and knocking down most of the cleaning supplies.

"What makes you think I want your number?" he asks, amusement seeping into his voice as he raises an eyebrow.

I roll my eyes and pull out the small mirror I carry with

me everywhere along with my favorite lip gloss and quickly apply a fresh coat. "Unless you were about to ask for a high five for what we did, I don't see what else you have to say to me."

My eyes lift from the mirror, and I make the terrible mistake of locking onto his gaze. His eyes are the most beautiful shade of light brown. Dangerous and thrilling, with a hint of mystery. He's the epitome of a bad boy if I've ever seen one. He looks like the type of guy you try to find for a good time, not to settle. High cheekbones, a chiseled jawline. A nose so defined you'd think Michelangelo himself took his sweet time sculpting this perfection of a man.

There. I said it. The man truly is perfect. It doesn't mean anything, though.

He raises his hands in defeat with a small smirk playing at the corner of his perfectly shaped lips. "Okay, you got me."

I sigh, opening my clutch and dropping the mirror and the lip gloss inside. I should've left my bag behind. But I paid a ridiculous amount of money for it, and damn it all if I was going to walk away without it.

I turn around to open the door, but before I do, I look over my shoulder. "You were a solid 7 out of 10." I'm lying through my teeth, but I'm not about to stroke a man's ego. "But I don't do repeats, so it's going to be a hard pass for me." With that, I open the door and walk away.

The fact I had the best sex of my life means nothing to me. I *know* men like him. They're the type who love to play with women every chance they get.

But I'm no ordinary woman.

In my world, *I* play *them*.

Sophia

As I enter through the revolving door of my best friend's apartment building, the concierge greets me and grants me access to the elevator since he recognizes me. I practically live here and even have my own key. I'm surprised Aria hasn't taken it away from me, considering I barge in most of the time.

Glancing at my watch, I cross my fingers, hoping I'm not too late. I may have forgotten the time I was supposed to be here because I didn't write it on my calendar. Every time, I tell myself I'll remember and jot it down later—and I *always* forget. The endless cycle continues. Will I ever be on time for anything in my life? Probably not. But by now, my friends know this about me.

"Open up!" I pound on the door, opting not to use the key this time, because if my speculations are correct, I have a pretty good idea who will be opening it.

Isabella opens the door and blocks the entrance, crossing her arms. "Do you have any idea how late you are?"

Isabella Walton, one of my best friends. She's feisty. Temperamental. Type A personality. A grump by heart but has a soft spot for romance novels. And surprisingly, an amazing baker. Seriously. The woman makes the *best* red velvet cookies. I *dream* about those cookies.

"I don't, but I'm sure you're about to tell me," I reply, batting my lashes and giving her the best puppy eyes I can muster.

Isabella glares at me with her intense green eyes without saying anything and moves aside, letting me in.

Aria walks into the living room and shoves a margarita in my hand. "The *maid of honor* is finally here!" She beams.

Aria Petrov, my childhood best friend. She's fiery. Quirky in an endearing, cute way, and has the kindest heart you will ever meet. But most importantly—she's a bride now.

That's right. My wonderful and insane best friend is getting married to Damian Romano—her former boss and former top bachelor of Chicago. Self-made billionaire, smart, handsome—the whole package. Hell, the man is so perfect he was going to take the blame for a crime he didn't commit to protect her. They are the perfect couple, and they complement each other in the best way possible. Not only that, but Aria has grown so comfortable with her body and her looks. She has always had a fire in her; she simply needed a push in the right direction to fully embrace it. And that's a job Damian has taken to heart. The man is the grumpiest person I've ever met, but when it comes to her? A huge teddy bear. He would do anything for her.

If only I could be so lucky.

You don't even want to open yourself to the possibility of falling in love, stop acting the martyr.

It's not that I'm not open to it. I'm simply not open to the inevitable heartbreak. Falling in love is for fools. For most people, anyway. My best friend was lucky enough to find a man who loves her fiercely. If I had a 100% guarantee I could have the same, I would be open to the idea. My heart has been broken too many times, starting with the most important man in every little girl's life. The one who's supposed to love you and protect you. The one who's supposed to show you how unconditional love looks and feels like.

Trauma, party of one. That's me!

"Maid of honor is very late, is what she is," Isabella points out, shutting the door.

The maid of honor title makes me equally excited and nervous. While I love my best friend wholeheartedly, I'm not entirely sure why she chose me. It honestly seems like a job for Isabella. I'm all for planning the most over-the-top bachelorette party, but the actual wedding? A recipe for disaster.

"Sorry I'm late, Ari." I grimace, giving her a tight hug, then drop onto the couch, getting comfortable.

Aria's loft is luxurious in a simplistic way. Her living room is an open space with an L-shaped couch and a loveseat in front of the floor-to-ceiling windows with a perfect view of the windy city. Her walls are decorated with her own paintings, giving the space a vibrant edge. It always makes me proud to see Aria unafraid to show off her art. All thanks to her fiancé, Damian, who helped her recognize her worth, even though I had been telling her for years. She needed to find her soulmate—her person—to finally be able to see it. She's now one of the best up-and-coming artists in the industry, painting and sharing her love for art, despite all the struggles she went through.

Aria sits next to me as she waves her hand dismissively. "You know I don't care, but this one"—she glares at Isabella over her shoulder—"will hang us both if we don't stick to the schedule."

Isabella shakes her head in disbelief, walking toward us

as she ties her long, straight blonde hair in a messy bun. "How do I care more about this wedding than the bride?" She juts her hip out, planting a hand firmly on it.

"Damian is your best friend, even though neither one of you acknowledges it. It's like a silent treaty between two very grumpy people," I quip then take a sip of Aria's famous margarita, savoring the strong citrus flavor.

Aria nods animatedly. "That's true."

"Enough chitchat. Let's get started. I brought my famous red velvet cookies." I perk up at her comment, but she points at me, squinting. "You can only eat them if you actually get to planning. Now, come on," she says, striding into the kitchen.

Aria and I look at each other as we roll our eyes and follow after her.

All the Pinterest pictures Aria printed to get some ideas are laid on the kitchen island, and we go over them, talking about what we like and dislike as we sip our margaritas. I honestly can't believe my best friend is getting married. I feel like it was just yesterday when she walked through my apartment door, stating she *hated* his guts and couldn't be with someone so insufferable. Now, though? I can't imagine someone more perfect for her. The way they love each other is nothing short of amazing. And while I'm more than excited for her, another side of me can't help but feel jealousy—that's too strong of a word, more like longing—to have what she has.

Let's get real. You and relationships will never mix. Or did you forget what happened last time?

Three years later, I still haven't forgotten. It's kind of difficult to get over something so... I can't even find the right wording for it.

Traumatic. Horrible. Impossible to believe.

"Why don't you hire a planner? Your man can afford it," I joke.

Aria shakes her head, hitting my shoulder with hers playfully. "No, come on! This is supposed to be fun!"

I have a different idea of what fun looks like than Aria and Isabella. I'm more into the *let's go on a girls' trip and have the time of our lives* vibe, while the girls are the *let's go to brunch and drink a good cup of coffee* type. Somehow, we still fit. I keep them young, and they keep me tamed. It's the perfect balance, if you ask me.

I will always be the loud and obnoxious friend. Having fun and experiencing life helps push away those helpless thoughts. Is trying to erase your problems away the best way to cope? Probably not. Doesn't mean I'm going to stop trying, though.

I bite my lip nervously. "Honestly, I suck at this, but anything for you, *Red*." I laugh. "Have you guys picked a date yet?"

"Gee, I'm glad the nickname is catching on," she retorts dryly. "And no." She groans. "We're still not sure if we want a fall or winter wedding."

I snicker at her comment. I can't believe I never thought about calling her Red. With her perfect, curly auburn hair and the red lipstick she always wears, the nickname is fairly obvious. I swear, whoever started this is a genius. I think it was Damian's head of security, or maybe his cousin? I heard the story from Isabella in passing. I'm not really part of the group they have going on. My schedule is too hectic, and the rare times they get together, I'm always too busy.

Aria perks up, her hazel eyes gleaming with something I can't quite place. "Are you able to make it to the birthday dinner tonight? I would *love* for you to meet the birthday boy. Please tell me you're not working, it's Saturday. You can't work on weekends!"

Ah. That gleaming is mischief.

Working at one of the top media websites in the country is anything *but* glamorous. That's mostly because Max, my boss, sucks. The hours are ruthless, and I work more often than not and barely have a social life. It was supposed to be a temporary job, but four years later, I'm still there. I honestly thought I was going to be someplace else by now, but I have too many responsibilities to ever quit and pursue what I want.

I mull it over for a moment. If only they knew all I did today was work when I was supposed to be outlining my book. I have lots of ideas. What I don't have is the time or the energy to pursue the author career I keep saying I want. And even though I worked all day, I still have so much left to do. But I *did* tell myself I needed to start cutting back.

I can also smell her intentions from a hundred miles away, and I'm not sure if I like where this is going. She has been throwing comments here and there about how she thinks I'll get along with Damian's cousin—the birthday boy. In Aria's world, that's code for: *I'm trying to set you up.* Ever since she got her own person, she's determined we all find ours, too. The sad reality is, even if I found someone I could get along with, I will *never* open my heart. I still have too many fresh wounds waiting to be mended, and it's safe to say they won't be closing anytime soon. That's why casual sex is in, and relationships are out.

"Aria Petrov," I scold, eyeing her suspiciously, "Are you trying to set me up?"

"No," she replies innocently before taking a sip of her margarita.

"Aria, come on, you can't possibly be trying to set them up," Isabella chimes in with an incredulous tone.

I gawk at her, flicking my hair dramatically. "You don't think I'm a catch?"

She sighs, rolling her eyes. "I never said that, but let's just say if you were to look up the definition of *player* in the dictionary, a picture of him would pop up."

Aria's shoulders deflate with a long sigh. "But maybe Sophia can keep him on his toes," she says hopefully. "She's pretty much the female version."

I throw the fakest and loudest gasp, clutching my imaginary pearls. "*Ugh, as if!*"

My *Clueless* reference earns me an eye roll from Aria.

Quoting '90s movies and TV shows is a favorite hobby of mine, which no one—especially not Aria—appreciates.

Isabella thins her lips, holding back a laugh. Knowing her, that's the best reaction I'll get. We make quite the trio, if you ask me. I'm the loud, obnoxious one. Aria is feisty when she needs to be but mostly sweet. Isabella, though, she's the grumpiest. Which was surprising at first. She was so shy and quiet when I met her. But now, I embrace it. An Isabella without her signature frown is a scary one.

"You're both impossible," Aria mutters, opening the fridge and grabbing a water, then closes it and leans her hip against it. "Come to the birthday dinner, please."

Resting my palms on the edge of the kitchen counter, I shake my head. "No."

"You can't say no to a bride, it's bad luck!" she exclaims.

I frown. "*Pft.* Says who?"

"I don't know." She shrugs. "But I promise I have no tricky business."

Aria is looking at me with those big puppy eyes, and she knows I can never say no to them. I know she's trying to set me up, but what's the worst that can happen? If he's a player like Isabella claims, chances are we'll have a one-night stand and move on. And if I'm being honest, I doubt anything will happen, because this past year has been a weird one. The men I've slept with have been mediocre at best. The excitement I used to feel doesn't hit the same anymore. Sometimes I think, *hey, maybe you're ready to settle down*. But I know better than that.

"Fine." I sigh, letting my head drop between my shoulders.

"Good luck," Isabella says, sarcasm lacing her tone.

I grab the kitchen towel from the stove handle and throw it at her. "Shut up before I make you go with me, because if I remember correctly, isn't your dear Matteo best friends with him?" I arch an eyebrow.

Her eyes snap to mine, her body tensing at the mention of Matteo. "Over my dead body, am I going to be in the same room as that asshole."

"Isabella, you do realize he'll be at the wedding, right?" Aria chimes in, unsure.

"Yes, I'm aware," Isabella drawls, sitting on the kitchen island stool.

"Why do you dislike him so much?" I ask.

Isabella pulls her phone from her jeans pocket, her gaze flicking away from us as she focuses on the screen. "I'm not going to talk about it."

Aria and I exchange a knowing look. This always happens when we try to find out what the hell happened between them. While I haven't personally witnessed their dynamic, Aria tells me it's not pretty. And I don't doubt it. I love Isabella to death, but her temper can be a lot sometimes. She's always simmering in anger, which as her best friend, makes me hurt for her. But I guess everyone copes differently. I'm not about to reprimand her for something I also do. While she relies on anger, I rely on jokes and keeping a smile plastered all over my face even when it hurts.

"8 p.m. at Lorenzo's, don't forget," Aria says while pointing her index finger at me, successfully deterring the conversation. "I'm sure you guys will get along *really* well."

I hold back an eye roll. I love my best friend—truly, I do —but she still thinks I'm teenage Sophia, the hopeless romantic who wanted to meet her prince charming. But the more I witnessed at home, the more I knew it was all bull-shit. When my father died, I also witnessed—and cleaned up—the mess he left behind. So much heartbreak. Dark-ness. Sadness. Some people are not meant to fall in love and find their person. I happen to be one of those people.

And every day, I try to be okay with it.

2

Lorenzo

Walking outside my stuffy restaurant with a glass of whiskey in hand, I take a deep breath as the bustling city sounds and wind welcome me. When I moved to Chicago, I was so excited. Eager to start my life and looking forward to what this city had to offer.

Now, knowing I'm stuck in this stuffy city, going to stuffy parties and stuffy meetings, makes my skin crawl. I didn't even want to celebrate my goddamn birthday today. But my best friend, Ivy, insisted. Try saying no to her. I dare you. It's impossible. All I wanted was to stay home and exist. Something I've been doing a lot lately. Simmering in the exhaustion I can't seem to shake off. Instead, I'm stuck at a birthday dinner I didn't even want. The only thing giving me some sort of relief is that at least it's happening in my own restaurant. Most people would say it's lame, but the restaurants are the only thing I still enjoy in this life I get to call mine.

I loosen my tie and slide it off, unfastening three buttons on my dress shirt before taking a slow sip of whiskey, savoring the burn as it warms its way down my throat. The sharp scent of car exhaust fills the air, stinging my nostrils. I used to love the city's relentless pace and no-bullshit attitude. But now? It feels like background noise to the thoughts I can't escape.

"What is your problem, man? Jesus," I mutter to myself, scrubbing my face.

A lot of things. Do we really need to go through the list right now?

A sudden sharp laughter followed by a sniffle cuts through the air, pulling me from my trance. I look around my surroundings until my eyes land on a woman. The fading city lights barely light up where she's sitting on the sidewalk. All I can see is her silhouette and her long, wavy dark hair.

I take a hesitant step forward. "Are you okay?"

She doesn't turn around. "Yes." Her voice quivers with a sniff, but she tries to recover with the fakest laugh I've ever heard.

"You're sitting on the sidewalk in the middle of the night, crying," I point out. A brief silence follows before I add, "And laughing."

She forces yet another laugh. What is it with this woman and her fake laughs? "I'm not crying. Now could you please leave me the hell alone?"

"Hey." I raise my hands in defense, which is pointless, because she's not looking at me. "I'm trying to be nice here."

"Be nice somewhere else. I'm trying to have a moment here," she snaps, still refusing to look at me.

Why am I dying to look at her right now? And why does her voice sound so damn familiar?

"You're the one sitting outside a restaurant"—I point to the restaurant doors—"on a Saturday night, in the middle of a busy city. Maybe try having a moment somewhere more private next time," I retort.

She lets out an exasperated sigh. "For God's sake," she mutters as she stands and brushes off her dress, trying to remove any trace of dirt.

She's petite, even with the black boots she's wearing. As she steps closer, the overhead lights of the restaurant gradually illuminate her face, revealing her features. When she looks up, my stomach *flips*, my heart almost skipping a whole fucking beat. This is the strongest emotion I've felt since last year. *Fuck*, what is happening right now? The world around me fades, my body suddenly hyperaware of the eyes locked on me.

Her eyes are like chips of ice. Piercing, cold, and a haunting shade of blue. They're the kind that pierce right through your soul, leaving you exposed and vulnerable. But that's not what throws me off-guard. What does is that they are the same eyes that have been stuck in my head for *exactly* 365 days now. The ones I fell for on this very day, a year ago. The ones that looked over her shoulder in amusement when I tried to get her number and left me standing— *starstruck*—as she walked away from me.

Now here I stand, dumbfounded, staring at the woman I fucked senseless in a cleaning closet at a club *exactly* one year ago.

My breath falters as I take her in. I never forgot what she looked—and felt—like. But seeing her in the flesh is so much better. Her brown hair frames her face beautifully. Her lips are plush and an inviting shade of a soft, nude pink. She's wearing a short, black dress that hugs her curves perfectly and an oversize leather jacket.

She studies every inch of my face, with a small frown. The moment she realizes who I am is obvious, because her expression starts to change. We both stand there, our eyes roaming each other shamelessly, drinking each other in. The only sound interrupting our deafening silence is the people walking and chatting around us and cars honking.

Before I can say anything, the restaurant door swings open and Aria and Damian step out. As they approach us, I don't miss the way she brushes under her eyes with her knuckles and plasters a huge smile that doesn't reach her eyes.

"Sophia! You're here," Aria says excitedly, throwing her arms around Sophia in a hug. "And I see you've met the birthday boy." Aria's grin is playful, her eyes dancing with a trace of amusement.

I can practically hear the laughter inside my head, my brain having entirely too much fun with the situation. Chicago is not a small city by any means. The chances of running into someone you had a one-night stand with are, hell, *slim*. I can attest to this fact, because I've had my fair share and have yet to run into any of them.

But here she is. The woman I haven't stopped thinking about. The only one-night stand I've had where I felt an uncontrollable, charged chemistry. I've never in my now thirty-six years of life—happy birthday to me, I guess—felt such a strong connection with someone. Having casual sex has always been a means to an end, nothing more. With her, though, it was anything but ordinary.

I'm a man who believes in destiny. There's something out there that's much bigger than us and can decide if luck is on your side or not. And right now, standing in front of her, I have no doubt. If this doesn't scream destiny, I don't know what will.

"Sophia as in, Aria's best friend, Sophia?" I ask, tilting

my head. I've heard much about Aria's best friend. And for the life of me, I can't believe this is who it is.

"And you're the birthday boy I've heard so much about?" Her tone is casual, a forced smile still plastered all over her face as she tilts her head, too. But it's hard to miss how stiff her movements are and the tension in her shoulders.

Can't say I don't enjoy the sight of her right now.

A small grin plays on my lips, amusement overtaking me.

Look at you, feeling something for once.

Thank God. I was beginning to worry.

"You guys talk about me?" I look at Aria and Damian, my tone playful. "I'm touched."

"I'm sure you are," Damian replies, dryly.

"I've been dying for you two to meet!" Aria exclaims excitedly.

With the way Sophia's searing me with those piercing-blue eyes, I highly doubt she shares her best friend's sentiments.

With a small, knowing smile I take her hand and bring her knuckles to my lips, giving her a soft, quick kiss. "Lorenzo Mancini, but you can call me Enzo. It's a pleasure to meet you, Bella[1]." My lips tingle, already missing the brief touch of her skin.

Is she going to tell these two how we met? Or will she pretend she doesn't know me? Am I deranged for hoping it's the second option? There's something about playing games. It gives me a rush, a hit of serotonin straight to the brain.

She takes her hand out of my grip. "Sophia Evans, it's *my* pleasure to meet you." She bats her eyes with that forced smile still in place.

------

1. Beautiful.

Oh. *Oh.* This is good. This is more than good. This is *fun.* Let's see how long she'll play along.

3

Sophia

This has to be some sort of sick joke.

Maybe if you blink enough times, he'll disappear.

Yeah, I don't think that will be happening.

Life has a funny way of bending me over and screwing me. Surely, the universe finds it hilarious to put me in the most idiotic, nonsense types of situations. This is what I tell myself as I meet the eyes of the man who pinned me against the wall of a cleaning closet at a nightclub and *fucked* me a year ago.

The famous Mr. Three-Orgasm Guy.

Oh, God.

I slept with—from what I hear—the biggest player in the Chicagoland area. I sure know how to pick them. It's always been an ongoing joke between me and Aria. Granted, the joke started when I went through one of the worst breakups of my life. And it was funny for a while. The perfect way to cope. I'm the queen of finding ways to turn something traumatic, or sad, into a joke. It's how I can be the life of the party. But dread settles at the pit of my stomach at the realization that it's not a joke anymore.

What is the matter with me? What's so fundamentally wrong with me that I can't even pick the right one-night stand anymore?

A lot of things are wrong with you. This is not *a path you want to tread.*

No. It isn't.

"Shall we go back in?" Lorenzo suggests, tilting his head to the restaurant entrance.

"Oh, yes! I was coming out here to get you. Why did you disappear on us, Enzo?" Aria asks, crossing her arms.

"I'm going to take a wild guess and say destiny wanted me to be out here, right in this moment, Red," he replies with a light, amused tone, his eyes finding mine.

This man is messing with me for the hell of it. If he thinks I'm going to break in front of these two, he has another thing coming. Besides being the loudest of the group, I'm also the most stubborn—though I will deny it until the day I die. I wonder who's going to break first? I'm sure as hell not about to tell Aria and Damian how *well* I know him.

His hand finds my lower back as he opens the door of the restaurant and guides me inside. The touch makes my skin hot, even though he didn't make direct contact with it. Knowing this, makes me want to crawl out of my skin. The last thing I should be doing is feeling like this, so I swat his hand away and shoot him a withering glare. A small, mischievous grin plays at his lips as he raises his hand in innocence.

I force yet another laugh as I take some very much-needed distance from him. "That's the stupidest thing I've ever heard."

I'm trying not to stare back and gawk at him, but it's useless. I can't help it. I forgot how handsome he is. He's ridiculously tall, about six-foot-three, if I had to guess. His dark navy suit fits in all the right places, hugging his broad shoulders and thick, muscled thighs. His white dress shirt has a few buttons undone, a small gold-plated cross pendant chain peeking through against his tattooed chest. His hair is slightly messy in an *I'm-hot-and-I-can-rock-this* type of way. But those eyes are what hold me captive. They're as beautiful as I remember—a light-brown color with a touch of gold.

"You don't believe in destiny?" he asks, taking a seat.

"No," I answer, taking the farthest seat from him.

He frowns, rearing back in surprise. "Talk about being pessimistic."

"Talk about being delusional," I retort.

Destiny my ass. I'm just unlucky, and the world wanted me to get a hefty reminder of the fact.

"You seriously don't believe in destiny?" His eyes gleam with mischief as he licks his bottom lip. "Not even at this moment?"

"Not even a little bit," I confirm, practically shooting daggers at him with my eyes.

If I believed in destiny, it would be ironic. With my upbringing, I've always felt everything has been working against me. I'm aware of how egocentric I sound right now, but with the shit I've been through, it's extremely hard to believe otherwise.

Aria is silently taking in our strange exchange, moving her head back and forth. Damian is, well, being Damian, and remaining enigmatic.

Instead of answering, Lorenzo zeroes his thrilling eyes at me and raises an eyebrow, silently asking me, *Ready to give up yet?* And I simply stare at him back with a blank expression. I will never give up. Not because it's not in my nature, but because, honestly, *fuck* the patriarchy. Men have been on top for far too long.

"Do you guys know each other?" Aria asks.

"No," we speak at the same time without breaking eye contact.

I can see Aria from the side of my eye trying to get my attention to drill me with silent questions. When you've been best friends long enough with a person, you can have a silent conversation by looking at each other. This woman knows me well. If I look at her, my cover will be blown. Aria is the one person I can't lie to. She can always smell the bullshit coming from a mile away. I know I'm going to have to confess eventually. It's not like this is going to be the last time I'm going to see Lorenzo.

This is so messed up.

A waitress appears at our end of the table and asks, "Anything I can get you guys to drink?"

As Aria and Damian request what they want, we're both still staring at each other.

"What about you, handsome?" the waitress asks Lorenzo, her tone flirty and playful.

He breaks eye contact and looks at the waitress, a smile playing on his lips. "I'm good. But a gin martini with a twist for the pretty lady over here." He nods my way.

One, did he seriously call me a *pretty lady*? And two, he remembered my drink order?

"Pretty lady? Are we in 1929 or something?" I snap.

"Or something," he muses.

"How do you know her drink order?" Aria scrunches her nose in confusion.

"Wild guess," Lorenzo replies with a casual shrug.

Yeah. And the three gin martinis he bought me a year ago

before burying himself inside of me. That's what I really want to say, but I stay quiet instead.

The waitress takes drink orders for the rest of the party, her eyes finding Lorenzo every chance she gets. Once she finishes and leaves, she starts to sway her hips, obviously trying to catch Lorenzo's attention. Hell, it even catches mine. She has such a nice ass, I'm almost tempted to ask about her gym routine. I shift my gaze to Lorenzo, hoping to catch him staring at her, but instead, his eyes are settled on me. His gaze is so intense, it makes every nerve in my body feel alive for a moment. I straighten my back, flicking my hair away from my shoulder as I hold his gaze and raise an eyebrow. Any other normal person would be embarrassed, but him? He flashes me with a stupid, dangerous smile, the infuriating dimple on his left cheek making an appearance as he keeps holding eye contact without any ounce of shame.

This man sure is something else.

Memories of that night invade my mind. Like the way his hand grasped the nape of my neck, possessive yet gentle, before sealing his lips on mine. The way his body pressed against mine as he so easily lifted me and pinned me against the wall while our tongues continued to explore each other's mouths. Warmth overtakes me, and I can almost taste the faint sweetness of smoky whiskey on my lips, just as I did that night.

Why is this happening to me?

I would have been happy to never have crossed paths with him ever again. Yes, the sex was hot, and yes, the man is practically sculpted like a Greek god, but that's the extent of it. I don't do repeats. It's my one non-negotiable rule. Even if I've come to regret it from time to time since that night. But now, knowing full well who he is? Yeah, that door is shut. I already threw away the key and everything.

Lorenzo drops his elbows on the table. "So, how long have you guys been *best friends*?" He directs his words at me. "And how come we've never met?"

I start picking at my nails with a bored expression, refusing to answer him.

"Sophia has a really busy schedule. She works for *Vogue Elite*. She rarely gets the chance to hang out with us," Aria chimes in, ever the sweet girl who wants to keep the peace.

He nods, visibly impressed. "What do you do there?"

"Junior journalist," I answer.

He scrubs his face for a moment, pondering. "Someone recently reached out to do an article about me at *Vogue Elite*. Max Steiner."

Oh no. No, no, no.

Oh, you unlucky bitch.

Aria goes to say something again, but I stomp on her leg with a *shut the fuck up* look.

"Oh, that's Sophia's boss," Damian chimes in instead. "Did you accept?"

Man, my best friend sure has a blabbermouth of a fiancé.

He gives Damian a pointed look. "You know I didn't." Lorenzo's eyebrows lift, his eyes filling with curious interest. "Though—"

Before he can continue, a beautiful woman with curly, black hair strides to our table, interrupting us. "I've been looking everywhere for you. We're supposed to be singing 'Happy Birthday' and cutting the cake now," she exclaims, griping Lorenzo's forearm.

He rolls his eyes, standing. "You're lucky I like you, Ivy."

"*Please.* You're the lucky one to have such a wonderful

best friend like me." She crosses her arms, and I decide at this moment, whoever she is, I like her.

We all stand and walk to the table where the cake is. And while everyone is singing, his eyes, accompanied by a knowing, playful smirk, never leave mine. Not even when he leans over and blows the candles. Not even when everyone around him is congratulating him.

I have a feeling this is not going to be my last encounter with Lorenzo Mancini, nor the last time he's going to push my buttons. One player can recognize another, after all. He's having entirely too much fun with this, and it's only fair I have my own share of fun.

Bring it on, player.

I'm ready.

Sophia

Running in four-inch heels is *not* for the weak. The only reason I'm wearing these fancy shoes is because my boss emailed me at midnight to inform me about a crucial last-minute meeting. He said, and I quote, "*You must bring your A-game.*" He speaks like an overgrown teenager who peaked in high school most of the time, and I honestly don't understand how he's able to keep his job. Especially because I know for a *fact* he doesn't do anything.

It was hard to not get pissed off when I received that email. I'm a lot of things. Very high-energy and somewhat intense, some people would go as far as to call me obnoxious, but I will never play when it comes to my job. I take so much shit from that place, any other normal person would have walked away by now. If I was the only one depending on the income, I would probably have left by now. But that's not the case. So I keep working—and keep getting taken advantage of.

As if on cue, my phone rings with a call from the person who depends on this much more than I do.

"Hey, Mom," I answer breathlessly, trying to speed walk to get to work on time.

"Hi, honey. You sound out of breath. Everything okay?" she asks with a sweet, soft tone.

"Yeah. I'm running a little late for work. Have an important meeting to get to."

"Train issues again?" she asks.

"Yup." I sigh.

Living and working in downtown Chicago has its downsides—too many transit delays and owning a car is out of the question. I'd rather spend the money on something useful, like Mom's appointments or groceries. Traffic's a nightmare, and rent near *Vogue Elite*, right in the heart of downtown, is sky-high. So, I'm stuck with public transit.

"You okay? Did you take your medication today?" A hint of worry laces my tone.

She lets out a soft laugh. "Yes. Stop worrying about me."

Funny. I don't think I will ever stop. The only reason I don't live closer to home is because *Vogue Elite* pays enough, allowing me to cover all her living expenses, and make sure she lives a stress-free life. The last thing I want is to see her go back to the way she used to be. I love my mother, I truly do. She's extremely sweet, and it's not her fault she had a hard life. I know she hates depending on me, but I will never stop caring for her.

"I'm calling you for a reason." She sighs. "Your sister, uh, called me again."

I stop dead in my tracks, almost bumping into someone as my heart rate picks to a dangerously fast pace. Biting my bottom lip, I try to control the involuntary reaction I get every time my sister is mentioned.

Just count backward, Sophia.

10, 9, 8...

Why is she calling Mom? She also called this past weekend, but Mom had told me she didn't pick up. It didn't ease my stress any less, though. I ended up sitting on a sidewalk in downtown Chicago, crying my eyes out with the uncertainty and anxiety of it all.

7, 6, 5...

What sort of trouble did she get herself into now?

4, 3, 2, 1...

How am I going to clean this mess? How can I make it go away? Think, Sophia. *Think.*

Taking a deep, shaky breath, I ask, "Did she say what she wanted?"

"Only wanted to see how I was doing."

"Right," I answer, trying to keep my voice even.

Whenever Amelia starts lurking around Mom like a vulture, I know she wants something. And it's usually money. She knows how to play me well by now. She reminds me of our deadbeat father. A sadistic, selfish man who thrived on the suffering of others. But there was one target he loved inflicting pain on more than any other—Mom.

I start walking again, in quicker steps this time as I glance at my watch. "Listen, Mom, I have to go but if she calls you again, promise me you'll tell me?" I stress.

"Yes. I will. I love you."

"Love you, too," I reply before hanging up. "God help me," I murmur to myself as I drop my phone into my purse and gaze at *Vogue Elite's* towering building, wondering what the hell I'm going to do.

Nausea settles in the pit of my stomach at the thought of my sister trying to reenter our lives. She briefly reappeared in my life a year ago, because she had a huge fight with her on-and-off boyfriend for the past three years, Miles. I stupidly let her stay with me, and everything was going fine.

Then we went out one night, and when I woke up the next morning, she was gone, along with a few of my more expensive clothing items. The ones I worked my ass off to have. I'm not materialistic by any means, and things are replaceable. But when you live your whole life scrapping for money, you learn to appreciate things. Become attached to them. And I really miss my fucking Louboutins.

My breakfast is threatening to come out, and the nervous sweats are already here. I can't afford to be all sweaty and disgusting for this meeting. Glancing at my watch, I have about ten minutes before I need to meet with Max and this mysterious person.

I drop my purse and lunch box in my cubicle and quickly walk to the restroom and lock myself in it, resting my forehead against the cold, dark wood door. I'm spiraling. This is what I do when Amelia reappears. I go into panic mode. She knows how to play the game, because she knows damn well I don't want anything stressing out Mom.

I laugh out loud as I turn around to take a look in the mirror. Tears are threatening to spill, so I reach for the paper towel dispenser and grab one, soaking up the tears before they ruin my makeup. Another laugh bubbles out of me, like the ridiculous person I am. It's impossible for me not to laugh when I'm on the verge of a breakdown. I'm all too aware it's insane, but it's something I've done ever since I was a kid. Even when the sadness wants to blow over, my coping mechanism tries to take over. Always with the laughter. Like a damn clown.

The worst part of this situation is that I'm self-aware she takes advantage of me, yet I keep letting her. It's like I'm a kid all over again, having to be the mother and take care of her. It was fine when we were kids. After all, Mom was barely present when our father died—I never understood why, but I've always been too afraid to ask her. The day he died was ironically the best day of my life. It sounds crude, and like I'm the worst person to walk this Earth, but I have enough trauma baggage to back up these claims.

When he died, someone had to take care of Mom and Amelia, so I shouldered the responsibility. It was my cross to bear, and I carried it. But Amelia is an adult now, and to this day, she still hasn't grown up.

I can't deal with this now.

Or ever. Don't deal with it at all, Sophia. Ignore her.

Except, I can't, because if I don't deal with the problem now, she will involve Mom somehow, and that's the last thing I need. It pisses me off how selfish my sister is. I know she was little when our father died, but there's no way she has forgotten everything we went through with him. I always tried my best to take the screaming, the punching, and the name-calling, but I wasn't perfect. She witnessed enough.

I walk out of the restroom and go back to my cubicle to grab my phone and physical planner. With Max, I always have to document everything. The man changes his mind more than not, and somehow, he manages to make it my fault. I've been down this road *many* times.

Any other journalist would be *ecstatic* to meet with the editor in chief and get to work closely with the person who's supposed to lead us and inspire us. Except, he's anything but a leader. Being a good employee under Max's leadership is a curse. One I've been carrying for far too long. I enjoy the job in itself. The research, interviewing, editing, and of course, the writing. If being an author wasn't my dream, becoming an editor in chief would be a close second. The reason I hate my job right now has nothing to do with my responsibilities and everything to do with my boss.

Taking a deep breath, I plaster a fake smile on my lips, like I always do, and stride toward his office as I mentally prepare myself. I softly knock on the door as I'm opening it. Walking in, I'm met with my editor with an exciting look in his eyes.

He waves his hand to where the other person is sitting. "Sophia, great, you're here. I want you to meet Lorenzo Mancini."

My steps falter for a moment as my head snaps to *him*. And I'm met with the same light-brown eyes, and *God*, how do they look even better during the day?

He's dressed in a dark-gray suit and vest, with a black tie that matches his shoes. His hair is slicked back, which I hate. The messy hair he had during dinner suits him way better. He looks like the type of man who has his shit together, and for some stupid reason, it annoys me.

"After much pursuit, Lorenzo—"

"Mr. Mancini for you," Lorenzo interrupts him with a dry, bored tone.

Max's ears turn red from embarrassment. "Right. Mr. Mancini, my apologies." He lets out a fake cough. "Like I was saying, Mr. Mancini has agreed to do an article about him for our fall edition."

"What's that got to do with me?" I ask with a frown.

"He specifically requested you do the piece," Max replies with a grimace.

I take a step back in surprise, clutching my things tightly to my chest. It's not normal for junior journalists to do the main editions, that's more for more senior journalists. I've only been working here for about four years, and while I'm considered as one of the best, you need to be working at the company for five plus years to be considered for a senior position. The fact it's a fall edition, and we're almost at the end of spring, makes me wonder just how substantial the piece will be. It's a privilege to do this. Every writer's dream. The opportunity of a lifetime—except, I'll have to work with *him*. That's a recipe for disaster.

I blink a few times, trying to make sense of what Max said. "Wow, I, uh. Thank you for thinking of me, but I can't accept it."

"I've read all the articles you've written over the years. You're a great writer. And if you're not willing to do it, well, I'm afraid this is not going to work." Lorenzo shrugs as he stands and starts buttoning his suit.

Max looks at me expectantly, with a hint of irritation that Lorenzo doesn't notice because he's focused on me.

Anger slowly simmers through my veins. This is such a blatant attempt to get closer to me. Read my articles? *Pft.* Yeah, right. He's playing those stupid games again, and while it was fun during his birthday dinner, this is completely different. This is my place of employment. I have people depending on me, and I can't afford to lose my job over something like this.

"I'm afraid this is not up for discussion, Sophia," Max says through gritted teeth.

Pick your battles. This is not one you can win.

I grab a strand of my perfectly styled hair with a nod, placing it behind my ear as I take a seat. "I'm sure you have an idea of where you want to go with this." He's my boss, after all. Even if he's a raging dick, I have to listen to him.

Lorenzo sits back down, and I can feel his eyes burning me, but I refuse to look at him.

Asshole.

I cannot believe he's here. *Jesus H. Christ.* This is a little too damn far.

"Definitely." Max nods eagerly. "I want you to focus on

what it is like to be Lorenzo Mancini, the billionaire. What is it like to live like him?"

"We should have coffee and chat more," Lorenzo chimes in.

I plaster on the most insincere smile I can manage, setting my eyes on him. "Yeah, sure."

"That's a great idea. I know the perfect spot," Max says, standing from his chair.

"No need for you to come. It's not like you're writing the article, right?" Lorenzo drawls lazily, not even casting him a glance, like Max is a pest he can't bother himself with.

Max's steps falter for a moment, a flush creeping across his cheeks as he sits back down. "Right. Of course."

I turn my face away and bite my lip, trying to hold back my laugh. I don't know much about Lorenzo, but I've noticed having a filter isn't his style. It's as funny as it is endearing.

He stands. "I have time right now."

Of course, because he's the king of the world, and the rest of the common people just orbit around him.

"Shocker," I murmur.

"What was that?" he asks with a playful lilt in his voice.

"I said sure, coffee sounds *great*," I reply through gritted teeth.

He nods toward the door. "After you."

Here the fuck we go.

5

Lorenzo

If someone had told me Sophia Evans looked even better in business attire than in the short little black dress she wore for my birthday dinner, I would have laughed. But damn. She looks so elegant and put together. The way her long brown hair settles on her hips makes me want to bend her over one of these desks and have my way with her.

You already slept with her once, and you don't do repeats.

Semantics. There's a first time for everything. This is the woman who has been stuck in my head for a year; sleeping with her one more time wouldn't be the worst thing in the world. The universe practically handed her to me on a silver platter, and who am I to question its intentions?

When I discovered she worked for *Vogue Elite*, I researched every single article she's written. I even found the pieces she did for her college newspaper when she was a student. And I read all of them—every single one of the 450 articles.

I found myself quickly becoming obsessed and intrigued by her writing. She can make the most mundane topics shine. She's an amazing writer, and even for a useless web media like this, there's magic in her words. But let's face it, I don't do interviews. Everyone knows that. I've never been interested in what people have to say about me. Not that it stops them from writing gossip columns. I let people write and believe what they want. I don't give them the ammunition. Whatever conclusions they assume, it's all them. People often wonder why I let the media get away with so much, and the answer is simple—I don't give a fuck. I know they're twisting the truth. Does it drive the board at Vortex a little crazy when I'm always the center of every gossip media website? Yes. And honestly, knowing those stuck-up sons of bitches aren't fans of me, but are stuck with me, makes the situation far too entertaining.

Vogue Elite was no exception to my no-interview rule, but as I was ready to turn them down, I found myself saying yes instead. Am I using this as an excuse to get closer to her? Maybe—okay, yes. Absolutely.

I'm playing with dangerous fire here, but *fuck*, I bet we'd burn so good together.

I'm obsessive by nature; once I set my eyes on something, I won't let it go. They'll have to rip it from my cold, dead hands. And even then, who knows what will happen?

She walks to her cubicle, grabs her purse, and stalks to the elevator without casting me a glance, like I'm a fly on the wall in her world. I quietly follow, waiting beside her for the elevator to arrive. The air between us crackles with tension, and I can't deny it makes my body spike with excitement. Stepping into the elevator, I press the button for the plaza. And as the doors close, her eyes lock onto me with intense fury.

She crosses her arms tightly across her chest, and her white button-down shirt has a few buttons open. Her tits get pushed together, and the sight is out of this damn world. "What are you playing at? I thought you turned down the interview."

A relaxed smile tugs on my lips, my eyes dropping to her mouth-watering cleavage. "Not sure what you mean." I shrug nonchalantly. "And I changed my mind. Problem?"

"Oh, please." She puffs, rolling her eyes. "*I've read the articles you've written over the years. You're a great writer,*" she mocks in a gruff voice.

I roll my lips, trying to hold back my laughter. "Are you trying to impersonate me?"

"Yes, but it's hard to imitate a stuck-up, self-centered man like you," she snaps, flicking her fingers in front of me. "And my eyes are up here, *asshole.*" She points to her eyes with two fingers.

I smirk at her comment, my eyes still zeroed in on her cleavage just to get under her skin. Any other man might be insulted, but not me. There's nothing I love more than the fire of a woman who pushes back. Insults only make me more eager to provoke a reaction. There's nothing like the thrill coursing through my body right now at the bite of her voice.

I click the emergency button, causing the elevator to stop abruptly. "What's your problem?" I ask with a light tone, my eyes finally finding hers.

"I didn't peg you for a stupid man, but in case I wasn't clear, *you're* my problem." Her voice drips with disdain as she glares at me with her intense, blue gaze.

"Why?" I reply, feigning innocence.

She uncrosses her arms and brushes her hair with her fingertips, letting out a sigh of exasperation. "This is great," she murmurs to herself. "Pretending is not going to get you anywhere, Lorenzo."

The way my name rolls off her lips, so raspy and sultry, even with a hint of fury, makes my cock twitch.

You're losing your mind here, Lorenzo.

Yeah, I know. And I'm 100% on board with it.

I raise my hands in defeat. "Okay, you got me. You're *really* good at this game."

"What game?" she asks with an incredulous look on her face.

Oh, is this how she wants to play it? Okay.

"Now who's pretending?" I raise an eyebrow.

Her shoulders stiffen as she crosses her arms again and looks away without a word.

"I'm talking about the game where you pretend I didn't fuck you senseless in a cleaning closet of a club a year ago," I deadpan.

Her cheeks turn a bright shade of pink, and it's the prettiest color I've ever seen. Her eyes turn a shade darker, almost like a blue-gray color combination. I take two steps closer, her citrus and sweet scent invading my senses. She smells like...summer. I could close my eyes and imagine myself on a tropical island filled with wildflowers, palms, and a calm breeze. It's intoxicating, and I can't get enough of it.

"The game where you pretend your pussy wasn't clenching around my cock as I was giving you a mind-blowing orgasm," I rasp, barely above a whisper.

She takes two steps back, flustered, and presses the button to get the elevator moving again. "Someone sure thinks highly of himself. If I remember correctly, I gave you a 7 out of 10. Not exactly mind-blowing, is it?" She flicks her hair, hitting me with it in the process. Can't say I'm mad at the act. Her hair smells like fucking heaven. "And I'm not pretending anything. I'm just trying to have more class than you by trying to do the right thing and move past it."

"So you *do* remember." I snort a laugh at her ridiculous comment. "And Bella[1], I know I wasn't a 7. If I remember correctly, I gave you three solid orgasms." I lift and wiggle three of my fingers as I get some distance from her, too, because the proximity affected me in other ways I didn't think possible.

"Oh, you're cocky, too. *Figures*," she retorts dryly.

"I'd rather you call me confident." I grin.

The elevators open, and she quickly walks out, not waiting for me. She's fairly shorter than me, even with those heels, so I quickly catch up.

Before I can retort, she turns around, pushing a finger on my chest. "Whatever game you're playing at, I want no part of it. If this is your way of cornering me to confess I remember you, well, you already won. Now leave me the hell alone." Anger flashes through her gaze, her eyes turning into an even darker shade of blue.

Why can't I stop looking at them? She's ready to push me off a cliff, but all I can focus on is the wild intensity of them, a mix of danger and beauty that's impossible to ignore.

"Your eyes are so...*blue*," I find myself saying, mesmerized.

Her eyes meet mine for a split second before she rolls them. "You can differentiate colors, *good for you*." With that, she stalks out of the building in fury.

I stride after her. "Sophia, wait!"

"Leave me the hell alone, Lorenzo. You're insane if you think I'm having coffee with you now, or ever for that

---

1. Beautiful.

matter." She grabs her phone from her purse, unlocking it and opening a ride-share app.

I snatch it quickly and hold it in the air. She tries to reach for it, but she's so short, I easily tower over her. It's kind of cute how hard she's trying, though.

"Listen, I'm sorry. I got carried away, okay? But to be fair, you had no problem fucking with me the other night, so sue me for thinking you were still cool with it," I retort.

She groans, exasperated. "That was before you decided to come to my place of employment and demand I write your article. Which, by the way, is the lamest way to get close to me. Couldn't you have asked Aria for my number?"

I frown at her comment. "I chose you because you're a great writer."

And because part of you wants to get closer to her.

Yeah, well...no one has to know that.

A humorless laugh escapes her lips. "Oh, for the love of God, stop pretending. Have you even read any of my pieces?"

Her question throws me off, making me take a step back with a frown. How can she go from walking and talking with so much confidence to whatever this is? Without a word, I hand her the phone. She quickly grabs it and opens the ride-share app again.

Before she requests the car, I say, "Your debut statement piece in *Vogue Elite* was about three years ago during New York Fashion Week. You wrote about Marc Jacobs and the brilliant way he uses fabrics to convey feelings. It was quite moving. And that's coming from a guy who knows nothing about fashion."

She lifts her gaze from her phone, her eyebrows raising in surprise. "Okay, well—"

I raise my hand, interrupting her. "Or how about the

time you wrote about the real story of Marilyn Monroe and how she suffered from misogynistic directors, and everything she accomplished as a woman in the fifties?"

She looks at me at a loss of words, shocked and confused. Funny, because I'm the one feeling pretty lost right now.

"Yeah." I snort a humorless laugh. "I do my research. You don't get to this level by being careless."

Her shoulders stiffen. "It still doesn't give you the right to talk to me like that, especially now that we'll be working together."

I nod in agreement, a ping of regret flooding through me. I accept I tend to get carried away when I'm playing with fire. The thrill of the game is exciting. This is how I work. No filter and consequences be damned. Pushing her was unnecessary, but it's like I have an angel on my right shoulder and a devil on the left.

And in my world, the devil always wins.

6

Sophia

If there's one thing I don't have time for, it's entertaining an overgrown, immature child.

"Let me make it up to you. How about dinner instead of coffee?" he offers.

My lip twitches with doubt. "I don't think that's a great idea, Lorenzo."

"Call me Enzo."

"I'd rather not," I deadpan.

Having dinner with him is dangerous territory. If I have any chance of surviving this, I need to draw the line as soon as humanly possible.

This is what you get for having random one-night stands, Sophia. Here are the consequences of your damn actions.

Don't I know it?

"Strictly professional. We'll talk about the article and that's it." He raises three of his fingers. "Scout's honor."

A small laugh bubbles out of me at his ridiculous gesture. "Were you in the scouts?"

His lip twitches with a small laugh. "Oh, God no. But I do promise," he says, sounding sincere.

I drop my shoulders with a sigh. The reality is, we need to talk about the article and come up with a plan. We'll probably have to meet a few times so I can interview him. It's not like I can avoid him forever. And more than anything, I take this job seriously.

He takes out his phone, handing it to me with the new contact page open. "Just give me your number and we'll plan for this weekend."

"This sure is a very complicated and creative way to get my number." I glare at him, grabbing his phone.

Our fingers graze for a moment, and the simple touch makes me shiver from head to toe, making my body tense.

Lorenzo is a handsome man, there's no denying that. After all, I let him give me multiple orgasms in a tiny cleaning closet for a reason—and it wasn't for shit and giggles.

Oh, God. What is wrong with me? This meaningless sex needs to *stop*. That's what toys are for. While my best friend is falling in love and getting married in a few months, I keep having these useless and meaningless one-night stands, knowing full well I wish for *more*. *More* than meaningless sex. *More* than random one-night stands. I want the type of love that consumes you wholly, to be with a man who makes my stomach flutter and my heart burst with a simple look. I want to feel that sting of electricity authors talk about in romance novels with every touch, every kiss, every look. To be protected and adored. But we can all agree those types of romances are just that—*fiction*.

"Nah. I'd rather you use the term original." He winks.

With a scowl on my face, I finish putting my number in his phone before handing it back to him.

He shakes his head with a laugh, grabbing it. "I'll pick you up Friday at 7?"

"Do I even have a choice?" I mutter.

He laughs again and starts walking backward, not breaking eye contact. "See you later, *Blue*."

Blue? Seriously? That's the stupidest nickname I've ever heard.

He's pretty far now, so I shout, "My name's Sophia. Or did you forget already?"

He shrugs with a smile that makes his annoying dimple pop before getting in his car and driving away, leaving me standing in the busy streets of the windy city wondering what the hell I got myself into.

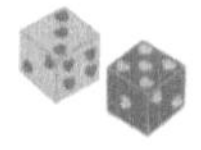

For the better part of my day, I worked mostly on doing some research Max needed, because God forbid he asks anyone else. On top of doing my regular job, I have to do these extra tasks he asks of me, and I always end up working insane hours. My concentration was shit, though, and between Lorenzo's shenanigans and the looming knowledge of my sister reappearing in our lives, I've been slowly losing my mind. As soon as the clock hit four in the afternoon, I ran out of work as fast as humanly possible.

Inserting the keys on Aria's door, I announce, "I'm coming in, if there's anyone indecent, it's time to hide. And yes, I'm talking to you, Damian."

As I'm opening the door, I hear Aria's fit of giggles and Damian's exasperated sigh.

Covering my eyes with my left hand and with my other hand extended, I walk into the apartment, moving it left and right, trying not to bump into anything. "Everyone decent?"

"Yes," Damian drawls. "That happened *one* time. Are you ever going to let me live that down?"

"Never," I quip. "I am forever scarred."

I drop my hand, my eyes finding my best friend on the couch, a cozy blanket draped over her as her head rests on her fiancé's shoulder. My heart tugs with longing at the sight of them. It would be nice to spend my days with someone, cuddled up and watching my favorite comfort shows. To find someone who can love me passionately and unconditionally, despite all my annoying little quirks.

Sounds like a nice little dream.

"I thought it was girls' night, but I can leave," I say, pointing to the exit with my thumb.

Aria gets up with the blanket still wrapped around her, walking up to me and shaking her head. "No, stay. Damian was about to leave anyway. It's just us today, though, Isabella can't make it. She had a dinner with her family she couldn't skip."

Oh, thank God.

If it's just the two of us I can tell her about my...*situation*. I love Isabella to death, but she's going to sit me down and tell me why, for the hundredth time, I need to stop sleeping around. I know she cares, but sometimes a girl doesn't want to hear it.

Damian walks after Aria, giving her a quick kiss before striding to the exit. He stops in front of me abruptly, his eyes eyeing me cryptically. "How do you know Enzo?"

My stomach flips at the sound of his name—well, *nickname*. "Your cousin?" I tilt my head, pretending to ponder. "I don't know him at all."

He glares at me, raising his eyebrows in suspicion, but

doesn't pressure the topic and leaves. At the sound of the door locking, my shoulders sag in relief.

Aria crosses her arms with a knowing grin. "Why did you lie to him?"

I pull off my heels with a satisfied groan and drop them at the entrance, flexing my numb toes to get the feeling back. I head to the kitchen and open the fridge, where I find the usual wine we love so much. Skipping the glass, I crack it open and drink straight from the bottle. It feels more badass this way.

Aria follows me to the kitchen and watches me as I chug. "One of those days, huh?"

I wipe my mouth with the back of my hand. "You have no idea."

"Wanna talk about it?"

Aria and I have been best friends since childhood—two girls from a small town in Kentucky who even went to the same college. She knows everything about me, the good, the bad, and the ugly. Telling her about Lorenzo should be easy, but she's always there when I mess up, and it makes me feel like a charity case. I can't afford to let my real emotions show, because people depend on me—my mom depends on me. I have to keep being the Sophia everyone expects: loud, funny, and always smiling. If not, they might see my scars, and that's a vulnerability I refuse to expose.

I turn around, rest my hip against the kitchen island, and look up for a moment, trying to gather the strength to confess this to my best friend. "I lied to Damian. I do know Lorenzo."

She laughs, folding the blanket and placing it in one of the island stools then mirroring my pose and crossing her arms. "I figured. Do you forget I know you pretty well?"

I roll my eyes without a reply.

"So," she prompts. "How do you know him?"

"You remember Mr. Three-Orgasms Guy?"

"Of course. You slept with him like a year ago, he gave you three amazing orgasms, and you still regret not getting his phone number—" She stops talking abruptly, her eyes bulging.

I grimace before taking another big gulp of wine. I need the liquid courage if I'm going to try to get through this conversation without wanting to crawl into a hole and die.

"Wait." She gasps. "You're telling me *the* Lorenzo Mancini is Mr. Three-Orgasms Guy?"

"You can't tell Damian," I rush to say, already regretting my confession and feeling guilty for asking her to lie to her fiancé of all people. "It's embarrassing enough as it is."

Aria takes the bottle of wine from my hands, taking a sip of her own. "I won't tell him, I promise. It's not my secret to tell." She shrugs. "I can't promise Enzo won't tell him, though. They're practically brothers."

I grab a stool and sit, resting my arms on the island counter as I massage my temples with my index fingers. That's what I was afraid of. I just love it when my stupid decisions bite me in the ass. As if I don't have enough to worry about. I stupidly decided to unblock Amelia's number and she's been calling and texting nonstop. That's the one thing I can't tell Aria, even if I'm dying to. She's Amelia's number one hater. Granted, she has every right. While I know Aria tries to be supportive, she'll never understand why I put up with so much. No one understands. And I don't expect them to. This is a problem I will always shoulder on my own.

"And I'm not done." I sigh. "You remember when he said Max had reached out to him to do an article on him or whatever?"

She nods, looking at me expectantly.

"He basically told Max he'd only accept it if I was the one to write it," I say, biting my lip. "So now, on top of everything else, I have to work with the guy, too."

Her shoulders shake with a soft laugh. "I'm not surprised. That sounds like something Enzo would do."

Yup. *Figures.* Another thing I was afraid of. Lorenzo Mancini seems like the out-of-control playboy he's known for. While that's what makes him exciting, it's also what makes him dangerous. He's a distraction I don't need. My life is already a clusterfuck of drama. I can't handle any more of that. Even when my body tells me to give in, to have fun.

Playing this game is dangerous. A danger I *cannot* afford.

7

Lorenzo

Staring at the big chandelier hanging from Vortex's ceiling, I'm lost in thought—only *one* thought, the one with a pair of deep ocean-blue eyes and a smart mouth.

"Earth to Enzo," Matteo calls out to me, snapping his fingers in front of my face.

"You sure are a persistent little fucker," I murmur.

"Funny." He laughs. "You didn't find me persistent when you had me look into Red's best friend. What do you want with her anyway?"

I shrug. "Call it curiosity."

Or that I'm trying my best to find everything I possibly can about her for some forsaken reason.

You know damn well why.

The itch to get another fix is the unfortunate reason. I seem to have a particular love for struggling. The last thing Sophia wants to do is give me the time of day, and somehow, that makes me want to get it even more.

A sharp, bitter laugh erupts out of me at the thought. I sound like a damn toddler. Isn't that sad?

He snorts at my comment. "Spill the beans, Enzo."

I lift my arm, calling Ivy to take our order. She has been working at Vortex as a bartender for a few years now. It took a lot for the board to agree to hire her. With Vortex being one of the most exclusive billionaire clubs, the board is picky in every aspect, including in who they employ. One day, she arrived at my apartment with a simple bag of clothes. She didn't want me asking any questions, and I didn't, out of respect. I hooked her up with a job and a place to crash for a few months. She's been my best friend since I moved to Chicago when I was barely eighteen, and this is how our friendship has always been. We know each other's darkest secrets, but we don't ask questions. We talk about it when we're ready. And Ivy's story, it's not mine to tell.

Ivy looks our way and nods, already knowing our usual order. Matteo likes his rum and Coke, since he's a little bitch who hates drinking whiskey. How I'm best friends with this guy is beyond me, because we couldn't be any more different. I, on the other hand, love a good whiskey neat. Simple. *Manly*—like my father used to say. Whatever the fuck that means. It does the job I need it to do, so nothing else matters.

A humorless laugh threatens to escape me as I realize I've turned out just like my father, using alcohol to numb the clusterfuck that is my life. What a fucking disappointment.

"You're seriously not going to tell me?" Matteo pressures.

I close my eyes, sagging my shoulders in defeat. "I'll need something to drink first if I'm going to confess this to you."

He lets out a low, long whistle. "Oh shit, this better be good."

Ivy approaches us, a smile lighting up her face. "Hello,

boys." When she places the drinks in front of us, she frowns at me. "What's wrong with you?"

"Thanks, Ivy. And that's what I'm trying to find out. Our boy over here has been cryptic," Matteo says, taking a sip and then looking my way, pushing my shoulder playfully with a fist. "Are you ready to confess whatever has you looking like a miserable idiot?"

I grab the whiskey glass and swirl it twice before drinking it in one gulp. The burn goes down my throat, slowly finding its way to the pit of my stomach. There's nothing better than the kick of a good old whiskey.

"You guys remember the girl I fucked on my birthday last year?"

He ponders, then nods animatedly when he remembers. "Yeah, you said she rocked your world, best night ever."

"The one who gave you a 7 out of 10? How could I forget?" Ivy laughs, grabbing a cleaning towel and drying some wine glasses before placing them where they belong. "I've never met her, but I love the woman already. Someone needs to put you in your place from time to time, Enzo."

I snort at the reminder. I still can't believe she looked me straight in the eyes and said, "*Yeah, solid 7 out of 10, but no thanks.*" Then shamelessly dared to repeat it the other day. I've never been rejected like that. The one time I was considering getting a girl's number, she rejected me instead. The irony is most definitely *not* lost on me.

I thread my fingers through my hair, releasing a frustrated sigh. "That girl has a name, and it's Sophia fucking Evans."

Matteo is midway through his rum and Coke when his eyes bulge in surprise. He spits out the drink, bursting into laughter. I glare at him as his shoulders shake with mirth and he wipes away tears with his napkin.

"The girl from your birthday dinner? Aria's best friend?" Ivy gapes at me. "No wonder you couldn't take your eyes off her," she squeaks.

"Please, let me be there when you tell Red," Matteo begs, hands clasped together like an idiot. "She's going to rip you a new one."

Ivy tilts her head, contemplating. "I don't know Aria well. But I do know Damian, and he's the one that's going to rip you a new one."

"I'm glad my misery is bringing you joy," I snap at Matteo, shaking my head with a scowl.

"Ivy, get back to work," Elisa, her manager—and a pain in the ass at that—scolds her. "What have I told you about fraternizing with the gentlemen?"

"It's fine, Elisa," I drawl. I honestly dislike her. If it were up to me, I would fire her. But it's not only my decision. The whole board has to agree.

"Mr. Mancini, with all due respect, it's clearly stated in the employee rulebook that this isn't allowed."

"And as the vice president of this damn club, I'm telling you it's fine," I snap. "Now, go about your business." I make a shooing motion with my hands.

Elisa, the smart woman she is, thins her lips and walks away without saying another word. I'm honestly surprised she was bold enough to say something in the first place. Not every employee here has the guts to talk to me like that.

Ivy looks around the room. "It's getting kind of busy, so I'll leave you two to it. I want updates, though!" she exclaims, serving me another drink before walking away.

Once she leaves, I look at Matteo. "Here's the thing, she pretended not to know me. Granted, I started the whole thing, because I wasn't sure how she was going to react, but she continued to act normal the rest of the night."

"Where was I during all of this? I cannot believe I missed this."

"You'd already left for that work emergency." I wave a hand dismissively. "Can we get back to the point here?"

Matteo bites his lip, trying to hold back his shit-eating grin. "Well, she *did* give you a 7 out of 10. That's a C minus. You're losing your game, lover boy."

"I'm not here for a lesson, genius." I hit the back of his head. "And me? Losing my game? *Please*," I scoff. I'm honestly a little offended he said that.

He raises his hands in defeat. "Hey, don't be mad at me. Be mad at yourself. Maybe you were having an off night."

Shaking my head, I grab the drink Ivy placed in front of me and take a sip. "I regret to inform you she *does* remember." I sigh, running a hand down my face. "And she dared to remind me of my piss-poor rating," I grumble under my breath.

Matteo's blue eyes sparkle as he presses his lips together.

"You're enjoying this, aren't you?" I ask in disbelief.

"Abso-fucking-lutely," he says with a shit-eating grin. "I can't wait to meet her."

I just know those two are going to gang up on me and fuck with me every chance they get. Add Ivy to the mix and they're going to have a merry fucking time.

"Are you going to tell Damian?" he asks, his tone serious now.

I give him an incredulous look. "Are you crazy? He'll go straight to Red as soon as I tell him."

"More like he'll punch you and then go to Red," he quips very matter-of-factly. "Ivy was right, Damian is going to lose his shit when he finds out. The girls are practically sisters, and you know how protective he gets of Aria. Our boy is pussy-whipped."

"Thanks for the great input." I grunt. "And stop talking about Damian being pussy-whipped, when *you* wished you were pussy-whipped by a certain grump with blonde hair."

That shuts him up. He rolls his eyes, choosing to drink instead. *That's what I thought.*

I know Damian better than that, though. He'll be disappointed, which somehow, makes it so much worse. Our relationship is not what it used to be. He acts more like a dad, and I feel like an overgrown teenager, disappointing the very little family I have left. But with how life has been lately, I can't bring myself to care, even though it makes me feel like shit. No one notices I'm drowning, so they assume I'm self-destructing. There's a huge difference between the two. But people will believe whatever they want.

I bang my head once against the bar. "I have to tell them."

"Yup. Because from the looks of it, I don't think Sophia will."

A hum of excitement floods through me at the mention of her name. Yes, the whole situation is fucked, but a part of me lives off the high that we're in close circles now. Her best friend is marrying my cousin. A cousin who is practically my brother. And now we'll be working together—a fact I didn't tell Matteo for a good reason. He likes to be the voice of reason sometimes, and I'm not looking for that right now. I'm all too aware of how risky this is.

If Sophia thinks she can avoid me forever, she's dead wrong.

Lorenzo

When my mind is a swirl of endless thoughts, I come to the restaurant and help. There's something so peaceful about coming here bright and early in the morning. It's a great escape from the real world sometimes.

I love getting my hands busy with prepping, washing dishes, or even deep cleaning. I'm not picky. Anything that can get me out of the suit and business mindset for a while. I'm not a chef, nor do I work in the kitchen when everything is up and running, but I enjoy helping the team from time to time, even if it's frowned upon. As the owner of Lorenzo's, I manage the business side of things—paying vendors, opening new restaurants, and constantly traveling to all the other locations I have around the world. But I would give it all up in a heartbeat to be in the kitchen, to become a chef. It's a thought I've never voiced.

Ever since I was a kid, I've had a passion for cooking. Creating recipes and playing with different combinations that could become the next best thing. But being a part of that world was never an option. I made my bed the day I let my father dictate my life and guilt-trip me into following his footsteps. I never imagined telling him I wanted to go to culinary school. The last thing I wanted was to be a disappointment. While he wasn't the most loving father, he knew how to use emotions to his advantage. My father wasn't a kind man, but he wasn't bad either. He was just...very business-minded. Very cold and calculated. Being vice president of Vortex consumed his life. So it consumed mine, too, by extension.

There was no escaping my legacy—that *is* the Mancini curse.

Our whole lives, it was always just me and my father. He never remarried after my mother's death. Instead, his work became the center of his universe. He taught me the ins and outs of how to act, feel, and think like a businessman. While other eight-year-olds would spend their life in summer camps and riding bicycles, I spent mine in business meetings. When Dad got sick, I took over the one thing that has carried the name for generations—the vice presidency of Vortex.

Many people would kill to be in my position. Vortex is one of the most exclusive clubs in the world, with chapters in places like Chicago, New York City, Tokyo, and Rome. Becoming a board member comes with connections, exclusivity, and fame every person dreams of. The reality is, being a part of such an elite group comes with many rules and limitations. For example, being the owner of a successful chain of restaurants was okay, but becoming a chef was not. Having the reputation of gambling and drinking was acceptable—to an extent—because at least it brought attention to Vortex, and that's all they cared about. We are allowed to act like we own the world because we have the means, the power, and the money to do so. It's as simple as that.

We are meant for more, meant to rule the world—their words, not mine. Sometimes, I wish they would shove their rules up their fucking asses. I couldn't care less about fame or money. But this is my life. This is what I promised my father on his deathbed. Even if he wasn't the most loving or caring, at least he was there. He was the only parent I had, and that's all that mattered to me at the time. Even now, years after his death, the thought of walking away from everything he wanted me to do feels wrong.

These thoughts have been drowning me lately. Thoughts I don't tell anyone, because no one will understand the pressure I put on myself. So I use other methods of escape—the partying, the gambling, the casual sex. But those have become less frequent lately, since they no longer offer the kind of relief they once did.

Lost in thought, I cut the ripe, red tomato with more force than needed, the slice ending up half an inch thicker than it should be. I know I shouldn't be handling produce right now, especially with my thoughts haunting me these past few days, but keeping my hands busy is the only thing giving me a sliver of peace.

My dinner with Sophia is tonight, which has me slightly on edge. Every time I close my eyes, I'm met with those same icy blue eyes of hers. I knew I was the obsessive type, but this is becoming a problem. Vortex is another source of my frustration, taking a lot of my time and energy. You would think such a prestigious, exclusive place would run smoothly in itself, but the constant pointless meetings are becoming the bane of my existence.

I drop the knife on the cutting board and clean the sweat prickling down my forehead with my forearm then remove my gloves as a tired, exasperated sigh escapes my lips.

"All good, boss?" Mikhael, the head chef, asks.

That's the million-dollar question lately. I'm not sure what I am. I can only think of one word—*tired*.

Tired of living the business-minded lifestyle but not doing anything about it because this is the promise I made to my father. I'm fulfilling my destiny. Doing what he wished for me. And who am I to deny the one thing he wanted? He put a roof over my head. He fed me. And for that, I will always be grateful and continue his legacy. Even when this world tires me. Even when I want to shout from the rooftop "*Fuck you all*" and walk away.

Before I can reply, I hear footsteps approaching the kitchen. I glance over my shoulder to see who it is, and when I catch sight of Damian's expression, I know I'm in for a world of pain.

"Ah, cugino.[1] What can I help you with?" I drawl.

Damian adjusts his cufflinks without replying. I've known him long enough to sense he's about to tear me a new one—I just don't know what for this time.

After a few beats, Damian tilts his head toward the empty restaurant. "A word?"

I let out a sigh and nod. Walking out of the kitchen, I step behind the bar to take two whiskey glasses and serve two fingers worth of the sweet and smoky golden liquid. I turn around and slide a glass to Damian.

He looks at me with a bored expression as he takes a seat in one of the bar chairs. "It's not even nine in the morning."

I shrug, gulping the whiskey in one swig. "It has to be five o'clock somewhere," I reply, grabbing his glass.

He follows my movement with his eyes, shaking his head.

"No point in wasting it," I say before drinking again.

---

1. Cousin.

He thins his lips and scrubs his face. "I came here to ask you a question."

"You could have called."

"I have the suspicion you would have lied, so I prefer to have this conversation in person." His tone is sharp and to the point. "How do you know Sophia?"

"Who?" I ask nonchalantly, even though my heart rate spiked at the mention of her.

"If you want to act stupid, fine by me," he replies with an amusing tone that doesn't reach his green eyes. "Sophia. My fiancée's *childhood best friend*."

"Oh, her." I scrub my stubble, pondering. "I've met her around. Can't remember where."

Damian folds his arms across his chest and leans back on his chair. "You slept with her, didn't you?"

I busy myself by flicking a nonexistent lint off my pants as a deafening silence falls between us.

"Yes," I answer truthfully, my tone devoid of emotion.

There's no point in lying. They were going to find out one way or another, might as well get it over with.

He lowers his head in defeat.

I've always been great at reading people, and Damian right now? The disappointment practically radiates off him. The irony is not lost on me either. Damian became the businessman he is today thanks to his ambition and his wish to be more, and I helped him through it. Now, he has his life together, a wonderful woman by his side, and his business is booming, and I'm just—little old me.

I'm extremely happy for him and how put together his life is. The man is stupidly in love, which was surprising at first. Shockingly, it suits him. But deep, and I mean very deep down, I'm a little envious. It's no secret I enjoy women. It's also no secret people perceive me as a careless playboy.

I've got my reasons for not opening up to loving someone. Reasons I keep buried deep. Reasons I will never say out loud.

But I can't deny that loneliness takes hold of me at the most unexpected times. And knowing he's getting married soon has brought back all those thoughts I've been trying to keep at bay for so long. I'm a thirty-six-year-old man who has never been in a serious relationship. No woman in their right mind will date me. I don't exactly scream husband material. Even if the knowledge stings sometimes, love isn't for men like me. How could it be?

"When?" he asks.

"On my birthday, last year, when we went to the club."

He lets out a long exhale. "Lorenzo, I don't think I need to explain this to you, but I will anyway." He straightens, stiffening his shoulders. "Whatever games you're playing with Sophia, you need to *stop*. This is Aria's best friend we're talking about here, not only that, but she—" He stops himself abruptly, shaking his head. "It's not my place to tell you her business, but she hasn't had an easy life, and she doesn't need you to come in and break her heart."

My ears perk up at his comment. I wonder how much he knows. Damian is like Switzerland, he never gets in the middle of anything, and the fact he's going out of his way to warn me off must mean Aria has told him enough.

The questions are on the tip of my tongue.

What do you know?

What do you mean she hasn't had an easy life?

The curiosity is killing me right now. A flicker of inexplicable annoyance runs through my veins at the thought of someone trying to hurt her. Every bone in my body tenses, because I don't understand where this feeling is coming from. I slept with this woman *once*, and she's been stuck in my head ever since. Now, she's stormed back into my life, and I find myself wanting to be around her and learn everything about her. It's absolute insanity. I barely recognize myself. Me, Lorenzo Mancini, the man who doesn't sleep with women more than once or care enough to know more about them, can't get this woman out of his head. Life is such a bitch like that sometimes. What a joke.

"What makes you think I'm going to hurt her?" My voice takes on a challenging tone.

Why am I the only one to blame here? She slept with me, too. And we're both consenting adults. I'm so sick and tired of people trying to meddle in my business.

He gives me a pointed, knowing look. "I'm not even going to answer that. The last thing I want to do is fight with you," he replies, getting up from the chair. "All I'm saying is, *please*, keep things professional with her. Otherwise, when Aria storms in here to cut off your balls, I'm not getting in the way."

I purse my lips and nod. "Anything else?"

I have no plans of hurting her whatsoever. I'm not a monster. People have this perception of me, and while I couldn't give less of a fuck, it hurts that my cousin—the man who's supposed to know me best—can't see the obvious. Contrary to people's belief, I do have a conscience, and I understand how complicated it would be if we were to get involved. But people will always believe what they want to believe, and I'm honestly tired of giving people explanations they don't deserve in the first place.

"As a matter of fact, yes. Aria wanted to invite you to dinner at our place on Sunday. Are you going to be here?"

"I don't know yet." I shrug, leaning against the wall behind the bar. "I have to go to Panamá, check in on the progress of the new restaurant."

"Reschedule it, then. She's inviting everyone. We have some announcements."

"Everyone?" I ask a little too quickly.

"*Enzo...*" he warns.

"What? I'm just curious. It's going to be pure entertainment having Matteo and Isabella in the same room." The lie slips through my lips easily.

He shrugs half-heartedly. "That's what I told her, but she said they are going to have to suck it up and act like adults."

I snort at his comment. Yeah, right. Matteo and Isabella not at each other's throats? That's a sight I would love to see. But I could care less about them. All I care about is the five-foot-tall brunette with a special set of eyes.

I make a split-second decision. "I'll be there."

What the fuck are you doing, Lorenzo?

I guess we'll find out.

9

Sophia

Max pops his head out of his office, snapping his fingers to get my attention. "Sophia, can I see you in my office for a minute?"

"Yup," I say over my shoulder as I grab my planner and a pen, knowing full well this will take longer than a minute. It's already bad enough I had to stay late on a Friday, now I have to deal with whatever misogynistic comments he's going to throw my way.

I walk into his office, closing the door before sitting down. "What's up?"

"This article about Lorenzo Mancini has me pulling my hair. Honestly, I don't understand why he had to choose you. Sophia, I swear, if you fuck this up..." He shakes his head, not finishing the thought.

All I want to do is grab that Tom Brady signed football that's sitting front and center on his desk and hurl it at his head for that comment.

Fuck it up? *Seriously*? That's rich coming from him.

People often wonder how he's the editor-in-chief. There have been rumors he slept with the VP of *Vogue Elite*, and others say one of his family members is part of the executive board. The way he acts most of the time is questionable at best. Not only that, but he's always been extremely unprofessional with women. This man is an HR liability. A lawsuit waiting to happen.

"I wonder what you did to have gotten this opportunity," he murmurs to himself.

Misogynistic asshole, party of one.

I take a deep breath, quickly counting backward. Has this method ever worked for me? Not really. I'm not sure why I keep trying. To keep some of my sanity, I guess. To feel some sort of normality.

I clear my throat. "What can I help you with, Max?"

"Oh, right." He shakes his head. "Sophia, I cannot stress enough how important this article is."

I hold back my eye roll. "Yes, I know."

"Okay, so what do you have planned?"

I'm silently thanking myself for deciding to do all this research. Otherwise, I would have been extremely unprepared, and that's not the ammunition I want to give Max.

"I know you said you wanted to see behind the scenes of what it's like to be a billionaire like him. But what if we take it a step further? Talk about his other accomplishments. He's more than a simple rich man, there has to be a personality and a person behind all of that."

He starts spinning his pen, pondering for a moment. "This seems risky."

"High risk, high reward," I point out. "This is Lorenzo Mancini we're talking about here. He never speaks to the media. We need to take advantage of this opportunity and go in a different direction."

To my surprise, Lorenzo has never done an interview. Everything you find online is gossip columns and people spreading rumors. It doesn't matter how bad it gets, he doesn't clear anything up. I've done enough research to back these claims and show Max the only thing that's out there are baseless rumors. He has the typical playboy billionaire image. Doesn't take anything seriously, but it's successful nonetheless. It's boring and tasteless. If I'm going to write this article, I want to do it the right way.

"I'll run it by the higher-ups. In the meantime, you can start." He points a finger at me. "But I also need you to work on what I originally wanted just in case, and a gossip column, of course. Then we will decide how to move forward. Oh, and before I forget, I need the articles I sent you fully edited and proofread by Monday."

"Monday?" I ask, my voice taking on a high pitch. "You gave them to me yesterday."

He drops his pen on the desk, leaning back in his chair. "Can your little brain not handle a tad more work?" He shakes his head with a laugh and murmurs, "Women."

As I'm about to respond with what is sure to be a retort, my brain stops me.

It's not worth it.

So I clamp my mouth shut instead. Of course, he's going to drown me in work. But hey, I'm Sophia Evans, this is what I do. I let *certain* people walk over me for no apparent reason.

I nod curtly, rising from the chair and striding out of his office. Anger is coming out of my pores, and now I don't know how I'm supposed to get any work done. I'm so sick of letting people get away with shit. It's ironic knowing I can be brutally honest and challenging when I want, but I can't ever seem to put my foot down with certain people. Max is my boss—as in, he can fire me if he wants to. Amelia, well, she's my little sister. She can be a total bitch, but I have to be the bigger person.

Angry tears fill my eyes, and I sniff, closing my eyes tightly and trying my best to make them go away. I don't do well with emotions in general—anger, most specifically. It reminds me of my father. There was not a moment of peace at our house because of his unleashed wrath. Mom was always on the verge of a breakdown, Amelia was too little, and I...well, I coped in any way I could. Shutting down, mostly. I've learned how to hide my emotions well, so when they show up and try to find their way out, I push them down as hard as humanly possible.

You do not cry.

You do not yield.

You do not show weakness.

You have to be strong. Normal. Fake happy. You've done it for years now, what's one more day?

Shaking my head and straightening my shoulders, I walk to my cubicle, finding the biggest bouquet of blue roses I've ever seen. With a frown, I grab the note that's placed on top of the flowers.

Looking forward to tonight.

—Lorenzo

This is definitely unprofessional territory, but it doesn't stop my stomach from fluttering as I trace his impeccable handwriting with the tip of my index finger. I put the note back in the envelope, a faint smile tugging at the corner of my lips.

We're having dinner tonight, and that has my body on high alert. I don't know how he's going to act, and I also have no idea how I'm going to feel around him. This is gray territory for me, because not only do I have to work with him, but he's part of my circle now. I'm going to have to see him *constantly*.

As I'm sitting at my desk to get this endless amount of work done, I hear quick steps and voices approaching our offices. The office door opens, but I'm still flipping papers, not paying any attention to the chaos happening behind me.

"Ma'am, you can't come in here," Ethan, our office assistant, says quickly, striding after whoever came in like they own the place.

"Like hell I can't," the other voice yells, and the hair on the back of my neck prickles at the recognition of that voice.

Amelia.

My eyes dart upward as I quickly turn around. And there she stands, with a scowl on her face, yelling in the middle of the office.

Cursing internally, I grip her arm firmly and lead her out to the lobby. "What the *fuck* do you think you're doing, barging in here?" I whisper-shout, looking around for signs of Max. If he gets wind of this, he'll have a parade with this information.

She gets out of my grip. "You're not answering my calls."

I wave my hand around. "I've been a little preoccupied. Working myself to the bone to take care of Mom. *Remember* her?" I ask, my tone heavy with sarcasm. "What am I saying? Of course, you remember her. You called her, pretending you wanted to find out how she's doing."

She tenses her shoulders, lifting her chin in a sorry excuse of a challenge. "I hadn't spoken to her in a while."

"Stop trying to feed me that bullshit," I spit.

I take a moment to inspect her. It's been a while since I last saw her. She's gotten skinnier, and her hair is a box-bleached color, chopped up unevenly. The bags under her eyes are more pronounced than the last time I saw her, and her blue eyes are dull and lifeless.

"If you're here for money, I don't have any," I continue.

She shakes her head, her eyes darting around, refusing to look me in the eyes as she bites her nails. "I need a place to crash. Miles and I." She sighs. "We broke up."

"You two are always breaking up just to get back together," I say, feigning boredom. "Remind me again how this is my problem?"

I'm not a particular fan of Miles—or this relationship—for many reasons.

"This time is for good." She sniffs. "He got another bitch pregnant."

I press my thumb and middle fingers against my forehead, taking a slow breath in and out. "Amelia, no. You can't stay with me. I don't have the space or the mental capacity to deal with you."

Proud of you, girl. Keep going. Stand your ground.

"I don't want to stay here. The last thing I want to be is around you," she retorts, crossing her arms. "I want to stay at Mom's."

"No," I hiss, my shoulders tensing. "So help me God, Amelia, if you show up at Mom's," I warn.

She tilts her head, her eyes dancing with amusement. "What exactly are you going to do?"

That's a good question. There's nothing I can do from here.

"I'm not going to have you come into Mom's life and disrupt her peace. She doesn't deserve it," I say, trying to level with her.

"Okay, so what would you have me do?" she asks, desperation seeping into her voice.

I stroll to the elevators and press the down button. "I don't know, but I honestly don't care anymore, Amelia. You're an adult, *act like it*." The doors open, and I get inside. I need to walk away from this situation before my resolve crumbles. "I better not see you when I come back," I say before the elevator doors finally close.

Once the elevator starts moving, a small, frustrated sob escapes me. It kills me to see Amelia like that. It kills me to know our relationship has gotten so damaged. I barely recognize her these days. I don't know where I went wrong.

You were just a child yourself, Sophia. You tried your best.

My best was not enough.

I straighten my back, swiping my tears away as I take slow, deep breaths. By the time the doors open, I have a fake smile plastered on my face and step out of the elevator carrying another fresh wound in my heart.

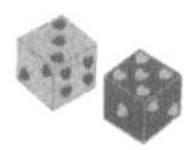

This day has been shaping up to be the worst. The cherry on top? I'm currently getting ready to go have dinner with Lorenzo.

Between Amelia's visit and the impending dinner, I don't know what to do with myself. I drowned myself in work today, and it helped for the most part, but Amelia has been texting me nonstop, and it has me on edge. I should've known better than to think that was going to be the end of our discussion.

My phone pings with another text. I'm about ready to

walk up to Lake Michigan and throw it in. Instead, I make the terrible mistake of looking at it.

AMELIA

Are you seriously not going to let me crash at Mom's? Sophia, come on. You're being such a bitch.

AMELIA

I don't understand why I even went to you in the first place. You're still bitter after everything that has happened. It's been years, move on.

Ha. If anything, I dodged a bullet. It may have broken my heart and made me swear off love in the process, but I can only imagine what my life would be right now if I were still in that situation. It's *not* a pretty picture.

My stomach churns, a wave of nausea rolling through me. I breathe in and out through my nose, trying to calm myself down. I throw my phone on the bathroom sink, leaving her message on read.

I grab my perfume and splash some on my wrist and the side of my neck then rub it in.

You'll cave eventually.

The looming realization hangs in the back of my head like a dark, stormy cloud. I know I'll cave eventually. Especially because if Mom finds out what sort of trouble Amelia is in, she's going to start worrying. So I have to go in and clean up the mess so it doesn't trigger her bad anxiety.

You could give her money to go away.

I would if it was possible. Every dime I have is counted for. Mom's psychiatrist is not cheap, but he's the best in the state of Kentucky. Not only that, but I have a maid who goes to clean her house weekly, and a nurse who stays most nights with her. And neither are cheap.

She doesn't necessarily need someone staying with her anymore—her panic attacks have become less frequent since she's been religiously taking her medication. But since I don't live near her, this arrangement gives me some peace of mind. Her anxiety is still severe enough that she needs help with simple tasks like driving to doctor's appointments and going grocery shopping. When her panic attacks were more frequent, they always happened at night. I can't blame her—nights at our house were always the scariest. It has always been a trigger for her. I'd rather be safe than sorry, even if it's more costly.

I don't mind covering for her things. I'm the eldest daughter. It's my job to take care of her, and I do it proudly. But I wish I could have something extra and throw it at Amelia so she can get the hell away from us.

I glance at the mirror, applying some lip gloss. I opted for a simple short, long-sleeved navy-blue dress with four-inch beige heels. My hair is in my usual soft waves, and my ears are adorned with my usual small gold earrings.

My phone rings with an incoming call, and I groan in frustration, because I know Amelia will keep insisting if I don't answer. Without looking at the screen ID, I pick it up. "*What?*"

"Whoa. *Feisty.*"

"Oh." I let out a sigh of relief at Lorenzo's voice on the other line. "It's just you."

"Just me? Please, you hurt me," he says through a hearty laugh. "I was calling to let you know I'm downstairs."

"Okay, I'll be right down," I reply quickly and hang up.

Looking in the mirror one last time, I give myself a much-needed inner pep talk.

Okay, Sophia. This is a normal, professional dinner. So what if you slept with him already? It was a random one-night stand.

No need to be nervous. And no engaging in unprofessional activities.

Walking outside, I spot Lorenzo leaning against his car. My knees, those two little traitorous bitches, tremble slightly, and I stumble like the idiot I am at the sight of him. He's wearing a dark-gray suit with a black button-down shirt, a few buttons left open. His hair is ruffled, and the look is so unmistakably him. I find myself staring at him like an idiot.

What are you doing ogling him, Sophia? Keep your cool.

My back stiffens as I stand before him and nod courtly.

His gaze locks onto mine with an intensity that sends shivers through me, igniting a storm of butterflies in my stomach.

"Hi, Blue," he rasps.

The moment is shattered by his choice of words, causing me to roll my eyes. "Will you ever call me by my name?"

"Nah. I think Blue suits you better." He shrugs casually, closing the distance between us, the gap now small enough for me to catch a hint of his intoxicating cologne. His eyes roam over my body, leaving a trail of heat in their wake. It's magical, the way Lorenzo can make me feel so much with a simple look. No one has ever been able to do that, and I don't know what to do with this newfound information.

He breathes in softly, his Adam's apple bobbing as he swallows. "You look stunning."

I pat his chest twice, internally chastising myself for touching him as an annoying charge of electricity courses through my veins. "That comment was completely inappropriate and a violation of our deal."

He raises his eyebrows, his eyes flickering with amusement. "What deal?"

"The deal where this needs to remain professional." For

some godforsaken reason, my hand still lingers on his chest. The rapid rhythm of his heart beats against my palm, filling me with a strange sense of satisfaction.

Do I make him nervous? *Interesting.*

He scrubs his face with a small laugh then places his hand on top of mine, grasping it softly. "Funny, because if memory serves me right, we never spoke about this."

"Because it was an unspoken agreement, of course," I reply weakly, the feel of his hand on top of mine rattling me to my very core.

"Mmm," he hums huskily, a smile tugging at his lips. His gaze lingers on my lips, and the look he has right now is anything *but* professional.

My breath hitches as his irises darken with an inexplicable fire, and our chests start heaving in sync. A wave of energy ripples through me, making every nerve in my body tingle. The tension that's quickly building and crackling between us is practically screaming at me to close the little distance and kiss him.

He's even closer now. His intense gaze roams every corner of my face, leaving me feeling raw and exposed. I close my eyes and let out a shaky breath, trying to kick away this exhilarating feeling. His other hand reaches out slowly, tracing my neck and collarbone with his thumb, leaving a trail of goosebumps. I open my eyes slowly, meeting his gaze, and my heart falters for the slightest moment. The way he's looking at me now is something I've never experienced before. It's not a look I can recognize, but it makes me feel exuberant nonetheless.

Before I know it, he takes a step back, taking his warmth away from me and dropping my hand. That brings me back to reality and I hastily take two steps back, wanting even more distance between us.

Oh, God. Here you are babbling about being professional and you almost kissed the man.

With a small, playful grin he opens the passenger door. "What about this?" He gestures at the car door. "Can I open it for you? I don't want you to think I'm propositioning you. I'm just trying to be a gentleman," he says with a teasing tone.

"Oh, yes, because you're known for that," I quip before getting in his car.

Lorenzo tilts his head, his mouth agape for a moment, before laughing. His laugh is so full of life and promises, it makes my stomach flip. It's like I've been transported back to high school when I had my first crush.

Snap out of it, Sophia.

If only it were that easy.

10

Lorenzo

I almost kissed Sophia.

My chest still tingles where she touched me. My hand feels strange, the feel of her soft skin lingering. My thumb still craves to trace every inch of her body. And my lips are cold, missing the warmth of the kiss that never happened.

You're such an idiot. Why didn't you kiss her?

Damian's comment from earlier today remains in the back of my head. She's been hurt, and I don't want to add another layer to that. Even though my body thrums with the need to say fuck it all and kiss her, consequences be damned.

But I can't. I won't. The perception people have of me couldn't be farther from the truth, and if I allow myself to do something like that, it would just prove them right.

"We couldn't have gone to your restaurant instead?"

I shake my head. "I'm always there, and I was craving some sushi."

"Yeah, right." She snorts a laugh. "Lorenzo, what are you playing at? I thought this was a business meeting."

Funny. I thought it was, too, until we shared that moment outside of her apartment.

"This *is* a business meeting," I confirm before taking a bite of nigiri. "So"—I wave my hand at her—"go ahead."

She drops her chopsticks on top of her napkin and leans back, crossing her legs. "I want to write about Lorenzo Mancini the person, not the billionaire. I honestly couldn't care less about how you made your billions."

Straight to the point. I like it. Sophia has this no-bullshit personality that I find, honestly, hot.

"But?" I prompt.

She frowns. "How do you know there's a but?"

"You forget I'm a businessman. I know how to read people."

Though reading Sophia hasn't been an easy task. She conceals herself well, for the most part. But the tense dynamic between her and her boss was fairly obvious, so I'm certain whatever he advised, she wants to do the exact opposite.

She gives an exasperated roll of her eyes at my comment. "Max wasn't too convinced, he wants me to write multiple articles that are drastically different."

"Let me guess, one of them is a gossip column?" I raise an eyebrow, giving her a knowing look.

She thins her lips and nods.

"Makes sense. *Vogue Elite* is a magazine, after all," I continue with a nonchalant shrug. "What matters is what *you* want to do."

The media thrives on gossip, chaos, and other people's misery. It's sickening. And I don't care for it. The thought of me doing this honestly makes my skin crawl, but then I look at Sophia and feel somewhat at ease. For some strange reason, I trust her. Maybe it's the fact I've read all of her work, or that I can tell she has integrity. I honestly don't understand why she works for a place like *Vogue Elite*. She's meant for so much more.

"It doesn't matter what I want to do," she replies with a flat tone.

I raise an eyebrow, setting my chopsticks aside and dropping my elbows on the table. "Why not?"

She drops her elbows on the table, too, resting her face on the palm of her hand. "Because it doesn't."

"I think it does matter, and I will do whatever *you* think is best." I lean back on my chair. "With that being said, I'm a simple man. What you see is what you get."

Her eyes gleam with something I can't quite place. "For some reason, I don't believe you."

Shocker. Who didn't see that coming?

I rest my hand on the table and start drumming my index finger against it. "You're not going to find what you're looking for."

She reaches for her glass of wine and takes a sip. My eyes follow the movement and focus on her soft, plush perfect lips. The same lips I'm still craving. And fuck, they're so pretty, all I want to do is get lost in them.

Get your head out of the gutter, man.

She shrugs lazily. "That's for me to find out."

What are you doing? This is risky. Stupid. You should walk away right now.

I couldn't even if I tried. Is this the best idea I've had? Probably not. I've kept my life private for a lot of reasons. Reasons I refuse to give a second thought. I don't think the world is interested in seeing the real me, and I'm not entirely too excited to share it either. This is a dangerous game, one a normal person would shy away from. But I think we've already established there's something stupidly wrong with me.

"Okay," I find myself saying.

Her eyes lock on mine in surprise, and then she nods. "Good."

"When do we start?" I ask.

"I'll let you know."

A smirk tugs the corners of my lips. "This will be an interesting dynamic."

"Tell me about it."

This will be far from ordinary. Yet it doesn't stop my body from buzzing with excitement.

Your play, Blue.

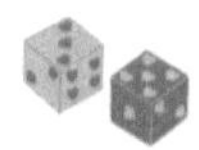

After I dropped her off, I texted Matteo to meet me at Vortex. He's loyal to a fault, so he didn't even bat an eye and was already there when I walked through the doors. Fridays tend to be very busy, especially on the fourth floor where the casino is located. The main floor, however, tends to be slower since everyone is upstairs gambling their money away.

The entrance of Vortex has a simple, classic style. Leather seats and tables are scattered throughout the room, offering a sense of comfort and exclusivity. In one corner, a bar gleams with an array of top-shelf alcohol, because nothing screams *entitlement* more than only keeping the best of the best. Some tables feature chess sets, providing an intellectual pastime for guests, while other small, round tables are perfect for intimate conversations. The décor exudes an old, classical charm with deep-brown hues and grand chandeliers casting a warm glow. It's not the typical style I would go for, but that's the beauty of this place. The style has remained the same since it was founded back in the late 1800s.

Matteo sits at the back of the room, where the plush leather seats and chess table are, our usual spot for when we prefer a game or two over conversation. He's currently typing away on his phone with a furrowed brow, deep in concentration. The man is truly a workaholic. *Carter's Corporation*, his cyber security company, is practically his baby. While people often judge him, I don't. He had to fight for his opportunities every second of every day and made a lot of sacrifices—some I know he regrets—to be here.

"Everything okay?" I ask, sitting in my usual seat.

He sighs, locking his phone and throwing it on the table next to him. "Yeah. I had to fire one of my analysts. He was working with the competition, completely breaking his NCA. You know, just my typical Friday."

I gape at him. "That was bold."

"Tell me about it."

He typically has the sunniest personality, a golden retriever by nature. But when it comes to his job, he's as ruthless as they come. You don't fuck with Matteo Carter if you cherish your life. He's been my best friend for years and even I can accept the guy can be terrifying sometimes.

"So, why'd you call me here?" he asks.

I straighten in my chair, looking down at the set of chess that's in front of me. I push forward the pawn from the left corner two steps. "Felt like playing chess."

He smirks knowingly, moving the pawn that's in front of his king. "Okay, let's play then."

I narrow my eyes as I move my pawn to match his. He then quickly moves his queen diagonally to the edge of the board. I frown, trying to see what his play is, and opt to move my pawn to challenge his queen.

With a smug grin, he moves his queen straight ahead to capture my pawn. "Checkmate."

I stare at the board. Once the puzzle clicks, I look back at him in disbelief. "I hate playing this game with you."

He laughs, leaning back in his chair and crossing his legs. "Chess isn't always kind," he remarks casually. "Can we talk about the real reason we're here now?"

Letting out a huge sigh, I lean back in the chair, the comforting embrace of the leather grounding me.

Matteo is almost like a brother to me. I confide in him for everything. He likes to fuck with me sometimes, but he doesn't judge. But I'm in so far over my head, I know he's going to call me out on my shit.

I chew the inside of my cheek. "I told *Vogue Elite* I would do the article they've been wanting to do for years now."

He offers a bemused smile. "*Vogue Elite*, as in where Sophia Evans works?"

My jaw ticks, and I simply nod.

"And let me guess, she's the one writing it?" he asks.

I nod again.

He lifts one eyebrow, tilting his head. "Walk me through what you were thinking when you said yes to this."

Where to even begin? I want to be near her and get to know her. I love to banter with her, because it's entertaining, and she also doesn't back down, making it even more fun. I haven't been able to get her out of my head, even though she has made clear where we stand. And let's not even begin to talk about what happened today. That's a can of worms I refuse to open at this moment.

"She's a really good writer." Technically, not a lie. "I think if anyone could make me feel comfortable with something I typically hate doing, it would be her." Also, not a lie.

He nods absently, and I can practically see the wheels turning inside his head. "Let me get this straight," he begins. "You never do interviews, because, and I quote, *fuck the media and everything they have to say.*" He punctuates his words with air quotes. "And in all the years I've known you, not once have you given the media what they wanted, but now you're totally on board because she's a great writer?" He narrows his eyes, rubbing his jawline.

Pursing my lips, I tilt my head, contemplating how to respond, because I have the feeling I'm walking into a trap. "Yes."

He completely stills, his cold, blue eyes settling on me. "Well, I'd be damned. I never thought I'd see the day."

I scowl at him. "What the hell are you talking about?"

"Lorenzo Mancini, the infamous playboy, wants to score *again* with the one woman who doesn't even give him the time of day."

My eyes roll at the ridiculous accusation. Listen, just because I enjoy sleeping with women doesn't mean I'm a playboy. I don't *play* women. I give them exactly what they're looking for—a good time. They know what they are getting into, because I always make my intentions clear. And when women are falling into bed with me, it's not because they are planning to marry me. They like to use me, and I simply let them. There's a difference.

"Trust me"—I snort a laugh—"I don't."

Mmm, then why did you want to kiss her so badly tonight?

A momentary lapse, of course. I'm human. Shit happens. I got clouded by... I don't know, her looks. Her scent. Her beautiful smile. Her bright-blue eyes. Her plush, pink lips.

Stop.

Fuck.

"Oh, please, Enzo. Spare me the lies." Matteo rolls his eyes. "You just want what you can't have, and honestly, I enjoy watching you squirm."

"You're having entirely too much fun with my life lately."

"What can I say? I enjoy the dramatics."

I glare at him. "You're a dick."

He laughs. "I'm not here to rain on your parade. I know I fuck with you a lot, but I mean, you're an adult. You know what you're doing."

"But?" I prompt—like I said, I always know when there's a but.

He fixes me with a piercing stare, all traces of mirth disappearing. "Be careful. This is Red's best friend we are talking about here. She'll be in our lives forever. Don't go making it awkward for the sake of proving a point."

I'm not trying to prove a point. Sophia is just...very intriguing.

And let's not forget about the fact that there must be a reason why she walked back into my life when I thought I'd never see her again.

Getting close to her is a dangerous game, because every time I'm near her it's like everything I know and the way I think goes out the window. I've never felt like this. I don't understand what this feeling even is.

But I'm willing to play, even when I don't know what the reward will be.

11

Sophia

I opt for knocking on Aria's door this time. As I wait for the door to open, I run my fingers through my hair, smoothing it out to keep it looking casually perfect. I don't know why I'm so nervous. This is just a regular dinner with a couple of friends, nothing to be excited about.

Maybe because you're going to see a certain man with a set of brown eyes you haven't stopped thinking about. The one you almost kissed, even though you told yourself you weren't going to engage in those types of activities. Remember?

Oh, right. *Ha.* Like I could ever forget.

Aria opens the door and greets me with a hug. "Hey, girl." She takes a step back and looks at me from top to bottom. "Interesting outfit. Looking to impress someone?"

I shoot her a glare, handing her the bottle of wine. "Yes. *Myself.*"

She squints at me, humming unconvinced. "If you say so."

As I walk into the apartment, I head straight for the kitchen, drawn to the charcuterie board that's spread out with my favorite cheese and multigrain crackers. I grab a cracker, scoop up a generous portion of that delicious, garlicky cheese with the knife, and slather it on.

Am I focusing on the food spread instead of the people around me? *Yep.*

Isabella approaches me. "Oh, thank God you're here."

I look up to see her annoyed face. "What's wrong?"

"I'm the reason for this sunshine humor of hers," a man says, walking into the kitchen. "Matteo Carter, nice to meet you, love." He gives me a boyish smile.

"Oh, the famous Matteo. I've heard so much about you," I say with a grin, wiggling my eyebrows and waving. "Sophia Evans, lovely to meet you."

Matteo laughs, taking a sip of his beer. "You've been talking about me, Isa?"

"If you count me telling her how insufferable you are, then yes, I've been talking about you," Isabella replies in a dry tone.

Even though Isabella spat an insult his way, Matteo's smile doesn't falter. I've heard Damian and Isabella say how Matteo is always smiling or joking, always the life of the party, and I can see what they mean. Funny, though, how that bright smile of his doesn't reach his eyes.

Matteo shrugs. "Whatever you say, Isa."

"Only friends get to call me Isa, and you lost that privilege a long time ago," Isabella replies before storming away.

Yikes. I guess Aria wasn't exaggerating when she told me chaos follows whenever they are in the same room. I step backward, inching out of the kitchen to dodge any chance of conversation and giving him an awkward little wave as I go. I turn around and bump into someone's chest with a loud *thud*.

"Watch where you're going, Blue."

My back stiffens at the sound of Lorenzo's voice. The

way he speaks, always with that light, flirtatious tone and the way his words drip like honey sends a shiver down my spine.

"Lorenzo," I say curtly.

"Blue," he repeats my new, dumb nickname he came up with.

I weigh my options for a moment. I can either go back to the kitchen and strike up a conversation with Mr. Sunshine, or stay here and spar with Mr. Playboy.

Boy, my options sure are looking grim.

But see, at least Mr. Sunshine over there doesn't infuriate me, nor does he make me feel things I'd rather not entertain.

Yup. Mr. Sunshine it is.

As I'm turning around to walk back into the kitchen, Lorenzo grabs me by the arm. The touch is brief and innocent, but it doesn't make it burn any less.

I get out of his grip. "I'd rather you not touch me."

"Is my touch taking you down memory lane?" he asks with a lighthearted tone, mischief dancing in his eyes.

I blink at him in astonishment. "You're breaking our deal with that comment."

His shoulders shake as he lets out a soft, velvety laugh that goes straight to my core, my body betraying me, yet again.

"Funny you say that," he comments.

I'm fairly shorter than him, even with my four-inch heels, so he has to lean down for his lips to hover just beside my ear. The way his warm breath hits my earlobe takes me back to that night. His woodsmoke cologne envelops me as I'm trying to mentally kick those memories away from me. The smell of pine and cedar hits me first. Such a rich, earthy aroma, like the comforting embrace of a roaring fire. It's faintly sweet, too, with a hint of burning maple. The scent perfectly suits him—strong, manly, dangerous, and surprisingly sweet.

"Rule number one about making a deal? Make sure the other party agrees. Otherwise, it's all fair game, Bella.[1]" His voice, barely above a whisper, is deep and husky.

He straightens, locking his light-brown eyes with mine, and winks before walking away and leaving me there standing feeling flustered.

Now that we're all here, we quickly sit to have dinner. It's nice, a lot of chatter and laughter, mostly from Matteo and Lorenzo trying to get a rise out of Damian. Isabella, well, she's her dark, cloudy self we all love, and Aria is the sweetheart of the group, but jokes from time to time with the guys to get a reaction out of Damian, too.

"Red, you know, I've been wondering how you can be with my cugino[2]," Lorenzo starts, trying to contain his laughter before he continues with the taunt. "You gotta tell me, is he that good in bed? That's gotta be it." Lorenzo shakes his head.

Damian fixes him with a glare sharp enough to cut. "You think you're so hilarious, huh?"

Matteo points at Aria with the mouth of his beer bottle, raising an eyebrow. "Care to confirm?"

"I can confirm Damian is a very passionate and thoughtful lover," Aria says in between fits of laughter, trying to catch her breath.

"Oh my God, *Damie!*" I chime in with a playful tone. "I'm so happy to hear my best friend is well taken care of."

The whole table is laughing now, except for Damian,

---

1. Beautiful.
2. Cousin.

who's as red as a tomato, but still has that broody, grumpy aura of his.

"You promised you wouldn't tell anyone about that nickname!" Damian exclaims, looking at Aria in disbelief.

Aria lifts her hands in surrender. "I'm sorry!" She grabs the black linen napkin from the table and throws it at me. "You are such a blabbermouth."

A loud laugh escapes my lips as my eyes fill with tears from all the laughing. As I'm trying to calm myself down, a small snort slips out between laughs. I haven't laughed like this in a while, and it's a welcoming feeling with everything that has been going on lately.

"*That'll do, piggy. That'll do,*" Lorenzo says with a laugh.

I lock my eyes with him in shock as the rest of the group groans in unison.

"You have to stop it with the quotes that no one gets," Matteo groans.

"I cannot believe we have another one in our group. Kill me now. Put me out of my misery," Isabella complains.

"Did you just quote *Babe* to me?" I ask.

Lorenzo frowns. "Yeah, why?" Then he looks at Isabella. "And what do you mean by that?"

"You'd be happy to know Sophia loves to quote famous movies and TV shows from the '90s," Aria chimes in. "It's kind of her most annoying quirk."

Her comment makes me falter for a moment, but I force a laugh instead. I know I have some annoying quirks, and my friends love me despite them, but the wound always opens the tiniest bit when someone points out things like that. And I know Aria doesn't mean any harm, it's not like I've spoken to her about it. This is how we work. I'm always the butt of the joke.

I look at her, faking disappointment. "*You're killing me, smalls.*"

Lorenzo chuckles, nodding. "*The Sandlot.* Nice choice."

"It's like you guys are meant to be," Damian chimes in, looking rather smugly at Lorenzo.

We both glare at him at the same time and say, "Please."

The rest of the group starts laughing as our gazes lock and we study each other. I'll be damned if what Aria said is true. Me being the female version of him? Not in a million years. This is a simple dumb coincidence.

"Okay, okay," Aria says, standing with her glass of wine. "Enough with the jokes. I have something I want to say. I'm so glad you all could make it here today. Means the world to me, guys, really." She lifts her glass. "To friendship."

We all smile as we pick up our drinks and toast.

Damian clears his throat with a small, deliberate cough. "We also wanted to let you all know we've decided to have the bachelor and bachelorette parties together. So, we will be going to Las Vegas at the end of August as a group. We're aware we don't even have a wedding date yet, but our schedules will get busier during the fall, so it makes sense." He shrugs.

Isabella chokes on her wine at the announcement, and Matteo's back stiffens. He glances at Isabella for the briefest moment before dropping his eyes to his drink, suddenly becoming very interested in the beer he's holding. I can feel Lorenzo's eyes burning into me, but if there's one thing I refuse to show, it's weakness—or how much I enjoy him not being able to take his eyes off me more than I'd care to admit.

"Everybody's cool with it, *right*?" Damian asks, his pointed look making it clear we don't have any other option but to agree.

We all nod and smile, and Aria's face lights up. I would do anything to make my best friend happy, even if it means spending more time than necessary with Lorenzo.

I tap Matteo's shoulder, leaning forward with my elbows on the table and my chin resting on my thumbs. "So, I hear you have a cyber company?"

He smiles charmingly. "I do. Built it from the ground up when I graduated from MIT."

"You and Isabella attended MIT at the same time, right?"

He nods, tensing a little at the mention of Isabella, who's sitting in front of him, silently watching our interaction.

"Yes. Totally built it from the ground up and abandoned people he claimed to care about in the process," Isabella remarks, abruptly standing and throwing her linen napkin on her empty plate. "I can't do this anymore," she mutters, grabbing her purse. "Thank you for a lovely dinner, guys," she says in a clipped tone then storms away.

"I'll walk you out," Aria says quickly, standing and following after Isabella.

Matteo's demeanor crumbles, his sunny personality nowhere in sight as he quietly gets up and picks his suit jacket from the back of his chair and puts it on. "I'd better get going, too. Long day tomorrow."

Damian gives Lorenzo a knowing look before standing and walking Matteo out.

I rise from my seat, silently gathering the empty plates and cups, the tension still heavy in the air. I head to the kitchen to start washing the dishes. Even though summer is starting, I get cold easily, so I decided to wear long sleeves today. I roll them up then take the hair tie from my wrist and put my hair in a messy bun.

From my peripheral vision, I see Lorenzo striding into the kitchen with the rest of the dishes. He drops them on the sink then rolls up his dress shirt sleeves. My eyes shamelessly follow his movements, admiring the way his veins trace intricate patterns beneath his skin, accentuating the muscles beneath. Small, random tattoos that I'm sure have some sort of meaning behind them adorn his tanned skin.

He lifts his gaze and catches me staring but doesn't say anything. Instead, he smiles knowingly. I straighten my shoulders and look at the sink, becoming very interested in the soapy, dirty water.

I haven't forgotten about our moment the other night. It's all I've managed to think about. I've been wondering what would have happened if we had kissed. Chances are, we would have ended up in my apartment. And that would have honestly been a huge mistake. But I think it's pretty safe to say, when it comes to men, I don't make the smartest decisions.

He approaches me and takes the sponge from my hands. "I'll wash and you dry. Okay?"

I lock my gaze with his, and God, I wish I hadn't. His eyes are so intense and warm at the same time. His right eyebrow has the tiniest scar, barely noticeable unless you really look for it.

I clear my throat and grab a clean drying towel. "Sure."

We quickly fall into silence as we work on the dishes. But here's the thing about me: I don't do well with silence. Chalk it up to my childhood, I guess. My house was loud, mostly with my father's drunken screams. When there was silence at home, it was never a good thing. Something bad would always inevitably happen. I associate silence with danger, and it settles a dread in the pit of my stomach. I know my friends consider me loud, and some people who don't know me well even find me obnoxious, but I can't possibly stay quiet or bear silence.

"That was intense." I nod toward the dining room.

"That was nothing, trust me," Lorenzo asserts, his voice laced with conviction.

"What's the story between them, anyway?"

Lorenzo lets out a long sigh. "It's not my story to tell. I'm sure Isabella will tell you when she's ready."

I nod, even though I would love for someone to clue me in on what the hell is happening. That's another thing about me—I don't do well with altercations. I always go into problem-solving mode. My brain is wired to automatically search for a way to make the situation right. With my upbringing, I was kind of forced to do so.

Lorenzo drops the sponge on the sink as he turns to face me, casually leaning against the counter. "So, when do you start drilling me with all your journalist-type questions?"

I scoff. "No one is forcing you to do this. You're the one that wanted to do it."

He raises an eyebrow, the one with the tiny scar, a soft smile playing on his lips. "Never said it was going to be easy."

Even though the smile is small, his dimple manages to make an appearance, and something in me wants to reach out and trace it with my fingertip. Instead, I slam the door on that thought before it goes any further.

"Never expected that, anyway." I shrug. "How about we meet tomorrow?"

"It's a date."

"It's not a date," I correct, dropping the towel on the kitchen counter and mirroring his pose, crossing my arms. "It's a business meeting."

He smirks, standing tall and closing the gap between us. He sure loves to get close to me at the most untimely moments. His intoxicating scent envelops me once again, and I lift my chin slightly, trying to maintain my composure, hoping he doesn't notice how my chest heaves. I refuse to take a step back. He started this, so he's the one who has to finish it. Backing down isn't an option, even though my body itches to reach out and touch him.

He brushes his knuckles against my cheek for a brief moment, giving me a quick chill. "Whatever you say, Blue."

Okay, then.

This will be fine. Totally fine. I can do this.

You literally can't.

Shut up, brain.

12

Lorenzo

I arrived at the coffee shop Sophia and I agreed on about thirty minutes before the actual meeting time. And it's safe to say, for the first time in my life, I'm actually nervous. I walked into this feeling rather confident, but now the realization that someone will have some insight into my life makes my skin itch. I don't think she's a vulture or anything. I'm aware this is her job. But her boss gives me the worst feeling I can't quite place.

The scent of freshly brewed coffee and baked pastries fills the air, mingling with the quiet hum of conversation around me. I glance at the clock, noting the time before looking up as the doorbell jingles, signaling someone's arrival. My heart quickens with anticipation.

The temperature inside the coffee shop rises a few degrees as I take her in. She's wearing an olive-green maxi dress paired with a white, knitted, cropped cardigan and black boots. Her long, beautiful brown hair cascades in its usual waves. While I've never been a hair type of guy, I guess there's a first time for everything. The only thing I hate about her outfit is that she's wearing sunglasses. She shouldn't be allowed to wear them. How dare she hide those beautiful blue eyes of hers?

Jesus. Are you even listening to yourself right now? You sound like a pathetic idiot.

I walk up to her as she's ordering, and before she can pay, I hand the barista a fifty-dollar bill and order a decaf, since I already had some caffeine today. With how nervous I'm feeling about this, the last thing I need is more caffeine.

"I can pay for my coffee."

"Blue, my chivalry will never allow something like that," I reply, grabbing her wallet and dropping it back in her purse. "You look beautiful today."

"Will you ever call me by my name?" she asks, exasperation creeping into her voice. "And stop complimenting me. Our—"

"Our deal." I interrupt her. "Yeah, yeah. I know. I haven't even technically accepted," I point out, raising an eyebrow. "And no. I will never call you by your name."

"Good to know, I guess," she retorts with a resigned sigh. "And I don't care if you haven't accepted our unspoken deal or not." She looks at me, but her sunglasses are still on, not allowing me to admire those perfect irises of hers. "Stop it."

I do my best to hold back a laugh, because really, there's nothing sexier than when she stands her ground. She thinks she looks so tough, when in reality, it makes her look more beautiful. Dare I say even cute?

We head to the pick-up counter to grab our drinks, and I tilt my head toward where I was sitting. When we arrive at the table, she sits and finally takes off her sunglasses. Relief washes over me at the sight of her eyes. There's a sort of tranquility they give me, even when they are nothing but intense. I'm making no fucking sense, but that's the best way to describe what I feel every time I can get a glimpse of them.

She opens her tote bag and takes out what seems to be a planning calendar and a journal. "Okay, so this is how it's going to work, I will have the tape recorder going as I ask questions. If at any moment you want something to be off-record, all you have to do is let me know so I can stop the tape recorder. Got it?" She points at me with her pen, raising an eyebrow.

I nod firmly, jokingly saluting. "Got it, *boss.*"

She shoots me a glare before hitting the on button on the tape recorder. "This is junior journalist Sophia Evans, day one of interviewing Lorenzo Mancini." She sighs, opening her journal, her eyes hovering over the page. "I see here you're technically Lorenzo Mancini III."

I nod. "My father named me after him and his father."

"Any particular reason why?" she asks.

I shrug. "Maybe he wasn't inspired that day, who knows?"

The truth is, he was obsessed with continuing the legacy. It was always about that. Nothing else mattered to him, not really. And what better way than to give me the same name as him and my grandfather? Talk about being original.

She bites her lip as she jots down her notes, and I find myself captivated by her every movement. Like the way her hand is wrapped around her pen as she delicately writes her notes. This woman is so effortlessly perfect, I wonder if she knows the pull she has on people.

"You were born and raised in Italy, correct?"

"This is public information already, Blue. Why are you asking this?" I ask with a bored tone before taking a sip of my coffee.

She stops the recorder and rolls her eyes. "If I ask for your deepest darkest secrets, are you going to confess?"

I thin my lips, trying to contain my laugh as I say, "For the right price, I might."

Her cheeks turn that cute pink color, and I can't hold my laugh anymore. It's too easy to rile up this woman.

"Okay." She snaps her journal closed with a little force. "I think it's time we talk about our deal."

"What deal was that again?" I knit my brows together, feigning ignorance.

She fixes me with an icy stare that makes my cock twitch. Mmm, being burned by her stare is not the worst feeling in the world. It's electrifying. Intense. Sharp. But what I like most about it is knowing her attention is fixed on *me*.

"You know the one. Here's what I'm thinking, okay? You refrain from any inappropriate comments so I can do this interview, and then we will go our separate ways."

I tap my left cheek with my index finger, pondering. "I thought you wanted to write a story about my life. The *real me* or whatever." I make air quotes with my fingers.

She begins drumming her fingers on the table. "Yes, and?"

"What makes you think interviews are enough?"

What are you doing, man?

I have no idea what the fuck I'm doing, I'm figuring it out as I go. That's the only way to live. Planning every single aspect of your life is boring. I'm the prime example of that—hence why I try to live in the moment as much as I can. My life has been controlled, my future planned, since I was a kid, and this is the only way I can get some sense of normality.

She nods, her shoulders sagging in defeat as she realizes I'm right. "Okay, so what do you propose?"

Before I can stop myself, I blurt. "Spend the summer with me."

13

Sophia

Am I becoming hard of hearing? Have I somehow entered the twilight zone? There's no way Lorenzo Mancini just told me to spend the summer with him.

My shoulders tighten as I lift my chin a bit. "Excuse me?"

He sits up straighter in his chair. "If you want to write a good piece, spend the summer with me. That's the only way you'll be able to get anything worthwhile. Sitting in these stupid interviews won't make any difference."

This is crazy. This man has officially lost his damn mind. I'm barely okay with being here with him, what makes him think this is a good idea?

It may be crazy enough to work...

No. It won't.

"Lorenzo, this is the stupidest thing you've said since I met you," I say flatly.

He shakes his head adamantly. "Think about it. You'll get to see my day-to-day, what I do during and outside work. My travels, what I get up to. It's a good idea." He waves his hand at my journal. "You'll get plenty of stuff, and I don't have to sit in these interviews that, honestly, are quite boring."

I take a sip of my coffee, hoping to soothe my suddenly dry throat. Of course, the coffee doesn't help, and I wish I had some water near me instead.

Those are some good points. I do want to write a unique, one-of-a-kind piece. Being his shadow is the perfect way to see more behind the scenes. I'll be able to get something good out of it. Because it doesn't matter how many questions I ask, he's not going to be honest with me. That feeling in my gut is telling me to do it. But the logical part of me is shouting at me.

Don't do it!

Stupidest idea ever!

Walk away right now!

"If we're doing this..." He perks up, and I quickly point a finger at him. "Don't get your hopes up, I'm not saying I am. But if I accept, we definitely need some ground rules. I'm done playing games with you."

"You can come up with whatever ground rules you need to make yourself feel comfortable," he says, his tone sincere. "Come on, Blue," he urges. "Be a part of my world for the summer. It could be fun," he singsongs, extending his hand so I can shake it in agreement. "Deal?"

I look at his extended hand, and before I know it, my hand takes a life of its own to shake his. "Deal," I reply, unconvinced.

He shakes his head with a grin. "Look at that. You made your first deal, the correct way."

Why do I have the feeling I just made a deal with the devil?

And worse, why am I looking forward to it?

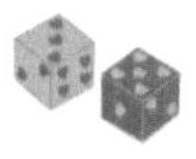

I think I made a mistake.

No. I most *definitely* made a mistake by telling the girls the crazy agreement I entered with Lorenzo Mancini. As soon as we shook on what I'm convinced is the stupidest deal I've ever made, I left the coffee shop with him promising he was going to reach out. I'm terrified, and I am almost hoping he regrets it and decides to do the interviews instead. I called the girls to have an emergency girls' meeting, and now here I am in front of a stunned Aria and Isabella.

"You did what?!" Isabella exclaims.

Aria remains quiet, looking at me dumbfounded. I've never seen her at a loss for words. It's actually kind of unsettling.

I groan, hiding my face with my hands in embarrassment. "Aria, say something."

Her hazel eyes widen, her mouth barely open. "I have no words," she mutters.

"I have something to say," Isabella starts.

Oh, here we go.

I nod, grabbing my glass of wine from the coffee table and taking a hefty sip, getting ready for her speech.

Isabella swirls her glass of wine, letting the red liquid move around as we both stare at her expectantly. "I want to be the maid of honor when you guys get married."

The delicious, fruity wine I'm currently drinking goes down the wrong way, and I end up spitting it out, patting my chest as I cough and struggle to catch my breath. "Isa, what in the *actual* fuck?" I manage to ask between coughs.

"I see it happening." Isabella shrieks excitedly. I can't decide what's more unsettling, a quiet Aria or an excited Isabella. "Oh my God, you're living the book dream. Two players who don't believe in love fall for each other."

Someone needs to wake me up, because I must be having a fever dream. I have no words for what Isabella spat out of her mouth. I don't even know how to start unpacking this.

"First of all," I say, lifting one finger. "Who knew you were such a romantic? This look is unsettling, please stop. And two." I lift a second finger. "There will be no falling in love. Especially because I've slept with him already, and I don't do repeats, much less love."

I realize my mistake a second too late. Aria's eyes bulge as Isabella lets out the biggest gasp known to man, placing her hand over her mouth in shock.

"You *slept* with Lorenzo?" she asks in disbelief.

"He's Mr. Three-Orgasm Guy," I confess with a grimace.

Isabella starts nodding nonstop as she tries to dissect this information. "My statement remains."

"For the record, I agree with Isabella," Aria chimes in.

"Oh, now you have things to say. Goodie," I mutter under my breath, crossing my arms.

"We should make a bet," Isabella says, patting Aria on her arm.

"Agreed. I bet he's going to say the L word first," Aria pipes up.

"Guys, hello!?" I shout, waving my hand so they can look at me, which doesn't work.

"And I bet they're going to have a Vegas wedding."

Isabella grins, clapping her hands a little too eagerly for my liking.

Aria gasps with equal eagerness. "I can totally see that happening!"

"Guys!" I shout again, causing them to startle and look my way. "This crazy talk needs to stop, *now*."

There are so many things I could say, I don't even know where to begin. For starters, I've been burned too many times to believe in love. Yes, it's been three years, but it doesn't mean it hurts any less. Not only that, but Lorenzo is a player at heart and I'm too pessimistic. We're the worst combination ever. We don't fit. We never will. And most importantly—*I don't want to fit*. Not with him. Or with anyone, for that matter. Even if my heart is begging me to open myself to the possibility, it should know better by now. That's never happening.

Always the maid of honor, never the bride. And I'm okay with that. Or at least I'm halfway there.

Always the person who takes care of others, not the other way around. Even though I'm surrounded by people who love me and would do anything for me, I can't bring myself to allow anyone to take care of me.

I'm the perfect daughter who sacrifices everything to take care of her mom, and I've grown to love that role. My mother didn't choose this life or her condition, and I'm more than happy to be there for her.

I'm the dumb sister who always comes to the rescue, even when Amelia doesn't deserve it. And I don't even do it for her sake, I do it for Mom's.

I'm the perfect junior journalist whose boss takes advantage of her, because I have no other option. If I have to deal with a misogynistic son of a bitch, then that's what I will keep doing.

I'm the girl who always has a smile plastered on her face, even when I'm dying inside, because the last thing I want to show is the cracks of my heart.

I'm a lot of things—just not happy. And I've learned to accept that.

I have *trained* myself to accept that.

Opening myself to someone is the opposite of that. I can mend my own heart and take care of myself. I don't need a man. Much less one who doesn't take love seriously. A reformed playboy is for fairytales. The type of love story you read in a good old romance book.

But the reality is so much more daunting than that.

14

Lorenzo

Every time I sit at a poker table and feel the cool green surface under my fingertips, I get such a high of adrenaline. This is hands down my only favorite part of Vortex—the casino.

In the center of the room, a huge chandelier hangs above the raised platform where all the games take place. The rest of the room has lounges scattered all around, where guests can sit and relax with a drink if they choose not to play. The lighting is soft, casting a golden glow that makes everything a bit more magical.

"Mancini, fancy meeting you here," Julian says sarcastically.

"Molina." I nod curtly. "I'm surprised to see you here."

A lot of people think I'm reckless with gambling and women. But Julian Molina? What I do is child's play compared to him. To be fair, the guy is a twenty-eight-year-old billionaire living off his trust fund. His family owns Molina Media Group, the largest digital marketing agency in the world. His parents, born and raised in Puerto Rico, moved to the United States for a better life when they were young. His father, the current CEO, worked tirelessly to get his MBA and build the company into the empire it is today. Julian is always the talk of the town. You can almost always find him in Ibiza or Greece, often plastered and getting himself into trouble. He's often the talk in gossip columns, always seen with a model or on Cala Tarida beach, jumping into the ocean butt-ass naked—true story, by the way. It happened recently. He's a god in the eyes of the media. They love to watch his every step, eagerly waiting for the inevitable trouble he'll get into.

"Yeah, well, Daddy dearest is out of town, so I'm able to fucking breathe for a change," he replies, amusement lacing his tone.

I raise an eyebrow. "What did you do now?"

Typically, when Julian is hanging around the streets of Chicago, it means his dad has a close eye on him because he did something he wasn't supposed to do.

He shrugs casually. "Got arrested in Spain for public indecency."

"Oh, Molina. You stupid motherfucker."

"To be fair, I was very drunk and I needed to pee." He laughs. "Come on, Mancini. Let's play some poker."

Before a response forms on my lips, Ivy approaches us. "Hello, gentlemen. Anything I can get you to drink?"

I frown. "They have you working up here today?"

"Yup. Elisa was *not* happy the other day, and now I'm stuck working here for the next two weeks." She rolls her eyes. "At least the tips are still good. Now, can I get you two anything?"

"How about your number?" Julian asks.

Ivy looks at him with a scowl. "Will you ever give up?"

I laugh at her comment. Julian has been trying to get Ivy's number since she started working here. The guy is a shameless flirt, but when it comes to her, I think he sees it more as a challenge since Ivy will bust his balls every chance she gets.

He leans forward in his chair, eating some of the distance between them. "Have you learned nothing? I will never give up, Ivelisse."

She hits him on the shoulder, hissing. "Don't call me by my full name. You know how much I hate it."

"But why, Princesa[1]? It's cute."

"Ay Dios mío[2]," she mutters under her breath. "I don't know what I hate more—when you call me Ivelisse or when you call me Princesa."

"Please." He rolls his eyes with a knowing smirk. "Tú sabes que a ti te encanta cuando yo te llamo Princesa.[3]"

She thins her lips for a moment. "Just for that, you can go get your own fucking drink." She turns her head, looking at me. "Whiskey neat, yeah?"

I nod. "You already know it."

She nods and walks away. Julian's eyes shamelessly follow every single one of her movements.

"Will you ever give up the chase?" I ask.

I honestly couldn't care less what Julian gets himself into, but Ivy is practically my sister and the last thing she needs is to get involved with someone like him.

He shakes his head. "Never. That woman is going to be my wife one day." His tone is so filled with conviction, I almost believe him.

"Good luck with that." I let out a small, amused snort.

---

1. Princess.
2. Oh my God.
3. You know you love it when I call you Princess.

"She knows what shit you get up to around here. You do realize you have a reputation, right?"

"I'll drop it all for a woman like her." He beams like the idiot he is. The day Julian Molina settles down will be a cold day in hell.

I opt to not say anything, because I know Ivy can handle herself. She's smart enough to know that mixing herself with Julian would be a recipe for disaster. Instead, I nod to the dealer to start the game. One of the perks of being the vice president of this club? If I'm sitting at the poker table, the game doesn't start until I give the go-ahead.

"Why don't you hand me your money now? You want to suffer through a game and claim I cheated?" I challenge, glaring at Julian.

The dealer places two cards face down to each of us and the rest of the players.

Julian peeks at his cards and smirks then looks at me. "We'll see. Maybe today is my lucky day," he says, betting two lavender chips, each worth a hundred thousand dollars.

I peek at my cards. An ace of spades and a king of hearts. It's a strong starting hand, so I call the bet, matching his amount without hesitation. People can call me cocky all they want, but I'm good at this game. Maybe even a little too good. I've always believed the reason I do so well is because, well, it's just money. It means nothing to me.

The dealer reveals the first three cards, and I glance toward the entrance as Damian steps inside with Aria. I lift my hand to get their attention, and my breath catches when I see none other than Sophia walk in right after them. She's wearing this killer short, blue satin dress that clings to her curves in all the right places, shimmering under the overhead lights. The hemline dances just above her knees, revealing those beautifully toned legs of hers. My memories flash back to that night, my hand traveling upward, touching every inch of her soft skin as I had her pinned against the wall.

Her hips move with a grace that commands attention, and looking around, I'm not the only one noticing her.

"Who's the babe?" Julian asks, intrigued. *This* is what I mean. This man will never stop chasing after every hot woman he comes across. *I'll drop it for a woman like her, my ass.*

My eye twitches involuntarily at the sound of Julian's voice. "None of your fucking concern," I snap, tapping the table twice to get his attention. "Get back to the game so I can beat you."

I have the sudden urge to finish this game as quickly as possible so I can go spar with her.

Well, that's a first.

Julian raises an eyebrow at me, his eyes flashing with a mysterious mischief. "Let's make this bet more interesting."

My heart rate picks up. Whatever he's about to propose, I'm not going to like.

"If you win, I'll stay away from her," he starts.

"I have no idea who you're talking about," I drawl, twirling a lavender chip between my fingers.

"I'm talking about the hot brunette that seems to have you squirming for whatever reason," he replies with a shit-eating grin. "But If I win, well, let's say she'll be going home with me tonight."

"Yeah? Weren't you just saying Ivy was going to be your wife one day? Moving on so quickly, lover boy?"

"You let me worry about that." He waves his hand dismissively. "What do you say?"

Yeah, over my dead fucking body.

Just say no to the bet.

If I say no to the bet, he'll go after her. I look at the cards. Ten of hearts, jack of diamonds, and queen of clubs. I have a good hand. My heart races at the prospect of entering a bet I'm sure to win.

Okay, but if you don't, he'll go after her...

I've never backed down from a bet, and I'm not about to start now. A few of the other players around the table fold, while others call. Then the dealer reveals the turn: a nine of hearts.

One card away from a straight.

Why are you so nervous? You're never nervous when it comes to gambling. You said it yourself, you don't care.

The stakes became much higher, and that's all I'm going to allow myself to admit.

"You're on," I reply, throwing two more lavender chips on the table.

He raises an eyebrow, but I see his demeanor changing slightly. He's *hesitating*. People always have a tell, and he's no different. Every time he's unsure of a hand, his shoulders tense, and if I'm right, he's about to scrub his face with his left hand right about now.

He scrubs his face as I expected before calling my bet. Finally, the dealer lays down the river: a ten of clubs.

Three of a kind, *thank fuck.*

For the first time in my life, my shoulders relax for the briefest moment during a game, and I catch myself before anyone else can notice. Julian goes all in, pushing the remaining chips to the center of the table. I do the same, feeling more confident than ever. The rest of the players fold, leaving it down to just the two of us. The tension is palpable as Julian reveals his cards, which are two pairs.

With a smirk, I flip over my cards, revealing my three tens.

Julian groans in frustration, rolling his eyes. "Well played, Mancini."

I casually rise from the table and button my suit, then pick up one of the lavender chips and give it to the dealer. I always tip a minimum of a hundred grand when I play high stakes like these.

I toss the remaining chips onto Julian's lap, letting them scatter across the floor, and plant a hand firmly on the poker table as I lean in close to his ear. My voice drops to a low, menacing tone. "If you ever come near her, or even *think* about her, you will answer to me. I mean it, Molina. Do *not* fucking test me."

A small smirk plays at the corner of Julian's lips. He nods at the chips that are currently scattered all over the floor.

I straighten, picking a nonexistent lint off my shoulder. "Keep them."

Like I said, I couldn't give less of a fuck about the money. But her? Off-fucking-limits.

Sophia

One of the reasons I'm the best junior journalist at *Vogue Elite* is that my research is always very thorough. Naturally, when Max assigned me Lorenzo's project, it was no different. I did a lot—and I mean *a lot*—of research. Most articles I found about him had one thing in common: everyone agreed Lorenzo was a gambling expert. I didn't believe it at first.

But now, standing in the corner of Vortex's casino, watching him play poker, everything falls into place. You can tell he's in his element. He radiates calmness, his face completely unreadable. The way he moves so effortlessly, looking at his hand without betraying a single emotion, and the way his piercing gaze follows the cards the dealer places, is mesmerizing. One thing is for certain, when Lorenzo Mancini takes a seat at that green table, the game is his.

The game just finished, and the dealer declared Lorenzo the winner, as expected. He stands from his seat and buttons his suit, and my eyes shamelessly follow his every move-ment. The way he gracefully grabs his chips and hands one to the dealer then tosses the rest into another player's lap.

All I can bring myself to do is focus on Lorenzo's hard gaze and the way his chiseled jaw clenches as he places one hand on the table and leans closer to the other player. He speaks with tensed shoulders and a look that could kill, sending chills down my spine. He emits danger, making my lower belly feel warm. Only a man like him could pull off this bad-boy vibe.

Once he's done talking, he straightens and starts scanning the room, and discomfort twists my stomach into a knot. He's probably looking for his date. Of course, he didn't come alone. I don't know why I thought otherwise. Before I can look away, his eyes find mine, sparkling for the briefest moment when they settle on me. That look makes my heart skip a beat, and my hand instinctively moves to my chest, rubbing the unfamiliar ache.

He strides over, flashing me his killer smile. "Hi, *Blue*."

A faint smile plays on my lips. "Hi, *Ace*."

He frowns, rearing back. "You were watching?"

Watching is an understatement. More like mesmerized by every movement of his, like a damn spell.

I laugh. "Oh, yeah. No wonder people say you're good. You get lost in the game. It consumes you, doesn't it?"

He fixes his light-brown eyes on me while I admire every detail of him. The light stubble on his chiseled face, the perfectly styled softness of his hair, and the sharp black suit he wears. His white dress shirt with a few buttons left undone—as per usual—giving me yet another glimpse of his golden chain resting against his tattooed chest. He leans casually against the wall, crossing his arms in a way that makes his suit cling to every hard muscle. My core tightens, the need present in the front of my mind. I'm acutely aware of how incredibly handsome he is. My mind wanders, trying to decipher how far his tattoos extend. Do they reach to his shoulders? Maybe his abdomen? During our one-night stand, we kept most of our clothes on, so I've never actually seen his body. I can't lie to myself—I'm dying of curiosity right now.

"You've been asking about me, Bella[1]? If you're curious, all you have to do is come to me, because I can show you *everything*," he says with a devious smile on his face, letting the innuendo hang between us.

I raise an eyebrow, trying to mimic his pose, but he's so impossibly tall I have to tilt my head back to look at him. "Been there, done that. A 7, remember?" I say with a smug smile.

His shoulders shake with a velvety laugh that's so infectious, it should be illegal. "You keep saying that, but I don't believe you."

I don't waver at his comment. If there's one thing I've learned from being around him, it's that he has no concept of a filter. And he's not wrong—Lorenzo is hands down the best one-night stand I've ever had, but that's the last thing I will ever admit. His ego doesn't need the boost.

I choose to ignore his comment, tilting my head toward the poker table where he had been sitting instead. "What were the stakes?"

He glances at the table for a moment, his jaw tightening as a flicker of something unreadable flashes in his eyes. Then he turns his gaze back to me. "You."

His comment is like a bucket of ice water, snapping me back to reality. If there's one thing men have, it's the fucking audacity. Really. Society has let men get away with entirely too much, making them believe they can step in and do whatever the hell they want.

---

1. Beautiful.

"I'm not some toy you get to bet for," I snap.

"Trust me, I did you a favor. You don't want to get mixed with Julian," he retorts very matter-of-factly.

"Who I mix myself with is *none* of your business. You're not my keeper."

He scrubs his face, groaning in frustration. "Forgive me for caring about you."

That word knocks the wind out of me. Men don't *care* about me. They mostly want to use me for my body and for a good time. All I am is the pit stop before they meet the woman of their dreams. And that's fine with me.

Yeah, if you say it enough times, maybe you'll believe it.

Someone *caring* for me is a concept I'm not familiar with. How could I be? I've never known what that feels like. I mean, my mom cared for me in the best way she knew how. But a *man* hasn't cared about me, ever. Not that I need it, though.

"I got involved with you, didn't I? How much worse can it get?" I fire back.

His gaze locks onto mine, and I can feel the color drain from my face as the realization of what came out of my mouth hits me. This is my pattern: I'm loud, hot-headed, and often speak before thinking. But honestly, what's an appropriate response to being told I was the prize in a bet?

Before I can open my mouth to say something, maybe to even apologize, he bursts into laughter.

"You're a feisty little thing, aren't you?" he asks, a knowing smile on his lips.

Confusion creases my face. "You're not offended?"

"No." He shakes his head, stepping into my space.

He lightly brushes his knuckles against my cheek, and his cologne, strong as always, captivates me. I fight to hold back a small whimper from the tempting aroma. I straighten up and lift my chin, trying to show him he doesn't affect me. Fake it 'til you make it and all that.

"I like you just like this. Unfiltered and all." His voice drops an octave.

"One of these days we're going to sit down and talk about those boundaries I keep telling you about," I manage to say, panting slightly. I'm trying my best to ignore the sudden need I feel between my legs. The way his knuckles feel against my cheek makes me wish he was grazing any other part of my body.

He slides his hand into his pocket, taking his warmth away as he casually shrugs. "I don't think you mean that."

Yeah, I'm not too sure I mean it either.

"You sure love to keep assuming things," I point out then turn around to start walking to Aria and Damian's table. Before I can get too far, he grabs my arm, gripping it softly.

"What are you doing here, anyway?" he asks.

"None of your concern."

His eyes gleam with that familiar playful glint as he bites his lip softly and shakes his head. Lorenzo's gaze is always intense, and when he looks at me like that, my body reacts. It's completely involuntary—or so I keep telling myself. He places his hand on my waist, guiding me to the table. I try my best to watch my steps, but my body is too entirely focused on his hand, where it's placed and how it feels. The burning sensation is relentless and charged, and it does nothing to help ease that achy sensation between my legs.

"Saw you playing with Molina. Did you win?" Damian asks.

Lorenzo brings out a chair and nods at it for me to sit. "Of course, I won. I'm quite offended you even had to ask," he replies with a scoff.

I glare at the chair then at him. "I don't need you to get a chair for me. I have arms, you know?"

"Like I've said before, Bella[2], my chivalry will never allow something like that."

I raise an eyebrow, meeting his gaze with a silent challenge. I'm not sure why I do this. I always try to find a way to spar with him. That's who I am—I can never make things simple. It's ironic, given how complicated my life has always been. In a twisted way, I keep returning to those patterns.

"*Blue*," he warns.

"Stop calling me that. I hate it," I hiss.

"I like that nickname, it suits you," Aria chimes in, which wins her a glare from me.

"Sit down," he says with a bored tone.

I start picking on my nails, already over the situation. "No."

"Must you make everything so difficult?"

Ouch. I mean, he's right, but still.

With an eyebrow raised and our eyes locked, I pull out the chair in front of me then slowly and deliberately take a seat.

He darts his tongue out to lick his lips then lets out a humorless laugh. Without saying a word, he sits in the chair he'd originally pulled out for me, shaking his head in disbelief.

"Aria wasn't wrong when she said you two are the same person," Damian comments.

We both cross our arms and say at the same time, "We are not." The movement is so in sync it makes Damian laugh, and that man never—and I mean *never*—laughs.

Aria hits his arm. "I told you that in confidence."

---

2. Beautiful.

"You owed me for the whole *Damie* thing," Damian replies with a casual shrug.

I laugh at their bickering. They act like an old married couple already, in the best way possible. My heart tugs at that familiar longing sensation I get every time I'm around them, but I quickly drown it with the drink Aria ordered for me before I arrived at the table.

As we drink and talk, Aria somehow convinces Damian to teach her how to play poker, so they leave the table, leaving me alone with Lorenzo.

"He's going to lose so much money." He laughs.

"He'll do anything to make Aria happy. I think money is the least of his concerns right now," I say, looking at the happy couple. Aria is confused as Damian animatedly speaks and shows her what each card means and the costs of the chips.

Lorenzo notices me staring at the game. "I can teach you how to play, if you'd like."

"No, thanks," I reply, folding my arms.

"You have to let go of this vendetta against me. Otherwise, you're going to have a terrible time this summer," he quips.

He does have a point there. I shouldn't be making things more difficult. If anything, I should try and be grateful he's willing to work with me on this article. Lorenzo is a very private person. It's a big deal that he's letting me do this.

I let out a resigned sigh. "You're right. But just to clarify, you *really* annoy me."

He grins. "If you say so."

"I do," I insist, narrowing my eyes at him.

His grin widens. "That's what I said."

"You don't believe me. Why?" I ask, frustration creeping into my voice.

"Never said I didn't believe you." There's something about the tone of his voice that rubs me the wrong way.

"Your tone says otherwise," I shoot back, crossing my arms tighter.

"*Blue*," he says, exasperated, running a hand through his hair.

I follow the movement, watching how he brushes his hair with his fingertips, remembering how those same fingers traced my neck and my collarbone in a sensual, exploratory way not that long ago. Call me crazy, but I swear he was about to kiss me that night. And what's even worse is I was going to let him.

"*Ace*," I retort, lifting an eyebrow and leaning forward slightly.

His gaze shifts purposefully from my eyes to my mouth then to my cleavage, where it lingers.

"Stop checking me out, Lorenzo. Have some manners," I snap, my cheeks heating with the way his eyes shamelessly linger there for another beat before looking up.

"Don't act like you hate it," he says with a cocky smile.

"Oh, please." I roll my eyes. "I've seen better attention from a stray dog."

He laughs, leaning in and wrapping me in his charming presence. "If you say so," he says then stands and drops a few hundred dollars on the table. "By the way, I'll be picking you up tomorrow, bright and early."

"For what?" I frown.

"For our summer adventure, of course." He winks. "And Sophia?" He thins his lips, trying to hold back a smile. "Maybe ease up on the resistance? I bet we'll both have more fun if you don't fight it," he says, letting another suggestive comment hang as he walks away.

You're playing with fire, Sophia.

Yes, I am. And I'm having entirely too much fun, even though I know I shouldn't.

16

Lorenzo

Am I being stood up?

That's the first question that pops into my head as I knock on Sophia's door—*again*.

"I swear to God, Blue, if you're ignoring me," I shout.

She opens the door, stretching her arm with a yawn. Her hair is in a messy bun, and she's wearing the tiniest pair of shorts with a white tank top that leaves nothing to the imagination. My cock stiffens at the sight of her peaked nipples, and I stifle a groan, wanting nothing more than to yank that top and have my way with her. If I remember correctly—and let's be honest here, this is all I've been thinking about lately—she more than enjoyed my tongue tracing slow, delicious circles on her nipples. Man, what I would give to feel her again.

What a way to keep yourself in check. Fantastic job, Enzo.

I shake my head, reality gawking at me. For one, she forgot I was going to pick her up. And two, she's opening the door to God knows who dressed like this?

I flex my fingers, making a fist. "Do you go opening the door to every random stranger looking like this?"

The half-asleep look on her face leaves instantly as she snaps her gaze to mine. Her eyes are as intense in the morning, and just as beautiful. I almost wish I hadn't looked.

"Nothing you haven't seen before," she replies nonchalantly.

I push her gently to the side and walk into her apartment. "Okay, but what if it wasn't me? That's not cool, Blue. That's dangerous."

She turns around and leans against the door frame, letting out a small frustrated sigh as she tries to flick away a stray hair that keeps falling in front of her face. When the hair settles back in the same spot, she scowls at it as if it's deliberately bothering her. I struggle to keep a smile in check, because the whole thing is too fucking adorable.

"Oh, why, yes, Lorenzo. Come in. Make yourself at home." She scowls. "And no one asked you to be my keeper."

Her apartment is tiny and very minimalistic. There are not a lot of decorations, which honestly surprises me. Sophia has this happy and loud personality, and I thought her apartment would reflect that. She has a small gray sectional couch and a wooden rectangular coffee table with some storage underneath, which is currently filled with books.

I walk to her living room, grab a random book from the coffee table, and throw myself on the couch with a smile plastered all over myself. "Why, yes, thank you. Totally will," I quip, getting comfortable on her sofa and opening the book at a random page. "And stop answering the door looking like that. I don't give a fuck if I sound like your keeper or not."

She closes the door with a groan and mutters to herself as she heads to the living room. Standing in front of me, she takes the book from my hands and crosses her arms. The movement pushes her tits together, and I'm trying to be respectful and not look, but fuck. I start to focus on her face instead. Sophia is very beautiful. And I don't mean in a sexual way. I mean, yes, she's hot, but this look makes her look very real. I think out of all the times the universe has allowed me to lay my eyes on her, this look is the best one yet. Her cheeks are slightly pink, like she's naturally sunburned, and she has a few freckles all around her face. They're very faint, barely noticeable unless you *really* look. And God knows I have no problem staring at this woman. Her eyes are slightly puffy, giving her this sleepy face, and somehow, her eyes shine more brightly when she's not wearing makeup.

She's too damn beautiful for her own good.

My legs seem to move on their own as I get up from the couch and stride over to her. I gently brush the stray hair from her face that has been bothering her and tuck it behind her ear, my eyes locking onto hers. "Your eyes," I whisper, amazed. "They shine so brightly in the morning. Has anyone ever told you that before?"

Her eyebrows knit in surprise as her gaze scrutinizes me. Her look is so intense, it's like I'm under a magnifying glass and she's trying to study every part of me, pierce my soul until she can discover every thought, every secret, and every scar. And in other circumstances, I would let her take everything from me—no questions asked. Instead of focusing on the looming realization, I take this rare opportunity to admire every inch of her face yet again. Her perfect face, may I add.

She slowly lowers her arms and stands there, still scrutinizing me with those beautifully haunting eyes. The gap between us is so small I can feel her chest lightly pressing against me, rising and falling with each small, hitched breath. I could reach out, grab the nape of her neck, and finally kiss her. It's killing me not to. I'm using all my self-control to hold back and be a gentleman.

She must sense the tension radiating off me, because she tenses her shoulders and takes a step back abruptly. "What are you doing here, Lorenzo?"

"Our summer adventure starts today, remember?"

"It's like five in the morning!" she exclaims.

"I did say bright and early," I reply, my voice lacing with amusement.

Her nostrils flare. "It seems we have a different definition of what bright and early entails."

"Well"—I wave my hand at her impatiently—"go get ready. Bring your passport and an overnight bag."

She furrows her eyebrows in confusion. "Why?"

I don't know why I thought this was going to be easy. Of course, she's going to question me every step of the way. I was an idiot for thinking otherwise.

"Why must you question me every single time?" I ask, raising an eyebrow.

"Why must you talk to me like you're my keeper?" she snaps back.

"Are you ever going to drop the attitude?" I counter.

"Are you ever going to stop being so annoying?" she retorts.

I give her the most unimpressed expression I can muster, and she crosses her arms and lifts her chin slightly in a challenge. She may be only five-feet-tall, but her personality is big and loud—in the best way possible. Who wants a quiet, dainty woman? That's boring. This is so much better. Unfiltered. Painfully beautiful. Smart. *Perfect.*

After a beat of silence, she relents. "Fine. Stay here.

Don't go snooping around," she warns, pointing a finger at me.

I raise my hands. "I would never."

She gives me a *you're-full-of-shit* look and walks back to her bedroom to start getting ready.

I can't possibly sit still. It's not in my nature, so as soon as she closes the door of her bedroom, I walk into the kitchen. The small stove and oven sits in the corner of the tiny room, and the counter space is limited, with just enough room for a cutting board and a coffee maker. A small, single-basin sink is tucked under the only small window, the natural light coming in slightly as the morning sun rises. Above the sink, a couple of open shelves hold four mismatched round plates and cups.

I barely fit inside this kitchen, but that doesn't stop me from opening the small black fridge and finding what I'm looking for. I grab the eggs and a few vegetables then grab the cutting board and start chopping some onions, peppers, and spinach, letting the colors mix vibrantly on the cutting board. Opening the cabinets below, I find where the pots and pans are stored, grab the small skillet, and heat up some olive oil before sautéing the vegetables until they're tender.

As I'm pouring the eggs over the veggies, Sophia walks into the kitchen. "What are you doing?"

Without looking at her and pouring in the rest of the whisked eggs, I say, "What does it look like? Breakfast. A frittata, if we're getting specific."

She approaches me, looking as I watch the eggs set around the edges. "What?"

I go to the fridge and grab the cheese, and as I'm sprinkling some on top, the oven beeps, letting me know it's ready to be used. Then I transfer the skillet to the oven.

"A frittata," I repeat.

"No, no. I heard you the first time. I just didn't think you would know what that was."

"I have hundreds of restaurants around the world. I'm not just a pretty face." I look at her, winking.

"Consider me impressed." She pats my chest twice. *"That'll do, piggy, that'll do."*

"I already quoted *Babe* to you once, so this doesn't count. I'm still in the lead."

She points her index finger between us. "And when did this become a competition?"

"Oh, Blue, you have much to learn about me," I reply, as I bring the frittata out of the oven and slide it out of the pan before slicing two pieces.

She tip-toes to reach for two round plates from the shelf and places them on the counter. I carefully lay the frittata slices onto each plate then carry them to the small dining table tucked into the corner of her living room. As I set down the plates, she heads off to grab some utensils.

"Then your *Babe* quote shouldn't count. I didn't know you had the same annoying quirk as me," she says as she sits, tucking both of her legs underneath her.

I gape at her, offended. "Annoying? More like fun as fuck."

She lets out a small chuckle that doesn't reach her eyes. "People like to often remind me that it's one of my most annoying quirks."

I scowl at her comment and sit. Who dares tell her she has annoying quirks? It's hard to explain, but somehow, the thought of Sophia quoting '90s movies and TV shows fits her perfectly in the most unexpected way. The woman is naturally funny, doesn't take shit from anyone, and is an overall badass. People are just idiots.

I reach for her hand and interlace our fingers, and I have

to take a moment before replying, because the charged electricity I feel by simply grabbing her hand is almost too much, but also not enough at the same time. I love the sensation, and I crave more of it.

"I think it's extremely funny and entertaining. Don't let people get to your head." I squeeze her hand. "Got it?"

Her eyes drop to where our hands are linked, avoiding my gaze. She bites her bottom lip, refusing to reply.

My other hand finds her chin, and I lift it, locking our gazes. "*Got it*?" I repeat.

"Yes," she whispers, her blue eyes shining with a different sort of light.

Her cheeks take on a slight blush as she breaks eye contact, almost like she's embarrassed. Which is a new look for her, because a woman like Sophia is all confidence and security. It's endearing, and another rush of wanting to kiss her surges through me. The urge to lose myself in her plush lips and remember their taste is almost overwhelming.

I take some much-needed space from her, dropping her hand in the process, not wanting to feel her perfectly soft skin against mine any longer. This electric energy that hangs between us every time we're near each other keeps intensifying, and I don't know how to make it stop. If I'm being brutally honest, I don't even think I *want* it to stop.

We look like two domestic idiots, sitting and having a simple breakfast together. I've never done something like this—eat with someone just because. It sounds both crazy and stupid, but it's true. Every time I had any sort of dinner with my father, work was attached to it. And when I was home, I was always with nannies or house staff, but always ate alone. I didn't have any friends. How could I? My father was always dragging me to his business meetings, wanting me to learn as much as possible. I couldn't spend time with family either. Damian was living in Chicago at the time, and I barely spoke to my other cousins from New York. It was always me and my imagination. I never noticed how weird it was until recently. I get together with the guys sometimes, but we always end up talking about business. I've never experienced the normal sitting down, having a normal conversation type of thing. But with Sophia, it feels strangely natural. I could get used to something like this.

Ha. Yeah. Right. Because you can do relationships. Get real.

Loving someone has never been in the cards for me. How can I do something I was never taught how to do? Between my dead mother and my father, who—let's face it—wasn't the most loving, I've never known what true love looks like. The thought should be depressing, but it isn't. You can't miss something you never knew in the first place. Even when the emptiness eats me a little. Even when I wonder what my life would look like if I believed or understood what love was. Would I be married by now? Maybe one or two kids? Would I even *want* kids? These are questions that haunt me, even when it makes no sense to let them get to me. They still find a way to invade my thoughts.

When she takes the first bite of the frittata, her eyes bulge in surprise. "*Holy shit, Ace.* This is delicious."

"Why, thank you." I bow my head sarcastically. "Let me get this straight, you refuse to call me Enzo, yet you created a whole other nickname for me?"

"*Yup,*" she replies with a shrug, taking another bite and letting out a groan of satisfaction.

"Oh, Blue. You're...something," I say with a soft smile as I look at her intently.

She raises her blue irises and locks them with mine, amusement flickering within them. "I must say, you're full of surprises. Who knew Lorenzo Mancini, gambler and player of the Chicagoland area, knows how to make a mean frittata?"

My food gets stuck in my throat at her comment, and I cough. "Excuse me?"

"Oh, yeah." She nods animatedly, and the way she's looking at me has me feeling like she's about to deliver a punchline. "Haven't you heard? If we look up the word *player* in the dictionary, a picture of you would pop up."

I gape at her in disbelief. "You're *mean*."

She gets up and extends her arm to grab my plate, and I catch a whiff of her perfume, a strong summery scent that envelops me. Anything summer-related reminds me of her now, and with summer just starting, she's everywhere. All I can think about lately. And boy, is that a terrifying fucking thought.

"I'm something, alright." She gives me a playful wink before walking away with the dishes.

"Yeah. You are," I whisper to myself.

She's beautiful, funny, challenging, and has absolutely no filter. But most importantly, she's true to herself. And that's pretty damn amazing.

Sophia

It took Lorenzo about an hour and a half to convince me to get on his jet. Then it took another thirty minutes for us to leave without him telling me what our destination was. How Lorenzo managed to not lose his shit while I gave him so much pushback, I'm not sure, but I'm impressed.

As I step off the jet onto the tarmac, the first thing that hits me is the warm breeze. The sun is bright and high in the sky, and I have to squint to adjust to the light. The rapid change in temperature causes goosebumps all over my body, but I welcome it. We get in the car that was waiting for us on the tarmac, and as we exit the airport, I'm greeted by the biggest *Bienvenidos a Panamá*[1] sign ever.

"Why the hell are we in Panamá?" I ask, turning to Lorenzo.

"I'm opening a restaurant here next month. As—"

"Wait, wait. Let me get my recorder," I interrupt, opening the overnight bag he made me pack. I don't think I have a

---

1. Welcome to Panama.

single good outfit, but it's just one night, so I'm not too worried.

He stops me with a firm hand on my arm. "Okay. I think it's time to talk about my rules."

With an eyebrow raised, I look at him. And I instantly wish I hadn't. The more time I spend with Lorenzo, the more things I notice about him. His brown hair is soft and always falls perfectly into place without any effort. The way it catches the light, it almost seems to have a faint golden tint. Memories of me fisting his hair as he was giving me the orgasm of my life flood through my mind involuntarily, and I look away, trying to calm these stupid, racing thoughts.

I start picking at my nails, trying to regain my composure. "Rules? You have rules now?"

He runs a hand through his hair absentmindedly. And what do you know? His hair falls right back into place. "Yes, rules. For one, no tape recorder."

I shake my head. "Absolutely not. I need it for work."

"Hear me out first. The rule is simple—you're going to live in the moment. Get to see everything I do. You're going to write down notes and questions you may have for me, and at the end of the day, you'll pick your question—only *one* question," he explains.

I gape at him. "Only *one* question?"

He nods. "Oh, and I get to ask you a question, too. That's my second rule."

I squint at him in suspicion. "I don't understand why you have to ask me questions. I'm writing an article about you, not the other way around."

"Because it's fun. It's a game we can look forward to at the end of the day," he replies with a boyish smile that makes my stomach flip.

"Does everything have to be a game with you?" I ask, exasperated.

"Is that your question of the day? It's kind of early, if you ask me. You may want to reserve it for later." He grazes his upper teeth with his tongue before flashing me another one of his perfect smiles.

I hesitate for a moment. *Wait.* Why am I hesitating? Do I actually want to play this game? That's ridiculous. The last thing I should be doing is entertaining someone like Lorenzo. I *know* men like him. For them, everything can be turned into a game. They treat people like their personal little circus.

"I'm not playing this game," I state firmly.

"Why not?"

"Because it's stupid," I retort.

"No, it isn't," he counters.

"Yes, it is."

"*Blue*," he warns.

"*Ace*," I reply, raising an eyebrow.

"Come on, live a little." He nudges my arm with his elbow gently.

Would it be the worst thing?

It'll allow me to be in the moment, observing his every move, how he interacts with people, and how he works behind the scenes. I can narrow down the questions and focus on the ones that will truly help me write this piece. I typically journal everything down at the end of the day on my work laptop and start forming my own opinion as I continue to research, anyway, so it's really not a big deal.

I can't lie to myself, it does sound fun and harmless—as long as I don't let him ask any deep personal questions. I'm not about to spill all of my darkest secrets to him.

I extend my hand. "You've got yourself another deal."

He takes my hand and shakes it, a small laugh escaping his lips. "Now that's what I call living."

The SUV makes a stop in front of a villa, and as I'm stepping out, my breath hitches at the sight. The white walls stand out against the bright-blue sky, and the flat black roof adds a sleek touch. Floor-to-ceiling windows invite the sunlight into the house. The yard is filled with white, purple, and bright-pink Madagascar periwinkles. The cement path is lined with white and light-gray rocks around the bushes, and soft lights surround them that I almost miss because it's still broad daylight. Lorenzo opens the door, and I'm greeted by a beautiful, open floor plan. The living room is spacious and bright, with a white L-shaped sofa that looks incredibly inviting. The kitchen is also huge, featuring state-of-the-art appliances.

I drop my overnight bag and take off my shoes at the entrance. "Wow, this place is amazing."

I'm no stranger to fancy things. Aria lives in one of the best high-rise buildings in Chicago, and Isabella owns her place. My place is the exact opposite of theirs, only because I'd rather put all of my money toward taking care of Mom. As long as I have a roof over my head and some food, I really don't need much else. But this place is fancy, like *I-don't-belong-here* fancy.

Lorenzo drops his bag next to mine and takes my hand, leading me to the crystal doors near the kitchen. "You haven't seen the best part yet. Let me show you."

It's hard to focus on anything else when my eyes are locked on our interlaced fingers. I know he doesn't mean anything by it, but my heart races at an abnormally fast rate anyway. As he opens the door, a warm breeze hits me, carrying a clean, crisp scent. My jaw drops when I look up. The inside of the villa is stunning, but this view is beyond words. There's a pool that cascades, making it look like it merges with the deep, beautiful, blue ocean. The bright-green lush of the mountains perfectly contrasts with the water.

I drop Lorenzo's hand and run toward the patio, getting closer to the pool and dipping my toes in. Even the water temperature is perfect. "This is just, wow," I say breathlessly.

"Beautiful," he whispers.

I nod and glance over my shoulder, expecting him to be admiring the view. Instead, his eyes are set on me. My cheeks flush, and while any other man would look away when caught, Lorenzo doesn't. No. He just...smiles. It's soft and kind, one that makes me wonder what he's thinking.

It makes me question if maybe, just maybe, I should break my one-night stand rule for him. Because that night was unforgettable, and I've never experienced such a charged and electric connection with anyone.

But I won't. The game started and ended the day we slept together. We're both players at heart.

And that will never, ever change.

18

Lorenzo

The flight to Panamá was long and tiresome, so after we arrived at the villa last night, we pretty much crashed until the next day.

The villa I rented is a short walk from the restaurant I'm opening soon, so we agreed to meet outside and head out first thing in the morning. A warm, sticky breeze drifts from the ocean, filling the air with the scent of salt and sun-baked sand as we head to the location.

Opening a restaurant in Panamá has always been a dream of mine. I found the perfect spot right on the beach, where we can offer outdoor seating with a beautiful view of Bocas del Toro, one of Panamá's many gorgeous beaches. It took a lot of effort to find this place, and I'm more than looking forward to seeing the final touches. Since we're getting ready to open in about a month, the construction should be almost ready.

When we arrive at the location, the place is bustling with activity. Construction workers are moving in and out, carrying tools and materials. As we approach the entrance, I stop dead in my tracks, taking a look at the interior that's *nowhere* close to being ready.

What the fuck?

Sophia stands next to me, her eyes wide with confusion as she surveys the space. "Didn't you say you're opening in a month?"

My eye twitches, and I clench my jaw before replying. "Yeah. I'm as confused as you are. Excuse me," I say, pulling my phone out of my pocket. My shoulders tense as I scroll through my contacts until I find who I'm looking for.

ME

Call me, now.

DIEGO (NEXTGEN BUILDERS)

I can't right now, what's going on?

A humorless laugh escapes my lips as I angrily type.

ME

You're kidding, right? Have you been to Panamá recently?

DIEGO (NEXTGEN BUILDERS)

It's on my schedule for next week, but the crew lead told me everything was going according to plan.

I shake my head and walk inside the restaurant, taking a video of the place. The kitchen is not built, not completely, anyway. The equipment that arrived last week is sitting in the corner, not even covered. The extension we decided to add to make the outdoor dining area bigger looks like they just started on it. Once I'm done taking the video, I walk out, because I can't stand looking at it any longer.

ME

Sends Video Attachment.

DIEGO (NEXTGEN BUILDERS)

It's being handled. I'll be there first thing tomorrow morning.

I don't even bother to reply, because I'm seething right now, trying to keep my cool. I'm going to have to cancel the training that's supposed to be happening tomorrow.

Fisting my hair in frustration, I look up and close my eyes, taking a deep breath.

"You okay?" Sophia asks softly.

I relax my shoulders a bit. "Yeah." I shake my head. "It doesn't matter. I just have to roll with the punches."

I'm meeting with Diego one way or another, because he owes me some *serious* explanations.

"I know I said we would go back to Chicago tonight, but I have to stay and talk to the builder, Diego. If you need to go back, I will get the jet ready for you, just say the word."

"Diego García? As in the owner of NextGen Builders?" she asks.

I squint. "Yes. How do you know him?"

"Who doesn't? He has the biggest construction business that's practically taking over the world. Everyone knows him." She shrugs. "And I can stay a few more days, I think it will be interesting to see you work behind the scenes."

Relief floods through me. I don't know why, but I was hoping she'd say that. Having her around will be nice. She's fun to talk to and keeps me on my toes most of the time, never afraid of giving me an ego check, and I always look forward to it. The company is a welcome change, since I'm always traveling by myself. It gets lonely, always being out and about and having no one to share your time with. It's why I typically fill the void with other extracurriculars that have become less and less interesting to me lately.

"This is not what I had planned," I say with a low chuckle. "I wanted to show you the restaurant."

She waves her hand dismissively. "You still can. Walk me through it and tell me what the ideas are. I have a pretty good imagination."

A small smile tugs at the corner of my mouth, and I tilt my head toward the restaurant. It's lunchtime right now, so the construction crew is not around as I walk her through.

Entering the area that's meant to be the kitchen, I wave my hand around. "It's going to be an open concept. Customers will be able to see what the kitchen staff is doing, from beginning to end." I point to a corner of the space. "We'll close off this area to create a private washing zone"—then to another corner at the far back—"that section will be enclosed for a ventilated dry store. With the weather here in Panamá, we have to ensure the ingredients are stored properly. The freezer will go right next to it," I add.

She looks around, nodding as she takes a small notebook from her purse and starts writing. She looks so beautiful with her eyebrows furrowed in concentration, her hand moving quickly, as if she needs to write all the words down before they escape her. Her hair falls onto her shoulders and down to her hips in soft waves. Sophia has this type of beauty that knocks the wind out of you without even trying. Her beauty is graceful *and* overwhelming. It's impossible to look away, even if I tried.

Before she finishes writing her thoughts, I let out a fake cough and look at anything but her. I don't want her to think I was gawking at her—even though I quite literally was. I continue the tour and give her as much detail as possible. This is one of the projects I'm most excited about, because

I'm finally expanding and dipping more into different types of menus. It's nerve-wracking to start a new project, but the exhilaration I get every time I open a new place makes up for it. The restaurant business is not easy, especially when you have hundreds of them to manage, but the food industry is where I'm most at peace. It's where I find my tranquility. The only thing I would change is I would love to be a part of the day-to-day and the creative side of things. Ditch the suit and wear the apron, opinions be damned.

I've never known what love is like, but if the passion and care I have for this job is anything like it, it's not the worst feeling in the world.

19

Sophia

My opinion about Lorenzo started to shift slightly after the restaurant walk-through. He's still the reckless playboy who likes to gamble and sleep around, but his demeanor changes completely when it comes to his restaurants. My question is...why? What makes one of the top billionaires of the windy city be one way in front of the public and do a complete 180 behind the scenes? Okay—that may be a bit of a stretch. He's still his playful, flirty self. That's one thing I'm sure will never change. But you can tell he's really passionate about this business.

We all have our reasons for hiding our true selves sometimes. Whether it's because we're afraid of rejection or embarrassment. I hide behind my work, my smile, and my loud personality, because I feel so empty inside, it's better to put on a mask no one can question. I'm Sophia Evans, the girl who loves to quote movies and TV shows, the girl who always jokes around and never takes anything seriously, and most importantly, the girl who sleeps around and plays men. But all of it is a coping mechanism I use to protect myself and avoid being burned. The brighter your smile, the less people worry about you. Even if your glow is fake, people are often too occupied to care. I've had a lifetime of practice, too. At home, I was always the brave one. The one who defended her mother when her father was too drunk. The one who always took the blame when her sister did something wrong, so she wouldn't be punished.

There's no reason to hide *this*, though. He's passionate about the food industry, so what? That's good. He has a purpose. Or at least that's how I look at it. It's difficult to comprehend why he doesn't share this part of his life. But this also means this is the perfect opportunity for me to bring light to it. Discover why he chooses to hide this part of himself.

"I don't really have much to show you for today. You can rest, get settled, or whatever. I have to attend non-negotiable Zoom meetings." He rolls his eyes. "But we can meet later?"

I nod. "That works. It would be good to get ahead on this article thing."

He frowns. "Already? You haven't even asked me anything."

"Still in the research phase."

"Good luck finding anything." He laughs. "I can assure you whatever you do find, chances are it's not true."

We arrive at the villa, and as we're both standing at the entrance, I shrug. "I know. You forget I'm pretty good at my job," I joke.

"That you are." He gives me a soft smile as he reaches for a purple Madagascar periwinkle and plucks it carefully. He holds it for a moment, and without a word, he steps into my space. His hand tucks a strand of my hair behind my ear, and then he carefully places the flower there. His fingertips graze my skin for a moment, leaving a trail of goosebumps.

"Purple suits you," he says simply before disappearing into the villa.

Oh, boy. Why did I say yes to this again?

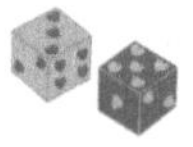

For the rest of the day, I journaled and dove deeper into my research, writing down every thought I had about Lorenzo and the mystery surrounding his life. There are still so many unanswered questions, but I'm sure I'll figure them out as we keep spending more time together.

As I'm drying my hair after getting out of the shower, I hear a soft knock on the door. I stride to the door and open it, finding Lorenzo standing in all his six-foot-three glory. He's wearing a pair of jeans and a black summer polo shirt that hugs his broad shoulders and strong arms. My curiosity about how far his ink reaches tames a little as my eyes roam. Besides the random small tattoos he has all over his arm, there's one that seems to be like a clock with roman numerals, some type of flower, and an ace of spades—how fitting. There's a tattoo on his tricep that catches my attention, but I can't get a good look because of the fabric that's hiding it.

And now my curiosity is sparked all over again. I just want to see all of his tattoos, just once. Is that too much to ask? Strictly for research purposes, of course.

Pft. Yeah. *Research.*

My eyes keep roaming the rest of him a little too eagerly. He's all tanned skin and strong, lean muscles. While he and Damian look somewhat alike, there's something about Lorenzo. His beauty is pure and raw, like a fire that hasn't yet been tamed, bright and intense, pulling you in without even trying.

He leans against the door frame of my room, crossing his arms. "You hungry?"

It takes me a moment to respond, because I'm totally checking him out and I'm sure I'm being fairly obvious about it. What can I say? The man is on his own level of handsomeness. I'm sure he knows it. Everyone does.

As if on cue, my stomach grumbles. "Actually, yeah. We got anything here?"

He shakes his head. "No. But I'm sending someone to do groceries tomorrow. Get dressed and we'll go out. There are some wonderful places around here."

"What category does it fall under for us to have dinner together?" I cross my arms, raising an eyebrow. "Careful, Ace."

He licks his lips, a hint of amusement glinting in his eyes as he steps closer, his presence overwhelming. "I'm assuming it's in a safer category than you blatantly checking me out when I knocked on your door," he murmurs, his voice low and teasing.

The scent of him—smoky and so intoxicatingly sweet—hits me as he towers over me, and suddenly my throat goes dry. I force myself to swallow, hoping it hides the nerves that kick up whenever he's near.

"Stop checking me out, Blue. Have some manners," he adds, a knowing smile pulling at the corners of his mouth.

"Don't act like you hate it," I retort, recalling what he told me that night.

He grabs a strand of my hair, twisting it around his finger with a playful hum. "On the contrary." He leans in, his mouth almost brushing my ear, his breath warm against my skin. "You can look all you want *and* touch all you want,

Blue." His whisper is low and inviting, carrying a weight of secrets that sends a thrill coursing through me.

"You're an impossible flirt," I say, a little breathless.

His grin is wicked, unapologetic. "Only for you, Blue. Think you can handle it?"

My back stiffens at his comment, and I take a sharp step back, squinting at him before shutting the door in his face with a mix of frustration and flustered nerves.

Walked right into that one.

His hearty laugh echoes through the closed door as he calls out, "I'll be waiting outside."

20

Lorenzo

Getting a rise out of Sophia is turning out to be one of my favorite things to do. Dare I say it's more fun than poker? She makes it so easy. When will she learn I'm not normal? Playing games is my thing. And as I've come to find out, it's her thing, too. She can deny it all she wants. Be stubborn about it. It doesn't make it any less true.

I know the group has been joking lately that we're the same person, and while I know Sophia is offended at the thought, I find it interesting. I've never met a woman like her. Someone who likes to challenge me and call me out every chance she gets and is unapologetic about it. It's my favorite trait about her—personality-wise, anyway. I can think of *many* favorite physical traits.

Her intense blue eyes.

Her long, shiny, perfect brown hair.

Her perfectly shaped lips.

Her round, perky ass.

The list is endless. It's no secret I'm attracted to her. We slept together, after all. And even though people consider me the biggest playboy of the Chicagoland area—as everyone often *loves* to remind me—little do they know, that's the farthest from the truth lately. I haven't slept with anyone since I crossed paths with Sophia. I'm not pining for her or anything. I'm smarter than that. She has made it very clear she's not going to touch me with a ten-foot pole, even when her eyes betray her sometimes and blatantly check me out. It's just a game. No one has ever taken me seriously. Women want me for one thing: sex. They don't care about getting to know me, why would they?

Women using me as a pit stop before meeting their prince charming should be depressing, but you can't be depressed at something you've always done. Something you're used to being. I'm not boyfriend material, much less husband material. Women come to me when they want to have the night of their lives, not when they're looking to settle down. And even though I've always felt this hole in my heart, and I've come to find it tiring from time to time, I've never understood what has been missing from my life.

Companionship, maybe?

Love? Extremely doubtful. That was an unknown concept at my house. While other kids were being unconditionally loved by their parents—hell, even grandparents—I was being trained on how to make mindful business decisions. On how to always make more money. On how to carry on the stupid family legacy. And what do I have to show for it? A stuffy vice presidency position. Oh, and my misery.

I'm overthinking shit too much. My life is great. I have no one to tie me down, nor do I answer to anyone. I *should* be happy about it. I *am* happy about it.

Are you, though? Or are you simply ignoring this hole in your heart you've been feeling more often lately?

Blame it on sexual frustration. I haven't slept with

anyone in a while, and my brain is spinning with all these delirious thoughts.

As I'm deep in thought, Sophia walks out wearing a simple, short yellow summer dress that makes her skin glow. My gaze drifts down to her legs, smooth and flawless, but I quickly look away, trying to push back the urge to run my hands all over them and remind myself how good they must feel.

"I feel extremely underdressed, and it's all your fault."

I frown. "How is it my fault?"

She glares at me. "You should have told me our destination so I could have planned accordingly."

"Where's the fun in that?"

"Says the guy with a perfect outfit."

I nod in understanding, biting my bottom lip momentarily before replying. "I'll rectify that."

"What's that supposed to mean?"

I rise from the stairs where I was sitting and start walking. "Don't worry about it."

"Are you always this cryptic?"

I shrug without bothering with a reply.

She lets out a small, frustrated groan that makes me laugh as she quickly strides to catch up. "Where are we going?"

"There's a perfect little restaurant around the corner that has, hands down, the best *Ropa Vieja* you'll ever try."

To be honest, every time I come here that's the only thing I eat, because I'm dying to figure out every single ingredient and make it myself. I could ask, but that takes away the fun. I like to explore the flavors and play with ingredients until I can nail them. It's the best part of being in the kitchen. There are endless possibilities and creations you can do until you find the perfect one.

"Ropa *what*?" she asks, confused.

I laugh as I open the door of the restaurant, placing my hand on her lower back and guiding her inside. "The English translation is old clothes. I know the name doesn't make it sound like the best, but I promise you it's good."

She scrunches her nose in the cutest way possible. "That doesn't sound good at all."

I roll my eyes at her comment. Of course, she argues with me. I don't know why I expected any less.

The restaurant is tiny, and soft, overhead yellow lights adorn the ceiling, giving the space a peaceful and romantic vibe. The brick walls are adorned with bright-colored paintings and small Panamanian flags all around. From the research I did while scouting for the perfect restaurant location, I found Boca del Toro is one of the most touristic places honeymooners visit. And every restaurant has this local but romantic feel.

It's fairly late, but the place is still bustling with activity. I request outdoor sitting, because I never tire of the view, the light breeze, and the smell of fresh ocean air. After a few minutes, they sit us on a corner table by the veranda with a perfect view.

While Sophia browses the menu, my eyes focus on her face. I hold back a laugh every time she furrows her brows when she can't understand a word. I mentally slap myself, trying to get my shit together and not reach out to trace her lip with my thumb every time she unconsciously bites her bottom lip in concentration.

"I give up." She drops the menu on the table. "I don't know what I want. You choose."

I purse my lips, holding back a chuckle. "Wise choice."

She rolls her eyes, crossing her arms and resting them on the table, slightly leaning forward. "Don't make me regret it. You're surprisingly very knowledgeable when it comes to food. So let's put that knowledge to the test."

"I mean, I'm not trying to sound cocky or anything, but did you forget I own hundreds of restaurants?"

"That doesn't mean you're an expert, now, does it?"

I raise an eyebrow, contemplating how to reply. No one knows the passion I have for cooking. It's not something I like to share. What's the point? I'm a businessman. My job is to take care of payroll, investments, and all the boring administrative shit that brings me billions of dollars every year. Sharing my love for cooking will pique Sophia's interest. I'm not here to be honest. I never claimed I was going to tell her the truth. The world thinks of me a certain way, and I prefer to keep it that way.

"Is that your question of the day?" I ask, threading my fingers through my hair.

She studies with squinted eyes, pondering. Her hair sways gently with the light breeze. "No."

I nod, drumming my index finger on the table. "When are you going to ask it?"

"When you least expect it."

Before I can reply, the waiter arrives and takes our order. We order a few rounds of *Seco Sour*, a typical Panamanian drink with a fruity yet sour taste. I figured this was something she would enjoy, since her typical go-to order is a gin martini with a twist. A few typical Panamanian appetizers, such as *Ceviche* and *Empanadas*. And, of course, the main reason we're here—the *Ropa Vieja*.

"Dare I say, Blue, Central America suits you," I point out.

The waiter arrives with our drinks and places them on the table, and Sophia takes hers with a gentle touch. Everything she does looks so smooth and effortless. She always seems so composed, but then she speaks, and her lively, fiery personality shines through, giving her an entirely different, vibrant edge.

"Dare I say, Ace, the real you suits you," she replies very matter-of-factly.

I raise an eyebrow. "What's that supposed to mean?"

"Is that *your* question of the day?" she asks, her eyes gleaming with amusement.

I grab my glass and take a sip of the fruity, slightly sour drink. As I gulp, I contemplate momentarily before replying. "Yes."

She's the one looking stunned now as she drops her elbow on the table and rests her chin on the palm of her hand. "Today, how you were talking about your newest business venture—"

I interrupt with a small laugh. "Not a new adventure."

She glares at me. "Let me finish." She takes a sip of her drink before continuing, and my eyes travel to her neck as she gulps. My cock comes to life with the idea of wrapping my hand around her pretty little throat and owning her mouth. Kissing her like my life depends on it. Kissing her until I can't breathe. Savoring her sharp tongue and getting lost in her.

"It's no secret you know what people say about you in gossip columns. But this side of you I saw today." She sighs, moving her head to the side and admiring the soft beach waves. "It's a good one, Lorenzo. One I can't fully understand yet, but still worthy of being seen."

My breathing falters for a moment, my heart stabbing my rib almost painfully. In my thirty-six years of life, no one has ever read me so openly. The fact she could figure out a small part of my life so easily after one day together puts me on high alert. My mind is screaming at me to shut this shit down right now, before it's too late.

"Why do you hide yourself?" she asks, plain and simple. Direct. Unfiltered. Just how I like her.

Words escape me somehow. My heart is soaring, demanding me to be honest.

Would it be so bad to be honest for once?

Strangely, I feel safe with Sophia. Anything I can say to her, she'll accept it without judgment. If anything, she would be understanding. There's something behind those eyes of hers, something I recognize.

"Because nothing about me is worthy, Blue," I rasp.

She looks directly at me, her shiny blue eyes roaming every inch of my face. "Somehow, I doubt that, Ace."

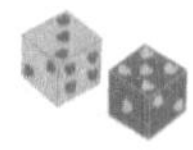

Dinner was amazing, and the company—unsurprisingly—was even better. Sophia ended up eating an entire *Ropa Vieja* platter without an ounce of shame, which made me smile so much that my cheeks are still hurting. She was so full by the time we walked out of the restaurant, she rested her head on my shoulder and interlaced our arms as we walked, claiming she needed the support if we were going to walk back. I happily complied, because any excuse to touch her is more than fine with me.

The villa has a small staircase that takes you to a private part of the beach, so now we're sitting on the sand, enjoying the sound of the waves and the calm breeze of the night. If I were still trying to drown my thoughts, I would probably be at a club getting drunk and trying to find someone to get lost in. But I've come to care less and less about the partying, the going out, and the sleeping around. The day I slept with Sophia, my brain chemistry shifted. I've never—and I mean *never*—felt such a charged chemistry with someone before. It has always been about chasing that high, about finding release. With her, it was like every nerve of my body came alive for the first time, and I'm dying to get another glimpse of that feeling again. How is that possible? We didn't know each other. We were two strangers looking for a wild night. Yet it changed everything for me. I've been sitting on these thoughts, these unknown feelings, since she waltzed back into my life, and they are scaring the crap out of me. No point in denying it.

I watch as she adjusts, sitting up to face me. She pulls her knees to her chest, wrapping her arms around them, and rests her head on her forearm. The soft lights coming from the villa give Sophia a beautiful glow, even in the dark of the night. I find myself studying her, wanting nothing more than to engrave her into my memory.

"Let's play a game," she whispers.

"Sure." I shrug. "What game?"

"I ask a question, we both answer it, and then vice versa."

My laugh echoes. "Curious about me, Blue?"

"Yes," she answers honestly, shrugging nonchalantly.

I nod. "Okay, shoot."

"What's your favorite color?"

"That's what you want to know? My favorite color?"

"Humor me." She pats me on the shoulder jokingly.

I shift and face her now, placing my hands on her legs, my fingertips caressing her smooth skin back and forth. Every time I'm near, I have the urge to touch her. I've never cared much about showing affection to someone. That was a strange concept in my house, after all. I can't even remember the last time I received a hug just because. These things are strange to me, but still, with Sophia, it's the most natural thing.

"I don't have a favorite color."

Her eyes roll slightly, followed by a light laugh. "Come on, everyone has a favorite color. Mine's periwinkle. Now spill it—what's yours?"

I can't help but smirk. It's funny, considering I gave her a flower of that exact color earlier. I let the silence hang between us for a moment before my eyes lock onto hers. "The color of your eyes," I say, opting for honesty.

Her brows knit together as her nose crinkles, making her look unintentionally adorable. "Blue? That's such a basic color. I thought you were more creative." She lets out an exaggerated sigh, her tone playful. "What a shame, Ace."

I shake my head, tucking her usual wild strand of hair behind her ear. My hand travels to the nape of her jaw, and I start stroking her soft skin. "Your eyes aren't just blue," I whisper. "They're deep and vibrant, like the ocean at its calmest. But when that fire flares up in you, they become more intense, like the sea before a storm. *Blue* doesn't even begin to cover it. And they are anything *but* basic."

She tenses under my touch, her breath hitching at my confession. Even in the soft lighting, I witness for the briefest moment how her eyes sparkle before she looks the other way, avoiding my gaze. "Uh, your turn to ask a question," she says weakly.

I roll my lips, holding back a satisfied smile. It's not often I get to witness Sophia looking nervous. Can't say I don't enjoy it. I also can't say I didn't mean what I said. It's the honest-to-God truth. Her eyes are unique, wild, and anything *but* ordinary. They fit her perfectly because she's *extraordinary.*

My hand drops to her leg again, continuing the caress. "What's one thing you've always wanted to do?"

She looks up, tilting her head as she ponders for a moment. "Skydiving."

I raise an eyebrow. "Someone likes the adrenaline, huh?"

She shrugs. "I've always said it's the Evans' curse. We all have our vice. Mine is feeling. I want to feel exuberant. *Alive*."

"What do you mean?"

She tsks. "This is not how this game works. It's your turn to answer."

Before I can register what I'm saying, I confess, "Work in the kitchen. Be a chef. Ditch the suits and put on an apron. Create new, exciting recipes."

Her eyes zero in on me, studying me. Scrutinizing me. Almost like what I said makes her look at me in a different light. "Why don't you?"

This is exactly what I feared. Exposing something so personal makes me feel like crawling out of my own skin. It's like a wave of discomfort rising up, making me itch with the need to escape, to disappear before the vulnerability can settle in.

I pull my knees to my chest and rest my elbows on them, looking over the ocean. It's so dark, I can barely see anything, but I know it's there from the smell, and the soft sounds of waves crashing against the rocks.

"Not what I was meant to do. I was born to carry the Mancini legacy. To think and act like a businessman. I was meant for something greater, or at least that's what my father used to say." The anger I feel every time I think about this starts to surface, but I fight to keep it down, steadying my voice. What I'm doing—being honest, letting her see the real me—makes my chest tighten.

Sophia's gentle hands cup my face, and she grips my chin, making sure I meet her eyes. "Don't let others dictate your life, Lorenzo. It's up to you to shape your own future and find your own happiness. Do you understand?"

The corner of my lip tugs with the softest, smallest smile.

"*Do. You. Understand?*" she asks again, the grip she has on my chin tightening.

I nod, grinning now. "Careful, Blue. If you keep this up, I might start thinking you actually care," I joke, trying to ease the tension. This whole game is getting a bit too real, too fast. And while opening up to her feels surprisingly natural, I'm not ready to lay bare all my scars. That would probably drive her away, and I selfishly want to keep her close. In such a short time, she's become someone I can connect with and confide in. She's become a part of my tiny, tight-knit circle.

She pulls her hands away from my face, and I immediately feel the absence of her touch, a wave of disappointment washing over me.

"Wouldn't that be something?" she says, tilting her head with a hint of amusement in her voice.

Her words make my heart clench. Maybe, *just* maybe, I've started to care a little more than I thought. Hell, I probably started to care the moment she stormed back into my life like a whirlwind, knocking the wind out of me with her laughter, her eyes, her smile—all of her. The thought is completely crazy, because she's only been around for a short time, yet it's like I've known her forever. Something about her pulls me in, and not knowing what it is drives me wild.

"You deserve to be happy, Lorenzo. Never stop chasing that." Her voice is steady, serious now, not a hint of the playful tone from before.

"Are *you* happy?" I ask.

She grazes her bottom lip with her teeth, contemplating. "I'm trying to be."

In this moment, I make a vow to myself to do whatever it takes to make her happy this summer—completely and utterly. But I also make a promise to myself. To chase happiness, even though deep down, I doubt I'll ever find it. It's not as easy as walking away from everything and starting fresh. The guilt would eat me alive. Like I still owe my father something, even if I'm not sure exactly what.

"Have you ever been in love?" she asks softly, throwing me out of the loop.

"No," I reply honestly. "I've never witnessed what love is like, so I've never given it a chance, and I don't think I ever will."

While I never knew my mom, I saw the cause and effect of loving someone so deeply to the point of ruin. Love *ruined* my father. I didn't have to witness it when he lost his wife to know he grew cold and distant. To know he depended on alcohol to numb the pain a little and focused all his energy on business. He was grasping for something to keep him above board. If that's what heartbreak does to you, then what's the point?

I look up. "You?"

She sighs, contemplating. "I thought I was, but the more I think about it..." She crosses her legs, and I mirror her, our bodies naturally moving closer. "No. I don't think I've ever been in love. I've just been heartbroken by people because the need for validation was so strong, I overlooked a lot of things." She shakes her head. "I don't think love is for people like me."

A dull pain settles in my chest at the tone of her voice. While I understand where she's coming from, there's no way in hell a wonderful woman like her won't find love. If anyone deserves it, it's her. Truly. Whoever sweeps her off her feet will be one lucky son of a bitch.

I shake my head. "You're wrong. You just haven't found your person, but you will."

A sharp, bitter laugh slips from her lips. "That used to be my dream, you know? Find my person, build a family. Live in a house with a white picket fence, hosting Sunday dinners with friends and family. Have my mom living closer to me." She lets out a long, wistful sigh. "But I've grown used to being alone. I've always had to take care of myself, and I don't think I could let anyone else do it for me. The whole idea feels...strange."

I interlace my fingers with hers, ignoring the burning sensation that travels from my fingertips to the rest of my body. Ignoring the charged electricity that happens between us every time we're near each other. "You deserve to be looked after. Loved. Worshipped. Cherished. Promise me to never stop looking for it."

She avoids my gaze and remains quiet.

Not good enough.

It's my turn to grip her chin tightly now, forcing her to look at me. "*Promise me*, Blue."

"Fine." She rolls her eyes. "God, this game sure took a turn."

I let out a short, sharp laugh. "We sure know how to live it up."

"I have another question for you." She bites her bottom lip, and it's so damn sexy I have to fight the urge to run my thumb over it. "Do you ever think about that night?" she asks barely above whisper. I almost missed it.

The air between us changes to something so thrilling and dangerous, I can almost taste it.

My voice drops an octave. "Not a day has passed where I don't think about what happened between us."

Her lips part softly, as if she wasn't expecting that answer.

Taking a bold chance, I allow myself to run my thumb across her bottom lip, just like I was dying to moments ago, and it's so smooth. I would love nothing more than to swipe my tongue instead before owning her fucking mouth.

"I think about these pouty lips of yours," I murmur, my hand sliding down to the column of her neck. "I think about kissing and biting this pretty neck." Slowly, my fingers trace her collarbone. "I think about kissing you right here, too," I say softly, my voice dropping as I follow the line with my touch. "I think about your moans and how perfect you felt coming around my cock and how much I'm dying to get another taste of you because once was simply not enough," I finish gruffly.

Her pupils dilate, her face flushing and chest heaving. All my blood rushes to my cock at the sight of her, and fuck, I meant it all. I need another taste. That would be the logical thing to do to get her out of my fucking system. We both can keep denying the attraction all we want, but we both know it's there. In every interaction, every retort, and every bantering moment.

"Then why don't you?"

Oh. My. Fuck.

21

Sophia

I can't believe those words came out of my mouth. But with the way he's looking at me, his eyes roaming every inch of my body with so much hunger, and the way his hand feels against my skin, I'm ready to throw it all out of the window for one more night.

"Blue..." He lets out a pained groan. "Choose your next words carefully, otherwise—"

I interrupt him. "Kiss me."

His eyes land on my parted lips, and he licks his own in anticipation. Contemplating. Wondering if I mean it. I must be losing my mind, but the need rooted deep in my bones is impossible to ignore.

I let out a slow huff. "I chose my words already, yet you're not—"

I can't even finish the sentence, because he eats the distance between us, our lips colliding in a fierce, desperate kiss. My hand finds his shirt, and I fist it as we fall onto the sand, kissing each other desperately, like we're each other's only source of air. He gets on top of me, careful not to put any weight on me as he swipes his tongue on my bottom lip, demanding entrance. I eagerly part my lips, and he wastes no time to crash our tongues together. I let out a moan he eagerly swallows like he wants to savor every sound that comes out of me. The ache between my legs intensifies as one of his hands finds my outer thigh and grips it, wrapping my leg around his waist. His knee presses against my center, close enough to give me some friction, but nowhere near enough of what I truly need. Need clouds my brain, and I start to shamelessly grind against his knee, hitting just the right spot on my throbbing clit.

His lips travel down my neck, and just as he had said, he starts kissing and nipping the soft flesh as his other hand finds the strap of my dress and pushes it down, exposing my breasts and peaked nipples to the summer brisk air.

"Goddamn," he growls, the sound going straight to my core. "Your tits are fucking perfect." Without another word, his mouth latches on one of my nipples while his hand plays with my other breast, squeezing it as his tongue keeps lapping and flicking over and over. His hand fits perfectly against my breast, like I was made for him and his touch.

That's a crazy thought.

"Oh, *God*," I moan.

His laugh, low and husky, makes my skin prickle. "No God around here, Bella[1]. Just me, playing with your perfect tits as you grind against my knee, desperate to come," he mumbles, hovering his mouth over my nipple, his hot breath against my soft flesh like a wonderful inferno.

I bite my lip, holding back a whimper. This is the last thing we should be doing, but it feels too good to stop.

His mouth closes around my nipple again, and he sucks

---

1. Beautiful.

on it once, *hard*. I try to stifle my cries with the palm of my hand, but he swats it away, clicking his tongue.

"I want to hear every sound that comes out of you. I want to hear how good I make you feel even though I'm barely touching you."

Before I can process what's happening, he flips us effortlessly, his back sinking into the sand as he guides me to straddle him, his growing erection sitting right against my aching core. I know I must be making a mess of his jeans right now, because the fabric of my underwear is lacey and thin.

"Grind on my cock, baby. Make a mess of my jeans and make yourself feel good," he murmurs before darting his tongue and licking the column of my neck with one languid, torturous stroke.

"Oh, *fuck*," I moan breathlessly. The feel of his tongue against my skin is hot and warm, making my body break out in goosebumps.

"You're wishing I was licking your pussy instead, aren't you?" He speaks in a sweet, taunting voice.

"*Yes*," I grit out through another desperate moan as I keep grinding against his erection. I forgot how big he is, and even with all these layers of clothes between us, I can feel every inch of his throbbing cock hitting against my clit over and over again.

"Don't worry, Blue." His voice is so deep and unrecognizable, it's doing wonders for my growing need. "I plan to feast on your cunt one of these days until you're begging me to stop. Then I'm going to make you fuck my face, because make no mistake—I'm *desperate* to fucking drown in it," he growls.

His words urge me to continue grinding hard and fast as my orgasm builds rapidly. My lower back tingles, and

Lorenzo somehow knows the perfect way to send me over the edge by grabbing my nipples between his thumb and index finger, playing with them until my orgasm explodes, making me cry out his name. As the orgasm keeps overtaking my body, he grips my ass so hard, I'm sure he'll leave some bruising. He starts grinding against my pussy, seeking his own friction. The fabric of his jeans rubbing deliciously against my thin lace feels so damn good, and knowing he's just as desperate for me as I am for him is so hot, another orgasm rolls through me as he lets out a guttural groan, his legs shaking from his own release.

As I'm riding down my high, reality crashes against me like a strong, cold wave.

Fuck. This escalated too damn quickly.

We dry-humped in the middle of a fucking beach. What the hell is the matter with me? What about our deal?

Oh, God. No. No. *No.*

My body starts to tense, and he frowns, trying to lock his gaze on mine. "Hey, are you okay?"

I quickly stand, adjusting the strap of my dress and brushing the wild strands of my hair away from my face. Of course, they don't comply and fall in front of my face as always, making me irrationally irritated. Without a word, and like the coward I am, I run toward the staircase, almost falling flat against the concrete as I find my way to the inside of the villa. Lorenzo tries to close the distance between us, calling after me, but I'm too embarrassed to look at him. To face him.

Before he can get any closer, I run to my room, shut the door in his face, and plummet to the floor. I lean my back against the door and look up as my heart starts beating violently, asking myself what the fuck did I just do.

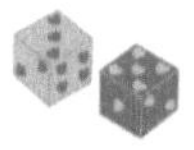

I got no sleep last night. I tried to get some writing done, but my brain was scrambled. I kept replaying everything in my head, because apparently, torturing myself is one of my new favorite pastimes.

The kiss. The dry-humping. The heart-to-heart conversation we had. A lot happened last night, and I don't know how to even begin to deal with it. I'm so embarrassed. After all the huffing and puffing I did about keeping things professional, I go and do something stupid like this. My mistakes will, without question, bite me in the ass like they always do.

Reluctantly, I drag myself out of bed and step out of my room. Still groggy but drawn by the enticing smell of coffee, I head into the kitchen. Lorenzo is leaning against the island counter with a cup of coffee in his hand and wearing a pair of dark Levi's, a green linen button-down, and a pair of—I do a double take to make sure I'm not losing my mind—*white Converse?* Even with a simple outfit, he looks so put together and—unfortunately for me—handsome. Heat creeks up my cheeks at the memory of everything that happened yesterday. I honestly don't know how I'm going to be around him for God knows how long now that we have to stay a few more days.

I somehow find the strength to stumble over to the coffee pot, open the cabinet in front of it, and grab the largest mug I can find. I pour myself a generous amount, not bothering with sugar or milk—I'm too eager for the caffeine to kick in. I take a big gulp, only to spit it out immediately, my tongue burning from the scalding hot coffee.

"*Fuck*," I murmur with a pained groan, darting my tongue out.

Lorenzo shakes his head with a laugh. "You should have checked first. That was reckless of you."

"What's reckless is how hot this coffee is," I exclaim through an exasperated breath.

"What can I say? I like my coffee extra hot."

I place the coffee mug on the counter with a loud *thud,* the coffee spilling on my hand, burning me. *Great.* I'm all over the place today, and it has everything to do with the man in front of me who gave me two delicious dry-humping orgasms and nothing to do with the lack of caffeine.

"That's ridiculous," I hiss, snatching a paper towel to wipe up the mess. "Were you raised by heathens?"

"Some would say that." He shrugs casually, hiding his smirk behind his cup.

I prop my elbows on the counter and shoot him a glare, resting my cheeks on the palms of my hands as a small huff escapes my lips. "Now I have to wait a hundred years, because you drink coffee that's hotter than *hell.*"

He grabs my mug and dumps the liquid in the sink then rinses it and places it in the dishwasher. "How about this? I'll buy you a cup of coffee on our way to our destination."

"And our destination is?"

He shrugs, opting for silence with a knowing smirk.

I shoot him a glance and roll my eyes. He's so cryptic about the stupidest things. I can almost guarantee he does it because he likes to mess with me. There's no point in arguing about it, because I know the chances of him telling me are slim to none.

Uhm, hello? Are we going to ignore the big elephant in the room?

"We need to talk about what happened yesterday," I blurt.

He leans against the counter casually, crossing his arms and looking at me expectantly. After a beat of silence, he says, "If you expect me to apologize, it's not going to happen. Because I'm not sorry."

I should find his brutal honesty endearing, but sometimes it's just too much—and that's coming from the girl who's equally as blunt.

I let out an exasperated laugh. "It can't happen again, Lorenzo. If we're going to spend this summer together, it has to remain strictly professional."

A heavy silence hangs between us, thick with tension. His gaze roams over me, the intensity of it setting my body ablaze. His tongue drags slowly across his bottom lip, and a part of me aches to be the one tasting him instead.

Seriously, Sophia. Get a grip. Buy a vibrator like a normal person and stop thinking about these things.

"Fine," he replies with a simple shrug.

I take a step back, a little shocked. *Huh?* I thought he was going to put up a fight. There was no denying what happened yesterday was crazy but hot.

As if reading my mind, he continues, "I told you I would follow your lead. The last thing I want to do is make you uncomfortable."

His reply should make me feel at ease; instead, a pang of disappointment hits me out of nowhere.

You have to make up your damn mind, woman.

If I have any chance to survive him, it has to remain professional. I have no other option.

"Good," I reply shakily.

He nods with a boyish smile that does nothing to calm my racing heart. "Now go get ready, we have places to be."

A resigned sigh escapes my lips as I walk back to my bedroom. "Give me thirty minutes," I say before disappearing back into my room to take a shower.

I'm honestly too tired to do anything today, but I'm still excited to see what new behind-the-scenes things I'll get to witness. Despite everything that has happened, spending time with Lorenzo isn't the worst thing in the world. And if we overlook the whole dry-humping fiasco, that moment of honesty he had with me yesterday almost felt like an olive branch. He's the type of guy who doesn't like to share anything about his life. Not willingly, anyway. And I will never force him. But it kills me to not know why he thinks like that. How can a man who's so successful, always has a smile plastered on his face, and loves being the life of the party talk like this about himself?

I brush my hair and put it in a messy bun, rolling the wild strands of hair with my index finger in hopes of taming them a little. The humidity and heat are unbearable, and I can't stand having my hair down another day. I've always loved my long hair, but when I'm in hot places like these, or during summertime in general, I always regret it. I dig through my bag, looking for the comfiest, weather-appropriate outfit, and end up with some jean shorts and a graphic T-shirt that says *Born To Read, Forced To Work*. I laugh, remembering Isabella gifting me this shirt as a joke. Who knew the grump of the group had a sense of humor?

I grab my phone and shoot a quick text to Mom. Typically, I talk to her every day, but yesterday was so hectic I forgot.

ME

> Hey, Mom. Sorry I didn't check in yesterday.
> I'm in Panamá (long story, I'll tell you later).
> How are you?

MOM

Hi, honey. How many times do I have to tell you that you don't have to check in with me every day? I'm fine. And Panamá sounds lovely.

ME

Did you take your medications? Did Bailey bring you the refills?

MOM

Yes, she did. And I'm taking the medications, I promise.

ME

Did Amelia call again?

MOM

Stop worrying about your sister.

ME

I'm not worrying about her. I just want to know if you've heard anything else.

MOM

I haven't. Now go enjoy Panamá. Send me pictures! I love you.

ME

I love you too!

Walking out of my bedroom, I bite my bottom lip as I contemplate asking her if she's lying to me, but I think better of it. I don't want to upset her.

Amelia went radio silent, and that unsettles me. She's scheming something, I just don't know what. Or maybe she got back together with Miles. I wouldn't put it past her. Their relationship didn't start with the greatest foundation, and it has only become more and more toxic.

I walk outside, and Lorenzo is leaning against a royal-blue Jeep Wrangler without the top with his legs crossed, wearing a pair of low bridge-fit Ray-Ban sunglasses.

"Wow, you look like a live-in Ken," I say, my eyes roaming his outfit. I bite my bottom lip, trying my best to contain my laughter.

He takes his sunglasses off and places them on top of his head, rolling his thin, almond-shaped eyes at me. "I knew the glasses were too much," he mutters, walking to the passenger side and opening the door for me.

The proud and stubborn side of me wants to tell him I can open my door, but I shut up instead. I've never had someone open a car door for me. And now I understand why women love this. You feel like you matter, even when it's something so simple. I've never known what that feels like. When I was dating my ex, I was practically his mother —always the one taking care of him. I paid for the dates and helped him pay for his apartment and bills. It's honestly embarrassing, now that I think about it. A level of pathetic I don't want to succumb to again.

I thin my lips as I hop on the Jeep. "I think what sealed the deal were those white Converse and this." I tap the car twice with my palm. "Groovy wheels, brother," I say through a loud laugh, making a peace sign.

He shuts the passenger door and walks around, hopping into the driver's seat and closing the door with a huff. "I've never wanted to flip you off so bad until now. Be glad I'm a gentleman."

I snort another laugh, pointing my index finger in the air before replying. "*You can't handle the truth!*"

He looks at me with an eyebrow raised, the one with the tiny scar that I'm dying to touch and ask what's the story behind it. "You just quoted *A Few Good Men*, didn't you?" he asks, a smirk etched on his perfectly shaped lips.

His smirk draws an earnest smile from me in return. It's a strange feeling to smile and laugh because I genuinely want to, not because I'm trying to convince others I'm perfectly fine. My heart tugs deep in my chest. I shouldn't get used to this. Real, heartfelt smiles have been rare for as long as I can remember. The fact he's one of the few people who can make me *really* laugh so often should make me question. But who am I to be questioning things right now? God knows my life has been anything but ordinary lately.

Not only do we share what most people would consider one of my most annoying quirks, but it's also turned into this little game between us—a game I probably enjoy more than I should. While I hear alarm bells around me, telling me to get as far away as possible from this situation and whatever is developing between us, I drown those thoughts instead and focus on staying in the moment. Lorenzo brings fun into my chaotic life, and it's a welcomed reprieve.

Before I can reply, he lunges forward, closing the distance between us, and I freeze, not knowing what he's going to do. A part of me wishes he'll say *fuck the deal* and kisses me. Instead, his hand reaches for my seatbelt. His forearm brushes my chest slightly, causing goosebumps despite the hot weather. Then he clicks the belt in place, making sure I'm secured.

"Just want to make sure you're safe." He flashes one of his killer smiles and the stupid dimple on his left cheek deepens.

Oh, God. This is going to be a long day.

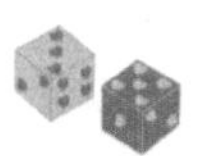

With a normal-temperature coffee in hand, I stand in front of a quaint little boutique displaying a *We're Closed* sign, but that doesn't deter Lorenzo from knocking on the door.

"Why are we here?" I ask, tilting my head to read the boutique's name.

He looks over his shoulder, locking his eyes with mine. "Is that your question of the day?"

I roll my eyes at him. "Obviously not."

The door of the boutique opens, revealing a tall woman with perfect blonde hair. She looks so put together in a light-blue summer cami dress, her wavy hair immaculate. I'm not usually one to feel insecure around other women, but standing here in a shirt that was given to me as a joke and my hair in a messy bun with stray strands everywhere, I can't help but feel it for a moment. That inevitable sting of inferiority when you compare yourself to a beautiful woman, especially one who has something you wish for—legs for days and the perfect height.

She flashes her perfect smile and waves us in. I hesitate, looking around but not moving.

Lorenzo is halfway inside the store when he stops and turns around. "Why are you standing there? Come on." He waves his hand for me to join him inside the store.

I cross my arms, frowning. "It would be lovely if you would clue me in as to why the hell we're here."

He looks up and closes his eyes for a moment, shaking his head, then strides back to me, placing his hand on my lower back and gently pushing me inside. I hate the power a simple touch from him has over me. It's unfair. And did I mention already that I hate it? Because I do.

Why are you lying to yourself?

I'm not lying. It does annoy me—among other things I'd rather not put into thought.

The inside of the boutique is cozy and inviting. Dreamcatchers and macrame hang from the ceiling, swaying slightly. The walls are decorated with framed prints of feathers, mandalas, and inspirational quotes. Wooden shelves display an array of accessories—beaded necklaces, chunky bracelets, and wide-brimmed hats. The clothing racks are filled with dresses, patterned skirts, and fringed tops, and most of the clothes have earthy tones and soft fabrics. There are lots of lace details and embroidered designs. A small seating area in one corner has colorful, patterned cushions and a low wooden table stacked with fashion magazines and lavender incense.

I turn around, gaping at him in disbelief. "Am I supposed to give you fashion advise so you can buy clothes for whatever bimbo you're fucking while we're here?" The audacity of this man. I know he likes to mess with me, but this is too damn far.

Did you think he was going to keep to himself this summer because you're around? Did you think you were special?

"You look extremely cute when you're jealous." He gives my nose a gentle bop.

"You're breaking our deal with that comment." I take a step back, hitting him on the shoulder. "And I am *not* jealous," I hiss.

He fake coughs, trying to hide his laughter. "Whatever you say, Blue. We're here so you can choose whatever clothes you need. It's my fault you didn't pack correctly." He shrugs. "So, shop away."

I look around, grabbing one random dress and searching for the price tag. "These don't even have price tags. Which can only mean one thing—I can't afford it," I say, putting the dress back.

He walks to the small seating area, sitting on one of the patterned cushions. "I had them remove all the tags, because I knew you weren't going to say yes without a fight," he replies without looking up, grabbing a random magazine and opening it on a random page.

Damn. Am I that predictable?

I lift my chin slightly. "I am *not* your charity case."

He looks up, and when his gaze finds my face, he gives me a knowing smile, like he was expecting this already. "Never said you were."

"I can't accept any of this."

I'm all too aware I sound annoying, but I don't do well with thoughtfulness. It makes me uncomfortable. Like I don't deserve it, because, well—*I don't.*

His eyes flash with mischief as he stands, deliberately looking me up and down. My heart hammers wildly, begging to be let free, and my breath hitches at the intensity of his stare. He scrubs his face, hiding his smirk. His muscles flex as he does this move, and I have to force myself to look away to avoid ogling him. I need to get laid, because all I seem to be doing lately is checking him out when I know damn well what happened yesterday was a one-time slipup and he's *off-limits.*

"Tell you what," he bargains. "If I choose something and it fits you, you're going to be a good girl and shop without any complaints. Deal?"

That *good girl* comment goes straight between my legs, making my core tighten and my cheeks blush.

"Good luck with that," I reply weakly.

"Do we have a deal or not?"

I nod without a reply, entertaining yet another stupid

deal. There's no way he's going to figure out my size just by looking at me.

You forget he also felt all of you last night.

I was *just* forgetting about that. But thanks for the reminder *thumbs up*.

He starts looking around the boutique until he finds a light-blue dress with spaghetti straps and a ruffle hem then walks to the dressing rooms and opens the curtain, hanging the dress inside. Refusing to meet his unrelenting gaze, I walk inside the dressing room, close the curtain, and quickly start taking my clothes off to try on the stupid dress.

The dress hugs my waist and breasts perfectly, and the length is right, too, about two inches above the knee. It's flowy and perfect for the hot weather.

With slumped shoulders, I open the curtain and glare at him without saying anything.

His whiskey-colored eyes darken as they hungrily take me in. Our eyes lock, and he licks his bottom lip then bites it gently. The move is so incredibly hot, it creates a pool between my legs. The urge to straddle his lap and bite his lip myself is strong. *Too* strong.

"We'll take it in every color," he says to the boutique owner, not breaking eye contact. He leans back into the cushion, crossing his legs and giving me an amused smile. "Guess you have to be a good girl now, huh?"

I keep making deals with the devil, but the worst part? I keep enjoying every second of it.

I cross my arms. "We do not need it in every color. I'm only going to grab this and another dress. This is already too much."

"You can grab whatever you want, it won't make a difference. I already bought the whole store," he replies casually.

I do a double-take, zeroing my eyes on him. "What do you mean you *bought the whole store*?"

He frowns. "Is that not self-explanatory?"

"Lorenzo," I say, exasperated.

"I bought every item in this store since I wasn't sure what you were going to grab." His tone is so light, you would think we're talking about the weather, and not about the fact he dropped *thousands* of dollars and bought a whole boutique.

I stand there, gaping at him, dumbfounded. My brain is still trying to catch up and form some sort of response.

He tilts his head, mirth playing in his eyes. "Cat got your tongue? That's a first. I'll have to buy stores more often if that's all it takes."

"For the love of God, don't do that ever again," I blurt. "What were you thinking?"

"I was thinking I wanted to take care of you and make sure you had proper clothing for the remainder of the trip."

There he goes again with that word. It rolls off his tongue with such ease, like it's nothing, and yet every time he says it, something in me recoils. I don't know what to do with the idea of someone looking after me. My skin prickles just thinking about it. I've always been the one to handle things, to make sure everyone else is okay. I've always been a fighter. A fierce protector. It's a role I take pride in, even when it gets exhausting. But the worst part? Deep down, there's a tiny, traitorous part of me that actually wants to let him.

I close my eyes for a moment, taking a deep breath. I'm at a loss for words, and the last thing I want to seem is ungrateful, so instead, I whisper, "Thank you. You didn't have to do this."

"Thank me by getting that dress in every color, because you look absolutely stunning." His tone is so sincere, it sends a swarm of butterflies fluttering through my stomach.

22

Lorenzo

Three hours and two shopping bags later, we're on our way back to the villa to drop everything off and go meet with Diego García to figure out a plan for the restaurant. The only reason it took us this long to get out of the boutique is that Sophia, unsurprisingly, fought me the whole time. She still ended up grabbing only the things she needed, plus a dreamcatcher for her mom, and made arrangements with the owner of the boutique to donate the rest of the clothes to any women's shelters around the area. The thought was sweet, and perfectly her. That's Sophia for you—always caring and thinking about everyone.

She kept on the blue dress I picked out for her, and it's currently doing wonders for my ego. She's wearing something *I* chose. Sure, I'd prefer her in something of mine—or better yet, nothing at all. Last night, I ended up jerking off hours after everything that transpired, because I couldn't get the image of her grinding on my cock and moaning my name with that perfect, sweet voice of hers. I had plans, *good* plans, to repeat and go further, because I was barely able to get a taste, and I needed more. But she shut down those thoughts this morning, and I'm going to respect her wishes. The last thing I want to do is make her uncomfortable, even though we both know it wasn't a mistake. She makes the rules, and I simply follow them. At this point, I would mindlessly follow her to the ends of the world.

My eyes find Sophia, and as she's looking around, unaware of what she does to me every time we're close, I take this chance to admire her beauty like a pathetic fool. Her perfectly small, round nose, her long eyelashes, and diamond-shaped jawline. Her naturally soft, pink lips have a perfect cupid's bow. Even her hair, in a messy bun, is perfect. The woman is so devastatingly beautiful, I wonder if she knows it.

Sophia stays outside to call her mom, and I walk inside the restaurant, trying my best to take deep breaths and not lose my shit at the sight of all the unfinished work.

"Diego, what's up, man?" I say, shaking his hand and giving him a quick pat on the back.

"Nothing much," he says, his brown eyes looking around as he scowls. "I fired the crew leader this morning, and I'm personally overseeing this project through completion. I had to bring in some extra help, but..." He sighs, taking his construction hat off and running his hand through his dark, curly hair. "It can be done on time for the grand opening. And we're almost done with the kitchen, so you may be able to get some training done in a day or two."

My shoulders sag in relief. "That's better than nothing. You gave me a hell of a scare there for a minute."

Sophia strides inside the restaurant, and Diego's eyes roam her body for a beat too long for my liking. My shoulders tense as I shoot him a glare. She's beautiful, I get it. Hell, I can't keep my eyes off her, and that's quickly becoming a problem. But when other men look at her, I want to take a knife and scratch out their eyes. Sounds reasonable and not at all crazy, right?

Diego thins his lips, holding back a grin and giving me a knowing nod.

"This is Sophia Evans, she works for *Vogue Elite*. We're uh..." I hesitate for a moment. What the hell am I supposed to say?

Yeah, I wanted an excuse to spend more time with her, so I agreed to do an article, and to top it off, I asked her to spend the summer with me, because I'm a sucker for punishment. And let's not forget about the fact we dry-humped like two horny teenagers last night.

I can't even bring myself to feel embarrassed. In all honesty, I wish we could do it again.

She waves awkwardly. "I'm a junior journalist. We're currently working on a fall edition article for this guy." She points at me with her thumb.

Diego's eyebrow arches in surprise as he looks at me. "And you're doing this willingly?"

"*Yup.*" I shoot him a withering glare.

We've been working together long enough that he knows how I feel about the media. We share the same sentiment when it comes to that. For Diego, it's harder. He's become so successful in such a short amount of time, the media is eager to get his claws on him.

Diego crosses his arms, his eyes sparkling with amusement. "You know, someone from *Vogue Elite*, Max something, has been hunting me to do the same."

Her shoulders tense at the mention of her boss, and I squint at her, but she avoids eye contact. "Yeah, that's my boss. He can be persistent." She forces a laugh, but her eyes are devoid of humor.

Diego presses his lips together, nodding. "Tell him I don't have time for that shit."

She nods with another fake laugh. "Noted."

Someone calls Diego, and he looks over his shoulder, barking an order. That's just how he functions. He's the best in the business because his tactics are ruthless and gives no fucks about what people think. He gets results, and it's exactly why I work with him even when he doesn't have the shiniest personality.

Shaking his head, he says, "It has been a nightmare finding reliable people. I pay above average for this line of work, but it doesn't stop them from doing a half-assed job."

I nod in understanding, choosing to stay silent. If I had to guess, people are not fans of his attitude and that's why he has so many issues finding reliable people. Regardless, he can afford to be that way. He took over his father's construction business and escalated it to a whole new level by the age of twenty-eight while being a single dad. He's as grumpy as they come, but the man is a legend. He's now a thirty-year-old billionaire from Sunset Creek, a small town in Colorado, still a single dad and taking over the world with his construction business one day at a time.

We do one last walk-through so we can be on the same page before the electrical work is completed and the kitchen appliances are installed. The plan was to soft open the restaurant at the beginning of July, but considering how quickly the month is approaching, pushing everything back one more month should give us enough time to finish the clusterfuck of a mess his crew lead left behind.

"I'll call you if we need anything," Diego says once we finish doing the walk-through, both of us hanging outside, leaning against the veranda.

Sophia stayed inside to take a call that seemed important, and I wanted to give her the space, even if the curiosity was killing me.

"Do you need me to stay longer?"

"Not really." He scrubs the back of his neck. "Only if you want to oversee the progress."

"Yes," I say without thinking.

The corner of his lips lifts into a subtle smirk. "Something tells me that decision has nothing to do with the business and everything to do with the girl."

"Don't know what you're talking about." I shrug nonchalantly.

I'm not ready to admit to anyone why I want to stay in Panamá for a few more days. This place is beautiful, and there are so many fun things to do around here. It would be a shame not to show Sophia around. I'm sure she would love it.

And it's the perfect opportunity to spend more time with her.

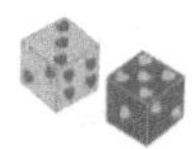

The rest of the day goes by in a flash. We go back to the villa, and Sophia seems quieter than usual. As soon as we arrived, she went to her room, and she hasn't come out since. I had back-to-back Zoom meetings with some vendors, as well as the usual bi-weekly meeting with Vortex's board members, which is currently happening. Being in this meeting is like a slow, painful death. I curse the day my great-great-grandfather decided to be a founding member. Couldn't he have left it at being a war hero? No. He had to take it a step further, cursing all the generations to come.

"Lorenzo, are you listening?" Amos William, the president of the board, asks, pulling me out of my trance.

"Yes," I drawl.

"Couldn't you have been here in person for this meeting? This is the third time in a row you have met with us through a webcam," James Smith, the treasurer of the board, says, annoyed.

"Well, considering I have a business to run, no. I could not have been," I reply through gritted teeth.

James Smith has always had it out for me. The fact I'm the youngest vice president they've ever had, and that he's not a particular fan of my way of living, means we butt heads more often than not. These people are so old school, it bores the hell out of me. In the beginning, when I took over the vice presidency, I was so eager to make changes, but they kept getting shut down to the point I started to let things go. To be fair, some of the rules are plain *stupid*. For example, you need to have a minimum net worth of five hundred million dollars to be a part of this club. We're losing so much revenue due to this rule. I ran the numbers and the logistics of things and made a whole presentation about it.

But did they care? No.

Stuck-up, old-ass sons of bitches.

"We need to do something about Julian Molina. He got arrested, *again*. I know any sort of press is good press, but this is getting out of hand," Amos says.

"I say we ban him," James suggests.

I roll my eyes, even though I know I'm on a big screen and everyone can see what I'm doing. "Julian Molina spends millions of dollars a year in the casino. He practically lives there these days. Something you, as the treasurer of the club, should know," I snap.

"No reason to take that hasty tone with me, young man," James spits.

"I'll take whatever tone I want to take when I have to point out obvious things. We're not getting rid of him, *period*," I say sharply, not leaving room for argument.

Amos rubs his eyes with his thumb and index finger, letting out a resigned sigh. "Those in favor of banning Julian Molina, raise your hand."

Only James raises his hand. At least the rest of the group has some common sense. That should bring me some sort of peace.

"Idiota[1]," I murmur.

The whole board glares at the screen, and I shrug with a shit-eating grin on my face. I have nothing to lose with these people. They can't get rid of me, even when I know they're dying to. I'm not too happy about being here either, so at least we have that in common.

"Alright, then. We'll give him a warning instead," Amos says, dropping his folder on the table. "Thank you for your time, gentlemen. We'll meet in two weeks, same time." He looks at the screen. "And try to be here next time, Lorenzo, yeah? You already know how important that meeting is."

I leave the meeting and snap the laptop shut without a reply. I'm so sick of these people. I've grown angry and so resentful at the life my father left me behind, I don't know how much longer I'll be able to hold on.

Sophia's words echo in the back of my head. *Don't let others dictate your life, Lorenzo. It's up to you to shape your own future and find your own happiness.*

---

1. Idiot.

Maybe she's right. Maybe it's time for me to...let go.

That's a crazy idea. You can't do that. This is what your father wanted.

Yeah, but when is it my turn to be happy? When is it my turn to follow my dreams and my passions?

I glance at my watch, noticing it's already dinnertime and I have yet to see or hear Sophia roaming around the house. Opening the crystal doors to the back patio, I find her sitting in one of the deck pool chairs, watching the sunset. Her hair moves with the air flawlessly, in a perfect movie slow-motion type of way. Her body is slightly shivering with the constant breeze, so I turn around and run to my bedroom to grab one of my hoodies. Once I find it, I head back out and shut the doors, causing her to startle and look over her shoulder. Her eyes lack their usual spark and are slightly puffy. Inexplicable fury rushes through my body as my eyes take her in. My first instinct is to run to her and hug her, but I hold back. My second instinct is to ask who did this to her so I can go take care of it, knowing I have no right.

You need to take a chill pill right now. She is not your problem to deal with.

Maybe I want to make her my problem. Would that be so bad?

I hand her my hoodie without a word. I'm ready to fight her on it, but she doesn't hesitate and puts it on. I stifle a satisfactory groan at the sight of her wearing something of mine. The hoodie looks ridiculously big on her, fitting her like an oversize dress and making her even more beautiful, if that's even a possibility. I never understood why men love to see their girls wearing something of theirs. But seeing her like this, something primal takes a hold of me. She looks very much like mine right now, even when I know it's not real.

"Thank you," she whispers.

I simply nod, sitting next to her and looking over the horizon, admiring how the sun slowly dips, casting a warm, orange glow over the ocean. My fingers itch to touch her, to caress her cheek, maybe even her hair. But the rejection that would inevitably follow would sting. So I keep myself in check, even when I'm dying to do nothing more than to be there for her and to take care of her.

23

Sophia

I don't show weakness to people. It's a craft I've mastered over the years. One I started learning when I was just a kid.

Being weak means you have to rely on someone to feel or be better. That's something I can't afford. I have to be the strong one, even if it kills me. But today, I couldn't anymore after speaking with my sister. I knew she was planning something when I stopped hearing from her. And I've been so busy, I kept pushing off the inevitable. Then I got a call from Mom's nurse today. Apparently, Amelia visited her, and she was not alone. She was with *Miles*. After I hung up, I was so furious I called Amelia right away, and we got into a screaming match.

It's not surprising she got back together with him. What pissed me off is she went home when I specifically told her not to. This may seem controlling of me and like I'm being a bitch, but the tornado Amelia always brings with her is one I can't deal with anymore. Her presence affects Mom, and in extension, it affects me. She storms in, destroys everything in her path, and walks away unscathed. It's hard to handle the situation from so far away. I've considered moving back home, but that would mean quitting the job that allows me to take care of Mom. I'm so tired of it all. Exhausted from trying to protect Mom from Amelia and make her believe something completely different. She doesn't truly know her daughter. If she did, it would destroy her.

"Feel like making dinner with me?" Lorenzo asks.

We've been outside looking over the ocean for almost an hour now, just sitting quietly. For once, I needed the quiet. For once, I wanted to get lost in my thoughts and feel sorry for myself. He came out, handed me his hoodie, and sat next to me without saying a word, which I honestly appreciate. I must look like a mess right now. The angry tears started flowing as soon as I ended the call. I hate that he's the one who got to see me like this. But I'm tired of faking it all. I needed those tears to come out. I needed to wallow in my anger. There's only so much one person can bottle up, and considering I never allow myself to feel, I'm surprised it took me this long.

"Sure," I reply with a soft rasp.

He stands and extends his hand, waiting for me to take it. After a moment of hesitation, I do. The touch brings me comfort and peace, but mostly? *Need.* I can't ignore my attraction for Lorenzo anymore. It's always been there. And yesterday didn't help; if anything, it fueled it. My stubbornness is quickly crumbling, and I honestly want to...feel *good* for one night. This is something I know he can do for me.

What's one more night, right?

That's insane, you need to shut that idea down right now.

What I need to do is shut down my brain for today.

We walk back inside, and as he pulls all the ingredients we're going to need out of the pantry, I grab my phone to look at myself in the camera and fix my hair. It's a little fuzzy from the humidity, but nothing I can't work with. My eyes are not as puffy, so at least I have that going for me.

"What are we making?"

"I was thinking a shrimp stir-fry," he replies without looking at me, studying the ingredients with a concentrated frown. "You're not allergic, right?" he asks, lifting his gaze to mine.

I shake my head and walk to the fridge, grabbing all the vegetables we're going to need. "I do like my stir-fry spicy, though."

"Same," he replies, dumping the shrimp in the bowl and running water through them.

I hum playfully, dropping the vegetables next to the cutting board. "I guess the group is right, we're more similar than we think."

His shoulders shake with a small laugh, the sound making me ache with need. His laugh is so carefree and velvety, I wouldn't tire of hearing it.

"We're both pretty amazing then. Because I don't know about you, but I'm a fucking treat," he says with a slight, playful shrug.

I grab a small kitchen towel, spin it, and snap it against his upper arm, laughing. "You're so full of yourself."

He stills his movement and snaps his eyes on me. "Did you just *whip* me?"

I shrug, spinning the towel again. "Did you like it? I can do it again." I wiggle my eyebrows playfully.

He places the bowl in the sink slowly, moving his whole body to face me now as he crosses his arms. "Someone's feeling bold today."

Oh, you have no idea.

I try snapping the towel against his upper thigh this time, but with his quick reflexes, he avoids it. Before I can react, he tries to yank the towel from my grasp, pulling me toward him in the process and making me crash into his chest. I stumble from the impact, but he quickly grabs my upper arms, steadying me.

"You good?"

A giggle bubbles out of me—what the fuck? Why am I giggling? I'm acting like I have some sort of high school crush. "Yeah. Damn, you're quick."

"Yes, I am." He successfully yanks the towel from my grasp and spins it as tightly as he can. "You should run now, I'll give you a three-second head start." His voice is husky, with an unspoken promise. The way it drops to a sensual, deep tone has my thighs clenching, already seeking some friction. The desire running through my veins so strong it's impossible to ignore any longer.

I take a few steps back, crossing my arms. "*Please*, I'm not afraid of you."

He chuckles, playing with the corners of the towel with his fingers. "You should be. This is going to hurt."

The way his eyes roam my body sets me ablaze. I welcome the burning sensation, because it's all I want—to feel the intensity of his flame. Make no mistake, Lorenzo and I? We'd ignite a beautiful inferno together.

"One..." he starts counting.

My back stiffens, but I don't back down. "You can count all you want, I'm not going anywhere."

"See"—he clicks his tongue—"I doubt that." He takes a step closer, like a lion hunting its prey. "Two..."

I should run. The thrill of knowing he could easily catch me makes me entirely too excited, to say the least. This interaction right here is slowly helping me forget about all of my problems. See? I knew Lorenzo would be the perfect recipe to forget about my life for a moment.

Instead of walking away, I take a step closer, lifting my head to meet his gaze despite our height difference. "Should I finish counting for you?" I drum my fingers against the kitchen counter, pondering. "Nah, I think I'd rather run." I shriek, darting out of the kitchen as quickly as I can.

His unrestricted laugh echoes through the villa as he takes slow steps toward me. "You can run, but you can't hide, Blue."

My heart races as I sprint to the living room, leaping over the couch to the other side, putting it between us. "I'm fairly short, but I can be fast. I think you're going to have to *really* try if you want to catch me," I say as I unzip his hoodie and take it off, dropping it on the couch.

"If you say so," he replies lazily, pausing for a moment to graze his teeth with his tongue before flashing me a mischievous smile. He's savoring every second of this, and I can't deny that it only fuels the thrill simmering inside me.

Before I can even blink, he charges forward, almost hitting me, but I swiftly move to the left and run back to the kitchen, open the doors to the patio, and run outside. I make sure to close the door behind me to win myself a few seconds. Darting my eyes around, I find a bush close to the pool and hide behind it. A few seconds later, he steps outside, expecting to find me, but when he doesn't see me, he stops in his tracks, frowning in confusion. My heart wants to burst out of my chest, and I place a palm on top of my mouth to stop myself from laughing. As he starts walking around the patio, my veins pump with adrenaline, and my breath hitches as I wait for him to position himself the way I want him to. When he finally stands in front of the bush, I leap onto him, catching him by surprise. He falls backward, sending both of us into the pool.

The rush of air whips past me as we descend, and for a

split second, I feel weightless—both physically and figuratively, like the weight of my problems is being lifted by the water. The cold water envelops me instantly, sending a refreshing shock through my body, quickly followed by the warmth of Lorenzo's body as I cling to him for dear life. He resurfaces, bringing me with him. Once we come up for air, I throw my head back, laughing with tears of joy welling in my eyes. Water drips from my hair and skin, and the chilly wind bites at my face, but it can't diminish the alive and carefree sensation vibrating through me.

He starts laughing, too, so carefree and unrestrained; I crave more of it. "You're such a cheat."

I let out a satisfactory sigh as I try to unwrap myself from Lorenzo. He grips my waist instead, keeping me in place. My body becomes aware of our proximity, and not even the cold wind can calm the heat I feel sizzling underneath my skin. Even with clothes on, I can feel every hard muscle of his body against mine. My nipples peak through the wet fabric, and I'm all too aware it's because of how close Lorenzo is, not the cold. He brushes a wet strand of hair from my face, his hand moving to the nape of my neck, where he begins to caress. Every time he touches me, my body reacts with a familiar burning sensation. In other instances, I would be trying to get as far away as possible, trying to maintain some sense of professionalism. But now? There's nothing that could keep me away from it. Not anymore.

Closing my eyes for a moment, I exhale a shaky breath as he presses his forehead against mine. We're so close, yet somehow, it's still not enough. I crave more of his presence. His scent. *All of him*—even when I know it's the last thing I should do. But this feels right. The perfect temporary fix I need. He doesn't do relationships, I don't either. It makes sense to give myself one last taste. To feel good and adored underneath his touch.

We both look up at the same time, the distance between us still so little. I lick my lips and drop my eyes to his, and he follows the movement, licking his own. He wants to kiss me. I can see it in his hungry eyes. The air is charged with an unspoken spark—the wild, tense silence that seems to fall between us constantly. The same spark we had at the club. The same spark we had last night. Lorenzo can make me feel so much with a single look—scratch that—with his *presence*. It's demanding. Dominant. And plain intoxicating.

"What about our deal?" I ask breathlessly.

He smirks knowingly. I don't need to specify my question, because it's clear enough. If we kiss, we'll be crossing that professional line I was nagging him about this morning. But *fuck* the line, and *fuck* the deal. I'm ready to throw it out the window and enjoy every second of this.

His Adam's apple bobs as he takes a slow, deliberate gulp. "Deals are meant to be broken," he replies, his voice a deep rasp, his eyes locked on my lips.

There are so many things wrong with that statement, but *God*, I could care less right now. Before I lose my momentum, I fist his wet hair and crash my lips into his, my heart hammering wildly. Lorenzo wastes no time and pushes me against the edge of the pool as the grip he has on the nape of my neck tightens. The touch is so primal, demanding, and needy, my skin starts to feel scorching hot. He licks my bottom lip, demanding entrance, and I eagerly welcome him, his tongue fervently crashing with mine. His hand leaves my neck, and I momentarily miss the touch before both of his hands grip my outer thighs as he nips my bottom lip for a moment before he continues kissing me like our lives depend on it. The kiss is punishing and every bit demanding. The satisfaction of it all pulls me under, drowning me in the feel of his lips, the heat of his strong body pressed firmly against mine. The kiss grows more desperate by the second, and so does my need for him. His erection is obvious, even with all the heavy, wet clothes between us. I'm out of breath at this point, and my lips feel extremely numb, but I don't dare stop.

Lorenzo stops abruptly, and I whimper at the miss of his lips. He grabs me by the waist and lifts me out of the pool. My clothes hug me, and my body shivers. Water drips in steady rivulets from his hair as he presses his hands against the edge of the pool. His muscles tense and flex, the veins in his forearms becoming pronounced as he hoists himself up. My eyes eagerly roam, appreciating every inch of his body. His clothes hug every ripped muscle, and my clit *throbs* with relentless need. I'm not sure how much longer I can hold on. My fingers itch to reach out and touch him. Something tells me he wouldn't be opposed to it.

"You're shivering," he points out with a concerned look on his face, standing and extending his hand for me to take. "Let's get inside."

A humorless laugh escapes me, because, yes, I am shivering, but not from the cold. My need for him is so strong, it's clouding my brain. I think my rational thoughts packed up and walked out, leaving me behind with nothing but a peace sign.

"I have my question of the day for you," I declare, ignoring his concerned look and his extended hand.

He looks at me expectantly.

There's no turning back now, Sophia. Are you sure about this?

I've never been so sure about anything else.

"Can you make me feel good just for tonight?"

24

Lorenzo

Fuuuuuuuuuuuuuuuuuuuuck.

I'm sure my soul left my body and came right back at the question Sophia threw my way.

Why are you standing there looking like an idiot? You're just staring at her. Say *something.* Do *something.*

I blink at her in shock. "What?"

She looks at me with a flustered expression. "You're going to make me repeat the damn question?"

No, I don't need her to repeat the damn question. I heard her *loud* and *clear*. Her question made my cock a little too excited, too. He's already getting too many ideas, and I'm trying to shut them down. Be the voice of reason for a change. She was just telling me this morning how she wants to keep things professional, and I'm trying so hard to respect her wishes. I'm grasping for anything at this point.

This is not you, at all. You would have jumped at the chance.

Yes. But this is different. The attraction I have for Sophia is intense, wild, and borderline obsessive. This is unknown territory for me, being attracted to someone I've already slept with. I'm aware I sound like a total dick right now, but it's the truth. I sleep with someone once and move on. But with her, it feels all kinds of wrong. Even I have my limit, and I think I've met it. Never thought I'd see the day a woman would make me question so much.

I point to the door. "Get inside and we'll talk about this."

She glances over her shoulder at the door then turns back to me, fire blazing in her eyes. "No."

This woman is so incredibly frustrating, I want to scream from the top of my lungs. She just knows how to push the right button sometimes. It's also what makes her a hundred times sexier, but this is *not* the fucking time to be acting stubborn.

I thin my lips, scrubbing my face in frustration. "You're seriously going to fight me about this?"

"Lorenzo, the only way I'm going in there is if I know for a fact you're going to *fuck* me. Otherwise, I'm not interested," she spits, crossing her arms.

"Trust me, there's nothing more I'd rather do than to *fuck* the sass out of you," I retort.

This is what I've been wanting, craving—*and wishing*—for. It's what I wanted to do yesterday. To fuck her until we had nothing left to give. But she's having an off day. The vulnerability has been clear since I walked out here. I'm not going to be the asshole who takes advantage of her in her most vulnerable state.

I'm not sure what the hell happened, and I know if I ask her she's going to deflect. Making her feel good would be, quite honestly, an honor. To make her forget her problems for a moment. It's what I'm used to doing. It's why women seek me out. Except, Sophia is different. This feels different for *me*. I don't want to give her what I would give to any other random woman. The high of the release will be good, but only momentarily. What she needs is to talk and be open about what's bothering her.

"I'll make you feel good under one condition," I say in a strained whisper. "You need to tell me what happened today."

"I'm not sure what you're talking about."

I pinch the bridge of my nose, taking a deep breath. "Dio aiutami[1]," I murmur to myself. "Stop feeding me that bullshit, Sophia. Something happened, and if you want me to make you feel good, that's my condition."

"You called me by my name," she points out, baffled.

"That should give you an idea of how pissed I am at you right now," I say, nostrils flaring in irritation.

She holds her gaze on me without saying anything. I look at her expectantly, raising an eyebrow. I'm not going to back down, not on this.

After a beat of charged silence, she stands and walks to the door. Opening it, she turns around, grabs the hem of her dress, and slips it off. I stifle back a groan at the way her peaked nipples are visible through her white-laced bra. The way the wet fabric hugs the swell of her breasts—tempting and perfect. Her lacy white panties are damp, too, leaving nothing to the imagination. My erection is painful against my jeans, and I'm beyond eager to strip away the underwear that's quickly becoming my undoing.

"You got yourself a deal," she replies sultrily and walks inside.

I raise a fist to my mouth and bite my knuckles as I try my best to not read too much into this. It's just one more night. I can make her feel good and move on. Yet I can't kick this queasy feeling that's settling in the pit of my stomach.

---

1. God help me.

Nerves, maybe? No. It's something else I have yet to figure out.

I follow her, closing the door behind me. My cock twitches at the sight of her hips swaying as she walks to her bedroom. Her perky, round ass looks perfect, and my hand aches to grab the curve of it and squeeze. To smack her ass until it's bright red and leave a mark behind. The things I want to do to this dangerous, beautiful woman are too many to count. The thoughts alone drive me to the brink of insanity and to a type of desperate need I've never known.

Her hungry gaze travels from my eyes all the way to my chest and my waist. "Would love it if you could get rid of your clothes, too."

"I bet you would," I reply smugly.

She rolls her eyes and closes the distance between us by fisting my shirt and pulling me forward. Even through the fabric, I can feel her peaked nipples against me, and my instinct is to get rid of her bra as soon as possible and grab one of them with my mouth, flick it in taunting circles with my tongue until it drives her crazy. But, if she wants to feel good, she needs to talk.

"What happened today?" I ask as my hand reaches her face, tracing her jawline with my index finger.

She closes her eyes, her breathing becoming choppy at my touch. "Family issues."

My index finger starts tracing her neck now as I bring my lips close to her ears and nip it softly. "You're going to have to be more detailed if you want more from me."

A small whimper escapes her lips, and I can't hide my triumphant smile. Touching her like this will help me figure out what she enjoys for next time. I know she loved how I kissed, bit, and licked her neck yesterday. But I wonder what else drives her wild? I want to study her body. I want to learn everything that brings her pleasure. I want to be the only one who gives it to her.

Where the hell did that last thought come from?

She's not mine to claim. There isn't going to be a next time.

I start giving her slow, peppering kisses on her jawline all the way down to her neck. She wraps her arms around my shoulders, and her damn intoxicating scent hits my nostrils when she's wrapped around me like this. She smells like temptation and my downfall. And I want nothing more than to drown in all of her.

"My sister visited my mom without consulting me," she says through a shaky whisper.

"Mmm," I hum, and as I keep kissing and nipping her neck, my other hand travels to the curve of her breast, using my thumb to caress and trace it. "And why is that an issue?"

When a beat passes and I don't hear anything come out of her mouth, I stop abruptly and take a step back. This wins me a groan, pulling yet another triumphant smile from me. I bet this has to be frustrating for her. She has a naturally challenging personality and doesn't like being told what to do. Unfortunately for her, I hold all the cards right now. While she doesn't realize this yet, I'm doing this for her own good. Not only that—but in this room, she will listen to me and do what I ask of her. That much I can guarantee.

I gulp, my eyes finding hers. I hope she can see the sincerity in them. "If you tell me what's going on inside that head of yours, I promise I'll make you feel good."

I barely recognize myself in this moment. The talking and the listening? That's not me. I'm more of a *let me fuck your brains out until neither of us can speak* kind of guy. With her, though, I want to listen. I want her to open up to me, to give me an insight into her life. Something about her calls to me. This unfamiliar pull—the need to want *more* from her. To stay close and actually care for her.

Get real. Taking care of someone is the last thing you're capable of.

It doesn't mean I want it any less. Even when the thought in itself is laughable.

"Okay," she replies, frantically nodding and taking a few steps back. "I can't believe I'm about to do this," she murmurs, more to herself than me. She takes a deep breath and says, "My mom, she's sick..." Her eyes, glimmering with doubt, find mine.

I nod at her to continue. I know she doesn't feel comfortable, but this is a good thing. She'll feel so much better afterward.

"She suffers from pretty bad anxiety. She needs help with a lot of things, like going to the grocery store and doctor's appointments. Mostly day-to-day stuff. This is why I work at *Vogue Elite* and—" She waves her hand dismissively. "That's beside the point." She sighs.

And what? The question is almost at the tip of my tongue. Something tells me this is also important. But she's getting her groove now, and I don't want to interrupt.

"I work there because it pays enough to allow me to provide for her so she can have a comfortable life. And my sister, well, she's not easy. Never has been." She laughs humorlessly. "I've always had to clean up her messes, and she takes advantage of me. Mostly because I let her, and because I don't want my mother to know the kind of person she is." She's talking a million miles per hour now, pacing back and forth. "Every time she reappears in our lives, something bad inevitably happens. I'm drowning in the uncertainty of things right now, and I just can't. I can't anymore." She stops talking abruptly and eats the distance between us in a few quick strides. Her eyes find mine as she places a hand on my chest, and the touch is so unbelievably electric, it rattles something in me. "My life is a mess, Lorenzo. All I do is think and control, stress and worry. For *one* night, I want to let go. So, *please*," she begs weakly. "Can you make me feel good now?"

How can I say no when she looks at me like I hold the answer to all of her problems? She has no idea how badly I've wanted to drop to my goddamn knees and worship her the way she deserves.

The vulnerability in her voice tugs deep at my chest, but what tugs even deeper is how proud I feel of her for being honest.

I collide my lips with hers in a soft, exploratory kiss. I want to savor every stolen moment from her, because I know after this night, everything will go back to normal. In the meantime, I will relish in the feel of her sweet, soft lips on mine, and the way our tongues meet and study each other's mouth. My hands travel to her back, and I unclip her bra, letting it fall to the floor. I grab one of her breasts and squeeze, and a husky groan comes out of me, which she eagerly swallows with her intoxicating kisses. My hand is a perfect fucking fit for them, and that makes me entirely too happy. When we fucked at the club, there wasn't much time for anything, it was a quickie and move on. Yesterday was even quicker, and I didn't get to see much of her. But now that I have her here in front of me, I'm determined to touch and admire every inch. My hand starts to travel south, making sure to touch her smooth, tanned skin. Arriving at her underwear, I play with the waistband as my mouth drops kisses from her lips to the column of her neck. I keep my kisses slow and deliberate until I arrive at her breasts, take one of her nipples, and slip it inside my mouth.

Flicking my tongue back and forth at a punishing, taunting pace. She moans, her hand reaching the back of my head and fisting my hair hard as she arches her back, seeking more friction.

I grab her by the waist, and we fall onto the bed, my mouth still lapping at her perfect, round peak. Her smooth skin tastes so sweet, I could savor her for hours. I graze her nipple with my teeth, winning me another delicious moan as her skin starts to break into goosebumps. My mouth starts traveling down, kissing her ribcage and abdomen until I arrive where I have been dying to fucking drown. Her underwear is see-through due to the dampness, and it clings to her lips, giving me a perfect view of her glistening pussy. She's so incredibly wet, her arousal runs down her inner thighs, making her skin glisten.

I tsk, tilting my head. "Look at you. All wet and ready for me, making a mess already." I lick my lips eagerly. "I think I should clean you up a little, don't you think?" I dart my tongue out and lick her inner thigh, where some of her arousal is, a gravelly groan escaping me at the delicious taste. "So goddamn sweet, I can't wait to get my mouth on that tight little pussy and get my fill. I'm fucking starving for you, Blue."

She props herself up on her elbows on the bed, her dilated eyes staring at me, burning me. I relish in the intensity of her blue gaze. It's quickly become my undoing, and I wouldn't have it any other way. Without breaking contact, I suck her clit through her underwear. The fraction of the fabric and my lips must feel good, because she clenches her thighs around my head as one of her hands reaches out and fists my hair, locking me in place.

"You trying to drown me, Blue?" I mumble with a laugh.

"Yeah," she replies, unapologetically. "You said you were

starving, thought I'd help. Because I'm desperate to grind on your face. Got a problem with that, Ace?" she asks, raising an eyebrow playfully.

The mouth on this girl, I swear. I am going to shut her up with my cock one of these days.

There's not going to be a repeat. Remember?

That seems less likely with every second that passes.

In one swift motion, I push her underwear to the side, exposing her bare, glistening lips. "Not a problem as long as you let me feast on this pretty cunt of yours," I reply huskily, wrapping her legs around my shoulders and tugging her ass to the edge of the bed.

Without giving her a chance to give me another witty comeback, I lick her center in one fell swoop, and it's a miracle I don't come at the feel of my tongue against her delicious slit. *Fuck.* It was a mistake to do this, because now that I've gotten a full taste, there's no turning back. She lets out a throaty moan, the sound going straight to my dick. It's so painfully hard and stiff, the lightest friction from my wet jeans hurts. She falls back onto the bed, one hand on top of her mouth to quiet her moans, the other one still fisting my hair. And she's not gentle about it either, but the painful sensation feels too good. Knowing she's using me for her pleasure and being unapologetic about it makes me want to make her feel more than good. I want her to reach the stars and come back. Give her the orgasm of her fucking life.

I push her hand away from her mouth as I bite her inner thigh playfully. "Did I tell you to be quiet?"

"Who knew you liked them loud?" she retorts, but her words have no bite. She's enjoying this as much as I am.

"No." I shake my head. "I like *you* loud," I growl, sliding two of my fingers inside of her. "Now be a good girl and play with your tits while I feast on this delicious pussy. If you stop, I stop. *Got it?*"

She nods frantically, her eyes rolling back.

Not good enough.

I curl my fingers, finding the sensitive spot, the touch driving her wild. "Use your words, Bella[2]."

"*Yes,*" she hisses through gritted teeth. "*Got it.*"

"That's my girl," I say gravelly, smiling triumphantly. I flick her clit with my tongue as I start fingering her. Her pussy is gripping my digits eagerly, and I growl as I keep feasting on her. The more of her taste I get, the more I want. I lap at her lips eagerly then suck her clit over and over, like the desperate, thirsty man that I am. The sound of my lips closing around the sensitive bud and sucking is straight up *filthy*, making me more excited. I keep fingering relentlessly, not stopping for even one second, enjoying how the sound of her wetness fills the room. If my cock feels a fraction of what my fingers are feeling right now, I would simply come right then and there.

She moans loudly, arching her back and rolling her nipples between her thumb and forefinger. All I can do is admire her flushed face, her damp hair, and the way her lips are parted, moan after moan escaping her. I'm fueled by her sound and by the way she tugs at my hair, so desperate and greedy. I graze her clit with my teeth, and she pulses and clenches around my fingers.

"Please don't stop," she begs, still tugging my hair like her life depends on it while riding my face. "It feels too good."

If only she knew I couldn't stop even if I fucking tried.

---

2. Beautiful.

With every thrust of my fingers and every lick, I grow more and more obsessed with her.

I curl my fingers, seeking her sensitive spot as I continue to alternate between sucking and flicking her clit up and down. The combination of the two drives her crazy, just the way I want it, and her moans become a sweet symphony. My girl is loud, and the sounds make me eager to get more out of her.

I look up, finding her hand nowhere near her peaked nipples anymore. "Did I tell you to stop touching yourself?" I growl. "If you stop again, I will bend you over my fucking knee and smack your ass until all you can see and feel is my handprint."

Her thighs clench around me at my words as she shuts her eyes with a tight nod and starts playing with her nipples again. I keep thrusting my fingers into her, hard and fast, touching her sensitive spot at a relentless pace. Her walls start to grip my fingers, and it's hard to keep up with the punishing pace as her body signals how close she is to orgasm. Wanting nothing more than to get a heady taste of her, I latch on her clit with my mouth one last time, sucking it hard.

"Lorenzo!" she cries out, and I almost lose control right there, just from the sound of her voice calling my name. I've never been particularly fond of it—that's why most people call me Enzo. But hearing it come from her pouty mouth, rolling off her lips? There's nothing better. All I want now is to hear her yell it again.

She starts grinding her pussy against my face, riding her climax, and my tongue licks her center, eagerly drinking her as she comes on my tongue. I never thought I could get high off something like this. The sight of Sophia coming undone before me. *I* did that. She's moaning *my* name and coming all over *my* face. It's a high not even gambling can bring. And this unknown, untamed feeling coursing through my veins is possessive and obsessive. I want—no, I *need*—to be the only one who brings her this kind of pleasure.

Once she's done riding her orgasm, she relaxes on the bed, letting out a content sigh.

"Who knew all I needed for you to obey me is to have my fingers inside of you?" I ask with a dark chuckle, resting my head on her thigh as I look at her.

"Shut up," she says with a laugh.

Her laugh is free, effortless, the kind that bubbles from deep inside, like a stream breaking loose from its confines. It's just like the one she had by the pool, and the one from this morning in the car. The same genuine sound that fills the air and makes everything around her feel lighter. And right here, right now, I make another silent promise to myself—whatever it takes, I'm going to be the one to make her laugh like this more often. I want to see her eyes shine and spark with pure joy. Sophia's laugh is something the world should hear. It's the kind of laugh I want to take a piece of and tuck into a corner of my cold heart. It's the kind of laugh that makes my problems go away. It's the kind of laugh I can find myself falling for, simply because it comes from her.

As I get up, she sits on the bed, tucking her legs underneath her, and when she tries to reach my jeans, I grab her by the wrist, stopping her.

She frowns, confused. "What are you doing? We had a deal."

"The deal was for me to make you feel good. And I did, didn't I?"

"The deal was for us to have a one-night stand," she challenges.

"You sure about that?"

I chose my words carefully. Sure, I told her I'd like to fuck the sass out of her, but I didn't say I would. What I did promise, though, was to make her feel good. I won't pretend it isn't torture to hold back from something I want so badly, but I'm not going to take it there. Not under these circumstances.

Her eyes flash with hurt, her irises turning a darker shade of blue. She grabs the sheets and covers herself, her cheeks flushing with embarrassment. "Fine. Leave, then," she says, tone cold.

"Blue—"

"No. I got it," she snaps. "You don't want to sleep with me. Would have been nice to know beforehand." She snorts a humorless laugh.

"You seriously think I don't want to fuck you?" I shamelessly point at the obvious erection. "Is this not clear enough for you? Was yesterday not clear enough for you?" I shake my head. "You have to be fucking kidding me," I murmur.

"Are we having the same conversation right now?" she retorts, tugging the sheet underneath her arms and crossing them. "You just rejected me."

With a low growl, I find her legs underneath the thin sheets that weren't hiding much of her in the first place and jolt her toward me, shutting her up with a deep, punishing kiss. I can still taste her on my tongue, and the mix of her arousal and her sweet lips is making my erection even more painful, to the point of no return—I *will* have to take care of this. I swipe my tongue inside of her mouth, wanting nothing more than to coat her with her own arousal. I want her to taste herself. To know *this* isn't a rejection. No. *This* is a promise. I don't understand what the fuck is happening between us, but I want to sit her on a throne and worship her until the end of my days. I want to open myself up and give her the best parts of me. The thought in itself is ridiculous, because there are no best parts of me. I'm just an empty shell, ready to break.

I rest my forehead against hers as we try to calm our ragged breaths. "I want you so much it physically *pains* me. I want you so much, I have to fist my cock at the thought of you every fucking night to stay away from you. I'm trying my damn hardest to honor our deal—"

She interrupts. "I think the deal has been broken for a time now, and we both know it."

She's not wrong. Still, I'm not going to do something she'll regret if she's not thinking clearly and if her heart is not in the right place. I'm not that kind of asshole.

After a beat of silence, I kiss her forehead. "I want you more than anything," I whisper, gripping her face with both of my hands and forcing her to look at me. To look at the sincerity of my eyes. To hear the pleading in my voice. "But the next time I *fuck* you, Blue, it's going to be because you want me—*us*. Not because you're looking to escape reality."

This is a promise I make for myself. For her. *For us*. As I let go of her against my own will, I understand now the queasy feeling I had in the pit of my stomach before. I am *not* done with her. One more taste was not enough.

It never will be.

This is the beginning of something new.

25

Sophia

Even with the beautiful Panamá weather, I've been holed up in my room all day, working on articles Max has been sending me to edit and proofread. Even though he was more than excited when I told him I was going to follow Lorenzo around this summer, my absence from the office didn't stop him from giving me all this extra work we both know belongs to him, not me. This has been a secret I've kept since Max became editor in chief. It all started innocently when I told him I wanted to dip my toes into editing because I used to have a side gig during college, and I wanted to keep honing that skill. It's not the same editing my work vs. other people's.

He quickly agreed—that should have been my first red flag—and started giving me assignments here and there until they became more frequent. And now? I edit most, if not all, people's work at the office while he takes all the credit. And while other times I would hate the fact I'm being drowned in work, it's currently a welcomed reprieve, because I've been able to successfully avoid Lorenzo all day.

The next time I fuck you, Blue, it's going to be because you want me—us. Not because you're looking to escape reality.

That comment left me stunned. Isn't that why he sleeps around, too? I can't speak for him, but when I sleep with people, it's because I *want* to escape reality, feel good for a fraction of a moment, and relinquish all control. I guess this means I have no way of getting him out of my system. He just had to be the voice of reason and ruin it. I practically— scratch that—I *actually* propositioned him, and he *rejected* me. The one time I decide to break my one-night stand rule and this happens. God, I'm an embarrassment.

Lying in bed, I brush a strand of hair away from my face with a frustrated sigh, staring at the ceiling, wondering what the hell my life has boiled down to. Single by choice and stuck with a job I could grow to love, if only I didn't have the worst boss in the world. I wanted to become an author, yet that dream is so far back in my head it's starting to accumulate spiderwebs. At this point, I'm not even sure it's my dream anymore. I don't even know what my dream *is*. I've been trying to survive and forgetting I have to continue to build my future. Except, I see no future in sight. I'm floating through life right now, and I have grown comfortable. *Too* comfortable.

There's a soft knock on the door, and I bring my pillow to my face and groan. The knocking annoyingly continues until I hop out of bed and open the door.

The corner of his full lips twitches as his eyes roam my body. "Glad to know you're alive. How've you managed to avoid me all day, I don't know, but consider me impressed."

"What a shame it's over," I murmur under my breath.

He purses his lips momentarily. "I checked in on the restaurant this morning, and they are working relatively fast. But we may need to stay a few more days."

"Cool."

"Out of all the things I thought you were going to do, giving me the cold shoulder was not one of them." He crosses his arms and leans against the door frame. "I had all these fun things planned for today, and you disappeared on me."

I let out a long, resigned sigh. "Didn't particularly feel like spending time with the guy who rejected me. And you forget I have a job."

He doesn't falter at my comment. Instead, he asks, "Ready to sleep with me because you want to?" He raises an eyebrow. "And isn't your job to be my shadow and write the article?"

"That's never going to happen," I fire back. To myself, I mutter, "And no, I have many other things to do."

"You keep saying these things with so much certainty, yet I never believe you," he muses.

I'm not sure I believe the things I say much either. I told myself I was going to keep things professional, and we know how that turned out. I lied through my teeth and told him he wasn't memorable. I've denied the attraction between us, day in and day out. I don't know why I keep doing this to myself. Would it be so horrible to accept I want to sleep with him because I want to and not because I'm looking for an escape?

I could keep doing this back and forth with him all day, but I'd rather keep it in the back of my head at this point. With a resigned sigh, I ask, "So, where are we going?"

He perks up, his eyes sparkling as a smile plays on his lips. "You're saying yes?"

"As long as what you have planned is fun." I shrug. "I don't see why not."

He rubs his hands together, giving me a mischievous grin. "Oh, it's going to be fun, alright."

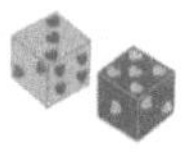

After spending all day in my room working and feeling sorry for myself, this is the last place I would have thought I'd end up.

Yet here I stand, helmet and goggles in hand, getting ready to *skydive*. Adrenaline curses through my body, and I'm shaking from excitement. While other people would be scared, I get such a high from doing things like these. When we arrived and Lorenzo said what we were doing, tears threatened to come out. This was something I told him in passing while we were playing our silly question game, and he kept it locked in his memory. No one has ever done something like this for me. I'm always the one going the extra mile for everyone—not that I mind, it's what I'm used to. And for once, I don't feel like fighting back. This has been my dream all my life, after all, and I want to take advantage of it.

"You good?" Lorenzo asks.

I shriek excitedly. "Are you fucking kidding me? I'm so excited I could throw up. This is the best idea you've ever had. Thank you."

He grabs my helmet and places it on top of my head with a chuckle. "It's no big deal." His hand grazes my cheek as he fastens the helmet, and the simple touch makes my stomach flip. Leave it to me not to be nervous about skydiving, but one touch from Lorenzo and I'm a goner. "Only a girl like you would say it's their dream to skydive. You're a woman full of surprises, Blue."

My traitorous little heart wants to leap out of my chest at the thought that he's willing to do something like this for me. If it were any other person, I would be running as far away as possible. But Lorenzo has brought down my walls low enough, and I can't help but feel thankful.

We sign the waivers as the guy at the front desk briefly explains what all the equipment is for. Our tandem instructors—which I learned is what they call the people who are going to jump with us—will go through everything and give us step-by-step instructions. The desk employee guides us to the plane we're going to be using, and there are two guys waiting for us.

A tall, long-haired blond guy strides toward me with a bright smile. "Hey, Sophia, right? I'm Matt. I'll be the one assisting your jump today."

I nod, giving him a soft smile. "That's me."

"Are you nervous?" he asks as he guides us to a table where he starts checking the equipment. Lorenzo is with his instructor at the table next to ours.

I shake my head. "I honestly thrive on chaos and adrenaline. It has always been a dream of mine to do this."

His gaze locks onto mine, scanning my face. An unexpected pang of disappointment hits me as I realize it doesn't stir the same feeling as when Lorenzo looks at me. "Wow, it's not every day I meet a beautiful woman who's not afraid of skydiving. You're a total badass." He winks.

I give him a small smile. He's flirting with me, and while I don't mind the attention, it still doesn't give me the excitement it used to. Much less the same stomach-dropping feeling I get every time Lorenzo flirts with me. The thought is jarring, and I hate it.

"Why, thank you," I reply with a small, forced laugh.

He laughs, his hand reaching for my helmet. "I'm just making sure it's secured."

I nod, glancing over to where Lorenzo is standing. He's watching us, shoulders tense. When I frown at him, his jaw clenches, and he practically shoots daggers at Matt with his eyes.

"Are you from around here, or just vacationing?" Matt asks.

"I'm here for work, actually."

"Yeah? For how long?"

I shrug. "Not sure yet. Could be some days or a week."

He nods as his eyes roam every inch of my body, making me visibly uncomfortable. But before he can say anything, Lorenzo strides toward our table and stands in front of me, giving me his back and completely blocking the guy's view. "Would appreciate it if you could stop flirting with her."

I take a step back, gaping at him as I tap his shoulder. "Lorenzo, what the hell are you doing?" I hiss.

He completely ignores me and crosses his arms impatiently. The shirt he has on today hugs his broad back and shoulders perfectly, and I can't lie, the energy oozing out of him right now makes him look dangerously sexy.

Matt laughs nervously. "Hey, man. I didn't know she was your girl. Sorry about that."

Lorenzo doesn't bother to correct him, instead, he bites out, "Even if she wasn't, you shouldn't be flirting with customers. You're clearly making her uncomfortable, and I don't appreciate it. Go find another employee, because you're not about to jump with her."

"There's no one else."

"Then we're switching," Lorenzo barks, turning around. His eyes are wild and a dark shade of brown I've never seen.

"Go with the other guy, Blue." He tilts his head to the other table.

He's pissed, and I don't know why that gives me a sense of satisfaction. Without a word, I go to the other table where there's an older guy.

"Gotta be careful what I say around you, I don't want to get your boyfriend mad." He extends his hand to shake mine. "I'm Harold."

I thin my lips, holding back a laugh. Instead of correcting him, I say, "Yeah, he's very protective." I shake his hand. "I'm Sophia."

There's no harm in living in a short fantasy where Lorenzo is more than whatever he is right now, right? What even are we? Friends seems like a looser term these days.

We go through the safety list, and once everything is ready, we hop on the plane. When it takes off, I close my eyes and exhale. If Mom were here, she would pass out from the anxiety. This is one of the things I can never tell her about.

"Okay, listen up," Harold's voice cuts through the plane engines. "When we get to the door, I need you to cross your arms over your chest, like this." He demonstrates, and I mimic the motion, arms tight against my chest. "Keep them there until I tap your shoulder. That's your cue to spread them out like you're flying. When we jump, keep your head back against my shoulder, and your legs tucked behind you. It's important for stability, so we stay aligned during free-fall."

I look up, my eyes finding Lorenzo. Matt is giving him the same instructions, but he has a scowl on his face, looking at Matt with a bored expression. The look on his face makes me laugh, but I try to keep it in check while Harold keeps talking.

"Once we're stable, I'll tap you, and you can open your arms. Just trust me and enjoy the moment," Harold finishes, giving me a warm smile.

I nod, trying to forget about everything and live in this moment.

Lorenzo goes first, and once they jump, I step to the edge. Everything looks so small and insignificant from this high up, and it makes me think for a moment how much more there is to this life. How, even when I'm drowning in my problems most of the time, there's more to look forward to. The wind roars in my ears, the deafening rush drowning out every other sound. My heart lodges in my throat with a wild rhythm that matches the adrenaline surging through my veins. The sky is the lightest shade of blue, with the whitest, most beautiful clouds I've ever seen, and the ground is a patchwork of green and brown that seems impossibly distant.

And before I know it...we fall.

For the briefest second, my stomach lurches, a free-fall that seems like it will never end. The air rushes past me, cold and sharp, biting my cheeks and tugging at my clothes. He taps my shoulders twice, and I open my arms wide as I start laughing to the point of tears. I laugh and laugh like never before. I'm weightless, suspended between earth and sky, untethered from everything that once felt solid and certain. It's an exhilarating feeling, one I don't want to let go of. All of my problems and swirls of thoughts wash away from me with every second we continue falling, and every sharp wind that cuts against my face. As my arms stay wide open, I let the wind catch me, lift me, and for a moment, I'm flying. Truly flying. Not just falling or drowning in the uncertainty of life and my decisions.

I'm...*living*.

This is the feeling I've been chasing. A reminder that I am *alive*, and I get to experience things like this. That I can take risks and be happy while doing them.

The parachute opens above me, yanking me back to reality. As we land, the world below me seems so peaceful now, almost serene, as a strange sense of calm settles over me. Once I'm settled, I quickly get out of the equipment, throw my helmet and goggles on the ground, and turn around, frantically looking for Lorenzo. When I find him, he's already out of the parachute, too, looking at me with a bright smile. Before I know what I'm doing, I start to run and run until my legs feel like giving out and leap into his arms. I wrap my hands around his neck and my legs around his waist, hugging him tightly. Lorenzo easily catches me, his hands gripping the curve of my ass to keep me firmly in place. The sensation of having his body pressed against mine makes me feel alive all over again.

My lips find his ear. "Thank you," I whisper shakily, on the verge of tears. "You have no idea what this meant for me."

His eyes find mine, and he gives me the most mouth-dropping, gorgeous smile he's ever given me. He kisses the top of my head then rests his chin on top of it. "Don't thank me. I'm just glad I was able to help you forget about your problems for a moment."

I knew he did this for me, but to hear that come out of his mouth makes my heart soar with so much... contentment.

It makes me feel understood.

But more importantly? It makes me feel seen.

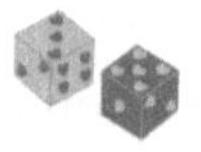

After we skydived—I still can't believe I get to say that now—Lorenzo decided he wanted to try to make *Ropa Vieja*. I'm currently cutting the vegetables as he's seasoning the meat. I thought it was mesmerizing to see Lorenzo take over the poker table, with his natural talent and commanding presence. But him in the kitchen is something out of this world. He's in his element, in every sense of the word.

"You're holding the knife wrong," he says, washing his hands and drying them on his apron. You would think he would look silly wearing one, but the man is so incredibly handsome, is quite the opposite. He looks ridiculously hot wearing a cedar-blue denim apron and a backward hat. He walks over and stands behind me as his arms wrap around me, his hand holding mine on top of the knife. His masculine, intoxicating cologne envelops my senses, and I hold myself back from doing or saying anything, because I selfishly want him to embrace me for a little while longer.

His lips are close to my ears, whispering, "Grab it by the handle and rest your finger against the side of the blade." His hand guides my thumb to where he wants it. With his other hand, he tucks my fingers under, forming a claw shape. "This will help you grip the vegetable as you cut and keep the control."

Lorenzo's voice is naturally deep and sultry, capable of making anything sound sensual. His whispers in my ear send tingles down my spine and ignite a fire in my lower belly. I only manage to bite my lip and nod, because I've lost the ability to speak with his proximity. We cut the peppers in silence, the only sound between us the steady rhythm of the knife against the cutting board.

"Got it," I manage to say hoarsely.

He buries his nose in my hair, inhaling. "Have I ever told you that you smell like summer?" he asks, his voice taking an even deeper tone.

I drop my knife and bite my lip again, stifling a small whimper. "Uhm, n-no. I don't think you, uh, have."

He chuckles softly, stepping back, and the moment he does, a wave of emptiness rushes in, leaving me cold in his absence. "It's funny how someone as fierce and wild as you can smell so intoxicatingly sweet."

I rear back as I look at him and tilt my head. "You think I'm fierce?"

He grins, his eyes glinting with admiration as he steps back in, just close enough that I can feel his warmth. "Oh, you are," he says softly, his voice a low murmur that makes my heart stutter. "You're fierce in a way that makes people take a step back. Like you could burn someone if they get too close."

My cheeks heat up at his words. "I...had no idea you thought that."

"I don't think it. I know it," he replies with one of his killer smiles, the one that makes his dimple pop.

With that, we go back to prepping the food in silence, but the air between us is charged with a tension thick enough to cut.

"When did you realize you enjoyed cooking?" I find myself asking, trying to avoid the energy that's flickering between us.

He drops the vegetables in the Dutch oven with a tiny bit of extra-virgin olive oil, the sizzling and earthy smell filling the air. "Is this your question of the day?"

I hop on the kitchen counter, swiftly grabbing my glass of wine and taking a sip before replying. "I have more than one question, so we should play another question game instead."

As he sautés the vegetables, his lips twitch into a smile, and he clicks his tongue, shaking his head. "Enjoying playing games with me, Blue?"

I throw a fake gasp at him, bulging my eyes. "*Ugh! As if!*"

He throws his head back with laughter, but the way his neck stretches and his Adam's apple bobs distracts me completely. "I was wondering when you were going to quote *Clueless.*"

"Damn it." I slap myself on the thigh. "You're so good at catching these. I hate this game."

He shrugs as he tosses the meat into the pot. "I *am* good," he confirms. "And I'll play the game—"

"Let me guess...*under one condition,*" I try to mimic his voice as I roll my eyes.

He squints at me. "We've been spending too much time together, that's the only reason you guessed it."

"Maybe you're just predictable." I shrug, crossing my legs and taking another sip of wine.

"*I'm having a good time...not,*" he murmurs under his breath while putting the broth in the pot, waiting for it to bubble.

"*Wayne's World.* That was too easy. *Score! You suck,*" I reply, pointing my finger at him. There's no way he'll catch this reference.

"That's from *Friends.* Monica Geller said it, if I remember correctly," he says, scrubbing his jawline while pondering.

"Damn it," I mutter. "You *do* suck."

His eyes find mine, and we stare at each other for a beat before breaking into a true, genuinely smile. Something that has been happening more often than not around him.

"And to answer your question," he sighs, "ever since I was a kid." He ponders as he takes the towel to clean his hands and drops it on his shoulder before crossing his arms. "I was so lonely, I wanted something to fill the little free time I had. Cooking became an escape, and eventually, my true passion."

The rawness in his voice and the way his body language turns tense, more serious, takes me by surprise. If he's loved this for so long, why deny it? That's the question nagging at me the most.

I hop off the counter and stand in front of him, tilting my head as I study him. "So why do you hide it?"

He shrugs. "I don't hide it, I just don't tell the world. There's a difference."

"No." I shake my head assertively. "You hide it. You hide behind this." I flap my hand around, trying to find the words. "Behind this playboy, doesn't take anything seriously, famous billionaire persona. The gambling. The partying. Do you even enjoy any of that?"

"Careful, that's your third question," he warns playfully. "Let's not get ahead of ourselves. I haven't even told you my condition."

"Do not give me that shit right now," I snap. "For once, stop playing your games."

He frowns and turns around without a word, reducing the heat and covering the pot.

I cross my arms and start tapping my foot against the cold, tiled floor. "Well?" I refuse to feel bad because of my tone. For once, I want him to take it seriously.

He turns around abruptly. "Cooking is more than my passion. It's the only thing that gives me any peace," he snaps, scrubbing his face with a weary sigh. "I'm exhausted, Blue. Tired of the lifestyle, the business, the suits. We've stayed in Panamá so long because—" He cuts himself off, shaking his head. "That part doesn't matter. But part of the reason is, I'd rather be here, getting the restaurant up and running. I'd rather be here, creating and cooking, than stuck back in Chicago wasting my days drinking, partying, gambling—doing whatever I have to do just to stand the thought of being trapped in this life." His words tumble out so fast he's almost breathless by the end. When he finally takes a breath, his shoulders relax slightly.

I'm at a loss for words. This is...not what I expected. Here I thought Lorenzo was simply a reckless man, living on the edge because he could afford to. But he's trying to escape his life, to have some sense of control, even though he knows damn well he's stuck. And to an extent, I understand what he means. People may think, *well, if you're sick of it, stop doing it*. But that's easier said than done. Sometimes, life gives us responsibilities we can't get out of.

My hand reaches his face, caressing his jawline. He closes his eyes, his breath hitching at my touch as he melts into it.

"That's terrible, Lorenzo. No one should live like that," I whisper.

He simply nods with his eyes still closed. As I caress his face, my head races with so many thoughts I can't keep up with them anymore. Lorenzo is not who I thought he was, and this new revelation tugs at my resolve. Maybe opening myself to him of all people will be my undoing.

It will destroy me.

I can feel it.

26

Lorenzo

This has been, hands down, the best day of my life.

We both lie on the pool deck chairs, admiring the stars. I would sell everything I have and move here to spend the rest of my days like this. Fuck the city. Fuck Vortex. Fuck everything. This right here? The perfect moment, with the perfect woman. I couldn't ask for anything better.

"It's safe to say that was the best thing I've ever eaten," Sophia says, rising from her chair. "Damn you and your good cooking, Ace."

"Hey." I sit up, turning around to look at her. "Where the hell are you going?"

"It's cold," she complains, hugging herself to keep the warmth. "Every night, the ocean breeze makes me freeze to death."

"Stay here," I order, darting into the living room and grabbing the blanket that's draped over the couch.

She shakes her head. "That blanket sucks. I'm just gonna go to bed."

I grip her shoulders, stopping her in her tracks, and

gently turn her around, guiding her toward the hammock strung between two palm trees with a view of the ocean. "No, come on. You disappeared on me all day, you owe me some quality time."

"Aw, did you miss me?" she asks jokingly.

My heart stammers at her question, because, honestly? Yes, I did.

I take off my shoes and hop on the hammock with the blanket then open it and pat the space next to me, completely ignoring her question. "Come on."

"Are you asking me to cuddle, Ace?" she asks with an amused look on her face.

"Oh, get over yourself. You don't want to share a blanket with me?" I fake gasp. "Do I make you nervous, Blue?" I wiggle my eyebrows playfully.

I absolutely want to be close to her. The hammock is perfect and comfortable for both of us. The night is clear, the ocean is calm, and I can't think of a better way to spend my time.

She narrows her eyes at me then hops onto the hammock beside me. I drape part of the blanket over her.

"For the record, no. You don't make me nervous," she retorts.

"If you say so."

She turns to face me, her hand resting on her cheek as she leans into it. "Stop assuming things."

I mirror her pose, and as soon as my eyes find hers, I want to slap myself in the face for looking. Her eyes, even at night, are the same haunting unique shade of blue. "Then stop lying. You can keep telling yourself these things, but we both know you don't mean them."

She looks at me for the longest time without saying a word, her gaze burning me with an intensity that makes me feel almost too exposed. We stay silent, our breathing slowly syncing. Around Sophia, being quiet brings me peace and comfort. I don't mind it. It feels personal. Everyone gets the loud and confident version of her, but only I get this. And while I like when she's loud and unapologetically herself, I also like this. The real her. She can't bullshit her way through me anymore. I know she puts on a front; I just keep letting her get away with it.

"Interested in making a deal?" she asks suddenly.

I raise my brows, caught off guard. "Am I going deaf, or are you trying to strike another deal with me? Here I thought you hated them."

"Don't be so sure of yourself. Chances are you're going to say no."

"Have you forgotten who I am? I can't turn shit down. I thrive in the chaos. We *both* do." I give her a pointed look.

What she doesn't know is I can't turn down anything when it comes to her.

She lets out an exasperated breath. "Never mind, I don't know what I was thinking," she mumbles quietly.

I hit her shoulder playfully. "No. Come on, tell me. Since when are you shy?"

Her eyes find mine with a silent determination, and she straightens her back while rasping her throat. The movement is so cute it makes me laugh. Dare I say she looks nervous? The way she twirls her hair with her index finger and purses her lips in contemplation, it's a new look on her.

"We have to spend a lot of time together this summer," she starts.

"Yeah?" I prompt.

"Why not have fun, then? Friends with benefits until we're done writing this article. Or, if you want to break it off before, fine by me." She waves her hand with a small, nervous chuckle.

I sit up so fast I nearly knock her over. If I hadn't grabbed her by the waist in time, she would have fallen. "What did you just say?" I grip her waist tightly.

She needs to repeat it, because there's no way. I must have heard wrong. My desire for her is so deep, my brain is coming up with all these crazy scenarios.

"I'm not going to repeat myself. You're either in or you're out."

"You're going to have to repeat it. Matter of fact, I never gave you my condition for all the questions you asked me. So this is it. You need to answer my question. *What. Did. You. Just. Say*?" I ask, pronouncing each word with gritted teeth, my grip on her tightening.

"Friends with benefits with an expiration date. We could break it off the weekend we're supposed to go to Las Vegas with the group, at the end of August. I should be done writing the article by then, so it makes perfect sense," she replies confidently, but her voice quivers slightly in the end. "We have fun with zero attachments. No falling in love. Just two people having casual sex."

"You're serious," I murmur more to myself than her.

She grimaces, expecting my answer. I'm trying to calm my fast-beating heart and the painful erection I have at the mere thought of entering this deal. I want to shout *Yes! For the love of God, yes!* but not without making sure this is exactly what she wants *and* needs.

She abruptly stands from the hammock, swatting my hand away from her waist. "I can't believe I did this again. Forget I said anything." She storms away back to the inside of the villa.

I rise to my feet, but the annoying blanket wraps around

me, causing me to stumble and land on the grass. That doesn't stop me from untangling myself as quickly as possible and running after her. Finally catching up, I grab her by the arm and turn her around. "What is the matter with you? You can't drop this bomb on me and then walk away!"

She pulls out of my grip, throwing her arms wide as a frustrated groan comes out of her. "Again with the bullshit! Are you seriously shocked? You're telling me right now you're not attracted to me? What are all these mixed signals you've been giving me, then? Another sick game of yours?"

I grip the bridge of my nose, biting the inside of my cheek, mulling it over for a moment as I try to muster a response that doesn't make me sound so desperate. I more than want her. I *need* her. One more night, multiple—whatever she needs. I'll take whatever she's willing to give me at this point.

"Of course, I'm attracted to you. But I told you, if we're doing this it's because you want to. Because you're ready to give in, and you're ready for the consequences." I close the gap between us, placing both of my hands on the back of her neck, gripping it softly and forcing her to look at me in the eyes. "Once we do this, there is no going back, Blue. I will ruin other men for you, and honestly? You will ruin other women for me, too."

What I don't tell her is that she already did, over a year ago. She ruined me so badly, I should be running away instead of entertaining this. But fuck, I will let her ruin me over and over again. I'll embrace the burn. I will hand her the fucking match myself and help her get away with it.

It's not lost on me either that I'm slowly, for once in my life, allowing someone in. What I did back there, in the kitchen? Confess what I've been keeping inside for so long?

Out of character for me. It should terrify me, giving her more ammunition to destroy me, but I couldn't give less of a fuck right now. She can do whatever she wants. My life is in her hands, she just doesn't know it yet.

She doesn't say anything, just holds her intense gaze on me, the fire in her eyes still imminent.

I tighten my hold on her. "What's it going to be?"

She remains silent. And with every second that passes, the need I have for her grows, my body itching to kiss her. My heart twisting in my chest as I wait for the magic words.

Please say yes.

Her hand moves to the back of my head, her fingers threading through my hair and giving it a gentle tug. The sensation of her delicate touch makes me roll my eyes with a low groan.

"Ruin me," she whispers breathlessly. "I dare you."

She barely gets the words out before I'm crashing my lips on hers. It's a punishing kiss, too. One I've been dying to give her since the last time we kissed. I flick my tongue across her bottom lip, and she moans, opening her mouth slightly and letting me own her. My hands find her hips, and I guide her backward until her back hits the kitchen island. I frantically hoist her up as our lips are still connected—kissing, nipping, and licking. Not wasting a second even though we're running out of breath. I fist her hair and give myself access to her neck, desperately tracing kisses and marking every inch of skin my lips and teeth graze over. She tugs my hair, her fingers playing with it as she wraps her legs around me, bringing me even closer.

"You need to take that fucking shirt off, *now*," she demands, her chest heaving, her peaked nipples visible underneath the thin fabric of her dress.

With a soft laugh, I take a step back, creating some

distance between us against my will as I pull the hem of my shirt and take it off. Her eyes ignite with fire while she starts tracing my abdomen, her hand traveling upwards until it lands on my chest.

"I've been dying to see how far your tattoos go," she whispers, tracing them with her delicate fingers. The touch is soft, but it doesn't make it any less electrifying.

"All you had to do was ask," I say with a low chuckle, my hands roaming her smooth legs, causing her to shiver and break out in goosebumps.

"That easy, huh?" she asks with a playful tone, tugging at my gold chain softly, bringing me closer to her again.

I brush my lips against hers. "*Yup.* That easy."

Before she can reply, my fingers find her already wet underwear, and I swiftly push them to the side, sliding two digits inside of her without any warning. She gasps through a moan, her head falling back as she wraps one arm around my neck, while her other continues to travel across my abdomen. Her feathery, explorative touch makes me shudder and become more addicted by the second. I never knew it was possible to be obsessed with something as simple as a touch, but with her, everything is better, brighter, and fucking perfect.

You've become obsessed with a lot of things lately. And all of them have to do with her.

"This is how it's going to work," I say in a hushed, husky tone, working my fingers in and out of her slowly. "While we're doing this?" I curl my fingers, and that wins me another moan. The sound is so deliriously sexy, it goes straight to my dick, making it painfully hard. "You will listen to me. You're going to be a good girl, enjoy yourself, and let me thoroughly fuck you. If I catch even wind of that sassy mouth of yours, there are going to be consequences."

"What are those consequences?" Her question comes out desperate, in between breathless moans.

My girl is already coming undone before me, and I'm just getting started. I meant what I said—I will ruin every other man for her. When she fucks another, she will think of me. When they kiss her pouty lips, savor her sweet skin and pussy, all she's going to be able to do is think of me, my mouth, my fingers, my cock. I close my eyes for a brief moment, trying my best to push away the thought of another man exploring her. She's mine—for as long as she lets me have her. And fuck, I'm going to do everything in my power to make it last.

"Fuck around and find out," I say with a dark laugh, dropping to my knees on the floor, bringing her closer to the edge of the counter, and opening her legs as wide as possible. "Keep your legs open for me. I'm fucking starved and ready for dessert."

I slide my fingers out of her, and her whimper turns into a moan as I flatten my tongue against her center, licking her fully in one, long and languid stroke. A gravelly moan escapes me, and I roll my eyes as I lick my lips eagerly. "You have no idea how much I was craving another taste of this sweet pussy of yours. You taste like my fucking undoing."

"God." She laughs through a throaty moan. "That filthy mouth of yours."

I bite her inner thigh playfully, looking up, and the view —oh, the fucking view—I have no words. It's too perfect to describe. "You sure you still want me to ruin you?"

Her eyes lock on mine as she replies shamelessly, "More than anything."

I close her legs for a moment, taking her panties off so I can see all of her, wet and ready for me. I open her legs again as far as they can go and place my hand on the curve of her ass as I take the other and press two of my fingers on her labia, spreading her open. Finding her sensitive bud, I wrap my lips around it and suck eagerly. I suck it hard and long, enjoying the way she writhes beneath me.

"*Yes*," she moans, arching her back. "You're doing so good, please don't stop."

I keep sucking her clit then flick my tongue back and forth playfully with enough pressure to build her orgasm, but not enough to take her over the edge. She fists my hair, pressing my face against her pussy as she shamelessly and unapologetically grinds against it. Her other hand finds the strap of her dress, and she slowly slides it down, exposing her perfect, round breasts and peaked nipples. She starts to play with them, just like last time, and the sight of her makes me smile. She's never looked more beautiful than now. With a flushed face, eyes closed, biting her lips, sweat trickling down her face to her neck and between her breasts.

A beautiful chaos. But perfect nonetheless.

I nip her outer lip then start flicking my whole tongue up and down, savoring every ounce of her. I dart my tongue inside her as I run my thumb over her clit with soft, quick circles. She writhes beneath me, but I grip her ass hard, giving her a silent warning to stay in place. Like the good girl she is, she takes the hint.

I want her to come undone beneath me. To see her fall apart before my eyes as she comes on my tongue.

"Come for me, Blue. *Drown* me. *Ruin* me. Because, baby, after this, I'm going to thoroughly *fuck* you until you can't remember your name," I say quickly before sliding in three fingers this time and finding her sensitive spot and sucking her clit one last time. This sends her over the edge, and she squirms beneath me, moaning. She's loud and unrestricted, and I love that.

I pat her thigh twice. "Don't you dare move. I'll be right back." I run to my room quickly and grab a condom.

I walk back and stop in front of her, taking in the breathtaking sight. Her chest rises and falls with each heavy breath, her nipples still hardened, legs spread open, her arousal glistening and making a tempting mess. She straightens and reaches for the hem of her dress, taking it off. And *fuuuuuck*. Perfect is too small of a word to describe her. She's so much more than that. Sophia is her own level of woman, no one can stack up to her.

My hand reaches and squeezes her mouth-watering tits. "One of these days, I'm going to fuck these perfect tits of yours," I say gravelly, licking my lips.

"Don't tempt me with a good time."

I look up and gulp hard, whispering, "*Jesus.*" I feel like one lucky motherfucker right now.

She bites her bottom lip and tries to jump off the counter as she reaches for my jeans, but I quickly stop her.

"I told you to stay put," I warn.

She raises an eyebrow. "What are you going to do if I don't listen?"

"I'll deliver on that spanking I told you about the other day," I say with a smug smile, getting rid of my jeans and boxers quickly.

She lies back, laughing. "I'll have to stop listening one of these days, then."

"I expect nothing less." I open the foil with my teeth and roll on the condom as fast as humanly possible, winning me another laugh from her.

"Someone's eager," she comments smugly.

Placing one hand on her hip and the other around my length, I stroke my cock twice before centering it with her entrance. "I've been dying to bury myself into this tight pussy of yours for the longest time. So, yes. I'm eager as fuck. Problem?" I ask, slowly working myself in.

"No problem at all." She bites her lip, moving slightly and burying another few inches inside of her. "As long as you get going, because I want to feel all of you."

The sound of her voice, so sultry and promising, snaps something in me. Without warning, I bury myself to the hilt, not daring to move as I let her adjust to me. As I adjust to *her*. The sensation is too much, too soon. It's better than I remember, and I want to stay buried inside of her forever if she'd let me.

"*Oh*," we both moan at the same time. Damn, she feels good. So wet and tight. The way her pussy clenches around my full length has my self-control slipping.

I place one of her legs over my shoulder, the position allowing me to drive even deeper, and I have to take a moment to inhale and exhale before moving because I can feel her *everywhere*. When I finally get my bearings, I look down at where we're connected, and I pull back, enjoying the sight of pumping in and out of her.

I hook both of her legs around my waist then grip her chin, tilting her head down. "I want you to watch how good you take my cock, Blue."

We both stare, engrossed in the way her pussy grips me as I slowly pulse in and out of her. It's a heavenly sight, and I could stare at it all night long.

"Look at that greedy little pussy of yours, taking every inch," I groan. "*Fuuuuck*, we fit perfectly, baby."

"Lorenzo..." she gasps, tilting her head back.

I grip the back of her head and force her to look down again. "I didn't tell you to stop looking."

She feels so damn good, so slick and wet, I'm losing my mind. I want her to admire how good we look together. How well we fit. How perfect we are for each other. My thrusts are slow and precise, because I want to enjoy this moment more than anything. Sinking myself into her warmth is too fucking perfect. Too fucking good. I want nothing more than to make it last.

"I thought you said you were going to ruin me, *hot shot*, so go ahead," she muses. "*Fuck* me."

With a deep growl, I latch my mouth onto one of her nipples and suck as my thrusts become faster. Her perfect tits bounce with every desperate thrust. I let go of her nipple with a loud *pop* and lean back. My hands find her waist, and I lift her hips slightly, the position letting me drive in deeper and hit her sensitive spot. I start to pump harder and harder, to the point where her moans become more and more frantic. She can't get a word in, because I'm thoroughly fucking her into this kitchen counter right now with every wild, desperate thrust.

"Look at me," I say through gritted teeth. "I want your eyes on me as you come around *my* cock. I want you to look at me as *I* ruin every other man for you. Let me see those pretty blue eyes of yours."

She obeys, her glassy eyes meeting mine, and fuck, they are the darkest shade of blue right now. I don't know which shade I prefer anymore. They are all perfect in their own unique way.

"Yeah, that's it," I whisper. "Fuck, you're perfect." My words are hitched and gravelly as I try my best to not come. She needs to come first. I *need* to feel her coming around my cock.

"I'm so close. Please, don't stop," she moans loudly, gasping for air as I keep pounding into her hard and fast.

"Oh, baby, we're just getting started. I'm going to fuck you all night long. I'm going to eat and fuck this pussy until you can't take it anymore. Until you're begging for me to stop." I sink my fingers into her soft skin, locking her in place as I hit the spot that has her rolling her eyes.

"*Yes*," she cries out, her eyes fluttering in pleasure. Her pussy clenches around me like her life depends on it as she starts to climax. My thrust becomes uneven and choppy as my balls tighten and my spine tingles, signaling my impending orgasm. Sex with Sophia is an out-of-body experience. Every touch, every kiss is so heightened and full of life. It's something I've never experienced before.

With one last, hard thrust, and as she's riding her orgasm, my legs shake uncontrollably as I follow after my own release. The orgasm is so hard, I get dizzy for a moment, and I drop my elbows on both sides of her head, trying to calm myself down as her pussy milks every drop out of me.

"*Merda*[1]," I groan, burying my nose in the crook of her neck, inhaling all of her. I want to be consumed by her fully. There's no other explanation for this possessiveness and need I'm feeling right now.

I slide out of her and get rid of the condom then grab her by the waist and keep her legs wrapped around me as I walk to my bedroom and stumble us both onto the bed. We both lie there, looking at the ceiling, trying to catch our breaths.

"That was amazing," she says breathlessly.

"I'm not done with you yet. I meant it."

"Good. Because I want nothing more than to be fucked by you until neither of us can speak," she replies with a grin.

This girl never fails to amaze me. Always unapologetically her. And I hope this summer, I can bring more light

---

1. Fuck.

into her eyes, because damn it all if it's not the best thing I've ever seen.

Sophia

I'm still trying to catch my breath from the two mouth-watering, most intense orgasms of my life when Lorenzo grips my waist firmly, lifting me with ease until I'm facing him and straddling his chest. "Time to ride my face, Blue."

I chuckle. "There's no way you're ready to go at it again."

With an eyebrow raised, he grabs my hand, guiding it to his already hard, throbbing cock. I stroke it twice, pre-cum leaking out of it and landing on my fingers. I bring the digits to my mouth and lick them clean. "I guess I was wrong," I say with a playful smile.

He guides me up his body until my pussy aligns with his mouth. "I told you, I'm just getting started." He starts to kiss and nip my inner thighs, making me clench as a small whimper bubbles out of me. I'm already so ready for him and for another mind-blowing orgasm. He doesn't have to do much to make me feel desperate for him.

"I'm dying for you to fuck my face," he mumbles against my skin, darting out his tongue across my inner thigh, lapping at it torturously. "I've been a good boy, patiently waiting for you to accept that you want this. And now that I finally have you, I've earned it, haven't I?"

My eyes find his as he keeps worshiping every inch of me with every soft kiss and lick, making me feel desired in a way no one ever has.

He tightens his grip on my hips, his voice a low growl as he repeats the question. "Haven't I, baby?"

"Yes, you've been a very good boy," I reply breathlessly. As soon as the words are out of my mouth, he sinks me down and closes his mouth around my clit as I thread my fingers into his soft hair.

A guttural moan comes out of me as his tongue circles my sensitive bud. I start grinding his face immediately and shamelessly, because it feels too good. He's barely started, and I'm almost there, ready to fall off the edge. He flattens his tongue, running it through my center with a delicious, slow stroke before pushing it into my hole as I moan and cry out his name. I tug on his hair so hard, I know it must be painful, but I can't bring myself to care. The more I tug, the more he laps at me like a man starved. His fingers dig into my hips so hard, I know he'll leave some bruising behind, and the sensation is sizzling. Knowing he's somehow marking me makes me feel exhilarated. He locks his gaze on me, his eyes a delicious darker shade of brown, filled with so much lust and hunger as he finds my clit and sucks down on it so hard, I arch my back and tilt my head back with a moan.

"Lorenzo," I cry out, desperate. "I need your cock. I want to taste you, please."

"You want me to fill that sassy mouth of yours with my cum?" His warm breath brushes against my pussy as he speaks, and I'm so overstimulated, I have to try my best to hold my moan back.

"Yes," I hiss, the word coming out so desperate, I barely recognize myself.

"Turn around," he orders gruffly.

Without a word, I obey. I get on my hands and knees on top of him, his mouth-watering cock right in my face. A ping of excitement floods through me, because I'm dying to show him how much I've been waiting to feel all of him, show him how much I want him.

"Now be a good girl and suck my cock while I keep eating this delicious pussy," he says before running his tongue all over my center again. I'm so sensitive, I involuntarily jerk forward, but he grabs me and brings me back, locking me in place. "I told you I was going to feast until you were begging for me to stop. Are you ready to beg?"

"No," I moan, shaking my head.

I grip the base of his cock and run my tongue from base to tip, leaving a trace of saliva as I desperately keep licking him, enjoying every second of it. I wrap my mouth around his tip and swirl my tongue, teasing him, edging him. I feel him groan against my pussy, so I do it again. Every time I repeat the motion, he flicks his tongue eagerly against my sensitive bud, which only spurs me on. I'm so close already; my lower belly starts to tighten and tingle.

"Your mouth feels so fucking perfect," he groans against my pussy, dragging his teeth across my sensitive flesh. "I'm going to fuck it so good with my cock one of these days."

I lick his cock from base to tip again, humming. "Again with all these empty promises that only tempt me with a good time."

"Wrong thing to say, Blue." He grunts before shoving his tongue inside me. With every pulse of his tongue, I come closer and closer to falling apart. His thumb finds my clit, and he starts doing soft but quick circles. All I can do is moan around his shaft. He must enjoy the vibration, because his cock pulses every time. I try my best to meet his punishing pace with my mouth, but he's so big and hard, it's useless. But I still try, wanting nothing more than to keep savoring him. Lorenzo keeps touching my sensitive bud at a relentless, but soft pace and my orgasm hits me out of nowhere, making panting noises come out of me. Once my orgasm subsides, I get off him, my back hitting the bed as I try to catch my breath. My heart feels like it's stuck at my throat, but God, it was every bit worth it. He towers over me, careful not to put any weight on me. He leans down, pressing a soft, delicious kiss to my lips that sends a dizzying rush through me. He tastes like smoky maple mixed with my arousal, and I get completely lost in the taste of us together. It's addictive and absolutely perfect.

He drops another quick kiss on my lips as his eyes dance with mischief. "Now, you said you wanted me to fuck your mouth." He stands, grabs one of the pillows, and drops it on the floor. "Get on your knees, baby, and put that pillow between your legs."

Even though I don't understand what's going through his head, I do as he says. Obeying Lorenzo makes me feel strangely powerful and wanted.

He grips my chin, lifting my head until I lock my eyes on his. "You look like a goddess on your knees for me, Blue."

I lick my lips eagerly. "Fuck my mouth, Lorenzo. I'm ready to ruin you."

His dark laugh echoes through the otherwise silent villa. "Oh, you've already ruined me so goddamn bad." The conviction in his voice makes my heart falter, but I push those thoughts away, because this is just sex. Nothing more. I open my mouth, ready to take him.

With a low moan, he sinks his hard, girthy cock inside

my mouth, pumping in and out of me slowly. "This is how it's going to go," he starts speaking in a low, husky tone. "As I fuck your mouth, you're going to grind that greedy little pussy against the pillow like the good, desperate slut you are. And you better make a good mess out of it and drench it, baby."

I look at him, my eyes bulging. I feel so utterly spent, I don't know how I'm going to come again. I try to get his cock out of my mouth to speak, but he fists my hair, keeping me in place.

He gives a quick, dismissive click with his tongue. "You don't get to speak, baby. You only get to choke on my cock now." He places my left hand on his thigh. "If it gets to be too much, tap twice, and I'll stop, got it?" His tone is soft but serious.

I try my best to nod as he keeps working himself in and out of my mouth. His face is still glistening with my arousal, and the sight of him, with his hard pecs, tattoos, and disheveled hair, is utterly destroying me. He starts pumping a little faster now, and I try to open my mouth as much as I can, flattening my tongue so I can take him deeper. The sound of his moans and my gags fill the room, and it's so filthy, my core starts to tighten again. And before I know it, I start grinding against the pillow. Not because he asked, but because I'm *desperate* for some friction.

"I knew you were going to listen. You're such a good girl, riding on that pillow as I use your hot, wet mouth for my pleasure. It turns you on, doesn't it?"

I moan around his length, looking at him through watery eyes and nodding desperately. I'm so turned on right now, it's borderline painful. His thrusts become faster and punishing, the tip of his cock hitting the back of my throat relentlessly. The faster he fucks my mouth, the harder I grind against the pillow. My clit is throbbing and so sensitive, but I can't bring myself to stop. Being on my knees for Lorenzo, knowing he's using me, seeing him desperate and coming undone before me is too good of a feeling. His pace is more punishing now, to the point that saliva starts to run down my chin, and the gagging sounds are becoming more and more loud.

"*Fuck*, Blue. This mouth of yours is so warm and perfect." He tilts his head back and moans. "Can I come in your mouth, please?" he asks through a quick, desperate whimper, and I nod just as quickly, wanting nothing more than to get a taste of him. "Such a good girl," he growls. "Don't swallow until I tell you to," he orders gruffly, and I nod again as his thrusts start to become sloppier and faster until he pulls back, only leaving the tip inside my mouth as his cock starts pulsing and spilling. I'm still grinding against the pillow like a desperate fool, the friction of the soft fabric against my clit feeling sensational.

He grips my chin, opening my mouth slightly. "Keep your mouth open and keep grinding like a good little slut. I want to look at you as you make a mess all over that pillow. Make yourself feel good for me," he commands, his voice rough with control.

I shut my eyes hard as I keep moving back and forth. My legs feel like they're on fire, but it's too good to stop.

"Look at me, baby. Keep those beautiful eyes on me—right where they belong." His tone grows huskier.

All I do is obey. It's all I can manage, because I'm at his mercy, and loving every second of it. I'm at a loss for words with how filthy and amazing this feels. I can't believe this is what I've been missing out on. That night we had at the club barely scratched the surface. I don't know how any other man is going to compare to Lorenzo. He's insatiable. His mouth deserves a medal, because the dirty talk is to a whole other level. And the way he can treat me like a queen one second and a slut the next is too good. He was absolutely right—he has *completely* and *utterly* ruined me, and I'm ready to thank him for it.

It doesn't take long for me to chase a delicious *fourth* orgasm. My body detonates, a million little fireworks exploding in my lower belly. I shut my eyes for a moment, trying to ground myself. Somehow, this orgasm manages to be just as strong as the other three, leaving me completely dizzy and in a state of pure bliss.

"That's it, baby," he coos. "You can swallow now. Get a good taste of what you do to me."

I tilt my head back to lock my eyes on his as I swallow every last drop. The saltiness, with a hint of sweetness, hits my senses, and I moan, still riding my release. He tastes better than I could have ever imagined, and all I can think about is how badly I want to taste him again. He extends his hand, and I take it as I stand on shaky legs. He delivered his promised and thoroughly fucked me, and I don't think I'll be able to move any longer.

"Oh, God," I groan. "I can't anymore, Lorenzo. Please. I'm wiped."

With a soft laugh, he scoops me up, and I cling to him, burying my face in the crook of his neck. "Let's get you cleaned up and we'll go to bed, no funny business, I promise."

He carries me to the bathroom, setting me gently on the sink countertop, then starts to run a bubble bath. The soothing scent of lavender fills the air as he adds soap to the water. He tests the temperature, making sure it's just right, and once the tub is ready, he looks back at me with a smile that makes my chest tighten, holding out his hand.

I take it, letting him help me down from the counter. He slides into the bath first, and I follow, easing into the warmth of the water with his steady hands guiding me. I settle back against his chest, the water and his body cocooning me in warmth. His arms wrap around me, pulling me closer, and I tilt my head back, resting it on his shoulder as I close my eyes and let myself melt into the comfort of his embrace.

He kisses the side of my head and mumbles, "You okay?"

I let out a content sigh. "Yes. This is perfect." I open my eyes and look up at him. "Thank you."

His lips find mine, giving me a soft peck. "No need to thank me."

My cheeks heat with a blush. "Why are you always so thoughtful?"

A small smirk plays on his lips. "Only with you, Blue. Just you."

I don't understand how I got this lucky and entered the deal of the lifetime with someone as thoughtful as him, but I'll soak up every second of it, and more.

28

Sophia

Light, peppering kisses from my cheek to my neck and the heat of a body pressed against me start to slowly wake me up. If this is what heaven feels like, I'd rather stay asleep forever.

"Wake up, sleepy head," Lorenzo whispers against my neck, his warm breath creating goosebumps all over my body.

"Can't. You fucked me to death last night," I groan, turning around and wrapping my leg on top of his and hiding my face in the crook of his neck.

His laugh is low and gravelly. "You had no complaints last night."

No, I didn't. I am thoroughly fucked and satisfied now, and all I want to do is stay in bed all day.

Sex with Lorenzo was...electric. Wild. *Fun.* In such a short period, I've grown so comfortable around him, it makes the chemistry between us a thousand times better. Can't say I'm regretting this deal, because if this is how it's going to be, I'm more than ready to have the summer of my life.

"Leave me here to die." I sigh.

"I have to go walk the staff through the restaurant today and talk to them. Are you coming?"

I scratch my eyes with my knuckles, yawning and getting out of the comfiest bed against my will. "Yeah. It's why I'm here, after all."

He follows after me, swatting my ass playfully before he wraps his arms around my waist and drops a kiss on the side of my head. "You go get ready, and I'll make us some breakfast. Yeah?"

I look at him with a soft smile and nod.

I walk back to my room and grab my phone from the nightstand, checking for any new text messages.

City Girls Chat

ARIA

We've been forgotten, Isa.

ISABELLA

She's too busy riding dick, Ari. Leave her alone.

ARIA

Who are you and what did you do with my best friend?

ISABELLA

Just calling it as I see it.

ME

There is no riding anything. 😊 I've been busy.

ARIA

And she liiiiiives! When are you coming back?

ME

Not sure. He had some issues with the construction, so we may need to stay a few more days.

ARIA

That's so romantic. Both of you, in such close quarters...a lot of things can happen.

ME

Talking from experience?

ARIA

Absolutely. The best idea Damian had when we were still hating each other's guts was to put us in such close quarters. 😏

ISABELLA

Sounds like straight out of my favorite romance novels.

ME

I will never get over the fact Isabella loves to read smut. 😅

ISABELLA

Are you slut shaming me? That's unbecoming, Sophia.

ME

No, girl. Live your life, by all means. You just don't seem like the type.

ISABELLA

Oh, let me guess, because I'm—as you guys like to put it—a "grump?" I'm not a grump. It's not my fault the world is filled with idiotic people.

Sophia changed the group name from City Girls Chat to Powerpuff Girls Chat

ME

Exactly.

ARIA

Enough about Isabella. You're seriously going to tell us you and Enzo haven't done anything?

ISABELLA

Bet you $10 she's lying. And what is with the new group name?

ARIA

Only $10? You're rich. Up that bet!

ARIA

And you seriously don't get the name of the chat? That was funny, Sophia. Good one. I love it.

ISABELLA

I'm not rich. My family is. There's a difference. And no, I don't get it.

I put my phone down with a laugh, opting to ignore them and get ready for the day. Lorenzo and I haven't exactly talked about how this deal is going to go, so telling the girls would be a terrible idea. Aria would get too excited if I told her, only to end up disappointed, because whatever this is between Lorenzo and me has a hard expiration date. This is the perfect way to have fun this summer and get each other out of our systems before we go back to normal. Who knows? Maybe we'll even stay friends. He's a fun and good guy to hang out with, so I can see it happening.

Then what is this crawly feeling you have on your chest?

I don't know, but I'm choosing to ignore it and focus on having fun instead.

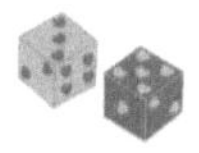

After a quick breakfast, we arrived at the restaurant, where the construction team was already hard at work with Diego barking orders left and right. He was working his butt off, too, alongside them, not scared of getting dirty and helping where they needed it the most. That's why Diego is the best in the business; he's not afraid of getting to work, despite his less-than-sunshine personality. It's why he's so successful—he didn't let his fame or money change him. From the research I've done about him, he's still the same down-to-earth guy from a small town, just expanding his business at an abnormally fast pace.

The place has been quickly coming together. They were able to finish installing the kitchen appliances, and now they are working on the outdoor part of the restaurant as Lorenzo and the head chef are giving a tour to the employees and talking about the idea and expectations for this place. I've been silently following them, taking notes, and witnessing how Lorenzo works in his day-to-day.

"The idea is to keep the local feel of Panamá, with typical foods and drinks, but also give it a little bit of an Italian spin," Lorenzo says, leaning against one of the industrial kitchen tables. "We want customers to feel comfortable and welcomed, and give them a time they will never forget."

The way Lorenzo commands a room with his presence and his voice is something out of this world. Everyone is looking at him and hanging on to every word he says like it's some sort of gospel. But he's also laid back and nice, making everyone feel comfortable.

"I will leave Roberto here to talk more about the menu and what the training before the official opening will look like, but if anyone has any questions or concerns, you have my contact information. I'm always available." Lorenzo finishes with a bright smile as everyone mumbles their thanks.

He and Roberto talk for a few minutes before he walks back to me. "Having fun?"

I nod, flapping my notebook in the air. "Yup. Took lots of notes, too."

"Good," he replies as we're both walking out of the restaurant. "I think we can head out for Chicago tomorrow. Do you have any idea what you would like to do on our last night here?"

"Actually, I do." I grin. "I want us go out so you can show me what a night out as Lorenzo Mancini, the billionaire player, looks like."

"I was expecting more of like *let's have lots of sex and then cuddle.*" He wiggles his eyebrows playfully.

"Cuddling?" I raise an eyebrow, hitting his arm with my shoulder playfully. "Are you going soft on me, Ace?"

He shrugs, a knowing grin plastered all over his face. "What can I say? I can't get enough of you."

My cheeks heat at his comment, but I manage to pull it together and not read too much into it. "Maybe you'll get lucky. Let's see where the night takes us." I wink before continuing to walk back to the villa, him trailing behind me.

I need this night out. Even though he's told me he doesn't enjoy it like he used to, I still have to see both sides of his life for myself. That was always the point of following him around. But there's also a selfish reason. Watching him in his usual element serves as a reminder of why our deal has to stay casual.

Because after just one wild night, I'm already hooked. Under Lorenzo's touch, I feel alive, and that's a feeling I could easily get used to if I don't keep my heart in check. I've always avoided love like the plague, but it doesn't mean I'm immune to it. I used to be the girl who wished for love, who dreamed of it. But little by little, as time goes on, I keep telling myself I don't deserve it. The uncertainty of love is overwhelming, and my clusterfuck of a life can't handle the heartbreak.

"Where are we going?" I ask as I walk out of my room, putting on my usual gold earrings. I'm wearing the only night-out dress I have, the one Lorenzo talked me into getting at the boutique. It's a simple white dress, with off-the-shoulder flared sleeves, and it stops about mid-thigh. I paired it with some chunky brown heels. My hair is down, a little frizzy from the humidity, but its usual waves are there, falling over my shoulders just the way I like it.

"You said you wanted the Lorenzo Mancini experience, so we'll be going to one of the hottest clubs around here." He's sitting on the couch, looking at his phone, but when he looks up and finds me standing in front of him, his eyes flare with heat as they roam every inch of my body. A simple look from him makes my body feel like it's been lit on fire, creating a need so powerful in my lower belly that I don't know how long I'll be able to hold on tonight.

He stands, and even with my heels, he still manages to tower over me. He's wearing a black, short-sleeve, button-down satin shirt, with three buttons open, and a pair of black pants and boots. My eyes eagerly roam his body, and I absentmindedly lick my lips.

He places his hand around the nape of my neck, the touch possessive yet gentle as he guides my gaze to meet his. "You look exquisite. I hope you weren't expecting me to stay away from you, because that will be an impossible task."

I bite my lip for a moment, holding back a smile. "You don't look half bad yourself, Ace."

His thumb runs across my bottom lip, the one I just bit, before he closes the little distance between us with a kiss. He slides his tongue inside of my mouth slowly, exploring and taunting. And just like that, the need I have for him intensifies.

He breaks the kiss, and I have to hold back a whimper at the miss of his warm lips. "I can't promise I'll behave if any guy so much as glances your way tonight. You sure you want to go out?" He raises an eyebrow.

His comment makes my heart falter for the slightest moment. I know he's joking, and I know he's playing his usual games, but my foolish heart decides to believe him—until the logical part of me takes over, smashing any useless and idiotic thoughts.

I place my hand on his chest, humming playfully. "That's funny, because we never said we were exclusive." Before he can reply, I walk away not looking back as I say, "Let's go, player."

29

Lorenzo

Going out was a colossal mistake.

As soon as we walked in, it was like Sophia put every man in this forsaken club under a spell. It didn't matter that I had my arm wrapped around her possessively, staking my claim—that's right, I have no shame in admitting it. I'm the possessive type—she just doesn't know it yet. But she'll learn sooner rather than later that even though this is temporary, I plan to keep her all to myself for the rest of the summer.

"Okay, pretty boy. Show me your moves," she taunts.

"I thought I already did when you slept with me in a cleaning closet of a club." I give a slight head tilt, my tone carrying a trace of humor.

She rolls her eyes. "Will you ever let that go?"

"Never." One of the best days of my life, no question.

"Glad to know, I guess," she retorts dryly.

I shake my head with a laugh. "Do you want something to drink?"

Her eyes gleam with mischief, and she nods eagerly, guiding us to the bar in the VIP area. As we're walking toward the bar, I notice how every guy stares at Sophia's ass. Her dress is short, and she has curves for days, so it's not surprising that they're ogling her. It makes me want to punch every motherfucker I come across. The only thing stopping me is knowing I'm the only one who gets to touch her tonight while they only get to look and suffer from afar.

They can look all they want, but *my* girl will only be coming around one cock tonight—mine.

Only yours for the summer, my sadistic brain tries to remind me, but I push the thought away quickly.

When we arrive at the bar, she lifts her hand, and the bartender practically trips on his feet like an idiot trying to eagerly get to Sophia as he focuses on how her tits are being pushed together by her dress. But I'm quick to stake my claim, trapping her against the bar with my arms and dropping a short kiss on her neck.

She orders four tequila shots with lime and salt, and as we're waiting for them, she turns around. "We need some liquid courage, because I plan on taking you to the dance floor."

A laugh bubbles out of me. "Do you know how to dance to this music? They're playing Spanish reggaeton, Blue."

She throws her head back with a laugh, and my instinct is to run my tongue along her exposed skin. I'm a man starved, and I can't get enough of her. Last night barely scratched the surface of the growing need I have for her. This is going south really quickly, and it makes no sense. Being friends with benefits should be the perfect solution for our little dilemma. A way to get each other out of our systems, yet I'm quickly growing addicted to her.

"With a few tequila shots in my system, I can dance to anything," she replies confidently.

The bartender drops the shots, and as I go to grab one

for myself, she stops me. I frown, and she shakes her head as her tongue darts out, licking her bottom lip before a mischievous smile plays on her lips.

"We're doing body shots," she says with a wink.

I gape at her. "I am absolutely *scandalized* by you right now."

She rolls her eyes. "*Please.* This is nothing, and you know it. Or do you need a reminder of everything that happened last night?" she asks with a knowing grin plastered all over her face before handing me a tequila shot. She slides the lime across the curve of her cleavage, and then grabs the salt, sprinkling it over the lime-drenched area, the crystals sticking to her skin like they belong there. Tilting her head back, she nods slowly, eyes never leaving mine. "You go first," she says, her voice a little breathless, then puts the lime wedge between her teeth.

A small, knowing smile plays at the corner of my lips. "Oh, I remember every detail of what happened last night. It will be engraved in my memory forever."

I take the shot in one quick swig, enjoying the way it burns my throat and settles in the pit of my stomach. I lower my head and let my tongue trace a slow, deliberate path over the salt on the curve of her cleavage, savoring the warmth of skin. The act alone has me wanting to do more, to latch my mouth on her soft skin and leave a mark. Instead, I cradle her chin with my hand and move closer slowly, our faces just inches apart. My gaze flick between her beautiful blue eyes and her mouth, the tension crackling between us. With deliberate slowness, I brush my mouth against hers, lips barely grazing her skin as I take the lime from between her teeth. My fingers linger on her chin, because there's something so satisfying about knowing I get to deliberately put my hands on her, and I want to do it at all times. The lime sits between my lips now, and I suck on it as my eyes burn into hers, wishing it was her pussy in my mouth instead.

She hops on one of the bar stools and takes the salt. "My turn. Tilt your head back," she orders huskily.

With a low laugh, I follow her lead. She rubs the lime on my neck then sprinkles the salt over it, takes the shot, and without hesitation, leans in. Her tongue flicks out, slowly tasting the salt from my skin. The warmth of her tongue against me sends a jolt straight to my hardening cock. I can't help but think about how that mouth—sinful and skilled—can do things that are almost too good to be real. And damn, I'm aching to feel it again.

"What about the lime wedge?" I ask.

She shakes her head, her finger hooking around my golden chain and giving it a gentle tug, pulling me closer until there's almost no space left between us. "I'd rather do this," she whispers, and before I can even ask what she means, her lips crash against mine.

Her mouth tastes like a heady mix of tequila, a hint of salt still lingering, but also so fucking sweet—like goddamn honey. It's tempting, sugary, and maddeningly perfect. Her tongue brushes against mine, taking control of the kiss, and for once, I let her. And damn, the way she kisses should be studied. Each kiss is like a drug—something I never knew I could crave so much. I've never been one to lose myself in a kiss, but with her, it's a completely different experience. Every nerve in my body is electrified, and my heart races, wanting to break free. We kiss like we're the only two people left in this world and like nothing else matters. Time stops, and it feels like destiny's whispering, *this is what you've been missing. Don't let it slip away.*

But the truth creeps in, the reminder that we're living on borrowed time. I only have her for two and a half months, and I know, deep down, even a lifetime wouldn't feel like enough. No matter how much I try to shove it aside, it's there, gnawing at me even as she holds me close.

With numbed lips and ragged breath, we order two more shots and take them quickly. She then grabs my hand and drags me to the dance floor without a word as "Escápate Conmigo" by Wisin and Ozuna starts to play. I recognize the song because they play it often when I go out with Julian to his favorite Latin spots. As the music begins, Sophia turns around and wraps my arms around her waist, her back flushed against me as she starts swaying her hips to the rhythm of the music, making me instantly hard. She wraps one of her arms around my neck, her delicate fingers gripping my hair softly as she continues to move with the music.

I drop my mouth close to her ear. "What do you think you're doing?"

She tilts her head back, looking at me with a flushed face and bright eyes. "I thought it was obvious. I'm showing you I *can* dance to this music," she says as she bends over slightly and starts moving her ass deliberately slow against my growing erection.

I throw my head back with a groan because, goddamn, she's not wrong.

As the tempo of the song starts to pick up, I rest my hands firmly on her hips, guiding her movements as she keeps swaying to the rhythm. She doesn't need any guidance, but I will use any excuse to touch her like the needy fucker I am. Her back arches slightly, giving me a perfect view of her ass as her hips moving in slow, sensual circles. She tilts her head back, and her hair brushes my chest while a small, devilish smile plays on her lips and the music takes over us. My grip tightens a little, pulling her closer as our legs move in step. She doesn't stop moving her hips even for a second. The space between us disappears as her back completely touches my chest.

"I bet if I slide my hand underneath your dress, I'll find you wet and ready for me," I whisper in her ear. Even with the background music, I know she can hear me. Every movement we do is heightened, and we're so focused on each other, it's impossible to pay attention to anything else.

A small moan escapes her lips as she reaches back and rests her arm on my shoulder, fingers brushing the skin of my neck softly, leaving a trail of goosebumps.

"I dare you to do it," she replies breathlessly. "Find out how wet I truly am. You know you want to, Ace."

Everything around me starts to fade. All I can focus is on her. She's like a siren calling my name, and I'm more than willing to get lost in her. Without a word, I grab her hand and start walking off the dance floor. The club is small, but it still has a VIP area with private booths, a bar, and a restroom.

As we reach the VIP restroom door, I push it open and call out, "Hello? Anyone in here?" When no response comes, I step inside, still holding her hand, and lock the door behind us with a quiet click.

"What are you doing?"

I turn around, my hand instinctively finding its way around her throat, fingers lightly brushing her skin as I push her back against the wall with a gentle but deliberate force. Her breath hitches, and I lean in, cornering her, the tension between us coiling tighter.

"I thought it was obvious," I taunt, my voice low as I throw her own words back at her, a smug grin tugging at my lips. "You dared me to find out how wet you are. And make no mistake—I am *dying* to find out, Blue." My other hand travels from the curve of her breast to her hips until I arrive where I've been dying to fucking touch. I lift the hem of her dress and cup her sex with her underwear still on, finding the fabric damp. I then press my index and middle fingers against her clit, which wins me a moan from her as I move them in slow, deliberate circles. I lift my hand between us, my fingers glistening with her arousal.

I click my tongue. "I knew you were drenched. You just loved grinding against my cock, didn't you? You loved making me crazy with that delicious ass of yours."

Sophia nods as she parts her lips slightly, bringing my fingers to her mouth and sucking them clean. Her tongue swirls around my digits, and everything she does makes my cock throbs, wanting nothing more than to feel that hot, wet mouth of hers.

"I bet you're wishing that was my cock," I say gruffly.

"You have no idea," she answers, licking her lips as her eyes travel to the painful bulge I'm carrying.

"Turn around and bend over," I order. While I'm dying to feel her mouth wrapped around my cock, I have other plans.

She obeys without a word, bending over revealing her perfect, heart-shaped ass. She's wearing a thong that barely covers anything, and I shake my head with a dark laugh. Of course, she did this. If there's one thing I know about Sophia, the girl loves to push my buttons.

"This barely covers anything. What were you thinking when you put this on?" I ask, my nostrils flaring in annoyance.

She looks over her shoulder, eyes hazy, face flushed from the alcohol. "I was hoping you would bend me over and deliver on that spanking promise."

I swallow hard, trying to hold back the groan threatening to escape. Before she can react, I lift my hand and bring it down on her smooth ass with a sharp smack. The sound echoes, and she arches her back, moaning as the heat from the strike spreads across her skin.

I rub slow circles over her soft skin, soothing her as I lean in close. "As much as I love hearing those beautiful sounds from that sassy mouth of yours," I murmur, my voice low, "those sounds are for me and only me. So be quiet. Understood?"

She drops her head between her shoulders, silent in her defiance. That earns her another sharp smack on the ass, and she whimpers, arching her back as she bites down hard on her bottom lip, trying to stifle the moan threatening to escape.

"Say you understand, Blue," I growl.

"I understand," she whispers softly, her voice barely above a breath.

"Such a good girl," I murmur as I drop to my knees and slide the flimsy fabric down her legs, taking it off. I run my hands up her thighs, feeling the warmth of her skin beneath my touch. I tap her inner thighs twice. "Spread your legs for me, baby."

She quickly obeys, and I get a perfect view of her glistening pussy that's making a mess out of her thighs. Placing my hands on the curve of her ass, I lick her slit with one long and languid stroke. Another small moan comes out of her, so I stand and grip her chin, parting her lips.

"Let me help you stay quiet," I whisper roughly, shoving her panties inside her mouth. Her eyes bulge, but her thighs clench, seeking friction. "Is your pussy craving my tongue? My cock? You're desperate for it, aren't you?" I give her ass another smack, because I don't tire of the sound, or how good my palm feels against her smooth skin. I love how well she responds to it, and how much she enjoys being controlled.

She nods eagerly, eyes closed, opening her legs even wider. I swiftly turn her around and drop to my knees again, lifting her and wrapping both of her legs around my shoulders. Locking my gaze on hers, I dive in, circling my tongue around her sensitive bud as I grip her ass, pressing her pussy against my face, letting her arousal suffocate me.

I would die a happy man if it meant I could drown in all of her. The sight of her is painfully beautiful with her chest heaving and her moans being muffled by the flimsy fabric she calls underwear.

My tongue strokes her slit back and forth, painfully slow. I'm enjoying how she tries to writhe but can't because I have her pinned against the wall. I wrap my lips around her clit and suck, the slurping sounds making the scene deliciously filthy. I want her on the brink of an orgasm, but not there quite yet, because I want her to come around my cock tonight.

I place her legs back on the floor for a moment, and she makes quick work of my pants and boxers as I grab the condom from my wallet. She points at her mouth, raising an eyebrow in question, and I nod, allowing her to take it out. This is one of my favorite things about Sophia. She has the sassiest mouth but also knows when to obey. Knowing she lets me have some sort of control makes my cock entirely too excited. It makes me feel good and like I accomplished the impossible. She's learned to trust me, and hell, I've learned to trust her, too.

She grabs the condom and opens the foil with her teeth, bringing out the latex and rolling it on me quickly. I don't give her a chance to stabilize herself before I wrap her legs around my waist and bury myself to the hilt in one fell swoop as I crash my lips on hers in a desperate kiss, eagerly swallowing every one of her moans. She kisses me back just as fervently, and I start pounding into her, desperate to feel her pussy grip my cock. We keep kissing each other, exploring each other's mouths to avoid making any loud noises. It's loud outside, sure, but I don't want to give people a show. This is a moment for us. I fuck her fast and hard, the sound of skin slapping against skin over and over filling out the room with the muffled sounds of the fast-tempo music from outside. We stop kissing to catch our breaths, and I rest my forehead against hers as I keep thoroughly fucking her. And we don't break eye contact, not even for a second. I do my best to contain the groans that want to come out of me every time I bury myself deep inside of her, and she just looks at me with parted lips. Breathless, low moans come out of her pretty mouth as her eyes roam all over my face. And fuck, I feel like the luckiest man in the world every time she looks at me like that.

"You're so goddamn perfect, baby." *Thrust.* "I love how eagerly your pussy takes my cock." *Thrust.* "And I especially love when you look at me with those pretty eyes of yours like you want me." *Thrust.*

"I do want you," she says through a low moan. "I feel so full. And you feel so good," she continues through soft moans.

She tilts her head back, and I place one of my hands around her throat, pressing softly. She wraps her hand on top of mine and presses even more, her eyes finding mine.

"You've already ruined me, Lorenzo. Now I need you to own me."

Hearing those words leave her mouth is what completely breaks me. I keep one arm wrapped around her waist to keep her in place then keep my other hand wrapped around her throat as I start thrusting harder and faster. I'm fucking her deeper than I ever thought was possible. Thrust after animalistic thrust, I want nothing more than to feel her come around me. I want nothing more than to see her become a mess because of me.

"Come for me. I want to feel your cunt gripping my cock, milking every ounce of me. I want you to make a mess, baby. *Now*," I say through a groan, and she...lets go.

She places one hand on top of her mouth to stop her cries as the orgasm erupts out of her. Her legs begin to shake, and I try to keep us both stable as I thrust once, twice more, chasing my own orgasm. Her pussy keeps gripping me as my cock pulsates, coming so hard I swear I see stars.

Once we get our bearings, she hugs me tightly, and I settle my nose in the crook of her neck, inhaling her in. I will never, *ever* get tired of this. My need for this girl will just continue to grow, and the thought is frightening, because Sophia and I will never be more than this, even when my heart has me believing it can be possible if I really try.

Even when I know I'm the last man on Earth who deserves such a strong, perfect woman like her.

With a yawn, I rub my eyes with my knuckles, trying my best to keep them open. I've been back from Panamá for about two weeks now, and my work keeps stacking. I don't know how much longer I'll be able to keep this up.

I glance at the time on the corner of my laptop. It's 10:45 p.m. on a Friday. The girls wanted to have dinner with me, and that was the plan, until Max dumped four articles on my desk that should have been edited a long time ago, but he forgot to give them to me. Sometimes, I think he does this shit on purpose. Maybe he feels threatened and thinks I want his position. He should know better by now—I need this job, and I wouldn't do anything stupid to risk it.

Amelia went MIA again after the big blowout we had, and I'm trying not to read into it. I'm going to act blissfully unaware this time around and assume she and Miles are completely thriving and I won't hear from her ever again. A girl can dream, right?

I stand from the chair I've been sitting in for the past four hours, groaning as I stretch my back. I wish I could afford a bigger place and have an office space; working on the dining table is not ideal. But it beats staying in the office until the night hours, I guess. With another yawn, I enter the kitchen and get another coffee pot going, because I'm going to need the caffeine if I'm ever going to finish this on time. Once the coffee pot starts brewing, my phone pings with a text.

LORENZO

Are you home?

ME

Depends. Is this a booty call?

LORENZO

Answer the question, Blue.

ME

I don't want to answer your question, Ace. Answer mine first.

I purse my lips, trying to hold back the giggle that wants to bubble out of me. I haven't seen Lorenzo since we came back from Panamá, and I honestly miss having him around. I've also been dying for another repeat of everything that happened between us the last few days we were there.

Okay. Did you just say you miss him? Are you okay?

Yeah, I mean...who else is going to push all of my buttons?

I'm supposed to be following him around to finish this article, but work has been so busy I've been canceling on him. I also don't know what to do with it anymore. There's so much to unpack when it comes to him, and it feels wrong to do it now. I have hundreds of pages written on my laptop, I just have to organize them. Selfishly, though, I want to keep this side of him in a little box and protect it from the rest of the world. He doesn't deserve to have his life put under a magnifying glass for people to judge. I think he's had enough of that.

But this is your job. And he agreed. You have to do it.

As I'm serving myself another cup of coffee, there's a knock on my door. I frown. It's almost 11:00 p.m., who the hell is knocking at my door at this time? I ignore it and walk back to the dining table to get back to work.

"Blue, stop ignoring me," Lorenzo says, pounding on the door.

I grab my favorite cardigan, put it on, and open the door, crossing my arms. "I don't have time for a booty call."

He lifts his arms where he's holding some takeout bags from Lorenzo's. "I'm here to feed you. Must you always think the worst of me?" he replies jokingly, pushing me to the side and walking in. "I wasn't sure what you were in the mood for, so I brought one of everything."

I close the door, following after him. "The whole menu?"

He shrugs. "Yeah. I felt like cooking after a long day," he says, shutting my laptop. "Where do you want me to put all of this?"

I stand there in shock for a moment. He thought of me and decided to cook the whole menu of his restaurant to make sure I had options. And he's acting like it's no big deal. This is the most thoughtful thing someone has ever done for me, well...ever. Is this how it feels being taken care of? It's unsettling, but also nice...like I could grow used to this.

Keep it together. This is not forever, and it's expiring sooner rather than later.

I make my way to the table, brushing his hand away from my things. "I got it." I grab all my work things, putting them in my bag. "Why are you really here, Lorenzo? It's

Friday night. Shouldn't you be, I don't know, partying it up and getting into bed with a *bimbo*?"

His soft laugh echoes through the apartment as he starts opening the takeout containers. "Jealous?"

More than anything.

The idea of Lorenzo sleeping with other women makes me green with jealousy, but I will never admit it.

I shake my head a little too quickly, scrunching my nose. "We never said we were exclusive. You can sleep with whoever you want." The lie slips out of me easily.

He stops opening the plastic container that has some delicious-looking pasta and looks at me. "Okay, it's time you and I define this deal a little better." He brings a chair out and tilts his head toward it. "Sit. Let's eat and talk."

"What have I told you about pulling chairs for me?"

"*Sit. Down.*" His tone is raspy and demanding, not leaving room for discussion. "I'm not above grabbing you like a sack of potatoes and dropping you on this chair."

Why does the idea of him picking me up, caveman style, make me a puddle? My core tightens with need at the thought, ready to give in. I'm tempted to stay stubborn to see if he'll deliver his promise. But something stops me.

He's trying to be nice. Let him.

I relax my shoulders and sit without a word. He brings the other chair next to me, also sitting.

"Okay." He drops his elbows on the table. "What do you want out of this deal?"

"Could you *be* any more direct?" I roll my eyes.

"Chandler Bing from *Friends*. Cute. You sure love quoting that show. Doesn't exactly count, though." His lip lifts in a soft smirk. "And stop evading my question."

I scowl at him as I grab and eat a piece of garlic bread.

He's a little too good at our little game, and it's driving me crazy.

I'm not sure what I want out of this. Does it kill me not to be exclusive? Yes. I don't want him sleeping with other women while we do this. And honestly, I don't want to sleep with other men either. Lorenzo is *fun*, and I want to be around that this summer. He's grown on me. He makes me *laugh*. He doesn't make me feel like my weaknesses are a nuisance. He doesn't judge me. He's simply there and knows what I need. Does it scare me, not knowing what will happen in the future? Not really. Neither of us is the relationship type. This is the perfect recipe for us to have some fun and then part ways at the end of it. Stay friends or whatever. I'm acutely aware we'll be in each other's lives forever, but it doesn't have to be awkward. We're both adults.

"I already told you. Friends with benefits until the end of August. We have some fun sex, and we end it before going to Las Vegas. We keep things strictly casual, we keep emotions out of the way." I shrug. "Sounds easy enough for two people who don't do the love thing, anyway."

"Do you want to be exclusive in the meantime?" he asks, plain and simple. That's Lorenzo for you. *Extremely* honest —and I mean that in every sense.

I shrug again, not answering, and biting another piece of bread instead. When did I become such a quiet bitch? I want to speak up, but I can't find the right words. *Yes*, I want to be exclusive. Is that so hard to say?

He takes the last piece of bread I have in my hand and drops it in the container. "Who knew you could go quiet on me?" he asks with a laugh. "That's fine. I'll speak—I don't want to fuck other women, and I most definitely don't want you fucking other men," he deadpans.

My eyes bulge, finding his and trying to find any trace of

mirth. His face is enigmatic and serious. Not the Lorenzo I've gotten to know and like.

His hand grips the legs of my chair, pulling it toward him to close the gap between us. "While I *fuck* you." His tongue flicks across his bottom lip, eyes dropping to mine, intense and unwavering. "While I make you come with *these*." He wiggles his fingers, the gesture slow and deliberate, his focus never leaving my lips. "While you come around *my* cock." His gaze snaps back to mine, locking us in a stare that makes my heart stutter. "You're *mine*," he growls.

His thumb runs across my bottom lip, sending a jolt of electricity down my spine.

"And Bella[1]," he whispers, his voice low, sultry, the kind that makes you lean in without realizing, "I'm a selfish motherfucker. I don't like sharing."

His eyes darken, full of that same dangerous edge I saw the night we met, thrilling and impossible to ignore.

After a beat of silence, he says, "Got it?"

"Y-yes," I reply weakly.

"Good." He smiles, leaning back. "What's the deal again?"

"Casual sex. No feelings. We're exclusive, and the deal expires the day before we go to Las Vegas," I confirm, my heart tugging at my chest, knowing time is flying by.

Only two months left.

"Good." He nods. "Let's eat, shall we?"

"You still haven't answered why you're here," I blurt. He could be doing so many things right now. Granted, I know now he doesn't truly like the party scene like he makes it seem to the rest of the world. But still, I could think of many other things he could be doing than being here.

---

1. Beautiful.

"Aria and Damian dropped by the restaurant today. I heard from Aria you've been working nonstop, so I wanted to check in on you." He shrugs.

"Oh, okay."

"And honestly? We haven't seen much of each other and I miss having that sassy mouth of yours around," he jokes, giving me a soft smile that makes his dimple pop.

I pick up a plastic fork and stab it into the pasta, twirling it around. Before taking a bite, I reply, "I kind of missed your annoying presence, too."

His eyes dance with amusement. "I know."

I roll my eyes at him and flip him off. "Forget I said anything."

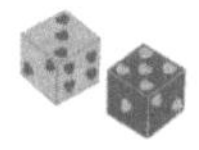

"I'm going to gain so much weight if I keep hanging out with you." I shoot him a glare as I drop onto the couch.

He barks a laugh, sitting next to me. "I didn't hear one complaint as you were scarfing down three pasta bowls." He grabs my legs, placing them on his lap and brushing them back and forth with his fingertips. The feathery touch is innocent, but it doesn't make me feel any less tempted to turn this night into something more. To get lost in his touch and his addicting kisses. To get lost in the way his eyes roam my body with heat and appreciation.

"Your food is too addicting. It's all *your* fault," I say, poking him in the forearm.

I rest my head on the couch and look at him. His head is resting on the couch, too, but his eyes are closed, so I take my time to just...stare at him. Lorenzo is a great cook. Now that I know this is his passion, I can see it all more clearly. I can imagine him being this big famous chef who travels around the world, teaching others. Come to think of it, the only time I've seen him happy, he was cooking—*both* times. Don't get me wrong, Lorenzo is overall an outgoing person, but most of the time, that sparkle doesn't reach those beautiful whiskey eyes of his. Knowing this tugs at my heart. The worrier side of me is starting to come out, and I need to shut it down. He doesn't need me to take care of him—I can't *afford* to take care of him, even when there's nothing I would like more.

"I can feel you staring at me. If you want to jump my bones, all you have to do is ask," he says through a playful grin, his eyes still closed.

I grab a decorative pillow and throw it at his head. "You wish."

His eyes snap open with a playful smirk still etched on his face, and he jerks my legs, a small gasp mixed with a laugh escaping my lips as he sits me on his lap. His warmth brings me a moment of serenity. My usual racing thoughts wash away every time he's around me. Somehow, he grounds me.

He buries his nose in the crook of my neck, something I've noticed he loves doing, and inhales deeply. I clench my thighs involuntarily, loving a little too much the feel of his hot breath against my skin.

"You smell so good." His voice is gravelly against my neck, and he presses soft kisses all over. "E tu sei così bella[2]." He grabs my legs and wraps them around his waist, making

---

2. You're so beautiful.

me straddle him now. His knuckles brush my collarbone before pressing a kiss there. "Perfetta[3]."

I whimper at the deep sound of his voice, my eyes fluttering as he keeps pressing soft kisses along my neck, shoulder, and collarbone. I have no idea what he said, but it doesn't matter. Anything that rolls off his tongue, especially in Italian, ignites a fire in my belly.

He presses his lips on mine in a soft and slow kiss. I never thought something so relaxed and sensual could make me clench with need. But here I am—*desperate* for him. Looking for any sort of friction, I start grinding myself against him, the swell of his growing erection giving me the perfect pressure against my clit, even with all the fabric between us I so desperately want to get rid of.

"*Blue*," he warns, biting my lip, his fingertips digging into the flesh of my waist, holding me still. "I didn't come here for this. We don't have to do anything if you don't want to." He places a strand of hair behind my ear, his beautiful, haunting brown eyes meeting mine. "I just wanted to see you and spend time with you. Because I honestly really fucking missed you." His tone is so sincere, my heart flutters.

I remove the firm grip he has on my waist and start grinding against his throbbing cock again, not breaking eye contact. "I know," I whisper, closing my eyes and brushing my lips against his. "I want this."

More than anything, I desperately want to regain focus on what this is—a simple deal, a casual fling. I need to remind myself this is just sex, nothing more. Even though I'm starting to doubt every step I've taken since I had this dangerous and thrilling idea.

---

3. Perfect.

31

Lorenzo

"Are you sure?" I ask, my eyes finding hers.

Her soft lips hover over mine. "Yes."

Without another word, I swipe my tongue across the seam of her lips, demanding entrance. She parts her lips without protest, allowing our tongues to tangle. Kissing her will never get old. The feel of her soft lips is out of this world, and that sweet taste of hers is one I can't get enough of. She moans, and I greedily swallow her sounds as I keep kissing and teasing her with my tongue. The kiss becomes more frantic and fervent with every passing second. My erection grows quickly as she starts grinding against me a little faster. Looking down, I see how her wetness coats her inner thighs and the tiniest, thinnest pair of pajama shorts she's wearing. I can tell she's not wearing any underwear, because the thin fabric of her shorts glues to her skin the more aroused she gets.

"Fuck, baby, you're making a mess. Is this all for me?" I ask, fisting her hair and exposing her neck, nipping and sucking the soft flesh. I know she loves it when I give her neck attention, and I'm more than willing to oblige. To leave my mark, so any fucker that looks at her knows who she belongs to, even if only temporarily. I've never felt such a possessive, primal sensation like this. I've never had a reason to be possessive. Being with other women was a means to an end, but with her, it's... So. Much. More.

"Answer me," I order, my voice gravelly.

"Yes," she whispers through her moans. "All for you. *Only* you."

Those delicious words coming out of her mouth are like music to my ears. Knowing how crazy I drive her makes satisfaction simmer through my veins.

"That's right," I croon against her neck. "And don't you ever forget that."

My thumb glides along her neck until I find the edge of her cardigan and slowly slide it off her. She's wearing a thin, white tank top, her peaked, perfect needy nipples showing through the fabric. I start to circle around one, touching her everywhere except where I know she needs it the most. This gets her going, her moans becoming a little louder.

"God, you're so fucking beautiful. I wish you could see yourself right now. Flushed face, grinding against my cock like the good girl you are, desperate to come."

"*Lorenzo*," she moans breathlessly.

I flip her onto her back, lift her hips, and take her shorts off. "Keep these legs open for me, baby," I say gruffly before diving in, not allowing her to respond. I latch my mouth on her clit like a man starved—because I am. I'm completely and desperately starved for another taste. These past two weeks have been *painful*, especially knowing our time is limited.

She fists my hair, locking my head in place. "Fuck, that feels good," she moans. "You're amazing."

Her moans give me the right amount of spur, and I keep

lapping at her, flattening my tongue and giving her one long, languid stroke before wrapping my lips around her clit and sucking as I slide two fingers inside of her. I start pumping my fingers at a punishing pace, dying for a heady taste of her arousal.

With one last, long suck, her legs lock into place as her whole body starts to shake, the orgasm overtaking her as I drink every ounce out of her.

"You taste so goddamn sweet." *Lick.* "Addictive." *Lick.* "And fucking perfect." *Lick.*

Once she starts to come back down from her release, I stand, towering over her and sealing my lips on hers. The kiss is slow, almost sweet. That's until she fists my shirt and sits me back down on the couch, deepening the kiss. My body almost trembles with how much I need this woman. With how much I want to get lost in her body and fucking worship her. With how much I've grown *obsessed.*

She drops to her knees, her hand traveling across my thighs and to the button of my pants. I lift my hips slightly, and she makes quick work of the pants and boxers, my throbbing cock springing free from its hold. Her eyes zero in on my shaft, and she licks her lips eagerly as she grips the base and brings the tip to her lips. She hasn't done anything yet, but my cock jerks in anticipation. It's been too long since I've felt her hot, perfect mouth around me. It's all I've been thinking about, because that mouth of hers is a dream. She gives my cock a gentle stroke, and pre-cum drips out of it. She's quick to flick her tongue around the tip and lick it. Her eyes flutter as she savors me, and I'm about ready to lose it.

Her tongue licks me from base to bottom in one swift motion, and I hiss, "*Merda*[1]."

---

1. Fuck.

"I've been dying to taste you again," she whispers sultrily before opening her mouth wide and sliding my cock inside. Her tongue is flat against it, and it travels all the way down then all the way up before she twirls it around my head once. This makes me jerk forward, because *fuck*, I want her to do that again. "I've been dying to see how much you enjoy watching me get on my knees for you, choking on your cock, taking you as deep as I can go."

"*Jesus Christ*," I mutter, a deep guttural moan bubbling out of me. "That mouth of yours, Blue. Who knew you had it in you?"

She doesn't say anything. Instead, with a small, knowing grin on her lips, she flattens her tongue once again. Her lips stretch around me as she starts taking me in deep, and damn, she's doing a fantastic job. Here I thought it wasn't possible for me to grow more obsessed, or more pathetically needy for this woman. But then she goes and does...*this*. Yeah. It's safe to say I'm a fucking goner.

"*Fuck*," I moan, my hand finding its way into her hair, fisting it gently as she continues to work me up and down with both of her hands and her mouth. "Your mouth is so perfect." My gaze locks onto hers, her haunting blue eyes entrapping me. "That's it, baby. Keep sucking my cock," I say through a low growl. "Such a pretty girl on your knees for me."

She moans around me, and the vibration makes my dick throb painfully, enjoying the sensation. One of her hands lands between her legs, and I watch in fascination how she slips two fingers inside of her and starts riding them as she keeps twirling her tongue around my tip before taking me all the way back to her throat.

I fist her hair a little harder now and start pumping in and out of her myself, because I don't tire of those delicious sounds that come out of her every time I take charge like this. This girl has me on my knees for her and doesn't even know it. Right now, I'm not the playful, successful billionaire everyone knows and loves. No. Right now, I'm a man who's so fucking starved I'm willing to take any pleasure she wants to give me. As long as it only comes from her. I don't want anyone else. I don't care about anyone else. All I want is... *her*.

My eyes roam all over her. Her watery eyes, her pebbled nipples through her white tank top, and the way she shamelessly keeps riding her fingers, seeking her own pleasure.

I lock my gaze on those beautiful eyes of hers again, amusement lacing my tone. "Does sucking me turn you on? You just can't help but touch yourself while choking on my cock, greedy girl?"

She nods eagerly, and my eyes travel down to where she's touching herself. She presses her thumb against her clit as her other hand strokes what's left of my length. The sight of her has me about ready to come, but I shut my eyes as I inhale and exhale through my nose, trying to ground myself. She removes her hand from the base of my cock and takes what's left of me with her mouth, and I tilt my head back, swallowing hard at the feel of her practically sucking the life out of me.

I can't take it anymore; I'm ready for more. "Goddamit, baby. You take me so well," I groan. "Can I go faster, please?" I ask, desperation seeping into my voice like a pathetic fool.

She places both of her hands on my thighs and looks at me, quickly nodding.

"You already know the drill. If it gets to be too much, tap my thigh twice. Okay?" I say softly. I know she can take it, but I want to make sure she feels comfortable.

Sophia is such a perfect woman, though, and can match

my energy and my drive like no one has ever done before. There are not enough words to explain how compatible we are, or how bad she has fucking ruined me already.

I start pumping at a punishing pace, just like the other night. I bite my bottom lip hard, but it's useless, my grunts and moans are relentless every time I hit the back of her throat. The gagging sounds coming out of her are quickly becoming my undoing. My balls start to tighten, signaling my orgasm is approaching quickly, so I stop abruptly, freeing my cock from her mouth.

"I would love nothing more than for you to swallow all of my cum, but I need to fuck you and feel you coming around my cock before I lose it. Do you have a condom?" I ask gruffly.

She nods, rising to her feet. She slips off her shirt and drops it on the floor as she strides to her bedroom. Before entering, she looks over her shoulder. "What are you sitting there for?"

I'm wondering how I got so lucky.

I'm wondering where the hell you've been all my life.

And I'm especially wondering how the fuck am I going to let you walk away from me at the end of the summer?

The last thought catches me by surprise, but I bury it all down and move on, because I have no other option.

Sophia

He shakes his head, following after me with a laugh as he takes off his clothes, too, both of us leaving a mess behind. He turns me around and crashes his lips against mine as we stumble into the bedroom. Even though it kills me to stop kissing him for a second, I turn around and quickly find the drawer I'm looking for, grab a condom, and toss it at him.

I think this is what I like most about us. It feels comfortable. Even as we're both in the heat of the moment, we're true to our characters. We connect. We can laugh. We can work in sync. I've never felt this type of connection with anyone, not even my ex—and I dated him for four years, convinced I was deeply in love. But now, I'm not so sure that was the case. Looking back, I think I was just searching for someone to fill the emptiness, to not feel alone for a change, and he happened to be there. With Lorenzo, though, it's different—deeper. And boy, does it scare my poor little heart.

"All fours on the bed, now," he orders, pointing to the bed, his eyes eagerly roaming every inch of my body.

Under the intensity of Lorenzo's gaze, I feel adored. Don't get me wrong, I've never had any confidence issues. I believe I'm beautiful just the way I am. Could I use a little more height? Maybe. That's as sorry as I allow myself to be. But the way he drinks me in, it's a feeling I don't tire of.

In other instances, I would fight him for the hell of it, but I'm so ready to feel all of him inside of me, I quickly obey, resting my head on the fluffy white pillow and arching my back. I've come to enjoy giving him control, and that's saying a lot, because I'm not big on trusting.

He stalks behind me, his hand brushing the curve of my ass as he starts peppering kisses all over my back. "You're so perfect, Sophia. And so goddamn beautiful. Fuck. How did I get so lucky?"

My heart quivers for the slightest moment at the sincerity of his voice. "You called me by my name," I say, turning my head slightly and looking over my shoulder.

He rolls his lips, holding back a smile as he drops one last kiss. "I wanted you to know how serious I am." With that, he enters me slowly and we moan in unison.

I love how open Lorenzo is in bed. He doesn't shy away from grunting and letting me know he's enjoying himself. It makes me want him even more. In this position, he's so deep inside of me, a sense of satisfaction washes over me. I love the feel of being filled to the hilt. He presses a hand against my back, making me arch even more. His movements are precise and slow, and I can feel every inch as he glides in and out of me. All I can do is moan into the pillow, because the sensation is all too much; I don't know what else to do with myself.

He places one arm underneath me, pulling my body flush against his, and a throaty moan—more like a cry, really—escapes my lips, because somehow, I feel him even more.

"Oh, God. I can't. It's too much," I gasp, wrapping my arms around the back of his neck.

"You can do it, Blue," he growls in my ear, one of his hands reaching my breasts as he starts playing with them, pinching my nipples just the way I like it. "Be a good girl and take every inch of my cock."

He nips my ear, and I clench around him at the feel of his mouth against my skin. His thrusts become more punishing, but also thorough, making sure I take every inch he has to offer me.

"God, you feel so fucking good." *Thrust.* "Tight." *Thrust.* "And *made* for me." *Thrust.*

It's funny, because I also feel like I was made for him. But the thought is too crazy to even entertain. We're just compatible in bed—or at least, that's what I keep telling myself to make this feel simpler. To make myself think I have some sort of control of the situation.

I tug his hair as he continues to pound into me, kissing and nipping my neck and shoulders. His lips don't leave my body, not even for the slightest second. This brings me an invigorating satisfaction. Knowing we're so desperate for each other that we must feel each other everywhere—at all times. His hand reaches for my clit, rubbing the sensitive bud, and my orgasm starts building at an abnormally fast pace as he keeps touching me in all the right places.

"Come for me again. Milk my cock, *please*, baby," he begs in my ear, sending me over the edge.

My pussy clenches around him, the orgasm overtaking my body as my legs shake, wanting to give out, but I don't let them. I stay put as his fingers grip my soft flesh and he starts pounding into me harder and harder. The delicious sounds of our skin clasping together, his grunts, and my cries mix and fill the room, making this moment feel more charged and erratic. There's nothing sweet about the way Lorenzo is fucking me right now. His moves are sloppy, primal, and desperate—I adore every filthy second of it. He thrusts twice more, and then a groan escapes his lips as he reaches his own orgasm. Once we both catch our breaths a little, he slips out of me and we fall onto the bed. Me, with a satiated sigh. Him, with a small laugh.

"You're amazing," he says, dropping a kiss on the side of my head before disposing of the condom in the small trashcan I have next to my bed.

I hum, hitting his shoulder playfully with mine. "Do you remember that night at the club when I told you I wouldn't give you my number and—"

He interrupts me. "You said, and I quote"—he clears his throat before trying to do his best impression of my voice—"*Unless you were about to ask for a high five for what we did, I don't see what else you have to say to me.*"

I roll my eyes, hitting him on the shoulder. "I hate you."

"Then you proceeded to give me a 7 out of 10, which I still think you lied, by the way." He gives me a pointed look.

I thin my lips, holding back a laugh. "I confess... I did lie."

"Knew it," he replies with a smug grin. "You can't fake this type of chemistry."

"*This* is why I lied. I knew you were going to be so cocky."

"Come here," he says gruffly, wrapping his arm around me and yanking me toward him, nipping my shoulder playfully. "It's not cocky if I'm stating facts, Blue."

"Get over yourself."

He tangles our legs together, our bodies flushed against each other. "Never. You like me like this, and you know it."

I opt not to say anything, because he's right. I do. I like him just like this. Funny. Unfiltered. Kind.

As we lie there, I rest my head on his chest, both silent now. I wait for the crawly feeling I get every time there's silence around me. Wait for the hair on the back of my neck to rise in alarm like it always does. But it doesn't come. All I feel is peace around him, and the thought jars me for a moment before I push it away. For once, I want to allow myself to be normal.

He kisses the top of my head, inhaling. "I gotta go, because I think the carbs are settling in and I'm falling asleep here," he croaks.

Before I know it, I grip his arm. "Stay over. It's late, I don't want you driving around at this time."

What the fuck are you doing, Sophia? This is not friends-with-benefits territory. You slept with him already. Why are you asking him to stay over?

"*Careful*, Blue. Otherwise, I'm going to start thinking you like me."

"Please." I wave my hand at him dismissively, even though my heart is beating wildly at his comment. Because he has no idea how scared I am, too. In fact, I think it's already too late. "If you die in a car accident, I'm going to feel guilty. I don't need that on my conscience, I already have enough problems."

He looks at me for a beat with a playful smile etched on his face. "If you want to cuddle with me, all you have to do is ask."

I shoot him an eye roll as I stand from the bed and make my way to the bathroom to begin my bedtime routine. "You're so full of yourself."

After taking a quick shower, we both stand in my tiny bathroom, brushing our teeth—him with his fingers, because I don't have an extra toothbrush. We look at each other through the mirror without saying anything, instead, we grin like two idiots. My heart still beats abnormally fast, something that has become normal every time I'm around him. We look so *domestic*, and even knowing that, I don't feel like running away.

I put on an old oversize hoodie from my college days while Lorenzo goes to find his clothes, only putting on his boxer briefs. For a brief moment, I regret asking him to stay over, because my eyes are shamelessly wandering from his chest down to his torso. I've always been so wrapped up around him and in the heat of the moment, I keep forgetting to study his tattoos. Now, I can see how the ink flows from his chest to his shoulders, wrapping around his perfect, muscled back. They all connect somehow, but it's hard to make out the details in the dim light of my room. He also has some small, random tattoos scattered all over his arms that I'm dying to study more closely.

He slips underneath the comforter, resting an arm behind his head. He brings me closer to him, but I prop my elbow on the bed and rest my head in the palm of my hand, looking at him as my fingertips start tracing a tattoo with roman numerals.

"What does this one mean?" I whisper, tracing the ink with a soft, feathery touch.

He looks down. "My mom's birthday. I wanted a

reminder of her. Never met her, because she died giving birth to me." He mirrors my pose, draping his leg over mine.

The simple touch of his skin against mine sets my body aflame. If I were any other person, I would think this is a sign from the universe. Like there's a deeper meaning behind every touch he gives me and how much I crave more of it. But destiny is a fairy tale, and this doesn't mean anything.

I hum. "Was it hard for you? Not getting to know your mom?"

He shrugs. "A little. When I was a kid and I would see every kid I went to school with their moms, I wondered what it would be like. Having a mom, I mean."

My heart tightens at the sound of his monotone, serious voice. Is this how Lorenzo acts around people? Detached? Like he doesn't care? It must have been so hard on him. My mom is my life, despite everything, and I don't know what I would do without her.

My fingers trace another tattoo, opting to not push the topic any further. This one is a kitchen knife. It's simple, but the shading is impressive. I've never seen anything like it. "What about this one?"

"I got it when I opened my first restaurant," he responds simply. "It was the best day of my life. I got to be behind the scenes for the grand opening. I was so in my element, I sometimes wish I could go back in time."

My hand reaches for his jawline, and I start stroking it softly. "I'm sorry."

He leans into my touch, his eyes never leaving mine. Even in the night, his eyes are the most beautiful light shade of brown. "For what?" he asks softly.

There are so many things I want to say, I don't even know where to begin.

For the fact that the cards life dealt you were not the best.

For the fact that you feel trapped in your life and don't know how to get out of it.

For the fact that you're such a wonderful man and you deserve so much more.

The last thought flips my stomach, making my heart clench, but I shut the door on it before it goes too damn far. Something I've become accustomed to doing around Lorenzo.

I shrug, opting to not reply. Instead, I say, "You haven't asked me any questions today."

He hums, contemplating. "What am I going to do with you?"

"What do you mean?"

"With this. With us," he whispers.

A million thoughts run through my head.

Does he feel it, too?

How everything is shifting?

Does he feel different about me?

Is he regretting this deal?

"You're going to let me be yours for now." I muster a fake smile, hoping he doesn't see through my bullshit. Hoping he doesn't see that if my life were any different, I might hope for more.

"And when it's over?" he asks softly, his brown eyes flashing with a hint of something. Vulnerability, maybe?

Impossible.

I turn around and reach for the nightlight to turn it off, needing a moment to digest the question. He wraps his hand around my waist, closing the gap between us. The warmth of his body against mine feels like belonging. Like this is where I'm meant to be.

"We'll look back and remember how this was the

summer of our lives, and how much fun we had," I answer simply, hoping he doesn't feel the way my heart is pulsing wildly.

He lets out a deep sigh and kisses the top of my head. I love it when he does that. "Non so come potrò mai lasciarti andare[1]."

"What does that mean?"

He clicks his tongue, shaking his head. "You asked too many questions tonight."

I hadn't noticed, but he's right. And he answered them all without hesitation.

I don't know what any of this means anymore. We say we're friends with benefits, but then I turn around and ask him to stay over. We say we're having fun for the summer, but then he opens up to me without any doubt, and it confuses me even more. I try to convince myself this is all part of the deal, yet the way he holds me in his arms has my heart believing otherwise. The way he holds me feels like forever. Like there are unspoken promises he's making.

I'm playing with fire.

I know it.

I can feel it in my bones.

Yet, I can't bring myself to stop.

---

1. I don't know how I'll ever let you go.

33

Lorenzo

The constant sound of a phone ringing wakes me from the best sleep I've ever had. At some point during the night, Sophia turned around and clung to me like a koala. She's resting her head on my chest with her arms and legs wrapped around me now. And fuck, this feels... meant to be. I've never stayed over or slept next to anyone. Never really saw the point. And I have the feeling if I were to do this with anyone else, it wouldn't feel the same.

With a deep, satiated sigh I tighten my grip around Sophia, inhaling her intoxicating, summery scent I've grown to obsess over. I close my eyes again, wanting to stay here a moment longer, but the ringing sound takes me out of it again. It's coming from the nightstand where her phone is being charged.

"Blue," I whisper, giving her cheek a soft peck. "Wake up."

She groans, turning the other way and putting the pillow on top of her head. "Go away."

A laugh bubbles out of me as I carefully remove the

pillow. She's definitely *not* a morning person. "Your phone has been ringing nonstop."

She turns around, opening her eyes slightly. They're puffy, and her hair is all over the place in the cutest way possible. I don't understand how she manages to look beautiful just waking up, but damn, she does. Painfully so. With a yawn, she reaches for her phone that's currently pinging with nonstop text notifications. And before I know it, she is darting out of bed with tense shoulders as her hands shake while dialing someone.

"Hey," she says, her voice trembling as she addresses the person on the other end.

I frown, waving my hand to get her attention and mouth, *What's wrong?*

She doesn't respond and turns away, her shoulders still tense. As she brushes her hair back, her fingers thread through it, holding it in place while she nods nonstop to whatever the person on the other end of the line is saying.

"Okay. Okay," she replies, her voice on the verge of breaking. "I'll be there as soon as possible." Then hangs up and turns around. Her eyes are red, tears threatening to escape her, but she doesn't let them. "You need to go."

I stand and make my way toward her, placing my hands on her forearms and caressing them. "Hey, hey," I say, trying to get her to look at me. "What's going on?"

"Please leave. I-I don't want you to see me like this, and I gotta go to Kentucky," she whispers shakily, taking a step back abruptly and avoiding my gaze.

The vulnerability in her voice makes my heart crack. Like hell I'm going to leave. She's got another thing coming if she thinks I'm ever going to walk away from her, especially when she's so distraught.

I grab her chin and force her to look at me. Her blue

eyes are gray and dull. A tear streams down her face, and I quickly wipe it away with the pad of my thumb. "If you stop pushing me away, maybe I can help."

She bites her lip, contemplating. "My mom had a pretty big panic attack. She's at the hospital, and I need to get there and figure out what the hell happened." She takes in a sharp breath. "And go into solving mode, like I always do."

This is the second time I've seen her this freaked, and it always has to do with her family. She's a closed book; sometimes it can be hard to get a read on her. Not that it stops me. I know a little better by now. She tries to put on this brave face and these fake smiles, even when she doesn't particularly feel like that all the time. I'm the last person to judge, because I know how it feels to create a false sense of positivity to hide the thoughts that keep you awake at night.

I walk over to where my clothes are, fish out my phone, and fire a quick text to my assistant. "We'll take my jet. It can be ready in an hour, so pack a bag, I'll go home and pack, too. We'll stay however long, whatever you need," I say quickly as I'm putting on my clothes.

"No." She shakes her head. "I can't ask this of you."

I stalk toward her again, grasping the nape of her neck. "You're not asking. I'm offering. *Let me help*," I plead. "Let me take care of you, okay?"

She has no idea I would drop anything to help her. She has no idea that for me, the lines have been quickly blurring, and even though all she wants from me is a fuck buddy, a friend, I would do anything for her.

She hesitates for a moment before replying. "Okay."

"Good." I wrap my arms around her and embrace her, dropping a soft kiss on her forehead. "Everything will be okay."

I say this to her, trying to calm her nerves. But honestly?

I'm saying it to myself, too. My heart clenches painfully, and the storm of emotions I don't understand leaves me, for the first time in my life, uncertain.

We're taking the steps to get onto my jet. Sophia has been quiet, and I've been on back-to-back phone calls rearranging a few things so I can have the rest of the week off.

"What do you mean you're not coming? This is *the* meeting of the year, Lorenzo," Amos says, aggravated.

I roll my eyes—thankfully, we're talking on the phone, so he can't see the disinterested look on my face. Taking my usual seat, I pat the one across from me, silently inviting her to sit there. The jet is big enough for us to have our own space, but where's the fun in that? I'd rather spend the whole ride looking at her.

"I think you all can manage without me," I retort dryly.

I knew missing this meeting was going to be an issue. Every year, we look over applications together to accept new members. New billionaires are rising every day around the world, but not all of them are worthy of holding the 24K gold–plated Vortex card—their words, not mine. I've always believed we're losing a lot of revenue opportunities by being so picky. But for them, it's not about the money, it's about the important connections we gain from accepting new members. It's all bullshit and nepotism at its finest.

"Lorenzo," He warns.

"Amos," I snap, my patience wearing thin. "I called you

as a courtesy. I'm not asking. I'm telling you an emergency came up, and I won't be assisting."

"You and I are going to have a conversation about your future as part of this board when you get back."

"Looking forward to it," I reply with a sharp, humorless laugh and hang up, throwing my phone on the seat next to me. Have them kick me out of the board if they want. I'll throw a fucking parade when they do.

"I'm sorry this whole thing is causing you so many issues," she whispers. I hate the way she says it like everything is her fault.

I lean forward, placing my hands on her thighs and starting to caress them. "Hey, this is *not* your fault. If anything, can I thank you for getting me out of that meeting?" I joke, trying to ease the tension.

She laughs softly, but it doesn't reach her eyes. "You're welcome, I guess."

"Look at me." She has been avoiding my eyes the whole ride here. While I miss her smile, I'm thankful she's allowing herself to be vulnerable enough to show me this side of her. I know it must be killing her. But she should know by now I will never judge her.

"It's already embarrassing enough you have to see me like this. But knowing I'm causing so many issues..." She sighs, contemplating her next words. "I don't know how I'll ever thank you."

I stand from my seat and crouch in front of her. My hand reaches for a strand of her hair, tucking it behind her ear before caressing her cheek with my thumb. "Don't you dare thank me. There is no other place I'd rather be." I give her a soft quick kiss, and even though this is probably crossing the rules we've set, I can't bring myself to care. I want to show her how much it means to me to be here for her.

Supporting her however she needs. "Have you heard anything else?"

She shakes her head without a word.

The stewardess approaches. "Mr. Mancini, the plane is ready for take-off."

I nod, getting back in my seat. "Can you bring a blanket, please? Thanks."

I reach for Sophia's seatbelt and put it on her. There's something so simple yet rewarding about making sure she's safe. Looking after her has become second nature for me, and I don't know how to deal with it. How do you take care of a woman as strong as Sophia? A woman who is as stubborn as they come and determined to do everything alone? I'm not sure, but I'll keep trying, even if she continues to push me away.

The stewardess comes back with the blanket, and I place it on top of Sophia, making sure she's tucked and warm, then sit back down.

"Lorenzo, stop babying me. I'm not some doll that's going to break." She shoots me a glare.

"I'm not babying you," I challenge. Leave it to her to fight me the whole time. "Now take a nap. The flight to Nashville should be an hour and a half."

"I'm not tired."

I give her a pointed look. "If you say so."

It doesn't take long after we take off for Sophia to fall asleep. And all I can manage to do for the duration of the flight is look at her. Her hair in a messy bun, the tiny wild strands that are always bothering her peeking through. Her soft, parted lips as she snores softly. The slight frown she has, even though she's sleeping.

This girl makes my heart ache for something I've never thought possible. What should be the summer of our lives is becoming something completely different. What started as a simple game to get closer to her to get my fix has become a lot more. There's not enough time in the world for me to get her out of my system. Sophia has infiltrated my body and soul so deeply, I'm terrified for myself. For her. Because one thing is for certain—I don't deserve this woman. She deserves someone who can be emotionally available and capable of loving. She needs someone who knows how to love, and that man is certainly not me. But I want to be selfish for a little while longer, hold her in my arms and give us the time of our lives before she can become another's.

I don't know how I'm going to let her go, but I will do it. Even if it kills me.

I may be a selfish motherfucker, but I will never stand in the way of the happiness she deserves. I would give Sophia the world, even if it meant not having her in mine.

34

Sophia

A sterile, antiseptic scent fills my nostrils as soon as I peek into the hospital room where my mother is staying. She looks so peaceful in the white-lit room, with the only sound coming from the machines and her soft snores. After making sure she's alright, I shut the door softly.

I feel like I can finally breathe again as my shoulders relax. What should have been a two-hour drive here turned into five due to a bad accident. Honestly, if it weren't for Lorenzo keeping me company, I probably would've pulled over at a gas station and had a mental breakdown in a dirty bathroom stall before arriving. I've been trying my best to keep these emotions at bay, but I'm not sure how much longer I can hold on.

"Is she okay?" Lorenzo asks. He hasn't left my side since we arrived, and I can't deny it's been nice. He brings some sort of... peace.

I nod. "She looks good. She's sleeping." Glancing over his shoulder, I spot the person I've been searching for since I got here and start walking toward her. "What happened?" I ask Bailey, my mom's nurse, who's been kind enough to stay until I arrived.

She sighs, fidgeting with her fingers. "I didn't want to tell you this over the phone, but Amelia has been staying at your mom's place."

"What did you just say?" I snap.

"Your mom didn't want you to know. And honestly, I didn't see the harm—Amelia has been keeping to herself for the most part."

"What do you mean?"

"When she showed up with Miles at first, your mom was confused, but Amelia didn't offer much of an explanation. But then she showed up the following night with a bag of clothes, and your mom let her in. I wasn't there—it was my day off. I think your sister asked your mom when I wouldn't be around and took the opportunity."

"Bailey," I groan, frustration seeping into my voice. "Why didn't you tell me?"

"Your mom asked me not to," she replies, her voice small. "But then Miles showed up drunk—"

I interrupt her. "She doesn't make the decisions, and you know that. This was extremely irresponsible and reckless. Now look at where we are." Without waiting for a response, I turn and walk away, needing some much-needed space from everything and everyone.

I search desperately for a corner—anywhere I can finally unleash the tears that have been building up since this morning. Spotting a door marked *Employees Only*, I try the handle anyway. It opens, and I slip into a small room lined with shelves filled with medical supplies. I close the door behind me and slump against it, sliding down to the floor. The tears spill out uncontrollably, flooding through me in a wave I can't stop. Sometimes I gaslight myself and say I'm exaggerating. That I'm acting like an overprotective, annoying daughter. Then I remember all I witnessed during my childhood, all she went through that led her to this bad anxiety, the things that trigger her attacks, and I lose my shit all over again. The memories I try to erase with every fake smile are still so fresh in my mind, it's like living in a constant nightmare.

Amelia is crying, so I wrap my arms around her, placing her head against my chest, trying my best to stifle her cries. He hates it when we cry. The screaming is so loud, I can't hear my thoughts. Please, God—or whoever is up there—make this end. Let it stop at the yelling. I can't handle this anymore.

"Amelia," I whisper. My body is shaking, and I don't know how to make it stop. "I need you to stop crying. Please," I beg.

"W-w-hy is h-he y-yelling a-a-t M-mommy?" she asks between sobs.

"I don't know, sweetie. But we have to be quiet, otherwise, we'll get in trouble."

Her whole body stiffens at my words, but at least she stopped sobbing now. I release a small sigh of relief.

We should be safe now.

I hear angry steps growing closer and closer to my room. My heart instantly drops. There's no way he heard us.

"Ronald, please, leave the girls out of this," I hear my mom cry out as the door flies open. We don't keep any locks on any of the rooms anymore. My father took them away when I locked myself in my room once and refused to come out.

"You!" My father seethes, pointing and stalking toward me. He grips my forearm so tightly, and I bite the inside of my cheek until I taste copper. I refuse to cry in front of my father or show any emotion to him for that matter. I have to be strong for Amelia. For Mom. For myself.

"Where was your mother today?" he screams in my face, the

stench of alcohol hitting my nostrils, which is no surprise. He gets paid on Fridays and always goes out, disappearing on us to God knows where.

"She was here with us all day," I reply honestly, trying to control my shaky voice.

He grabs my other forearm now, shaking me. "Bullshit! Stop lying to me."

"I'm not lying." My voice is small now, but still controlled.

Mom truly was here with us all day. Amelia has been complaining we haven't done anything fun this summer, and all we do is stay home. But I heard Mom talking to Nanny over the phone the other day. She was complaining we were so broke, we can't even afford groceries. That's why we've been cooped up in this forsaken house all summer.

He lifts his hand, ready to slap me, but Mom gets in the way and screams. "Stop! Please, I'm begging you, Ronald. Stop."

My father's bloodshot eyes bulge in fury. "You want to defend your whore of a daughter? You're going to regret that decision, stupid bitch."

I never understood why he loved calling me horrible names. He claims I look like Mom, and since in his eyes she's a whore, I guess I'm a whore, too, by extension.

He fists her hair and drags her out of my room to theirs, leaving the door open. Amelia's sobbing fills the air, not letting me think. I'm too terrified to move, too weak to pull him off her. So I stand there, paralyzed, as I watch him shove her against the wall and hit her over and over again. The sickening sound of bones breaking and blood splattering is all I can hear now.

Blood. There's so much blood. And I don't know what to do.

I shut my eyes as hard as I can, forcing myself to push down the horrible memory.

That night, when he finally passed out, I had to convince her to go to the hospital. I had hoped she would tell the truth. Instead, she lied and said she got mugged and refused to press any charges, claiming she couldn't see who the person was since it was so dark. I resented my mom so much that day, but the older I grew, the more I understood. Abuse was all she knew by then, and like so many victims, she lived in constant fear, convinced there was no way out. It might sound harsh, but I thank my lucky stars every day that my father died. Because if he hadn't, I know exactly where my mom would've ended up—in a body bag. The thought alone threatens to tear me apart.

I press my palm to my mouth, trying to stifle my sobs. I *hate* this. I *hate* this crawly feeling. I *hate* the memories being here brings. Resting my head against the door and looking up, the room's bright, white lights are blurry as tears still escape me. This is what happens when I bottle everything up and I can't hide it anymore. I'm so pathetic. I'm supposed to be strong, to be out there and plaster a smile on my face when Mom wakes up. But I need a moment to feel sorry for myself. I need a moment to let the inner Sophia, the broken one, come out and *feel* for once.

After a few minutes, I finally start to calm down. I pull out my phone to check my reflection on the camera. I look like a mess—puffy eyes, disheveled hair, everything. This isn't the usual put-together Sophia, and it annoys me. But that doesn't stop me from drying my tears as I start counting backward, always hoping it will help.

I stand and open the door, completely unprepared as Lorenzo, who had been leaning his weight against it, tumbles to the floor with a loud *thud*.

"Ouch," he groans.

"What the hell do you think you're doing?"

He gets up, rubbing the back of his neck. "I've been waiting for you to come out."

"How long have you been sitting here?" I snap, crossing my arms.

Oh. My. God. Did he hear you losing your shit?

He lifts his hands in surrender. "Not long at all. I just asked if they've seen a five-foot midget running around here and someone pointed me to this door," he jokes, trying to ease the tension that's flickering between us. But the laugh doesn't reach his eyes. Instead, all I see is *pity*.

"I'm so tired of that look you've had on your face since we got here."

He rears back in shock. "What the hell are you talking about?"

"Pity, Lorenzo," I reply, resigned. "You're looking at me like you pity me."

He eats the distance between us, forcing me to look him in the eyes. "I do not pity you, Blue. You are a strong woman. An amazing daughter, too. The only look you see right now is *worry*." He caresses my cheek, and God, I hate how much I love his touch. "I'm allowed to worry about you, because I care, okay? I know it scares you, but you're going to have to deal with it."

Tears well in my eyes once more as I sniffle and roll my eyes. "You think you know me so well."

"I do," he says, tone serious. "I know you hate it when people care for you. I know you hate to ask for help. You're the most stubborn and challenging woman I have ever met." He smiles at me now, all bright and light; it makes me feel lighter, too. "But that's not going to stop me from being here for you and taking care of you. You forget I enjoy challenges," he finishes with a joke, barking a soft laugh that bubbles a laugh out of me, too.

"Do you want to talk about it?" he asks.

More than anything. It's what I almost say. But I don't think I'm ready to unpack all of that trauma on him.

I shake my head and whisper, "I would like a hug instead, if that's okay." My cheeks heat at my words. This is not me at all. But I'm willing to put my stubbornness aside for one of his warm hugs.

He wraps his arms around me without a word, and I rest my head on his chest, inhaling his strong, masculine scent. The scent I correlate peace with. The scent that brings some sense of normalcy. The scent that has started to smell more often than not like belonging.

We stand there for a few minutes, and before he lets go, he gives me one of his famous forehead kisses I like more than I'd ever care to admit. "I was looking for you to tell you that your mom is awake. I saw a few nurses walk into the room."

My ears perk up, and I shove him aside, rushing to her room. I open the door and find a nurse taking her vitals as Mom casually talks with her, all laughs and smiles.

"Mom."

Her blue eyes flick to the door, and she raises her eyebrows in surprise. "Honey, hi."

I approach her and wrap my arms around her in a warm embrace. "You gave me a big scare there," I say with the fakest smile I can muster, taking a step back. I've gotten good at faking smiles around Mom.

"I'm sorry." She grabs my hand and squeezes it. "What are you doing here? How did you get here so fast?"

"A friend." My voice quivers for a moment. I'm not sure how much information I want to share. "He has a plane and flew me here."

"Did you say *he*?" She wiggles her eyebrows.

"He's actually here, and has been very helpful," I answer honestly.

More than helpful, is what I want to say. He's the anchor I didn't know I needed. I'm glad he stuck around even when I was being stubborn.

"I want to meet this mysterious man."

I give her a warning glare. "Whatever you're thinking, stop it." I sit on the edge of the bed and interlace my fingers with hers. "How are you feeling?"

There are a million questions I want to ask her, but I hold my tongue, because I don't want to add to her anxiety. I'll have to get my information from Bailey, who I'm still extremely unhappy with, but I know I have to give her the chance to explain.

"I'm good, honey." She wraps her other hand around ours, squeezing them. "Really. You didn't have to come all the way here. Won't you get in trouble with your boss?"

Chances are I will. I sent him an email explaining I wouldn't be in the office for a few days due to a family emergency, and all he asked was if I could work from home in the meantime. Mind you, I've never missed work or taken a sick day. But coming from Max, this is not surprising in the least.

I shake my head. "Don't worry about it."

"So, tell me about this *friend*." She beams.

Before I can tell her how ridiculous she's acting, there's a knock on the door.

"Come in," I say, standing from the bed.

Lorenzo pops his head in. "Hey. I'm going down to the cafeteria and I wanted to see if you guys needed anything."

"Oh my God, you didn't tell me how handsome he was." Mom pats my shoulder, and a blush creeps up my cheeks.

My mother, ladies and gentlemen—her favorite hobby is, apparently, embarrassing me.

"Come in here, young man."

I roll my eyes. "Mom, you can't say things like that in front of him. Seriously. You'll give him an ego boost, and he doesn't need it."

Lorenzo shrugs, flashing a boyish smile that makes my insides melt. "It's good to know at least one of the Evans girls has good taste." He takes my mom's hand and kisses it gently. "Lorenzo Mancini, but you can call me Enzo. It's lovely to meet you, Miss Evans."

"Oh, please. Call me Charlotte." She smiles back. "My daughter tells me you've been helping her out."

"Well, as much as she lets me anyway." He laughs, dropping her hand and shooting a knowing look my way.

"She can be kind of stubborn, I know." She sighs.

I scowl at them. "Gang up on me, why don't you?"

Lorenzo gives me a side hug and plants a kiss on the top of my head. "You're not as terrifying as you think, even with that scowl on your pretty face."

I look at him, shocked he would say something like that in front of my mom. He thins his lips and shrugs, not having a care in the world.

"Sophia, why don't you go with Lorenzo to the cafeteria and get me some gelatin? The red kind. That's my favorite."

I hesitate for a moment. I don't want to leave her alone for several reasons. Mainly because I'm afraid my sister will appear at any moment. Because if there's one thing I know for certain—she'll make an appearance at the worst time possible.

"You heard the lady, come on, Blue." He squeezes my shoulders and drags me out of the room.

"Oh," Mom gasps, her face beaming. "I love that nickname. It suits her perfectly."

"Thanks to that comment, you're getting a green gelatin now." I glare at her, shutting the door before she can reply.

As we're walking to the cafeteria in silence, I stop dead in my tracks and grab him by the arm, stopping him.

He looks at me with a frown. "Everything okay?"

Before I lose my momentum, I wrap my arms around him and embrace him tightly, burying my head in his chest, because apparently one hug wasn't enough. I don't think any amount will ever be enough. They make me feel safe, and that's a feeling I haven't experienced for a very long time. "Thank you for everything," I murmur.

Lorenzo's fingers find my chin, and he lifts my head, forcing me to look at him. His face has some stubble, but it doesn't make him look any less handsome. If anything, he looks more human. And I like that a little too much.

He presses his lips to my forehead, the soft kiss sending a flutter of butterflies through my stomach. It's becoming a problem. "Stop thanking me. I'm happy to be here."

My heart presses tightly against my ribcage at his words. I'm trying to not look for a meaning behind them, to not read too much into it. He's just being a friend, trying to be helpful. Nothing more.

Why does it feel like more? Why are you hoping *for more?*

Hoping can only get me so far. It's not real. I'm not delusional enough to think I'll be able to open my heart to him. When I'm older and think back to this time of my life, I'll remember it for what it was—the summer of my life, with the most wonderful man who, in a perfect world, I could have fallen in love with, if destiny were a real thing.

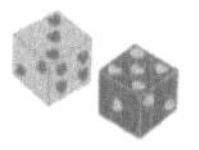

A nurse walks into the room and announces, "Visitor hours will be over in about ten minutes."

We all nod and mumble our thanks.

"Will you be okay?" I ask my mom with a frown etched on my face.

"Yeah. You heard the doctor earlier, it's going to be one more night. You kids go home and pick me up tomorrow."

The doctor came in earlier today and said everything was looking fine and that they wanted to keep her one more night as protocol. Relief took over me when they said that. I want her back home where she can be comfortable and get back to her routine.

"*Yo-hoo*," a voice I recognize anywhere says, opening the door.

And there she is, in the flesh, my fucking sister.

Lorenzo shoots a look my way, and all I can manage is to thin my lips before I say something in front of Mom I'm going to regret.

Before Amelia can walk into the room, I stalk toward her and stop her. "Hey, little sis," I manage to say with a light tone I don't even recognize. "Let's go outside and talk, yeah?"

She gets out of my grip. "I came here to see Mom."

"Visitor hours are over, anyway. You can always come back tomorrow." I grip her arm tightly, my eyes widening as I push her out of the room. "Mom, we'll see you tomorrow, okay?"

Looking over my shoulder, I see Lorenzo standing, deliberately blocking my mom's view so she doesn't have to see the tension between Amelia and me. When my eyes meet his, silently thanking him, he simply nods in understanding. This man is something else. And damn, my heart is picking up on these small things and making up a mind of its own.

Over my dead body is Amelia going to get anywhere near Mom. Once we walk out of here, we're going to have some words. Bailey told me everything and why my mom ended in the hospital. Turns out, Miles showed up at our doorstep completely drunk, begging Mom to speak to Amelia. He and Amelia had a screaming match outside. I'm still unsure of all of the details since this is the only thing Bailey was able to get out of Mom. But she witnessed everything, and the fight must have triggered her somehow, and this is why we find ourselves here.

Once we're completely out of the room and out of earshot, I stop dead in my tracks. "You have some fucking nerve showing your face around here," I snap.

"Oh, so you're the only one allowed to see our mother? Just because you take care of her? Get over yourself, Sophia," Amelia retorts, crossing her arms.

"She's here because of you," I say, jabbing a finger in her direction. "Did you think I wasn't going to find out? What were you thinking, staying at Mom's? No—worse—what were you thinking bringing Miles around her? Did you even stop to consider that for a second?"

"I didn't think he was going to show up drunk in the middle of the night!" she exclaims, exasperated.

"That's the point. You don't think! God, Amelia. You're so fucking selfish!" I yell, not giving a fuck that everyone is currently casting glances our way. "You think the world revolves around you. Wake the fuck up and look at where Mom is because of you," I seethe, widening my arms with a humorless laugh. "You need to leave."

She shakes her head. "I just want to apologize."

"I don't care—" Before I can continue, I look over her shoulder and see none other than Miles walking our way. "Did you seriously bring Miles *here*?"

"We got back together, not that it's any of your concern. He's supposed to be waiting for me in the car."

"Hey, *babe*," Miles says, dropping his arm around Amelia. "Oh, hi Sophia, long time no see."

I'm going to lose it. I think this is it. I've hit my limit. Don't get me wrong—I've been over Miles for a very long time. There was something so cathartic about grabbing all his music equipment and throwing it out the window of his apartment the day I decided to leave work early and drop by and, to my oh-so-fucking-merry-surprise, found these two fucking. The perfect way to get over my trashy boyfriend.

Yeah, that's right. You heard it here first, *folks*. Miles is my ex. The guy I spent four years of my life with, all while he was screwing my sister behind my back. As Rachel Green from *Friends* would say, *Isn't-that-just-kick-you-in-the-crotch, spit-on-your-neck fantastic?*

Yet, you haven't opened yourself to love ever again. Are you sure you're over him?

More than sure. I *am* over him; I just haven't forgotten about the betrayal. There's a difference. I don't open myself to love anymore, because how can someone hurt me if I'm always the first one to leave? It has been the perfect way to protect my heart.

"Both of you need to leave, now," I say, my voice flat and emotionless. I'm exhausted—tired of them, tired of everything. Can't a girl get a moment of peace? *Jesus Christ.*

"Aw, come on," Miles says, his lips curling into a sly smile as he gives my shoulder a playful tap with his fist. "Isn't this a nice little reunion?"

"Do *not* fucking touch me," I hiss, recoiling. "And for the last time, leave. I better not see either of you lurking around Mom again."

"You can't tell me what to do," Amelia snaps.

"She told you guys to leave," Lorenzo's voice cuts in, calm but firm. He steps behind me and wraps his arm around my waist, the warmth of his touch grounding me. I glance at my hands, realizing they're shaking. But the tremor starts to fade under the reassurance of his touch.

"Who the hell are you?" Miles retorts, glaring at Lorenzo.

"None of your concern," I reply, shooting them both a fierce look. "What's it going to take for you two to leave?"

"Babe, let's go," Miles says, gripping Amelia's shoulders. "You know how bitchy Sophia gets. We can visit your mom another day."

Lorenzo's jaw tightens as he strides toward Miles, grabbing the front of his dirty, worn shirt. "Apologize," he demands, his voice low and dangerous.

"What the fuck is your problem?" Miles protests, trying to wriggle free from Lorenzo's grip.

Lorenzo tightens his hold, now gripping the back of Miles's neck, forcing him to face me. "Apologize for calling her a bitch. *Now.*"

"Lorenzo, it's fine—" I start to protest, but his fierce look stops me. I've never seen him like this before; he's usually so laid-back and laughing. But now, anger radiates off him. His jaw is tight, and his eyes are a dangerous, darker shade of brown.

"Apologize," Lorenzo repeats through gritted teeth.

"I-I'm sorry," Miles stammers, his voice trembling.

With a sharp shove, Lorenzo sends Miles stumbling back. "Get out of here, both of you. And if I ever see either of you around again," he adds, his glare boring into Miles as he points at him, "I'll be breaking *your* nose."

"This is not over," Amelia mumbles, grabbing Miles's wrist as they leave the hospital.

As soon as they're out of sight, Lorenzo turns to me, his eyes scanning my face with concern. "Are you okay?"

"Yes. Are *you* okay?" I ask, gently placing my hands on his face and caressing his jawline. "You lost your cool for a minute there."

He relaxes at my touch, closing his eyes. "No one gets to insult you. Not in front of me." His voice is firm and full of conviction, making my stomach flutter with a mix of emotions.

It's safe to say at this point, we're both playing with dangerous fire. And we're already too far gone.

God, what mess did you get yourself into, Sophia?

A very big one. One that's going to obliterate my heart.

35

Lorenzo

As I stand in front of Sophia's childhood home, it's not what I imagined in the least. We arrived really late last night, and we were both exhausted, so I didn't get to really see the outside.

It's a small eastern farmhouse, the wood is worn, and the white paint is chipped away. The roof could also use some work. I'm not sure how it's still standing, to be quite honest. The lawn is overgrown and in need of some love, too.

"You don't have to stay, Lorenzo. Go back to Chicago, I'll be fine here with Mom for a few days," Sophia says, eyes on her phone. I swear, the woman never knows when to stop working. "You already stayed last night, and I'm sure you've got a million things waiting for you."

She's right. I have an impending list I couldn't give less of a fuck about. As long as none of the restaurants are burning down, the rest can go to hell.

I glance at her, and though her blue eyes remain dull, I notice the exact moment her body tenses when her gaze falls on her childhood home. I've never seen her so jarred. My girl is usually all smiles and confidence, but that hasn't been the case these past few days. She's been on edge, and when I try to pry information out of her, she shuts down. I'm out of my depth here, and I've been trying to be supportive, but she's going to have to start cluing me in. Especially after the fight she had with her sister in the middle of the hospital. I've never seen her lose her cool like that.

I grab the grocery bags from the trunk of the car and head toward the house. "Stop trying to kick me out. Are you getting sick of me, Blue?" I gasp, pretending to be hurt.

She rolls her eyes. "I'm trying to give you an escape."

If only she knew I don't want an escape. I want to stay right here, next to her. Supporting her in whatever she needs.

"Mom, we're home!" Sophia yells.

Charlotte was discharged this morning, and Sophia had Bailey come back to the house with her while we went to the pharmacy to pick up her mom's medication and anything else we might need. I told Sophia we'd stay as long as she wanted, but I know she'd stay forever if she could. Unfortunately, she has to fly back to Chicago in a few days, because her boss is getting impatient. It's frustrating, because Sophia's balancing her job and being there for her mom instead of taking time off. I'm keeping quiet about it, though. The last thing Sophia needs right now is more stress.

"In here!" Charlotte calls from the kitchen.

When we walk in, she's wearing an apron and cooking something that smells amazing.

"Why are you cooking?" Sophia scolds. "You're supposed to be resting."

"I wanted to make my famous pot roast for you two," she says with a warm smile, glancing back at us over her shoulder.

Charlotte is truly wonderful—sweet and kind. Spending time with her has been a joy. Her motherly spirit is something I've never really experienced before, and it's been comforting.

"I thought we were going to cook together," I say, setting the bags on the kitchen counter. "You betrayed me!"

Charlotte drops her head back with a laugh. "Oh no, I'm sorry! I just really want you to try it and get your professional opinion."

I had no problem telling Charlotte how much I love cooking when she asked me all sorts of questions about my life and what I do. When I told her I owned many restaurants around the world, she got so excited. We've been talking about food nonstop.

"Lord help me, there's two of them," Sophia groans dramatically. "I'm going to gain so much weight between the two of you and all the delicious food you guys keep making."

"You can use some meat on your bones, honey," Charlotte pipes up.

Sophia gapes at her, and I simply snort a laugh. My body feels light, and my heart feels full around these people. I never knew something so simple would bring so much joy. I have all the money in the world, all the connections, and everything is practically at my fingertips, but I would give it all in a heartbeat for moments like these.

I know, deep down, it wouldn't be the same without the woman who has become such an important part of my life. The realization I only want these moments as long as she's around washes over me, leaving me in a daze.

I'm so fucking screwed.

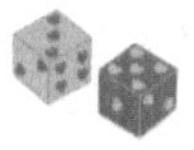

After devouring an absurd amount of pot roast—because, yes, it was *that* good—I'm scrubbing the kitchen stove. I insisted on taking care of the cleanup so Sophia could get some work done and her mom could rest.

We've been so busy, we haven't even talked more about the article. I know what I showed her in Panamá must not be enough to go on, but at this point, I don't know what else to show her. The thought of her writing what she has witnessed and what I've told her honestly terrifies me.

"Do you want any tea?" Charlotte strides into the kitchen and asks, startling me.

"Sure," I reply with a smile, dropping the sponge on the sink.

She nods, grabbing two packets of black tea and the tea kettle. She works in silence as I start washing the dishes that are left.

She places the tea kettle on the stove, turning it on. She leans against the kitchen counter, crossing her arms and staring at me. "Thank you."

"Oh, it's no big deal. That roast was delicious, worth washing every single dish," I quip with a low chuckle.

She shakes her head. "No. I meant thank you for making my daughter smile."

Her words are like a bucket of water being thrown at me. I stilt my movements for a second, casually shrugging. "It's easy to make her smile. She's a naturally happy person." The lie rolls off my lips without hesitation. I know better now. Sophia can be loud and laugh a lot, but it doesn't always reach those beautiful eyes of hers. But I have the feeling she wouldn't want Charlotte finding out.

"You and I both know that's not true," she replies, her voice laced with conviction.

She opens a kitchen cabinet, retrieves two mugs, and places the tea bags inside. After grabbing the tea kettle, she pours hot water into the mugs. She then grabs two spoons and a few packets of sugar before tilting her head toward the dinner table.

"I owe a lot to my daughter," she starts, her gaze drifting to the screen door leading to the porch where Sophia is sitting, absorbed in her writing. "I wasn't always like this, you know?"

I nod, opting to stay quiet. Sophia has been extremely cryptic about her life—granted, it's not like I've been actively asking her. I'm trying to be supportive and respect the boundaries she sets, because I understand.

"Sophia has shouldered a responsibility I didn't wish for her to have. Ever since my husband..." Her voice quivers at the word *husband*. "Died, she's done everything she can to take care of me. Her father was not a kind man. In fact, because of him, I am the way I am now."

"You don't have to share this if it's too painful," I say softly.

"I want to. I want you to understand why my daughter is the way she is."

"It doesn't matter." I shake my head. "Because to me, your daughter is wonderful. She's strong. Funny. Resilient. Challenging. She takes care of people and loves doing it."

Charlotte's gaze meets mine, and a heavy silence settles between us. "You love her, don't you?" she asks quietly.

For a moment, I'm at a loss for words, staring at Charlotte with a blank expression. The idea of loving anyone is foreign and overwhelming. Something I'm...unfamiliar with.

Being around Sophia makes me want to be someone worthy of her. I want to protect her, to be there for her in every way possible. I want to make her laugh genuinely, not the forced laughs she offers to everyone else. I want to see her smile, the kind that makes her eyes sparkle and tugs at my chest with a sharp, bittersweet ache. I want to be her support, her shoulder to lean on. I want to show her she's not alone in this world. I want her to know I can share her burdens and help her carry the weight of her pain.

But love? That's not something I can offer.

I clear my throat and take a sip of tea, my throat feeling unexpectedly dry. "We're just friends," I finally manage to say.

She takes a sip of her tea while keeping her gaze locked on mine. "You didn't answer my question."

I stare at her, struggling to find words. It's such a complex, tangled question for someone like me.

"When you walk into the room, her face lights up," she says, her voice catching as she fights back tears. "Do you have any idea when was the last time I saw her eyes full of life? She thinks I don't notice. But I know my daughter isn't happy, and as her mother, it breaks my heart. Because I know it's all my fault—"

I cut her off gently. "It's not your fault. She adores you," I say firmly, trying to reassure her.

She shakes her head with a humorless laugh. "I didn't set a good example for her. There's so much you don't know. I did the best I could with the situation we were in. But now, seeing how it's affected my daughters, I wish I'd handled things differently."

I grab her hand and squeeze it, reassuringly. "You raised

a wonderful daughter. And I know it would kill her if she knew you were talking about yourself like this."

She wipes her face with the back of her hand, standing. "Thank you for listening. You're a great man." She caresses my cheek in a motherly, tender way. "Thank you for loving my daughter. Even if you don't realize it yet." The way she speaks is like she's privy to a secret Sophia and I haven't figured out yet. "I'm going to bed, tell Sophia, yeah?"

She exits, leaving me alone in the kitchen, caught in a whirlwind of emotions I can't quite make sense of, but I'm eager to try.

Sophia

As I sit on my childhood home porch with my laptop in hand, the blank page stares at me mockingly.

Max asked how Lorenzo's article was going. And to be quite honest, it's not. I bullshit my way through excuses, reminding him all the work he's been giving me has set me behind. He was pissed about it but didn't pressure me into sending him a rough draft yet. So I have some time to work on this. With everything that has been going on, I'm barely above water right now. But this is important, and I have to do my job despite how our situation has...*changed*. Lorenzo deserves the best work. The best article yet. But I feel everything I come up with is so impersonal and tasteless.

"Blue," Lorenzo rasps, startling me.

I look over my shoulder, finding him leaning against the door frame with his arms crossed looking too handsome for his own good. "Jesus! You scared me."

He laughs. "It's late, you should get some rest."

"In a minute," I mumble, staring at the blank document.

I'm hoping for a miracle that'll get me writing in the next few seconds.

He closes the distance between us, shutting the laptop as he shakes his head. "Now."

I press my lips into a thin line. "You're so bossy."

"And you must be exhausted. Can't Max, I don't know, give work to other people?" he asks, frowning.

"If only," I mumble to myself as I stroll inside the house.

He follows me into my old bedroom. I don't keep much here anymore—never had much to start with. The room has two nightstands, a full-size bed, and a small desk in the corner where I work when I visit Mom.

"You say that a lot. Why? Does he give you a lot of work?"

"It doesn't matter." I wave my hand at him dismissively, placing my laptop on the desk.

He hums, unconvinced, shutting the door. "Do you want me to take the couch? The bed is kind of small. I want to make sure you're rested."

"You said the exact same thing yesterday, and I already told you the couch is uncomfortable. No reason for you to break your back," I say, climbing onto the bed, and patting the space beside me.

"If you want to cuddle, all you have to do—"

I interrupt. "All I have to do is ask. I know, I know." I laugh, rolling my eyes. "Will you *cuddle* with me, Ace?" I ask, wiggling my eyebrows playfully.

He climbs on the bed and wraps his arms around me. I let myself get enveloped in his intoxicating and masculine scent I've grown to love so much.

"About damn time you asked, Blue." He chuckles softly, locking his beautiful eyes on mine, allowing me to get lost in them.

Every second I keep looking at him, so many emotions wash through me at an overwhelming pace. When I met Lorenzo, this was the last place I thought we were going to end up. Over these past few weeks, he has become my sounding board. The thought is totally crazy. Who knew he was going to be the one there for me? Who knew he was going to be the only person I could feel comfortable enough to be myself?

I have my friends, yeah—who I haven't seen in like forever. I'm sure I will get in some serious trouble when I go back to Chicago. The girls have been there for me, but... It's not the same. Lorenzo fills a void I never knew I had.

"Can I ask you something?"

"Well, I do owe you a few questions. Go ahead," I reply softly.

"What's the deal with your sister?"

I sit, creating some space between us, and frown. "Where's this coming from?"

"There's a story there, and I want to know. I'm a good listener," he jokes with a soft smile tugging at the corner of his lips, his stupid and cute dimple making an appearance.

"That stupid dimple of yours always makes an appearance when I least want to see it," I point out, glaring at him.

His smile grows, the dimple deepening. "Are you obsessed with my dimple, Blue?"

"Yes," I answer honestly.

"*Wow*. You must not want to talk about your sister if you just admitted something like that."

I lay my head against the wall and groan. "Busted," I murmur.

He bursts out laughing, and I can't help but join in, the sound contagious.

"There's a lot you don't know about my family."

His eyes soften. "You don't have to tell me if you don't want to."

Strangely, I want him to know the rawest, darkest parts of me. It should scare me, but somehow, I feel a strange calm.

I swallow, fighting the tightness in my throat. "My mother...she's a survivor of domestic violence. My father was an alcoholic. He took his anger out on her, and on us."

Lorenzo's jaw tightens, his expression pained as he squeezes my hand, his fingers threading with mine, offering a silent anchor. "Fuck, Blue," he whispers.

"Mom protected us as much as she could, so we didn't get it as bad as she did," I say softly.

He shakes his head, interrupting me. "Don't do that."

I blink, taken aback. "Do what?"

"Diminish your problems. You're as much a survivor as she is," he says, his voice so gentle it nearly undoes me. "You deserve to feel, too."

I press my lips together. "I tried to be strong for Mom and Amelia," I continue. "I took on a lot to protect my little sister. I was the oldest. It felt like it was my job to shield her."

His thumb brushes over my hand in soft, steady circles, grounding me. The strength in his grip, his unwavering attention, gives me the courage to go on.

"When my father died, it was like a weight lifted, knowing he couldn't hurt us anymore. But then came the aftermath. Mom was shattered, and I never understood why she was grieving so deeply. He was a man who'd caused us so much pain... But who was I to question her feelings? So I took over. I became Amelia's rock while Mom coped with her own battles."

A tear slips out, and before I can brush it away, Lorenzo

does it for me—like he always does. He always knows exactly what I need and when I need it.

"Mom eventually started to get better, though the anxiety and panic attacks were still frequent. But by that point, it was too late. Amelia grew rebellious and started acting out." I shake my head. "Most of the time, I feel like I failed her."

"You did everything you could under impossible circumstances," Lorenzo murmurs, his voice a mix of firmness and compassion. "You did *not* fail her."

I give him a small, grateful smile. The way he cares for me, without hesitation or judgment—it's overwhelming in the best way.

"Our relationship has always been rocky," I admit. "And now... We're here." I take a shaky breath, gathering the words. "The guy she was with at the hospital...Miles. He's my ex-boyfriend."

His eyebrows raise in surprise. "Wait, *what*?"

"We dated, always on and off, but when I graduated college, he decided to follow me. At first, I was hesitant. It was a big move, so I made him get his own place, and I was roommates with Aria even though I spent all of my time over at his place. But it still gave me some sort of security, I guess, knowing I had a place to call my own. He had odd jobs here and there that didn't pay enough, but he was trying—or so I thought—to focus on his music. I supported him financially in any way I could." I gulp, looking away, feeling embarrassed. The only person who knows this story is Aria, and that was so mortifying. Telling him this, I'm bearing my soul out to him right now. Something I'm not used to doing.

Now that I know better, I can see it as clear as day—I

was so naive back then. Eager to please. Desperate for love. I accepted whatever crumbs Miles was willing to give me.

"Looking back, our relationship wasn't the greatest. I was barely making any money, yet every penny I had was being spent to help him cover rent here and there, to furnish his place little by little, plus taking care of Mom. It took a toll on me. We barely had sex and just fought most of the time. I thought he was under so much pressure trying to make the music thing work." I shake my head, laughing humorlessly. "Funny enough, Amelia had moved to Chicago not long after. Now I understand why she did, but at the time, it didn't occur to me. The few times they saw each other, they always acted so civilized in front of me," I say, my voice devoid of emotions.

These memories aren't as painful as they used to. If I'm being honest with myself, ever since I started spending more time with Lorenzo, I've been able to heal and let go.

Never thought I'd see the day.

"Then one day, I decided to leave work early to surprise him. I had just gotten a promotion, finally becoming a junior journalist. I worked day and night for it, and I was really excited. I wanted to celebrate it with him after such a busy week." I sigh, closing my eyes for a moment. "And there they were." I shake my head. "It was such a slap in the face." A sharp, bitter laugh escapes me. "So there you have it. My boyfriend of four years was sleeping with my sister the whole time, and I was too busy to notice."

"God, Sophia. I am so fucking sorry." He brings me in for a hug, and I let him. "You didn't deserve that."

"Maybe part of it was my fault, too," I point out. "I was so focused on work, only because I needed the raise to hire a nurse for Mom, and to keep helping him, too. I was so focused on building a future."

"*No.* Let me fix that statement for you. He was an insecure, half of a man that couldn't handle such a strong, wonderful woman like you." He shakes his head. "I wish I had punched him like I wanted to," he mutters. "Figlio di puttana."

"What does that mean?"

"Son of a bitch," he translates.

"I love when you speak Italian," I say with a soft chuckle.

His hand cradles my face, his eyes locking onto mine. "Sei la donna più meravigliosa che abbia mai incontrato[1]," he says, placing a gentle kiss on my left cheek. "Te lo meriti tutto[2]," he adds, kissing my other cheek. "Vorrei essere l'uomo che potrebbe darti tutto[3]. Vorrei essere degno di te[4]. Vorrei poterti amare come meriti[5]," he finishes, sealing his lips on mine with a slow kiss that makes my soul roar.

"Care to translate?" I ask breathlessly. Whatever it was, the way his eyes are simmering with an unspoken emotion tells me maybe I'm not ready to find out.

Stop lying to yourself. You're dying to know. You're hoping to find out if he feels the same way you've been feeling.

His forehead meets mine, and barely above whispers, he says, "Don't ask me to be honest right now. Because I can't bring myself to."

I respect his wishes, because I don't think either one of us is ready to handle what's happening right now between us. Without saying a word, I press my lips to his, kissing him like he's the breath of fresh air I didn't realize I needed so badly. My heart wants to come out of my chest with the

---

1. You are the most wonderful woman I have ever met.
2. You deserve it all.
3. I wish I could be the man who could give you everything.
4. I wish I were worthy of you.
5. I wish I could love you the way you deserve.

knowledge of how different this kiss feels. There are so many words being drowned with every second we brush our lips together. His hand travels from the crook of my neck to my curves, all the way down to my legs, leaving a trace of goosebumps in their wake.

He lays me down on the bed gently as his hands roam every inch of my body with such delicacy, I can feel the adoration in every touch. There's so much meaning behind every trace, my heart quivers.

"Lorenzo," I whisper shakily. "I need you."

"I'm right here," he whispers back, huskily.

"I *need* you inside of me," I correct, threading his hair with my fingers.

"I didn't bring any condoms. I didn't want you to think that's why I was here," he replies, caressing my legs, and *God*, his touch is so addicting. I wish he would never stop.

"I'm on the pill, and I've never done it without a condom," I say, taking off my shirt.

A low growl escapes his lips, tilting his head back. "I've never done it without a condom either. And *fuck*, I would love nothing more than to feel all of you. Are you sure?"

I nod silently, tugging at the hem of his shirt and pulling it over his head. My hands glide over his muscular shoulders, down his chest, and along his torso, until they reach his shorts. I trace his growing erection through the fabric, feeling his body respond beneath my touch. Lifting my hips slightly, I allow him to take my shorts off, leaving me only in my underwear. He stands, grasping my legs and bringing me to the edge of the bed. As he takes off the rest of his clothes, I inch forward, unclasping my bra and throwing the lace fabric on the floor. Lorenzo gets on his knees and starts to press soft, lingering kisses along my skin. Every kiss he gives me makes me shiver, my need for him growing by the second.

His fingertips hover over the waistband of my underwear, slowly bringing them down. "There's nothing I like more than getting on my knees for you." His husky words, so soft but rough all at the same time, make my thighs clench. He drops a kiss on my inner thigh now, his tongue and mouth teasing everywhere except where I need him the most.

I wiggle under his teasing touch. "Lorenzo," I pant. "Please," I beg.

"Mmm, I love it when you beg." His mouth latches on my sensitive clit, and his tongue moves in slow, but delicious circles. I arch my back as much as I can, trying to get more friction from him. But Lorenzo takes his time, lapping at me, savoring me as his hands continue to caress my legs. He takes his time to lick every inch of my center, slow and steady, like it's just us and we have all the time in the world.

"I need more." I tug his hair.

A dark chuckle comes out of his lips. "I know, baby," he replies gravelly, two fingers entering me. "I'll give you everything you need, and more." He continues to flick his tongue back and forth, not stopping to even breathe. He just licks and sucks and nips as he keeps working his fingers in and out of me.

"Lorenzo." My chest heaves. "I need you inside of me. Please. Let me feel you."

His fingers slip out of me, and he looks at me, his face glistening with my arousal. He looks so incredibly sexy, I let out a soft moan.

His tongue darts out, licking his lips. "Whatever my girl wants, my girl gets." He starts peppering kisses from my love handles to my stomach.

With every soft kiss he gives me, my heart clenches.

With every soft kiss he gives me, I feel seen. Adored. *Worshiped*.

His body hovers over me without putting any of his weight on me. Our faces are so close, I can clearly see his light stubble. My hand reaches for the tiny scar on his eyebrow, brushing it with my thumb softly as my eyes take in the beautiful man before me. His cock meets my entrance as his eyes find mine. And it feels as if, somehow, our souls are connected, with the way I can see every bit of adoration behind his intense, brown gaze. I close my eyes, not wanting to see the way he looks at me any longer. It's too painful. I wrap my arm around his neck, bringing him closer. He slowly enters me, and... It's like *magic*. I've never felt something like this before. The connection. All the feelings bubbling inside of me that I'm trying to make sense of are heightened as he starts to work himself in and out of me.

His lips find mine, and he kisses me with a soft, simmering passion. It's like my body is levitating on its own, seeing the world with a whole new perspective, with bright new colors. And we don't stop kissing. Not as he keeps sliding in and out of me slowly, taking his time. And that's when I feel it, deep in my bones. I can feel it burning— *piercing*—my soul. With every slow, deliberate thrust, I can feel everything we're not saying. With every consuming kiss, even as our lips grow numb, I can feel how this has become more. In the silence of the room, where the only sound is our slow, ragged breaths, I can see it, as clear as day, how hard I've fallen for this man.

His thrusts are still slow and precise as my orgasm starts slowly building up. "I'm coming," I moan softly against his lips.

His eyes, glowing in the soft light of the room, lock onto

mine as he starts to pick up the pace a little more, but his thrusts still feel different. They feel like so much more. This isn't about sex anymore. Deep down, I knew this deal would break me. Deep down, I knew my heart was going to end up in pieces.

As my orgasm builds and then crashes through me like never before, I keep my eyes locked on his, refusing to break the connection, even when it's killing me. Even when I know falling in love with him will haunt me for the rest of my life. As I clench around him, my moans fill the room. He thrusts once more, his glassy gaze never leaving mine as he finally lets go, spilling inside of me.

He slips out of me slowly and we both lie there, not saying anything. What is there to say? We both know everything has changed. We both know this is over. It's just a matter of *when*. Because neither of us do love, and never will.

Lorenzo Mancini is the one who mended my broken heart, and he's going to be the one to break it.

Sophia

Powerpuff Girls Chat

ARIA

Isabella, do you think Sophia is alive? She's disappeared on us once again. You're being a terrible friend, Soph. I'm heartbroken.

ISABELLA

Don't count on it.

ISABELLA

And what is up with the name of this ridiculous chat? I still don't get it.

ARIA

We've been abandoned. And I still can't believe you don't get it.

ISABELLA

It's terrible. I hate it.

ME

You sound exactly like Buttercup. The only thing you're missing is the black hair. And that's the reason behind this wonderful name.

ISABELLA

You sound ridiculous. Matter of fact, you sound just like Bubbles.

ME

Exactly. And I'm only missing the blonde hair. Duh! 😆

ARIA

Hello!? You're not going to give us any explanations as to where you've been?

ME

Crazy couple of weeks. Long story short, I'm in Kentucky. But I'll be back tomorrow.

ARIA

Yes. I heard, which reminds me: I'm pissed at you for not telling me. But care to tell me why Damian told me Lorenzo is there too?

ME

Because he came with me.

ISABELLA

throws book across the room This is more interesting than my book. Care to tell us why?

ME

Too long to explain via text.

ISABELLA

Code for: they're fucking.

ARIA

You really think so? 😦

ME

> I have to go guys, but I promise we will meet when I get back. Have some quality girls' time and all of that.

ARIA

> You owe us!

ISABELLA

> I cannot wait to be proven right. 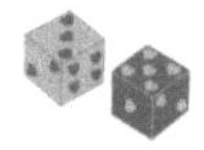

"I wish I didn't have to leave," I tell Mom, hugging her tightly. Her hugs have always been the best.

She kisses the top of my head. "I'll be fine. I have Bailey with me, she keeps me company."

I purse my lips, nodding. I had a serious conversation with Bailey. She, of course, kept apologizing profusely. Ultimately, I let her stay because Mom needs routine more than anything. But she knows not to lie to me again. We like her a lot, but when it comes to Mom, I have to protect her and won't let anyone get in the way of that.

This is our last day here, and I've been hanging out with Mom, keeping work and everything that has been happening with Lorenzo in the back of my mind. Max has been flooding my email inbox, nagging me about the work he keeps throwing my way like I'm his personal dog, at his beck and call when he wants it. I haven't had time to think much, but something has to change. I can't keep living like this.

I woke up today to the sound of the lawn mower, and

when I looked out the window, it was Lorenzo taking care of the overgrown lawn I've been putting off since it's hard to find someone cheap. I'm ashamed to admit it brought tears to my eyes when I walked into the bathroom to get ready for the day. He's just so...sweet. And does everything without being asked. He's such a protector and a giver. He shows the way he cares through actions, not words. This doesn't help my fragile heart, which already feels too much for the man. It's going to be so much harder to let him go when the time comes. The logical thing to do is break it off now, but I selfishly want to keep this going until we go to Las Vegas, like we agreed. I'm all too aware this is going to destroy my heart, but I want to embrace him and everything he has to offer for a little while longer. Let myself live in a fairytale for once.

The screen door of the entrance opens, and Lorenzo walks in with his face flushed and hair sticking to his forehead, his tank top hugging every hard muscle that's dripping with sweat. He brushes his hair away from his face, the movement flexing his bicep, and I have to do everything in my power to not lick my lips eagerly at the sight of him. He's all man and muscle. Something you would never think possible, since he's always in suits and meetings. The man puts Adonis to shame; that's the only way to describe how perfectly sculpted he is.

A boyish smile plays on his lips. "The lawn is all ready, Charlotte."

Mom strides over and gives his cheek a couple of light pats. "You're a keeper. My daughter is very lucky."

"Mom," I warn, heat rising on my cheeks.

"I'm going to get you guys some lemonade," Mom quips, completely ignoring me, which wins her a glare from me and a laugh from Lorenzo.

When she's out of earshot, I close the distance between

us and hug him even though he's all sweaty. I honestly couldn't care less. "You didn't have to do this. Thank you."

He hugs me back, kissing the top of my head. "No need to thank me. I already reached out to a lawn company and scheduled them to come weekly."

My shoulders tense, and I take a step back, shaking my head. "I can't afford that, Lorenzo."

He rolls his eyes. "Good thing you're not paying for it, then."

I gape at him in disbelief. "Lorenzo, no. Are you crazy?"

His knuckles brush my jawline, a trace of goosebumps taking over at the simple touch. "I want to help in any way I can. And I'm not asking you, I'm telling you this is what I'm going to do." He winks before dropping a quick kiss on my lips.

God, this man. What did I do to deserve to be treated like this? This has me holding back another set of tears.

Mom walks out of the kitchen with some cups and a pitcher of her famous homemade lemonade. "I hope you guys are thirsty."

"For your lemonade? Always," I reply, pushing once again all the emotions that want to find their way out of me and grab a cup instead, serving some of the delicious, citrusy juice and handing it to Lorenzo. "Get ready to try the best lemonade you will *ever* have."

Lorenzo smirks, taking the cup from my hand and taking a sip. His eyebrows rise in surprise. "Wow, yeah. This is amazing. Charlotte, I need the recipe for the restaurant I'm opening in Panamá. This would go so well with the menu."

Mom smiles, her eyes shining with excitement. "Anything for you, dear."

Even though they only met a few days ago, their relationship has quickly flourished. Mom is infatuated with Lorenzo. They love to talk about food, cook together, and gang up on me every chance they get. Surprisingly, Lorenzo has been in his element. He looks...happy. Rested. Like he belongs here with us. These past few days, I've been living in a daydream where Lorenzo and I make it work and end up together, and Mom lives close to us and we go have dinner with her on Sundays, and they cook together, always talking about food and joking. Maybe even have the rest of the group join us. And eventually, when we start having kids, we can make it a whole thing. Of course, I know these are silly wishes. But it's nice to dream sometimes, it feeds the soul.

"I'm going to take a shower, because the last thing I want to do is stink up the place," he says, dropping the cup on the coffee table and then kissing me on the cheek before walking to the room.

Mom sighs. "I love him."

I purse my lips. "Yeah, well, don't get used to it."

She looks at me for a moment, her eyes studying me. "We need to talk."

Oh, boy.

"About what?" I ask casually, grabbing a cup of lemonade for myself and sitting back on the couch.

"I need you to tell me what happened with Miles. Because whatever happened with him has you in this sort of funk I don't understand. I need you to stop hiding the truth from me," she says sternly, using the authoritative voice she used to use when I was a kid.

"Nothing much to say. We didn't work out," I mumble.

"Sophia Annette Evans," she chastises, popping her hip and resting a hand on it. "Then why did he show up here all drunk, begging for Amelia to take him back?" She raises an eyebrow. "I need you to stop treating me like a baby. I understand you're overprotective and want to make sure I'm okay, but I am your mother. I deserve to know what's happening in your life."

I laugh humorlessly, shaking my head and avoiding her gaze. "Drop it, Mom."

"Why are Miles and Amelia dating?" she presses. "Why didn't you tell me?"

I place the lemonade cup on the coffee table with a loud *thud*. "Because I don't particularly want to relive the fact that my boyfriend of four years was cheating on me with my own sister the whole time and I was too stupid to notice," I confess, devoid of emotion, my eyes finding her.

Mom gasps, her eyes bulging as she sits on the couch and grabs my hand. "Amelia did that?"

"Mom." I sigh, rubbing my temple. "Amelia is...a lot. You know? After Dad died, you were so checked out, and I don't blame you. You were grieving. But I dealt with her the best I could. She grew angry. Rebellious. I guess that never went away."

"I don't understand why she would do that." Mom gapes, shaking her head in disbelief.

"Because Amelia thrives in destruction. Just like Dad did," I say softly. I feel so guilty for putting this all on her. For shining light on the reality of the situation. Here's to hoping it doesn't bite me in the ass.

Tears start to fill her eyes, threatening to spill over. "I'm sorry, honey. I'm sorry you've been dealing with so much and you felt like you couldn't come to me. I feel like a burden when I should be supporting you, giving you advice."

I sit closer to her, bringing her into a side hug. "Mom, you are *not* a burden. I will always take care of you. You haven't had an easy life, and all I want you to do is be happy. You never have to worry about me."

"You haven't had an easy life either. Because of me. Because I never left your father. I—" She stops, breathing in and out slowly, trying to calm herself.

"We don't have to talk about this. The last thing I want is for you to end up in the hospital again," I say softly.

"No," she replies, her tone sharp. "We need to talk about this."

I start rubbing her back with soft circles and nod. I know her psychologist has told her she needs to face her past to keep moving on. Maybe it's time. Maybe she's finally ready. Part of me is hopeful. Part of me wants to believe this will be a distant memory, and all the abuse, the berating, and the hate will be so distant it won't affect her—*us*—anymore.

"I met your father when we were just kids. And we truly loved each other at some point. But everything just... changed. Your father was sick, Sophia. Alcoholism is a sickness. I've come to accept this. It destroyed him *and* us. I will never, and I mean never, forgive him for everything he put us through. But some part of me wanted to believe he was going to change." Her tears start to come out rapidly, but her voice remains controlled. So much different than before. I've never felt so proud. "And because I was clinging to a life that was long gone, I affected the two most important people. The only two people who mattered—my daughters. When your father died, I felt like a part of me died, too. But another part of me was also relieved he was gone, and I've felt so guilty over the years for that."

"You have no reason to feel guilty, because if we're being

completely honest right now, I also felt relieved when he passed away. It was like a huge burden was lifted. Even though I had to step in and take care of you and Amelia, I did it happily, because at least he wasn't here to harm us anymore," I confess, my voice barely above a whisper as I try my best to push down all of those emotions. While I'm proud of her for speaking up, I can't be showing those types of emotions in front of her. I need to be strong for her.

"I'm so sorry. I'm sorry you had to carry this burden for so long. But I will keep working on it, going to the doctor, and taking my medication. And eventually, maybe I can even work," she says hopefully.

I shake my head. "I will always take care of you. I never want you to worry."

"I want to, eventually. I want to leave this place," she says, barely above a whisper. "Living in this place, filled with so many bad memories, I want to let them go. Have a fresh start."

"God." I groan, leaning against the couch. "I never thought about that. I am such an idiot. I will find you a new place, okay?"

"No. You've done enough."

"Mom, you need to understand I will *always* do everything in my power to see you happy. I want to see you *live*. Because..." I inhale, holding back my tears. "When Dad was alive, you weren't living. You were surviving. We all were. So I need you to live now. For me, okay?" I whisper shakily.

After a beat of silence, she nods. "Okay."

We hug each other tightly, and as I'm letting go, she asks, "Can we talk about that boy now?"

I chuckle. "You really want to get it all out there today, huh?"

"Stop avoiding." She hits my shoulder playfully. "Do you love him?"

I start playing with my cuticles, avoiding her gaze. "Even if I did, I can't, Mom."

"But why? I've seen the way you look at him. I've never seen you smile like that. And the way he looks at you." She sighs, a wide smile playing on her lips. "That boy adores the ground you walk on. He loves you. I know it. Even if you guys are too blind to notice."

How do I explain to her that even if that were the case, it still wouldn't matter? I don't do love. I can't. I was supposed to be loved by my father, but we all know how that turned out. All my life I've sought validation, which is how I found Miles. I let him treat me like I didn't matter, but I never saw it clearly because I wanted the companionship. I wanted to be seen. I wanted the attention I never got from my father. I see it now, as clear as day, Miles wasn't good for me. He took advantage of my weaknesses.

Yes. But Lorenzo is not Miles, and he has proven that.

He's a protector. Fierce. Funny. Humble. True to himself. He doesn't make me feel like my weaknesses are a burden. If anything, he makes me feel like I'm capable of anything. In a self-destructive kind of way, I don't think I'm worthy of that. I'm stubborn. Can't process emotions correctly. And an overall complete mess. That's not what he needs. He deserves a woman who's the complete opposite. A woman who can love him wholeheartedly.

In a world full of boys, Lorenzo is a gentleman. The kind of man who seems almost fictional. The prince charming every children's book talks about. He's the guy who listens and makes you feel like you're the only person in the room. He's the guy who remembers small details. The kind of person who puts on your seatbelt to make sure you're secured. The kind of guy who remembers your dream and makes it a reality because he wants you to forget about your problems and live in the moment. He's the kind of guy who, when he smiles, it's warm and genuine. His actions speak louder than words, and when you're around him you feel... safe.

Lorenzo is the man you don't believe exists until you meet him.

"He's a wonderful man. Perfect, even. I just don't think —" I take a deep breath, gulping down the ball of emotion that's finding its way up. "It doesn't matter, Mom, okay? Please drop it."

She pulls me into an embrace, kissing the top of my head. "You deserve all he can offer you and more, honey. You deserve to be loved. Promise me you'll open yourself to it."

"I can't—"

She interrupts. "*Promise me*, Sophia."

I let out a long, tired sigh. "I promise," I murmur.

But I don't mean it.

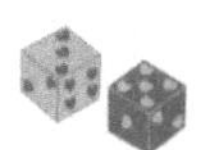

For our last day, Lorenzo decided to barbecue some steaks on the back patio. We even invited Bailey, per Mom's request. I'm glad to know she has someone she can rely on when I'm not here. It gives me peace to know I made the right decision to give her another chance.

"We forgot the sour cream for the mashed potatoes!" Mom exclaims, walking out on the patio.

As Lorenzo is flipping the steaks, he looks over his shoulder. "I can go get it when I'm done here."

Mom waves her hand dismissively. "Bailey can take me. You two love birds can stay here. Right, Bailey?" she asks, looking over her shoulder.

Bailey nods. "Of course."

"Mom, you don't have to. I can go."

She rolls her eyes, exasperated. "No. I enjoy going to the grocery store. We'll be back." She turns around with Bailey following after her before I can voice my complaints.

I approach Lorenzo and wrap my arms around him from behind. With him, I always crave his touch. It comes naturally to me. A million butterflies always take charge when I hug him and touch him, and I love every second of it.

He turns around, wrapping his arms around my waist and dropping a soft kiss on my lips. "Hi, *Blue*."

I smile brightly, lifting my chin so I can look at him. "Hi, *Ace*."

My eyes find his, and I get lost in those beautiful light-brown irises that are looking at me with so much adoration. And while it should make me happy, it only breaks my heart instead. We're more than halfway through the summer, and I'm still not ready to let go.

The sound of tires against gravel in front of the house catches my attention, taking me out of my trance. No way they're already back.

"Didn't they just leave?" Lorenzo asks, pulling the thought out of my brain.

I frown. "Yeah, let me go check. Maybe they forgot something."

I open the back door of the house and leave it open then walk to the front porch. My blood *boils* when I see who it is.

Amelia. And following her like a lost puppy is Miles.

I stride toward them furiously. "What the hell are you doing here?"

Amelia rolls her eyes like she has every right to be annoyed. "I'm really getting sick and tired of you acting like you own the world."

I laugh humorlessly. "Are you describing yourself? Take a look in the mirror. I think you've done enough, and I need you to leave before Mom returns."

"I'm not leaving. I have every right to talk to my mother." She squares her shoulders. "I need help, and you've made it crystal clear you're not willing to give it."

Oh, for the love of fucking God.

"You have no right to shit!" I yell, the emotions I've been bottling for years bubbling up. There's no taming this beast any longer. I've done it for long enough. "All you do is take and destroy, just like Dad!"

"Oh, and you're so much better with your big city job and your big billionaire city *boyfriend*?" she retorts, crossing her arms. "You're a *nobody*, Sophia. An unloved, attention whore that loves to control others. He'll get tired of you in no time. You're incapable of being loved, I think we've proven that already."

For the first time in my life, I see red. My pulse pounds in my ears, every beat sending a rush of heat straight to my head. My hand moves on instinct before my mind can catch up, and the next thing I know, my palm connects with her cheek with a sharp, unforgiving slap. The sting radiates through my fingers, and the sound of it echoes in the tense air between us. A suffocating silence follows, but the throb in my hand keeps pulsing. I ball my fist as tightly as I can, trying to stop the shaking that's overtaking my body.

I've never lost my cool with Amelia like that. But I'm so fucking frustrated. Hearing her say those things, the same thoughts I think about myself more often than not. I *am* unlovable. My scars are too many to count. My heart refuses to be beaten again, and that's what, at the end of the day, makes me incapable of being loved. But she should be the last one to look down on me and judge.

Miles gets between us, pushing me. "What the fuck, Sophia!?" he yells, getting in my face.

"I suggest you take a step back," Lorenzo's icy and sharp deep voice cuts through Miles's yelling.

And even in the warm summer daylight, it feels as if my surroundings drop a few degrees. Shivers run down my spine as Lorenzo eats the distance between us with menacing strides. The air is charged with a strange, dangerous electricity as Lorenzo's hands find my waist, gripping my hips possessively as he gently pushes me behind him.

"Control your bitch, because she hit my girlfriend!" Miles spits, getting in Lorenzo's face.

Before Miles can utter another word, Lorenzo's fist flies hard and fast, connecting with his jaw. Mile's head jerks back with the impact as blood starts rushing out of his mouth.

Before he can recover, Lorenzo grabs him by the collar of his shirt, shaking him like a rag doll. "You really need to learn when to shut the fuck up," he says through gritted teeth, his fist meeting his face again. "But don't worry, I'm more than happy to give you a lesson."

I reach for his shoulder, trying to ease the tension. "Lorenzo, forget it. It's not worth it."

His eyes snap to mine, wild and unforgiving, with a simmering anger that rattles every bone on my body. "Stay back," he orders gruffly. After a beat, his eyes soften, scanning my whole face. "Please."

I raise my hands in surrender and nod, taking a step back. My stubborn self, who loves to be proud and prove to the world she doesn't need anyone to take care of her, is nowhere to be found. For once, I want to rely on someone, and there's no one better than him.

He snaps his head back to Miles, his tone unwavering. "This is for calling her a bitch." His fist connects with his stomach. "This is for not knowing your place." His knee connects with his groin. "And this is for cheating on the most wonderful woman in the world and making her feel like she's worth nothing when we both know the only piece of shit here is *you*." He finishes, his fist connecting with his face one last time, right on the nose, landing with a loud crack. He pushes Miles, letting him fall to the ground.

Miles lets out a pained groan, blood dripping down his nose as he tries to control it with his ragged shirt. I can hear Amelia yelling at the top of her lungs, but I'm in a trance. Having an out-of-body experience as everything unfolds before me.

"You're going to pay for this, mark my fucking words!" Amelia yells, trying to push Lorenzo, but his towering build makes it impossible for her to do any sort of damage.

I step closer to her, ready to unleash my frustration all over again, but more than anything, I want to settle this before Mom returns. "You need to leave, Amelia. I don't want you to show your face ever again. Consider me and Mom dead. I'm done cleaning up your messes. I'm done doing favors for you when all you've done is take advantage of my kindness." My tears of anger start to come out, and even though I hate every second of it, I can't make them stop. "I will always love you because you're my sister, but you've done enough damage. Go live your life, and we'll live ours. Please," I say through a resigned sigh.

She gapes at me, fury flashing in her eyes. *Funny.* I thought she was incapable of feeling anything. "You think you're so much better than me, don't you?" she spits, her nostrils flaring. "You and I come from the same fucked up background, Sophia, so wake the *fuck* up." She flashes me a smile that is straight up *diabolical.* "Before you keep looking down at me, get off your high horse and realize that this"—she points between me and Lorenzo—"will be over in no time. He'll get tired of you, because no one wants to love someone like you." She sneers, that diabolical grin still playing on her lips as her words gut me, knifing my already beaten heart. "Good luck with your miserable life, sister, because you're going to need it." She grabs Miles's hand and drags him to their car and they both *finally* leave.

As soon as their car is out of view, I drop to my knees, my chest tightening as I struggle to breathe through my tears. Lorenzo drops next to me and brings me in for a hug.

He kisses my forehead and brushes my hair with his strong, big hands over and over again in a soothing motion. "You're okay, baby. You're okay. I'm here." His voice is soft and reassuring.

When I finally calm down, I whisper, "Lorenzo, you can't tell Mom what happened."

"Sophia," he says through a pained groan. "You can't keep pretending everything is fine."

My gaze snaps to his. "*Promise me.*" It's all I manage to say. I need him to understand how important this is. I want him to understand where I'm coming from, but the words just get stuck, refusing to come out.

He rubs the back of his neck, his lips twitching in doubt. "If that's what you want."

I rise from the ground, brushing the dust from my knees.

"Thank you," is all I say before turning around and walking back inside the house.

The rest of the night goes like normal. I put on my fakest smile and I laugh like everything is perfectly fine, even though the cracks of my heart are barely hanging on. And I take in every moment I can with my mom before I have to get back to reality and deal with the rest of my shitty life.

Sophia

"**S**pill the beans," Aria says, crossing her legs underneath her and taking a sip of the margaritas we just made.

I start speaking fast, wanting nothing more than to get this off my chest. "Lorenzo and I are fuck buddies. It was my idea, not his. I don't know what the fuck I was thinking. Well, yes, I do. I was thinking, *hey, wouldn't it be nice to have fun this summer?* But I think... I think I like Lorenzo now. And I don't know what to do with that information." I inhale, trying to catch my breath. "Who am I kidding? There's nothing I can do. I think we've established I don't do well with relationships."

Aria and Isabella look at me expectantly, not saying a word. I reach for my margarita that has been sitting on the coffee table, waking Isabella's dog Marley in the process, since she's been sleeping in my lap. There's an unspoken agreement that when we're hanging out at my place, Isabella must bring Marley. She's the sweetest black lab, and I love cuddling with her. I drink the whole cup in one sitting, waiting for them to say something.

"Have you talked to him about it?" Isabella asks.

I shake my head. "I think we both sort of felt how the vibe changed when he went with me to Kentucky."

"And how did that go?" Aria asks softly. She knows enough about my family and all my problems, and she knows how much I hate sharing that part of my life.

"He dropped *everything* to be there with me. He made my mom *laugh*, Aria. She loved him." I gulp, scratching my neck. This conversation makes me so uncomfortable, but I need some help. I'm desperate. "He defended my honor with Miles. He cooked and talked with my mom, they got along so well." I sigh. "He was the perfect gentleman. And the perfect person for me to rely on. He was there, no questions asked. He's *been* there this whole time."

"And how does that make you feel?" Isabella asks, crossing her legs and zeroing her green eyes on me.

"Scared," I admit. Because even though Lorenzo has brought so much out of me, and he makes me feel strong despite all of my weaknesses, it doesn't make it any less unsettling.

"Sophia," Aria whispers, standing from her seat and settling next to me, grasping my hand. "You can't feel like this forever. You can't seriously believe every man out there is going to do the same thing Miles did to you."

My eyes brim with tears, and I'm trying my best to hold them back, but I'm so tired of being fake around people, I finally let one fall.

It's so much more than that. I've never known what true love, from a man, looks like. Everything around me is tainted. What if letting myself love him becomes another path to pain? What if he breaks my heart, too?

Who are you even kidding? Even if you walk away now,

you'll still get heartbroken, because you already fell in love with him.

I don't want to regret him. Us. All the fun we've had this summer. I want to end this amicably so when I look back twenty or thirty years from now, I can remember how the most wonderful man made me feel.

"You need to open yourself to love. You're a wonderful girl who deserves the world. And if Lorenzo is willing to give it to you, why not let him?" Aria asks softly.

"I'm a mess, guys." There's no turning back now, it's time for me to be honest with my best friends. "I'm all too aware I don't process emotions well. I'm stubborn. Annoying. Loud. But all of that is something I do to keep people at arm's length. To make everyone believe I'm happy when I'm not. I'm far from happy."

Isabella stands from her seat, taking the other side and grasping my other hand. "You are stubborn, yes, we won't deny it, but you're an amazing woman, Sophia. You're always there for all of us. And even though you think you don't deserve to be loved and cared for, the way you care for all of us is amazing. How long have you felt like this? Why didn't you come to us? We are your best friends. We're here for you, through thick and thin."

"I've always felt like this," I confess, and when I look at Aria, her shoulders are deflated, her eyes welling with emotion. The look on her face guts me. "But I've always been good at masking. I didn't—*don't*—want to depend on people. Emotions are...a weakness for me."

Aria lets out a long sigh, taking a moment before replying. "Emotions don't make you weak. I'm sorry I never noticed. God, I feel like the shittiest friend."

I sniff, shaking my head. "God, no. You had your own problems, Aria. You're not a shitty friend. I just wanted to open up. If anyone deserves my honesty for once, it's you, guys."

"What about Lorenzo? Don't you think he deserves to know how you feel about him?" Isabella asks, ever the voice of reason.

Her question makes me question every moment between us. All our time in Panamá, where after he kept his promise and made me feel good, I disappeared on him like a coward, and instead of making me feel like shit about it, he sought me out to give me the experience of a lifetime. Because that's Lorenzo Mancini for you—thoughtful, kind, and selfless. He saw how lost I felt, and with his actions, he showed me how much he cared, and how much he was willing to help me.

He absolutely deserves to know how I feel about him, I just need to figure out how I will be brave enough to tell him.

39

Lorenzo

"Where the hell have you been?" Ivy asks as a way of greeting me as soon as I step into Vortex's main bar on the first floor, where she typically works as a bartender.

"Well, hello to you, too." I smirk, taking a seat at the bar.

Without a word, she grabs a glass of whiskey, but before she pours it, I say, "No. Just water, please."

Her eyes bulge, but she doesn't say anything and serves me a cup of water instead. Ever since I've been hanging around Sophia, the craving to drink my usual whiskey has been less and less. The thought is unsettling. I'm self-aware and know the only reason I used to drink so much was because I wanted to numb those crawly feelings that would eat me alive. Sophia, though, has given me more than enough reasons to be in the moment and...feel.

Yup. There's no denying anymore that what I feel for Sophia is more than a simple attraction. I'm way over my head, and I need help. My mind is a mumbling mess about this whole situation, so I have no other option than to talk to the people who know me best. And despite them loving to fuck with me, I know they can tread this situation carefully and help me figure out what the hell is happening to me.

"Hello, sweetheart," Matteo says to Ivy as he takes a seat next to me. He's such a shameless flirt, you'd never guess he's pining for a certain ray of—*not*—sunshine.

"Well, hello there. Aren't you all smiles today?" Ivy raises an eyebrow.

He shrugs. "You know me."

Damian grunts, taking the other seat next to me. "I don't know how you always manage to be shitting rainbows and rays of sunshine. You exhaust me."

Ivy rolls her lips, holding back a laugh. "Always lovely to see you, Damian."

He nods without saying a word. Most people think Damian hates everyone, but the guy can be decent when he wants to.

I silently take in their exchange, until Damian's eyes find mine. "You've been so cryptic about why you wanted to meet with us. What the hell is wrong? Are you in trouble?" he asks gruffly.

Matteo tilts his head, squinting his eyes at me as well. "You look different."

Ivy nods. "I agree."

I roll my eyes. "The fuck does that mean?"

"You look more relaxed," Matteo points out, his eyes dancing with mischief. "Have any fun in Panamá?"

"Forget about that," Damian says dryly. "I'm more interested to know why you were in Kentucky with Sophia. I thought we had a very insightful conversation not that long ago." He shoots me a withering glare. "Or did you forget already?"

Ivy lets out a small gasp. "You've been hanging out with Sophia?"

"Oh, yeah. Didn't he tell you? She has been working on an article about him, and they've been spending some time together," Matteo quips.

"Damn, you've been keeping this from me." Ivy hits my shoulder. "That's rude."

"How do you know when you're in love?" I blurt, interrupting them. Might as well get it out of the way.

They snap their heads my way, gaping at me, all of them at a loss for words.

"We have to backtrack here, because I'm confused," Ivy says, dropping her elbows on the bar and resting her chin on the palm of her hands. "And *very* intrigued."

I fist my hair in frustration. "Okay, long story short. Me and Sophia have grown rather *close* this summer. She suggested we make a deal, a friends-with-benefits thing. I accepted because, to be honest, I couldn't get her out of my head. I thought this was the perfect way for us to have fun this summer while working closely together. Except now, I have all these feelings I can't explain."

Matteo snickers, and I glare at him. "I'm getting real sick and tired of you always laughing at my problems."

Damian hits the back of my head, and I hiss, "Motherf—"

He interrupts. "Qual è il problema con te?[1]"

"Well, right now I'm in pain thanks to you," I hiss, rubbing the back of my head.

"I told you to not play games with her. I could kill you right now," Damian snaps, nostrils flaring.

Ivy cuts in, her voice soft. "Hey, hey, guys. Let's calm down now. Let's hear him out first."

---

1. What is the matter with you?

Damian thins his lips, giving me a clipped nod to continue.

I let out a long sigh, mulling over my words. "Everything changed...somehow. The more I understood her, the more I wanted to be there for her—to protect her, to be the shoulder she could lean on." I shake my head, feeling more out of my comfort zone than ever before. "When she walks into a room, my heart aches for her. When someone hurts her? I want to burn the whole fucking world. Not being near her at all times kills me. I miss her so much right now, it hurts to fucking breathe. It's hard to explain," I finish, exasperated and looking at everything except them. This was a mistake. What the hell was I thinking?

This crawly feeling is not getting better as time passes. If anything, it keeps getting worse. We've been back from Kentucky for almost two weeks, and we haven't seen each other much due to our busy schedules. I ended up having some electrical issues with the restaurant in Panamá, so I had to set everything back. Sophia has been slammed with work, which is nothing new. I don't understand how she does it all. The article, at this point, is in the back of our minds. I don't know what she has planned, and I'm afraid to find out.

"Wow," Ivy begins. "When did everything change?"

"When I dropped everything for her and flew with her to Kentucky to take care of her mom," I reply without a second thought. "But if I'm being honest, since the day I laid my eyes on her again. There was something about her that called to me, guys. As if the universe was telling me *this is your sign, take it.*"

"Do you love her?" Matteo asks.

I run my fingers through my hair, shrugging half-heartedly. "I don't know."

Ivy nods, her fingers tapping against the table. "When is this deal of yours supposed to end?"

"Tomorrow." I look at Damian, finding his face enigmatic. Not an emotion in sight. "We agreed we would end this before going to Las Vegas."

"And will you be okay with just walking away and letting her, I don't know, meet someone else and fall in love?" Matteo asks, his tone probing.

"She will be in your life forever. I'm marrying her best friend," Damian chimes in, tone deadly serious. "Will you ever be okay seeing her with another man?"

My heart beats erratically at the thought. Jealousy claws at my heart, refusing to let go. "Fuck no," I spit, gripping the glass of water so hard, my knuckles are going white.

"Then what are you going to do about it?" Matteo presses.

"I don't deserve her," I whisper more to myself than them. "How can I love such a wonderful woman, when I don't even know—"

"Cut the bullshit, Lorenzo," Ivy interrupts, her voice serious. She grabs my hand and squeezes it. "I'm so sick of hearing this *I don't know how to love* speech. You're a wonderful man with a great heart. Or did you forget everything you've done for me?" She gives me a pointed look.

"You're one of my best friends, it was the right thing to do," I reply easily.

"You are unselfish and kind, always caring about others. You *do* know how to love, and you *do* deserve to be loved. It doesn't matter how your upbringing was. That doesn't define you," Ivy urges. "It doesn't matter that you didn't grow up with a mom or that your dad was a manipulative asshole. Because despite all of that, you've become someone you should be proud of."

I scoff at that. How can I be proud of myself? I feel like every day of my life I'm being drowned by the expectations my father left me. But no one knows that. No one *except* Sophia. That's how much trust I have for her.

"I agree with her, man," Matteo adds. "We've barely seen you this summer, but you look different. There's a different light in you, and I think it has everything to do with the woman you're trying to deny you love."

They both look at Damian. Ivy bulges her eyes and tilts her head my way, as if saying, *Aren't you going to say something?*

Damian lets out a long sigh, his hand reaching out and gripping my shoulder. "I know how you feel. When Aria walked into my life, I never thought I would end up here. You know more than everyone what I went through, and how unattached I became when it came to...feelings."

He's right. I witnessed firsthand how much of an asshole his father was. I never liked the man. I never understood what my aunt ever saw in that man. I witnessed how Damian changed after being belittled by his father. But I was also thankful to be a witness to how Aria changed him for the better. How love changed him for the better.

Maybe, just maybe, it could change me, too.

"And I believe you," Damian whispers roughly. "The way you talk about her, I see it in your eyes. You love her, Enzo. The way you feel? The overprotectiveness that is taking over you? That's exactly how I realized I fell in love with Aria. There's nothing I wouldn't do for that woman. You punched the fuck out of her shitty ex, for God's sake. Which"—he snorts a laugh—"I'm proud of you for that. It was long overdue."

My eye twitches involuntarily at the mention of that fucker. It's hard for me to believe such a wonderful, strong, and confident woman like Sophia was ever with that sorry ass of a man.

"How do you know about that?" I frown.

He rolls his eyes. "You forget Sophia and Aria are practically sisters. She told her all about it."

"Did she say anything else?" My tone is hopeful. I know I sound like a pathetic fool, but the curiosity is killing me.

He thins his lips, shaking his head. "I already said too much."

I simply nod, because he's right. Anything Aria has told him was in confidence. The last thing I want to do is cause issues between them.

"You're in love, Enzo. This is *good*." Ivy pats my hand twice.

I shake my head. "You guys don't understand. Even if I did, I don't know how to show her. She..." I sigh, mulling over my words. Wondering how much I want to share. All the time I've spent with Sophia has given me an idea of how she works. "She's a closed book. Doesn't open up. I don't know how to show her we could be more."

"It's simple. You need to show her with actions, not words," Ivy replies. "You need to show her why you're the man for her and why you're perfect for each other."

"And you need to be honest," Damian adds. "Do not be like me. I lied my way through so much, I almost lost Aria for good."

I nod, remembering how Damian almost took the blame for something he didn't do. He was willing to lose everything for the woman he loves. He just went the wrong way about it. Instead of being honest, he tried to shoulder all the responsibility.

Matteo speaks now, his voice is soft, eyes lost in thought. "If she's important to you, you need to be there for her. Fight for her. You will regret it if you don't." He shakes his head, his eyes focusing on me. "That much I can promise you."

"What if I scare her off?" I ask. Her walking away from me is my biggest fear. I think that's why I've been putting off telling her how I feel. But I can't keep pretending I don't want more.

Ivy shrugs. "If she feels the same way, she may be scared, sure. But she'll open herself to it."

I don't know if my heart can take her not feeling the same way. The logical part of me is telling me she does feel the same. This is not one-sided. But what if, despite how she feels, she refuses to give us a chance?

"Damn, Ivy. When did you become a love coach?" Matteo asks.

"You idiots wouldn't know what love is even if it hit you in the face. Someone has to step in and be the voice of reason."

"Care to help me?" Matteo begs, clasping his hands together.

She laughs. "Of course. Lay it on me."

Me and Damian snort at that.

"Good luck with *that*," I say.

"The girl he's pining for couldn't hate him more—it's humanly *impossible*," Damian adds.

Matteo glares at both of us, hissing, "*Shut up*."

"People do say there's a fine line between love and hate," Ivy pipes up.

"Does that mean I have a chance with you?" Julian says, appearing out of nowhere.

"Where the fuck did you come from?" I frown.

"He's always here when I work." Ivy rolls her eyes.

"Dude." Matteo barks a laugh. "That's borderline creepy."

Damian shrugs. "I think it's endearing."

"Says the guy who stalked his now fiancée," I mutter, shaking my head in disbelief.

Julian shoots Matteo an annoyed glare. "Can't I hang out with my favorite girl?"

If I didn't know any better, I would think Ivy's cheeks are blushing. "You're an idiot, Julian. Déjame en paz[2]."

"I'll wear you down one day," he replies confidently, winking at her.

"In your dreams, pretty boy. I don't date Puerto Ricans."

Matteo tilts his head, confused. "Aren't *you* Puerto Rican, though?"

Ivy gives Matteo an exasperated look. "Exactly."

"You wound me," Julian says with an exaggerated sigh, rubbing his chest in circles.

"I have a feeling after you find your flavor of the night you'll be *just* fine." She makes a shooing motion. "Now, leave me alone."

He thins his lips and shakes his head, walking away.

"That guy has it bad for you," Matteo points out.

She shakes her head. "He just wants what he can't have."

I nod. "I agree. I consider him a friend, but that guy is a mess. Don't fall for it, Ivy."

Matteo gives me an incredulous look. "If you could change, why can't he?"

"Enzo has always been a good man. Julian is an overgrown child, end of story," Ivy snaps, her tone serious.

We all share a look as Ivy busies herself cleaning some whiskey glasses. Ivy tells me everything, but there's something I must be missing here. It's rare to see her losing her cool.

---

2. Leave me alone.

"What are you going to do about Sophia?" Matteo asks.

I scrub my face with my left hand, pondering. "I just need to keep showing up for her."

Damian gives me an approving nod. Knowing him, that's the most I'm going to get out of him.

"Attaboy," Ivy squeaks. "You got this."

I'm a determined motherfucker, and I'm ready to make the ultimate play—make Sophia Evans, the girl of my dreams, give us a chance.

40

Sophia

LORENZO

How you doin'?

ME

We really have to stop with the Friends references. Do we not know any other shows?

LORENZO

I won't have you disrespect my favorite show like that.

ME

It's my favorite show too! How cool is that? 😊

LORENZO

So what you're saying is we're having a Friends marathon tonight?

ME

I could be convinced…

LORENZO

I will pick you up at your office.

ME

I haven't said yes.

LORENZO

You're acting as if you don't miss me.

ME

I don't. 🙄

LORENZO

You're cute when you lie. But that's fine. I won't be taking no for an answer because I miss you. See? I can accept it.

LORENZO

I'll pick you up at 5, Blue. 😉

I stare at my phone screen with a blank expression.

Where the hell did that come from?

The thought of spending time with Lorenzo after everything that's happened sets a million butterflies loose in my stomach. And the looming realization we're going to Las Vegas tomorrow makes me queasy, to say the least. The truth is, I've missed him. A lot. But I also know we're supposed to break it off when that's far from what I want, and I don't know how to deal with that fact.

Max strides into my cubicle, making himself at home as he perches on the edge of my desk, crossing one ankle over his knee. "Are my eyes deceiving me? I can't believe you're here."

I keep the eye roll I want to throw him in check. "Yeah, sorry about that. Had a family emergency."

"I don't care." He rolls his eyes. "Tell me, how's the article going? And the gossip column?"

I look around, and the office is pretty empty. This is my chance to tell him the truth.

"The article is almost done, only needs some editing,

which I'm currently working on, but the gossip column...not so much. I can't write something like that, Max. It's not my style, and you know it." I lift my chin slightly, keeping my voice as even as possible. I won't back down. Not on this.

"Let's go to my office to talk some more," he grits out, tilting his head.

Once we enter and he shuts his door, his real colors show, as always. "I don't give a fuck if it's your style or not, Sophia. You get paid to write. Are you incapable of following simple instructions?"

Something inside me snaps as I hear the words come out of his mouth. Anger. Annoyance. But overall, I'm *fed up*. I'm tired of being the good little Sophia who lets people eat away at the kindness of my heart. With everything that went down with Amelia, a huge weight has been lifted off my shoulders.

I'm done being pushed around.

"It's funny you say that. Because you get paid to be editor in chief, and yet, I do all the work for you."

His face turns bright red, his eyes bulging in shock. "What did you just say?" He stalks toward me, eating the distance between us. He's a tall man, sure. Not as tall as Lorenzo, though, and honestly, it doesn't intimidate me in the least.

"I'm tired of playing your puppet, Max. I'm not writing the gossip column, and I'm done doing your job."

"I will make your life a living hell if you don't comply."

"I would love to see you try," I reply in defiance. "The emails are there. All the evidence that you've been dumping the work on my lap for years. I wonder how the VP will react if she ever finds out?"

Taking a stand after being taken advantage of for so long feels like a fever dream. My heart is beating like crazy, knowing this confrontation will probably bring horrible consequences. But I can make it work, I always do. Even if he decides to fire me right now, I can pack up my things and move back to Kentucky, get a two-bedroom apartment, and live with Mom. Get a waitressing job, or anything to survive in the meantime. Everything is cheaper in Kentucky, anyway.

Why is the thought of moving to Kentucky so depressing, then?

My life is here. My friends. *Lorenzo.* The idea of walking away from him kills me. My heart aches at the thought.

Max's nose flares in annoyance as he holds my gaze, but I don't quiver. "Very well. You better bring the article of the lifetime, Sophia. Otherwise, you won't like the consequences."

That's it? He's not going to fire me?

This is a win. Take it and run away!

Something's not right. Out of all the scenarios I've cooked in my head, this wasn't one of them.

Don't overthink it.

I simply nod and walk away, feeling more confident than ever.

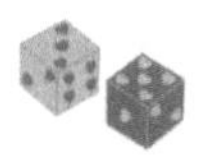

Lorenzo's article is done.

A sense of relief washes through me as I stare at the completed work. The first thing I'll do tonight is show it to him. If he hates it, I'll have to figure something else out. But

I think I did good. I feel good about it, and my gut is rarely wrong when it comes to this sort of thing.

As I'm printing the article to give a physical copy to Lorenzo, I hear the door of the office open and steps getting closer to me. The hair on the back of my neck prickles in anticipation, and I don't need to turn around to know who it is. Lorenzo has such a specific, commanding presence that can take the air out of my lungs and make my skin fill with goosebumps with his proximity. I turn around and find Lorenzo leaning against the wall, arms casually behind him, dressed in black pants and a burgundy short-sleeve knit top that shows off most of his ink. I've never been drawn to tattoos before, but that's only because I've never seen someone like Lorenzo wear them the way he does. I can't picture him without them—they suit him perfectly. The small golden chain I love to tug sits around his neck, gleaming against the fabric of his shirt. When my eyes meet his, the intensity of his gaze—hungry and electrifying—makes my thighs clench with need.

"Hi, Blue," he rasps, a small but killer smile playing on his lips.

I swallow hard, trying to find words. "Hi, Ace."

He closes the small gap between us, arms still tucked behind his back. When he stands in front of me, a small bouquet of purple Madagascar periwinkles appears between us—the same flowers that decorated the villa in Panamá. The same flower he tucked behind my ear that night.

I look up, tilting my head. "For me?"

"Of course," he answers simply.

Before I can take them off his hands, he stops me and reaches for a flower, plucking it carefully. Just like last time, his hand tucks a piece of hair behind my ear and places the flower there.

"God, you're beautiful," he whispers gravelly.

I swallow hard, trying to drown the way my cheeks heat. "Thank you. I love them."

He nods, giving me a sheepish smile before asking. "You ready?"

I nod, grabbing my purse and dropping the article inside. I almost grab the laptop out of habit, and I hesitate for a moment, but I keep true to my word and leave it. It's sort of a surreal, proud moment. Knowing I'm putting myself first for once, forgetting about work and actually enjoying life. As we walk out to take the elevator, my shoulders tense as I see none other than Max waiting for the elevator, too.

"Oh, Lorenzo, long time no see, man," Max says.

The elevator door opens, and we walk in.

"Max." Lorenzo gives a curt nod, his voice sharp and to the point.

Max frowns at Lorenzo's tone, his eyes finally landing on me, like he's now noticed I've been standing here the whole time.

Shit.

Vogue Elite doesn't have any hard rules against fraternizing with the people we're writing about. It's all too vague to enforce, considering the range of stories we cover. But Max isn't the type to care about rules anyway. I can almost see the gears turning in his head, plotting how to use this situation against me. After all, I threatened his job, and if there's one thing I know about working for a misogynistic asshole like him, it's that he's proud to his very core.

Stop overthinking. Nothing has happened.

"I hope Sophia has been nice to work with," Max says with a smug, knowing grin.

"She has," Lorenzo replies, his face enigmatic.

"I bet," Max murmurs, shaking his head slightly. "Have a good night, Lorenzo." His gaze shifts to me, his tone pointed. "Sophia, don't forget to turn in the article on Monday." As the elevator doors slide open, he steps out without another word, leaving a tight knot of tension twisting in the pit of my stomach.

"The article is ready?" Lorenzo asks.

I nod. "I was going to talk to you about it tonight." I pat my purse. "I have a physical copy for you to read and get your approval. It doesn't come out until the end of next month."

He shakes his head. "You don't need my approval. I trust you."

My eyes find his in shock. "Are you sure?"

He nods, a soft smile playing on his lips as he drapes his arm over my shoulder, pulling me close. "Now, come on," he says, guiding us toward the exit, "we've got a *Friends* marathon to start."

I offer him a simple smile, though inside my thoughts are racing. Knowing I've earned Lorenzo's trust makes my heart tighten. If this summer has taught me anything, it's that he keeps his walls up for a reason. He doesn't trust easily. And the fact he's let me in—deemed me worthy—fills me with a strange sense of pride.

You have to tell him how you feel. Before everything goes up in flames.

I have no other option but to tell him tonight, because tomorrow we're supposed to go to Vegas, and I'm far from done.

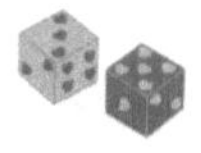

We've managed to watch one whole season of *Friends*. It doesn't matter how many times I watch this show; the jokes will never get old. My belly hurts from all the laughter, and we've been competing to see who can quote more—and fortunately for me, I'm winning. I changed into one of Lorenzo's dress shirts that practically fit me like a dress, and he changed into a white shirt and a pair of gray sweatpants that leave nothing to the imagination.

Damn gray sweatpants. They are every woman's undoing.

It's been a chill night. We ordered a ridiculous amount of food and snacks, and we're currently washing it all down with some boba tea only because I was craving some. It's one of the best nights I have had in a while, and for once, I feel some sort of normalcy. Something I could get used to, *only* with him.

"Try my boba," I say, shoving the drink in his face.

He pushes both my hand and the cup away. "No."

"Why not?" I pout.

"Because brown sugar boba sounds like it's going to be obnoxiously sweet."

"Exactly. It's amazing." I give his arm a playful smack. "Come on, one sip. For me?" I persist, bringing the drink back toward him.

He rolls his eyes but leans forward, wrapping his mouth around the straw. The second the taste hits, he grimaces, shaking his head as he pushes the cup away again. "God, that's even worse than I imagined."

I roll my eyes. "Okay. Mr. Black Tea With No Sugar. That one does sound disgusting."

"Hey!" He laughs. "I'm a simple guy. Leave me alone."

Before I can reply, thunder rumbles in the distance. I glance over my shoulder, watching as flash after flash illuminates the city skyline in shades of purple. The rain starts sprinkling, lightly at first, but true to Chicago summers, it starts to pour in no time.

Lorenzo's condo is nothing short of luxurious. We're in the living room, sprawled across a massive sectional couch that's big enough to sleep on. Behind me, floor-to-ceiling windows stretch across the wall, offering a perfect view of the rainy city. The muffled sound of rain drowns out the noise from the TV, the laughter that follows another one of Chandler Bing's jokes fading into the background.

I stand, making my way to the window, and press my fingertips against the cool glass as I watch the raindrops race down. There's something so peaceful about it, like the storm outside is washing away all the chaos of the day. I sense Lorenzo's presence approaching, and we both stand there, quiet, enjoying the view.

Breaking the silence, I say, "I used to love dancing and playing in the rain when I was a kid." I close my eyes, a bittersweet smile tugging at my lips as I recall the few good memories of my childhood.

Amelia loved it, too. We used to beg Mom to let us play outside, and she'd always give in, despite the inevitable outcome—one of us getting sick. But it was worth it, every time. It's a shame, knowing that's the same sister who I had to cut out of my life. She will always have a space in my heart, but I can't say I regret my decision.

Lorenzo's hand slips into mine, his fingers lacing with mine as he gently pulls me away from the window. His touch is like a lifeline, something I've grown dependent on —something that feels like home.

"Where are we going?"

He glances back at me with a knowing smile. "You'll see."

We climb the stairs and keep walking until we find another smaller set. At the top, he opens a door that leads us to a rooftop. Soft, twinkling lights are strung around, casting a warm, golden glow that blends beautifully with the cool, misty rain. Some cushioned chairs circle a bonfire pit. The view is the best part of it all, though. Simply breathtaking. The entire Chicago skyline stretches out before us, towers and skyscrapers glowing beneath the stormy sky. Thousands of lights flicker in the rain, each one a reminder of the city's restless energy.

Lorenzo pulls out his phone, and "Hunger" by Ross Copperman begins playing through hidden speakers, catching me by surprise.

"What are you doing?" I ask, laughter bubbling out of me.

He grabs my hand, leading me to the center of the rooftop. The rain starts falling harder, droplets running down my hair and skin. I close my eyes, savoring the cool sensation as goosebumps spread over my body.

"Let's dance," he says, his voice low.

My eyes snap open as I raise an eyebrow. "Are you serious?"

He rolls his eyes, yanking me into him. I yelp as he barks a laugh that makes my stomach drop with butterflies. He wraps one arm around my waist, pulling me closer. My left arm circles his neck, and I rest my right hand on his chest, feeling the quick rhythm of his heartbeat beneath my palm.

"Dead serious," he whispers with a bright smile that tears down whatever was left of my walls.

As the music plays on and we sway together, my gaze locks with his, and it's like the universe is teasing me. Every feeling I've tried so hard to bury rises to the surface until I'm left raw and vulnerable in his arms, unable to ignore how much he truly means to me.

The rain falls steadily, each drop cool and refreshing against my skin, but none of it compares to the warmth I feel when I look at him. I watch his face as he spins me, the joy in his eyes, and I remember how easily he makes me laugh, and how free he makes me feel. Every moment around him makes everything else disappear. It's like the world has narrowed down to just him and me.

I don't want it to stop.

I don't want *us* to stop.

After everything, I was so convinced love and I were done. But then there's...*him*. A man who's not asking for my heart. No. He's earning it, bit by bit, with every kind word, every smile, and every time he makes me feel strong. Safe. *Taken care of.*

And it hits me, right here as we dance under the rain, how far I've fallen for him, to the point of no return. If he asked me to give us a chance right now, I'd say yes in a heartbeat. Because even though I've been hurt before, he's shown me that maybe, just maybe, it's worth letting myself be loved again. And maybe, after all that running, loving him is a risk I'm willing to take. Because he's worth it all.

The song finishes, but we keep moving slowly in circles, not breaking eye contact. The world dulls around me, and I see nothing but him as his lips meet mine in a soft kiss. We kiss like we have all the time in the world. It's not our usual passionate, desperate kisses. It's...sweet. Exploratory. In that kiss, every hidden feeling surfaces, making my heart take flight.

His forehead meets mine, and in one breathless sigh, he says, "I can't do this anymore."

My body goes rigid as he keeps dancing. I can't move. Have I read this all wrong? Of course, I did. Why was I expecting anything different?

I take a step back, but he doesn't let go of my hand. "Is this why you wanted me to come over today? Some sort of goodbye thing?" I force a laugh, placing a hand on my stomach as I try to calm my breathing. "If so, it wasn't necessary. I know this was another game for you." I'm babbling now, and I'm trying my best to shut up, but if I stop talking, I'll start crying instead. "Hell, maybe it was for me, too. A fun game. Yeah. A really fun game."

He grips my hand, frowning. "What are you talking about?"

"You. Me. *Us.* Whatever this was, it's over now. Got the message, loud and clear." I pull out of his grip and hug myself. Having this conversation under the rain is probably not the best idea, because now I'm shaking.

He takes a step forward. "You didn't let me finish."

I take a step back. "You don't need to finish. I understand. We were supposed to break it off before going to Vegas. You did the right thing."

"Blue—"

I shake my head, my voice barely a whisper. "Don't." My chest tightens, and I hate myself for not being able to hold back the sadness gripping it like a vise. I look up as a flash of lightning splits the sky, illuminating the rain as it pours down around us. With a sigh, I turn around and start walking away.

At least it was nice while it lasted.

Lorenzo is quick to eat the distance between us and stand in front of me, gripping my shoulders. "*Sophia.*"

My name rolling off his lips makes me stop, because he *never* says my name. It always catches me off-guard when he does. He takes this opportunity to grip my chin, forcing me to look at him. Droplets of rain fall from his hair, and even with how disheveled he looks, clothes hugging his frame and hair sticking to his forehead, he still manages to look painfully handsome. And I can't take it. I can't take looking at him any longer. So I don't. Even as he tries to get me to look at him, I keep doing my best to avoid his gaze.

He sighs, dropping his hand and stepping back. "If you'd let me finish, I would've told you I'm head over heels for you."

My eyes snap to his, searching for any sign of humor, but there's none. His jaw is clenched, shoulders stiff, his expression dead serious.

"*Goddamn it, Blue.*" He gestures between us. "I can't keep pretending this is all I want from you." He fists his hair, tilting his head back, his Adam's apple bobbing as he struggles for the right words.

I let out a small gasp at this confession. "Lorenzo—"

He interrupts me. "I know I'm not worthy of you. God, you're so far out of my league it's comical." He laughs, but it doesn't reach his eyes. He grips the nape of my neck with both of his hands. I look up, locking our gaze. His eyes are wild now, and his chest is heaving rapidly. "Be mine, Sophia. And I will work every goddamn day to be worthy of you. Let me prove to you I can be the man you need. Let me look after you. Please." His voice breaks at the end. "Be mine," he repeats.

Little does he know, he has nothing to prove. I'm the one who feels like I'm not worthy of all he has to offer me.

Because without any attachments, he has offered me the world. I've always been his. I don't think there was ever any question.

"What about our deal?" I ask breathlessly, barely above a whisper.

It's a stupid question. I don't know why I ask it. Maybe I want some sort of reassurance that this isn't just a game to him. Maybe I need to convince myself I still have control over the whirlwind of emotions tearing through me. But I had to ask it—for myself, for us.

His eyes lock onto mine, and the silence between us grows heavy. Our breaths are shallow, in sync with the sky's rumbling above, but I don't dare move. I don't dare speak. My heart pounds in my throat. Hope builds inside me, and the weight of anticipation crushes me. I don't blink. I don't look away. I get lost in the depths of his brown irises that have grown to feel like a home I never knew I wanted.

With a strained, low whisper, he rasps, "This was a broken deal from the start, Blue. Because you were always destined to be mine."

His words hit me harder than the thunder rumbling above us, and my breath catches in my throat. Every ounce of doubt I had dissolves in an instant, leaving me with nothing but the raw, overwhelming need for him. My heart races, pounding against my chest like it might burst from happiness.

The words are stuck in my throat—there's so much I want to say, but I don't know how. My body takes a life of its own, and before I realize it, I wrap my arms around his neck and crash my lips against his. The kiss is explosive and desperate, like never before. Lorenzo's hand tightens around the nape of my neck, anchoring me to him, while the other slips down to my lower back, pulling me flush against him. I can feel every muscle of his body against mine with how drenched our clothes are. His tongue invades my mouth, and I melt into him, into his firm yet soft lips and the way our tongues dance with each other. I can't get enough. Every time his lips meet mine, it's like my heart flutters uncontrollably. I'm losing myself in him. And I simply don't care.

My fingers tangle in his damp hair, pulling him closer still, causing him to groan, which I eagerly swallow with my lips. Heat pools in my stomach, and I feel like I'm on fire despite the cool rain cascading over us. The intensity of it all makes me feel alive in a way I never thought possible, like every nerve is awake, every sensation heightened. He takes a step back, a whimper bubbling out of me at the miss of his lips on mine.

With a ragged breath, he asks, "Is that a yes, Blue?"

"That's a yes, Ace," I say with a smile so big it makes my cheeks hurt.

He brings me in for another kiss, and we get lost in each other's bodies. All. Night. Long.

41

Lorenzo

"*Vegas, Baby, Vegas!*" I shout, arms spread wide as we stride into one of Damian's hotels. It pays to have a cousin in the hotel business, not that it ever stops us from doing our thing. But, you know, it's still a nice perk.

Matteo groans beside me, rolling his eyes. "This whole weekend is so fucking stupid," he mutters then gives my shoulder a shove. "And cut it with those stupid quotes only your girlfriend gets."

The word *girlfriend* still feels surreal. I'll never get used to hearing or saying it. I, Lorenzo Mancini, have a fucking girlfriend. Who would have thought?

The girls went to the spa while we checked into our rooms, but the flight here was...well, *interesting*, to say the least. Matteo and Isabella didn't even look at each other once, and that's probably why he's been sulking since we arrived.

I grin, draping my arm over his shoulder and giving him a playful tap. "You're just bitter because you're the only single one left."

He glares, shoving my arm off. "You just had to figure out you're a relationship guy the day before we go to Las Vegas, didn't you?"

Damian, ever the voice of reason, raises an eyebrow and adds dryly, "Have you *actually* tried talking to Isabella instead of sulking like an idiot?"

Matteo huffs, shaking his head like Damian's suggestion is the most absurd thing he's ever heard. "Do you think I have a death wish? I know better than to get near her. My plan is to stay as far away as possible."

"See," I say, barely hiding my grin, "that's going to be a challenge, since this is a combined bachelor and bachelorette party."

Matteo's eyes narrow as he turns to Damian. "That reminds me... Really? You couldn't have said no?"

Damian shoots him a glare. "No. Because I loved the idea. That way, we didn't have to spend any time apart."

"Pussy-whipped," Matteo mutters under his breath, and I can't help but snicker. Damian responds by smacking the back of Matteo's head.

"*Motherfucker*," Matteo hisses, rubbing the spot. "You really have to stop doing that."

"I'm not pussy-whipped," Damian says with a deadpan expression. "I just love hanging out with her."

I snort, unable to hold it back. Hearing my cousin—the grumpiest man alive—use the words "pussy-whipped" is too funny. "You kind of are."

"Get off that high horse, because you're following his footsteps," Matteo fires back.

"Never said I wasn't." I wink at him before walking to the check-in counter.

Honestly, if I could scream from the top of my lungs how stupidly in love with Sophia Evans I am, I would. In a heartbeat. But I want to take it slow. The last thing I want is to scare her away. Now that I have her, there's no way I'm letting her go. Hell, if I could marry her right this second, I would.

The idea sounds crazy—like, certifiably insane, almost —but what can I say? I've never felt this way before. And it feels...good. Too good. Maybe even too good to be true. But I'm done doubting everything. I'm done feeling sorry for myself.

I'll do whatever it takes to hold onto this, hold onto *her*.

We grab the keys to our rooms, and I head to the room quickly to set up something I planned at the last minute. It may or may not have been my idea for the girls to go have a spa day; that way, I could have time to set up. As I'm on the floor, contemplating why the fuck I decided to do this, there's a knock on my door.

Opening the door, I find Matteo. "If you're here to keep sulking, at least help me with this." I tilt my head, letting him come in.

"Dude, what the hell are you doing?"

"You wouldn't understand," I say, sitting on the floor and grabbing another piece of paper, knowing damn well I'm going to fail even though I've watched the tutorial about a million times. "Are you going to help or not?"

He rolls his eyes, sitting next to me. "Only because you look like an idiot and you're doing it wrong."

"Okay, Mr. Genius, have at it."

That was the wrong thing to say, because Matteo, on top of being a know-it-all, loves a good challenge. So almost two hours later, we're pretty much done with an hour to spare. We've mostly been silent, something Matteo hates most of the time, except when he's stuck in his head.

"So," I break the silence. "Do you want to talk about it?"

He doesn't look up from his task, biting the tip of his tongue and frowning in concentration. "No."

"It's not healthy to bottle things up," I press.

Matteo shoots me a glare but remains quiet. He knows better by now that nothing will stop me, not even his death glare.

"Why don't you talk to her? It's been so long, I'm sure if you explain—"

His head snaps, his cold blue eyes finding mine. "Drop it, Mancini. I mean it. Just because you finally found someone to understand you and be with you, doesn't mean the rest of us are as lucky," he spits, standing abruptly. "Now, if you'll excuse me, I've had about enough of this project of yours and the opinions no one fucking asked you for." He stalks out of my hotel room angrily, slamming the door behind him.

I sigh, shaking my head. He's my best friend, and God knows I love him, but goddamn can he be stubborn.

BLUE

You never brought me the room key!

ME

I know, I didn't want to ruin the surprise.

BLUE

What surprise?

BLUE

Ace, answer me!

BLUE

Not cool, dude. Not cool.

ME

I'm on my way, calm down, Blue.

BLUE

I like it when you call me Blue.

ME

How much have you had to drink?

BLUE

Just some champagne, not much.

ME

Enough to be truthful, I see.

BLUE

Forget I said anything. Your ego doesn't need any more of a boost. What was I thinking?

ME

You like me like that.

BLUE

Unfortunately…yes. Yes, I do.

Sophia

"Is closing my eyes really necessary?" I roll my eyes, though a playful smile tugs at my lips.

Lorenzo presses his lips together, already exasperated. I can tell I'm getting on his nerves. I get a little annoying after champagne. And I've had enough to be the right amount of buzzed. "Yes."

"Okay, okay." I surrender, closing my eyes as his hand gently lands on my lower back. The warmth radiating from it is dizzying, and every bit electrifying as it always is. If anything, it's heightened now that I get to call him mine. He gently guides me into the room, and though I'm desperate to peek, I keep my eyes closed. "Alright, open," he whispers in my ear, and the sound alone gives me goosebumps.

I blink my eyes open, and my breath catches as I take in the sight. Soft lights are scattered all around, casting a romantic, golden glow over the room. But what really steals my breath are the delicate, tiny, paper-made purple Madagascar periwinkles scattered everywhere. They cover the entire space—countless and impossibly beautiful.

"How did you do this?" I laugh, the sound catching in my throat as tears threaten to well.

"Matteo helped me, because I suck at stuff like this. You'll notice the messed-up ones—those are mine." He laughs.

"Then those will be my favorites," I say, beaming at him, meaning every single word.

His brown eyes soften, and a blush creeps onto his cheeks. His shy smile makes my heart skip a beat. "It's stupid. I don't even know why I did this."

I throw my arms around him, hugging him tight and kissing his cheek. "Because you like me," I tease.

He lets out a hearty laugh, kissing the top of my head. "I think *like* is too little of a word."

A smile that makes my cheeks hurt tugs at my lips. "Yeah?"

He nods, his grip on my waist tightening slightly. "I more than like you, Blue."

He doesn't need to say it out loud. It's all in his eyes—the love, adoration, and deep wanting radiating from him. In such a short period of time, Lorenzo has become my constant. The one who, without even trying, makes me feel seen, safe, and cherished in ways I never thought possible. He's become the person who knows me in ways no one ever has.

"I more than like you, too, Ace," I whisper, the words filled with a weight of certainty as I keep my gaze locked on his, my heart pounding hard in my chest. We don't need grand declarations—everything we feel is there, in the unspoken language of our shared smiles, touches, and glances.

And for me, that's more than enough. If there's something I've learned throughout my life, it's that trust is nothing without proof and love is nothing without action. In his arms, I found a home and the warmth I knew deep down I always wanted but never looked for because I never felt... worthy.

His lips find mine in a soft brush at first, teasing, almost hesitant, like he's savoring the moment before fully sealing our mouths. It sends a rush of heat through me, and I can feel my pulse pounding in my ears. His kiss becomes both tender and hungry, and I melt into it. When his tongue glides along the seam of my lips, it's slow, deliberate, asking for permission but with a quiet demand. I part my lips, giving in without hesitation. The taste of him, mixed with the faint hint of champagne still on my tongue, fills my senses, and I moan softly against his mouth. His hand tightens on my waist, pulling me closer, and I feel like I could drown in this moment—his touch, his kiss, the way he holds me like I'm something precious. It's overwhelming— the intensity of it and the way he consumes me so effortlessly.

"We should stay in," he says, dropping soft, peppering kisses from my mouth all the way down to my neck. The feel of his lips against my skin makes me an instant puddle, aching with need.

I laugh, wrapping my arms around his shoulders. "Aria will be pissed."

His lips keep delivering soft, intoxicating kisses from the column of my neck to my shoulder as he breathes me in. "They'll be fine without us." His hand trails over the curve of my breast through my dress, and the simple touch sends a shiver through me, a moan escaping my lips.

"Fuck it," I mutter, pushing him onto the bed with a swift motion. Straddling him, I crash our lips together in a deep, desperate kiss. The guttural sound that escapes him makes my thighs tighten around him, and I press into him, deepening the kiss. We bite, nip, and explore every corner of each other's mouths, my fingers fumbling clumsily with his shirt buttons. After my third failed attempt, frustration kicks in, and I grab the fabric in both fists, ripping it open. Buttons fly in every direction, but we're too consumed to care.

His hands roam my body, tracing from the curve of my breasts to my hips before he finds the hem of my dress and lifts it, leaving me in nothing but my lacy, blue underwear. His gaze darkens as it sweeps over me, taking in every inch.

"Did you wear this for me?" His voice is low and musky.

I shrug, a sheepish smile playing on my lips. "Yes."

He bites his lip, shaking his head slightly. "God, you're so incredibly beautiful."

The sincerity in his voice always gets me. And it's not just the words; it's how he touches me, how he holds me. His appreciation, his need, his want—it radiates through every caress, every look.

Before I can respond, Lorenzo flips us effortlessly, spreading me out beneath him. My hands immediately move to his belt, working quickly to rid him of his pants, and within moments, he's down to his boxer briefs.

His palm glides over my skin, fingers trailing delicate, feathery touches that leave me aching for more. Each kiss he plants on my body feels like fire, igniting everywhere his lips touch. When his hand reaches my inner thighs, I'm already on edge and in desperate need for his touch. I crave it all—his dirty, praising words, the way he worships me with every look, every move.

I lift my hips slightly as he slides my underwear down my legs, leaving me bare and exposed to him. My thighs instinctively clench at the way he licks his bottom lip, leaving a trail of moisture behind as he drinks me in. Without breaking eye contact, I sit and reach for the clasp of my bra, unhooking it, and let it fall to the ground.

He hovers over me with careful precision, making sure not to put his weight on me. His mouth finds one of my peaked, sensitive nipples, teasing it with slow, taunting circles with his tongue while his fingers roll the other between them, sending jolts of pleasure through me. I arch my back, seeking more friction, the sensations over-whelming, every touch toe-curling, making me crave more of him.

My fingers tangle in his hair, silently begging him to never stop. His touch leaves my nipple, a small whimper bubbling out of me at the miss of his touch. Lorenzo's fingers brush against my sensitive clit in slow, torturous circles, sending waves of pleasure coursing through me. The sound of my moans fills the room, mingling with the slick, wet noises of every teasing touch he gives me. He flicks my nipple with his tongue playfully, smirking as he takes in my writhing body beneath him.

"Mmm, look at you," he murmurs. "So wet and ready for me. What do you need from me, baby?" he asks, his voice so deep and husky I can't help but moan.

"I need you," I reply breathlessly. "All of you."

My fingers slide down from his hair, trailing along his neck and shoulders, tracing the familiar patterns of his tattoos. I'll never grow tired of this—of memorizing the ink on his skin, of touching him like he's mine and mine alone.

Lorenzo's fingers trail over my center, his touch slow and torturous, gathering my slickness with each stroke. His finger brushes my bottom lip, smearing my arousal across it. He watches me intently, his gaze dark and full of intent as his breath grazes my skin until his lips claim mine, his tongue licking away the taste of me. He lets out an appreciative, satisfied groan before moving to my ear.

He nips at my earlobe, his voice low and rough, sending a new wave of shivers down my spine. "You already have all of me, Blue," he whispers, his words dripping with hunger. "You're going to have to be more specific."

Heat rushes to my cheeks, my face burning with the intensity of my desire. I don't hesitate, my need too overwhelming to care. "I want to ride your cock, and I want you to fuck me good and hard."

His throat flexes with a groan, the sound raw and full of lust. His hands grip my waist, and before I know it, he flips me over, placing me on top of him. I'm straddling his hips, and my core tightens at the feel of his erection pressed against me. He lifts his hips slightly and I take off his boxer briefs in one swift motion. I grip the base of his cock, centering it at my entrance, and start to sink down, a low moan escaping my lips as I continue to slowly take him in.

He brushes the hair out of my face then slides his hand down to my throat, gripping it just tight enough as he pulls me closer, our lips barely touching. "I want you to take every goddamn inch and ride my cock. Take it all, baby. I'm all yours."

His filthy words push me over the edge, and without a second thought, I sink down, taking all of him. "I'm so full," I moan against his lips, my breath shaky and desperate.

He shuts his eyes, breathing heavily through his nose. "You're such a good girl, taking all of me. Letting my cock fill this perfect pussy," he whispers, his voice thick with need.

I kiss him hard, my hips grinding slowly at first as I adjust to his size and stretch around him. The friction is electric, and my body tingles with every motion. Once I'm comfortable, I plant my feet on the bed, hands pressed firmly on his chest, and start riding him harder, sliding all the way out only to sink back in deep, over and over. The wet slap of my ass meeting his skin echoes through the room, mixing with our breathless moans. Every sound lights me up, pushing me to move faster, harder, chasing that high.

Lorenzo grabs my waist, holding me in place. "Give me a second." He brings me closer, pressing his forehead against mine. "You feel too fucking good. I'm going to come if you keep going."

I smirk, brushing my fingertips through his hair before biting his lip teasingly. "Come on, Ace. Don't quit on me now. I need you to fuck me hard."

His eyes flash with hunger as he wraps his arms around me and lifts me then slams me down onto his throbbing cock without any warning. The pace he sets is brutal, his thrusts rough and punishing. "Is this what you want?" He grunts in my ear. "For me to fuck you good and hard until my cum's leaking down your thighs?"

"Yes, please," I beg, my pussy tightening around him at his words.

He hums with a dark chuckle. "Your cunt is so needy for it, isn't it?" he growls, fucking me even harder, his balls slapping against my soaked pussy with every smooth thrust as my moans fill the room until I'm begging him not to stop.

"Eyes on me, Blue," he commands, his voice rough and full of authority. "Let me see your pretty face while my cock fills you up."

My eyes lock on his, even though it's hard to keep them open with how perfectly he's hitting that spot inside me. My lashes flutter, and he grips my cheeks between his fingers, forcing my gaze back to him while he continues to fuck me without mercy. "I said look at me."

I obey, my eyes roaming over every inch of his face—his

furrowed brows, the heat in his glassy eyes, the way his lips part as he watches me. Seeing him so lost in pleasure, so raw and full of desire, sends me spiraling. My climax starts to build quickly, climbing higher with every wild thrust.

"I'm gonna come," I gasp, my eyes glued to his in a silent plea, the edge so close I can't think straight.

He bites his lip, his grip tightening on me. "That's it, pretty girl. Milk my cock and make a mess, baby, *please*," he begs through a low guttural moan, slamming into me with one final thrust that sends me tumbling over the edge. My orgasm rips through me, my pussy clenching and fluttering around him as his cock swells and spills deep inside of me.

We ride it out together, moaning through the intensity of our release, our bodies moving in perfect sync, lost in the bliss of each other.

He slips out of me, kissing the top of my head. "Stay right here."

I mumble an "okay" and close my eyes, trying to catch my breath.

A few minutes later, Lorenzo returns from the bathroom with a warm washcloth. When I go to reach for it, he stops me. "Let me," he says softly.

I simply nod, and he quietly cleans me as I just stare at him, my heart filling with so much emotion, I don't know what to do with it.

Once we're clean and settled under the covers, he pulls me close, pressing his body against mine, his warmth wrapping around me like a blanket of calm. Lorenzo rests his chin gently on top of my head as my hand drifts over his, fingers tracing the lines of his skin as we cuddle in comfortable silence. The peace he brings me feels like home, and my heart flutters with so much love, it feels impossible to keep it inside much longer.

Those three little words hover on the edge of my lips, but something holds me back. It's not because Lorenzo doesn't deserve to hear them. He does, more than anyone. But there's a small, insecure part of me that's still afraid, still wondering if saying it will make things too real, too vulnerable.

So, instead, I stay in his arms, letting the words linger on the tip of my tongue, unspoken. Maybe soon I'll find the courage to let the words slip out, but for now, I hold on to this—us, together, in this quiet moment that says more than any words ever could.

43

Sophia

You'd think having a combined bachelor and bachelorette party would be boring, but the guys have forced Damian to take one too many shots, and it's the first time I've seen him genuinely smile. It was unsettling at first—still is. I mean, Damian and *fun* don't exactly go hand in hand. But here he is, laughing with a glass in his hand, and I can't lie—it's kind of nice to see him loosen up for once. Hopefully, when he marries my best friend, he'll be able to remove the permanent stick he has stuck in his ass.

Isabella, on the other hand, has been another interesting development. The pressure of being near Matteo must've gotten to her, because she's been drinking herself into oblivion. And to my surprise, she's actually fun when drunk. She's been dancing, laughing, and forcing me to take shots with her. Most of the time, I sneakily toss them into a nearby bush when she's not looking, because, well, someone's got to keep her tamed, right? It's hilarious to think I'm the responsible one tonight. Who would've thought?

I glance at Matteo, who's been trying—and miserably

failing—to avoid her all night. He looks like he's locked in an internal battle—either step in to help or stay as far away as humanly possible. Judging by the glares he keeps sending in her direction, he's leaning toward the latter.

After dinner and hopping into a few casinos, we ended at a club—because we girls insisted we wanted to go dancing. And if there's something we know by now, the guys are incapable of saying no to us. It's around one in the morning, and Lorenzo and I have been exchanging looks all night, silently plotting our escape. But before we can act on it, Aria catches us.

"No!" Aria shrieks, cutting through the music as she points a finger at me. "Stop looking at each other like that! You"—she jabs her finger in my direction—"are not leaving. No, ma'am. You guys ditched dinner last night, this is not happening again." She shakes her head adamantly.

"Red, you're being such a cockblocker right now," Lorenzo says with an amused, joking tone, and I can't help but snort a laugh.

Aria casually shrugs, a mischievous grin tugging at her lips. "While it makes me happy you two finally figured it out, it's *my* weekend—"

Damian suddenly interrupts, throwing his hands in the air. "Hey! It's *mine*, too!" His voice is a bit louder than necessary, making us all turn toward him.

Aria thins her lips, fighting back laughter as she pats Damian's head like a scolded puppy. "I know, Damie. No need to shout."

"Don't call me Damie, I am *begging* you." Damian tilts his head back, groaning.

I can't hold back my laughter. "Jeez, he's such a lousy drunk."

"Oh, you have no idea. This is *nothing*," Matteo mutters from beside us, his eyes glinting with amusement.

"Hey." Isabella hiccups—another lousy drunk. "If Aria's nickname is Red, and Sophia's nickname is Blue..." She pauses, lost in thought, her brow furrowing as if she's solving a complex math equation.

I glance at Lorenzo, who's already stifling a laugh.

"Does that make me Yellow?" Isabella finishes with another hiccup, blinking at us in earnest.

Matteo rolls his eyes, exasperated. "God help us," he mutters under his breath, though I catch a hint of a smile tugging at the corners of his mouth.

"What would you call me?" Isabella asks, zeroing her green eyes on Matteo.

Matteo freezes, the rim of his glass hovering near his lips. For a moment, he stares at Isabella, caught off guard by her sudden lack of attitude. Hell, we're all caught off guard. This is the first time she's spoken to him without biting sarcasm or that cold edge in her voice.

He lowers his drink slowly, eyes narrowing slightly as if he's trying to figure out if this is some sort of trap. "What would I call you?" he repeats, his tone cautious.

Isabella nods, her eyes still locked on his, an unexpected softness in them. "Yeah. What do you think my nickname should be?"

He lowers his drink slowly, a hint of something flickering behind his gaze. His voice is quiet but steady when he finally responds, "Sunshine."

Her eyes widen, and for a second, the drunken haze seems to clear as recognition flashes across her face. "You used to call me that," she whispers, her voice soft, tinged with surprise and something else I don't recognize.

Matteo holds her gaze for a moment. "I know," he murmurs.

We're all looking at each other expectantly, wondering what the hell is happening right now. Is this the start of a new friendship? Maybe whatever happened between them —something Isabella refuses to tell us—will finally be a distant memory? But then Isabella looks the other way, tensing her shoulders, and Matteo drops his gaze, sighing in resignation, and the brief moment passes.

"Okay." I clap my hands, stepping forward and snatching the drink from Isabella's grasp. "You're officially cut off."

Isabella laughs, shaking her head as she stands. "Fine."

Matteo stands, too, a frown forming on his face. "Where are you going?"

Isabella glares at him, and just like that, the tension snaps back into place. "Wouldn't you love to know?"

"It's one in the morning, Isabella. You're not going out there alone."

"Good thing I'm not asking for your permission," she spits back.

Matteo rubs his beard, sighing in exasperation. "If you could stop being stubborn for one second—"

"Wouldn't you like that?" She crosses her arms defiantly.

"Yes, I very much would," he retorts.

"I can go with you," I offer, hoping to ease the tension between them.

"No," Matteo says immediately, his tone leaving no room for argument. "I'll go with her."

Isabella whirls around. "I'd rather be alone."

Matteo doesn't hesitate. "Over my dead fucking body," he snaps, following after her. "There's no use arguing, Isa. I'll be going with you whether you like it or not."

With that, they both storm out of the club.

"Will those two ever figure it out?" I ask.

Lorenzo shakes his head with a knowing grin. "Damian and I have been trying for years now. They're both way too stubborn."

Aria waves a hand like it's no big deal. "Trust me, they will."

There's something undeniable about them. When they're in the same room, they're like magnets trying desperately to stay apart, yet life keeps pulling them back together. It's only a matter of time before they stop fighting it.

"Hell will freeze the day that happens," Lorenzo comments.

"A lot of things can happen. I mean, look at us now." I shrug.

Aria beams excitedly. "I always knew you two were meant to be."

Lorenzo wraps an arm around my waist, kissing me on the cheek. "I will forever be grateful the day you walked back into my life," he says with a sheepish smile.

My eyes find his as I smile at him, my cheeks hurting from how happy I feel.

This is it for me.

He is it for me.

And my heart couldn't be any happier.

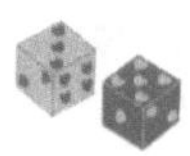

Though we barely slept last night, we had already planned to meet for brunch. Since I've been so busy these past few months, we haven't had our usual Sunday brunches, so it was overdue.

"I'm actually shocked you made it," I say, watching as Isabella approaches our table. Aria and I have been sitting for about ten minutes, just drinking coffee and catching up.

Isabella slumps down into the chair without a word, sunglasses still on. Aria and I exchange confused looks.

"So..." Aria ventures, unsure how to start.

"Where did you disappear to last night?" I ask. "We never heard from you again."

Isabella stays silent, reaching for the coffee pot and pouring herself a heavy cup. Slowly, she pulls off her sunglasses and takes a sip. I study her, trying to figure out what's different about her, and that's when I see it.

"No." My breath catches, eyes locking on her left hand.

Isabella follows my gaze and stiffens, dropping her hand into her lap, like that will make me forget what I just saw.

Aria frowns, confused. "What?"

"Isabella Walton," I gasp, leaning closer. "Tell me you didn't."

She grimaces. "Technically, I'm Isabella Carter now."

Aria's jaw drops. She's at a loss for words.

"You married Matteo fucking Carter?" I sputter, staring at her in disbelief.

Isabella pushes her hair back with a sigh. "Can we drop it?"

"No!" Aria and I shout together.

Isabella groans, rubbing her forehead. "I'm really not in the mood for this."

Aria tries again. "But—"

"Drop it," Isabella cuts her off sharply.

I frown, unwilling to let it go. "We deserve to know—"

Isabella interrupts me. "This is between me and Matteo. Leave it alone, guys. Please." Her voice quivers.

Isabella never—and I mean never—shows any vulnerability, so when her green eyes find mine with a silent plea, I nod in understanding.

I sigh, taking a long sip of coffee. "You know, I keep telling you guys we should start brunch with mimosas, but no one listens..."

Aria nods, thinning her lips. "I'm starting to see the wisdom in that."

"How's the article going?" Isabella asks, looking at me.

So we're completely changing the topic.

I nod. "It's finished. I'm turning it in on Monday when we fly back. I was going to do it this morning, but I left the computer at work."

"You? Leaving work at...work?" Aria gapes at me. "Who are you and what did you do with my best friend?"

I shrug nonchalantly. "It was time to take a break for once."

They don't know the extent of it all. They don't know I've been doing Max's job for the past few years. Will I ever tell them? Not sure. I don't want to give Max any more thought. What he did was unfair, as we all know now, so why keep giving it any thought?

My phone pings with a text.

LUCY (COWORKER)

Nice article. Ruthless. I loved it!

I frown, confused.

ME

What are you talking about?

LUCY (COWORKER)

Uhm, the article exposing Lorenzo Mancini?

My stomach drops, the nausea hitting me all at once. The girls keep chatting, but I feel like I'm underwater right now, the voices being drowned by the beat of my own heart. With shaky hands, I search *Vogue Elite's* website.

"Fuck, fuck, fuck," I mutter, my voice trembling as tears fill my eyes. I scroll through the article, each sentence making me feel sicker.

Aria grabs my phone, her eyes scanning the screen. "Did you write this?"

My hands tremble as I shake my head, and my chest tightens, a suffocating pressure that makes me wonder if this is what a panic attack feels like. I've always managed to keep my emotions in check, to stay steady and detached. But now, as my palms grow clammy and my pulse pounds erratically in my ears, drowning out everything else, there's no mistaking the anxiety gripping me like a vise.

I open my mouth to say something, but all that comes out is a breathless sob. Tears start to run down my cheek, but I'm paralyzed. Breathing is becoming harder by the second, my eyes becoming more and more blurry with tears. Without a word and not caring how people are probably looking at me, I stand abruptly, grab my purse, and run out of there as soon as possible with only one thing in mind.

I need to find Lorenzo.

44

Since the girls decided to have brunch, we figured, why not do the same? I know, it's completely out of character for us. We're not exactly the brunch type. I'm running a bit late because I've spent all morning on the phone with Diego, trying to decide whether we need to push the restaurant opening back another month. Thankfully, it looks like we're on track, which honestly feels like a miracle at this point.

As I walk into the restaurant, I spot the guys sitting at a table. Their conversation seems serious—low voices, tense shoulders. They notice me approaching and immediately straighten in their seats, frowns etched into their faces.

"What's wrong?" I ask, sliding into a chair.

"You good?" Matteo asks, his tone careful.

I grab a menu, flipping through it casually. "Why wouldn't I be? Sorry I'm late. I've been on the phone with the contractor all morning." I roll my eyes. "Good news is, I don't have to push back the opening again. Thank fuck. I was starting to worry."

Damian reaches across the table and snatches the menu from my hands. "You been online today?"

I shake my head, confused. "No, my phone's been blowing up, but like I said, I've been busy—" I stop midsentence, catching the look on their faces. Both of them are watching me expectantly, Matteo with a grimace, Damian faking a cough. "What's going on?"

I pull out my phone, scrolling through the endless notifications. One message catches my attention.

AMOS

Care to explain this? *link attached*

I frown, clicking on the link. "Oh, Sophia's article is out? It's not supposed to be out until next month." A grin spreads across my face. "This is a nice surprise."

Matteo tilts his head, eyebrows drawn together. "So you've read it?"

I shake my head. "She wanted me to give it a once-over before it went out, but I told her she didn't need my approval. I trust her."

"You might wanna read it now." Damian's voice is rough as he leans in.

The tension in the air is thick, and I'm starting to get the feeling that something's off, so I open the article and start reading.

Lorenzo Mancini: The Ultimate Player?
By Sophia Evans

When the name Lorenzo Mancini is mentioned, it comes with tales of power, charm, and—above all—ruthless ambition. This Chicagoland billionaire has climbed to the top by being relentless, but as they say, sometimes you can climb so high that you forget what's beneath you. Known for his string of conquests in both sex and business, Mancini treats life like a game he's already won. And everyone else? They're just pawns for his advantage.

As one of the youngest vice presidents of Vortex—the infamous, invite-only billionaire club—Mancini has shown a talent for winning, but he's also garnered whispers of being careless, even cruel, in his decisions. Sources within the industry paint a picture of a man who is "tactless" and "unscrupulous," willing to bulldoze anyone in his path to stay on top. And he doesn't just accept that image; he thrives on it. Mancini wears his heartlessness like a badge, and people keep falling for the charm, unaware of how quickly he'll move on when they're no longer useful.

His "success" in the restaurant business doesn't change much. Sure, he knows what he's doing, but let's not pretend there's any deep passion behind it. It's just another way for him to look good, keep people interested, and keep his name in lights. What you see is what you get—a man who's only loyal to himself.

His avoidance of the media isn't just strategy—it's survival. He knows that if anyone looks too closely, the whole polished act might unravel. Behind the tailored suits and smug smile is a man whose only real accomplishment is manipulating everyone around him. And maybe that's all he ever wanted.

Lorenzo Mancini isn't just playing the game; he is the game —a man defined by power plays and shallow connections, and when it all falls apart, he'll have no one left but himself.

The eerie calm that settles over me feels deadening. Like my body is slowly shutting down, one sense at a time. I never got it before—how movies and books make betrayal seem so dramatic, over the top. But now, sitting here, my heart clenching and hurting, I understand it all too well.

My neck burns as heat creeps up it, the reality of it all sinking in. And my heart—it's breaking. *Literally* breaking. I didn't know that was even possible, to feel something inside you shatter like that.

I shake my head in disbelief. "No. No way." I drop my phone on the table, scrubbing my hands over my face, trying to shake off the growing panic.

"Maybe there's an explanation," Matteo points out, trying to be the voice of reason.

"Yeah," Damian adds, his voice softer than I've ever heard it, it's almost unsettling. Just as he's about to say more, his phone rings. He picks it up, his tone shifting. "Hey, Darling, I can't really talk..." He pauses, listening closely and looking at me as he shakes his head, giving me a knowing look.

"What the fuck is going on?" I mutter to myself, the words barely leaving my lips as I try to make sense of it all.

Damian hangs up, his eyes meeting mine with a resigned look. "Aria said Sophia left brunch, completely losing it. I think you should talk to her. There has to be an explanation."

Matteo frowns. "This makes no sense."

"She couldn't have written this," I say, but it's more to myself than anyone else. I'm trying to convince myself. Trying to hold on to something.

But wouldn't she? That article wasn't exactly wrong. You thrive in that sort of chaos. You've used your charm in both business and sexual conquests. You've had every chance to walk away from this world you claim to despise so much, yet you haven't. She's not wrong.

But I told her. I told her I was tired. I shared all of my secrets with her. So why would she still write something like this?

Because it's the truth. You've been lying to yourself this whole time. It's time to wake up and face reality.

I shake my head, trying to shut off my sadistic fucking brain. I'm trying to breathe through the tightening in my chest. In and out. But it's no use. The insecurities are crawling their way up, threatening to pull me under. It's so easy to let them. To let them drown me. To accept love—*real* love—was never in the cards for me. To accept that Sophia, like everyone else I thought I could trust, took advantage of me.

Fuck.

"I need to get out of here." I push back from the table, already half-standing.

Matteo's voice stops me for a moment. "And what are you going to do? You're in no state to talk to her right now."

"I don't give a fuck," I snap, storming out of the restaurant.

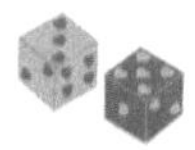

The walk back to the hotel is a blur. My mind is a mess, too loud and too hurt to think straight. Anger starts to simmer beneath the surface, barely held in check. But I need to confront her—I *have* to. Even if it destroys me.

When I reach the hotel, I take a deep breath before opening the door, hoping it will steady me. But the second I step inside, the charged air between us stirs everything back up. The anger, the hurt, the betrayal—it crashes over me all at once, suffocating.

Sophia looks up, standing abruptly. "Lorenzo—"

I raise my hand, cutting her off. "Save it," I seethe, my

voice sharper than I mean it to be. "Why'd you do it, Sophia?"

"You think I did this? Seriously?" She frowns, confused.

I make the colossal mistake of looking at her. Her eyes, those hauntingly beautiful blue eyes I've come to love, are glossy with unshed tears. But the sadness in them claws at what's left of my heart—and not in a good way.

I ignore her question, too focused on my self-destructing anger. "Was it really necessary to write something like that?" I snort a humorless laugh. "I mean, I knew you were good, but even for you it's a little too far, don't you think?"

I'm not thinking straight. Anger, shame, and self-preservation are trying to take over, and it's easier for me to let it. To destroy. After all, that's all I know how to do, right? I'm ruthless. Careless. I don't care about anyone. Might as well live to the fucking reputation.

"Lorenzo, I didn't write that article. You *know* I wouldn't." Her voice cracks, barely above a whisper.

"It sure doesn't look that way from where I'm standing." I wave my phone in the air, pointing to the screen. "Your name is right here, clear as day."

"I don't know what happened, but I will get to the bottom of this. Just... Can you please trust me?"

I pace the room, dragging a hand through my hair, avoiding her gaze like it burns me. I can't look at her anymore. It physically hurts. "I thought I could trust you. I thought..." My voice falters, threatening to break. *I thought you loved me.* But I can't say it. "I don't know what to think anymore, Sophia."

She steps back, her breath catching like my words slapped her. Words—they're the most dangerous weapon when wielded right. And I'm losing control, letting them tear through her, through us.

"Are you fucking kidding me right now? After everything, you don't trust me?" Her voice trembles, disbelief coloring her expression.

I shake my head, my voice tight with anger. "I *did* trust you, and look at where it got me—"

"I didn't write it!" she yells, frustration seeping into her tone.

"And I don't fucking believe you!" I roar back, my own voice harsh and unyielding.

"Wow." Her laugh is sharp, almost bitter, and there's a hint of breathlessness in it. "So... That's it, then?"

"Yup." It's all I can manage, my voice tight as I struggle to keep the knot in my throat from breaking free.

She takes another step back, her face twisting with hurt, a fierce glint flashing in her eyes. "Out of all the people in the world, I thought you'd be the last one to hurt me."

"Back at you," I spit.

I can't control the words that keep coming out of my stupid mouth. The insecurities, the doubt—they're too loud, drowning out every rational thought. The words I need to say, the ones that could stop this, are trapped, stuck in my throat.

And maybe I don't want them to come out. Maybe it's easier to let go, even when I feel like I'm holding the shattered pieces of my heart in my hands, bleeding from the jagged edges. Even though, deep down, a part of me knows if I stopped for one second, if I could let the rational side of my mind catch up—I'd maybe be able to see the truth. But I can't. It's easier believing people think the worst of me, because that way, I never give them a chance to see the real me.

A fuck-up. A good-for-nothing no one has ever loved, and who can't love, even when he thought he could.

"Honestly, fuck you, Lorenzo," she says, her voice quiet but full of venom.

I flinch, but the anger surges, burning hotter, pushing me past the point of reason. I snort, cruel and bitter. "You already did. Multiple times." The words leave my mouth before I can stop them, sharp as a knife, and I know they'll hurt. I *want* them to hurt. Because I'm sadistic in a self-destructing kind of way.

A sharp, angry laugh comes out of her as tears start to stream down her face. "God, I'm so fucking stupid. I thought you were different," she says, her voice gaining strength. "But you're just like everyone else, aren't you? So quick to believe the worst, so quick to throw me away. Another man with empty fucking promises." She lets out a sharp breath. "After all, you wanted to look after me. Take care of me for once, right?" She shakes her head in disbelief. "That's a whole lot of an elaborate lie for a *quick fuck*," she spits.

I flinch at her words, each one of them slicing whatever's left of me, slamming into me like a punch to the gut, leaving me breathless. Instead of fighting back or swallowing my pride and trying to find a solution, I stay silent, letting the weight of my insecurities crush whatever's left of us.

The silence between us is deafening. I still refuse to look at her, because if I do, I will crumble. I will beg for her to stay, and she doesn't deserve this. She deserves a better man. A man who can properly love her. A man who can protect her from the worst. I want to be that man. God, do I want to.

But how can I protect her from myself?

I can't believe I let myself believe I was capable of loving someone. I will always think the worst of people. It's in my nature. It's how I was raised. And this... This is how it's supposed to be.

My eyes find hers, and her gaze is like arrows shooting

straight into my heart. Not missing a single shot. She nods knowingly, and without a word, she starts frantically gathering her things. Every movement, every item she throws into her suitcase, chips away at the fragile pieces of my resolve.

But I stand still. I don't dare move. I don't even breathe.

This is it. This is what you wanted.

So why do I feel like I'm slowly dying? Like I'm watching the whole summer we spent together unfold before my eyes? Every laugh. Every touch. Every kiss. All of it flashing in front of me like some kind of cruel reminder of what's slipping through my fingers, like fine, cold sand.

She turns away, her back stiff as she walks toward the door. I can feel it—the finality in her steps, the way her shoulders shake slightly, as if she's barely holding it together.

"Sophia, wait..." The words are out before I can stop them, but she doesn't turn around.

Her hand is on the doorknob when she speaks. "No." Her voice is sharp, unrelenting. "We're done."

She steps out of the room, leaving me in the suffocating silence, the weight of reality crashing down on me—I just let the best thing that's ever happened to me slip away.

45

Sophia

These past seventy-two hours have been pure hell.

I spent a ridiculous amount of money on a last-minute ticket to get back to Chicago. It was unsurprisingly expensive and it's definitely going to set me back for the foreseeable future. Not like it matters anyway, because I've had a lot of time to think due to the lack of sleep.

I've always been a fighter, you know? I have always had a fight-or-flight response for everything. It's how I stay productive, it's how I've managed to survive, but this... This was the last blow that obliterated me. If I had any fight left in me, I would be trying to deliver justice. I would be trying to explain and make amends.

Fuck that and everyone else, too.

I walk into *Vogue Elite's* building with one thing in mind. I don't knock on Max's door when I storm into his office. He looks up, surprise lacing his face for a moment before he shoots me a knowing, smug grin. "To what do I owe this pleasure?"

Without a word, I slam my letter of resignation on his desk.

He looks at it, tilting his head, amusement creeping into his voice. "Oh, leaving us so soon?"

"Why'd you do it?" I ask, not giving him any context.

"I'm not sure what you're talking about," he says.

I roll my eyes. He knows damn well what he did.

"Good to see you haven't lost your writing talents, at least."

After the slight mental breakdown I had over it, I had time to mull it over. He must have gotten into my laptop, grabbed all my notes, and twisted them to the point of no return. Max is a lot of things, but he's not stupid. He was looking for an opportunity to fuck with me and took it.

He rubs his chin, giving me an enigmatic look. "You really thought I was going to let that little empty threat you gave me the other day fly?"

"It really doesn't matter now, does it?"

I was determined to go to the VP and show her everything, but when I logged in to my work email, everything was gone. It's my fault, really, if you think about it. Leaving the laptop here, I practically handed it to him on a silver platter.

"I suppose not." He laughs as he points at the letter. "You sure this is what you want?"

Instead of answering, I turn around and walk out that door for the last time, because I'm officially done with it all. I'm done with the city. There's nothing for me here. It doesn't matter how good of a writer I am, journalism jobs in Chicago are a rarity. There's a reason I started as an assistant and worked myself to the bone to rise through the ranks. All the hours wasted, the tears, the anger, and the stress were for...nothing. Because I'm tired, and I'll be grabbing my things and not looking back ever again.

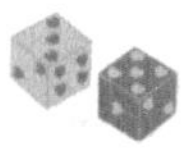

Sweat prickles down my neck as I tape a box labeled *BOOKS*. Packing is taking me less than I thought, because my apartment is the size of a box and I've always been sort of a minimalist. The less I had, the bigger my apartment looked. All I have left to do is sell the furniture, which will help me get some extra money that will help me cover for Mom's mortgage one more month.

Who would have thought, at the ripe age of twenty-six, I would be moving back to my childhood home? The thought alone makes me shiver. It's only temporary, though. As soon as I get a job, I am moving us out of that damn house.

As I'm folding my winter clothes, I hear some keys rattle and the front door opening. I don't even bat an eye, because it was only a matter of time before my best friends came to check in on me. I disappeared on everyone, and they have been calling and texting.

Everyone but him.

I should be thankful he was smart enough to take the last thing I said to him seriously. But it stings. I thought, after everything, we deserved a little more than this. It doesn't matter, anyway. He made his feelings quite clear. I have only myself to blame, thinking this time it was going to be different.

Before I can spiral any deeper, I slam the door shut on those thoughts. I can't afford to think about him, because when I do, it feels like a thousand tiny needles are piercing my chest. Giving it any more thought is just going to slowly kill me.

Doesn't matter if you don't think about it. It's killing you all the same.

I sigh, giving a final shove to all those emotions and slapping on a smile as I walk out of my room. Both of my friends are standing in the living room, their faces twisted in concern as they take in the mess around them.

"What's happening here?" Aria asks carefully.

"Oh." I wave my hand around. "I'm moving," I manage to say with a casual tone.

Isabella's eyes flash with a hint of hurt as she takes a step back. "Were you planning on telling us?"

"Of course, silly." I force my practiced laugh.

They both stand there, staring at me expectantly. For the first time in a long time, I can feel my mask slipping. I fake a cough as I walk back into my room and busy myself with more packing, folding boxes and shoving clothes inside, trying to keep my hands moving.

Aria follows me, snatching the coat I'd spent twenty minutes folding out of my hands.

"Hey! That took me forever to fold!" I snap, trying to grab it back.

"I'm not doing this with you," Aria says firmly, pointing a finger at me. "You're not going to pretend everything's fine when I *know* it's not. I've given you three days to cool off, but enough is enough. *Sit.*" She points to the bed with authority.

"Bossy much?" I mumble but comply, crossing my legs beneath me.

She levels me with a dry, exasperated look. "You forced my hand."

Isabella lingers in the doorway, arms crossed. "Matteo told me what happened."

I snort, shaking my head. "I can't believe those words came out of your mouth. You? Talking to Matteo?"

She shrugs nonchalantly. "We're married now," she says, as if that explains everything.

"Yeah, and you *still* haven't explained what happened there."

Aria snaps her fingers in front of my face, pulling me back. "No. I'm not letting you deflect. While I'm dying to know what's going on with *those* two, I'm more worried about you. Where are you going? Why are you packing?"

"I'm moving back home."

"To *Kentucky*?!" they both exclaim at the same time.

"Where else?" I shrug. "Turned in my resignation letter this morning. My lease is ending soon. It works out perfectly."

"Oh, for the love of God," Isabella mutters, rubbing her temples. "So, you're quitting your job and running away because you and Lorenzo broke up?"

"It's complicated," I say, keeping my tone neutral as the weight of the truth presses against my chest painfully.

Aria's nostrils flare in frustration. "You better start filling in the blanks, because none of this makes sense."

"I'm done talking about it," I mumble, getting up to resume folding.

But of course, Aria isn't about to let it go. She's as stubborn as I am. She grabs the clothes I've just folded and tosses them onto the floor. "I'll keep doing this all day if I have to."

"Are you *five*?" I snap. "Do you know how hard winter clothes are to fold?"

"Talk. *Now*," she orders.

"I didn't write the article. Max did. I tried to explain that to Lorenzo, but he didn't believe me." I shrug, my voice tight as I avoid their eyes.

What I don't say is how deeply I fell in love with him. How his words cut into me like glass, leaving me in pieces. What I don't say is how utterly shattered and numb I feel. What I don't say is I *am* trying to escape. I want to leave this city and never look back, because I believed in something that was never real. He made me fall for him, and now all I have to show for it are my scars.

"Why did Max do that? I know he's always been an asshole, but that's too far, even for him," Aria points out.

"For the past few years, I've been doing Max's job," I confess. There's no point hiding it anymore. My life at *Vogue Elite* is over. "That's why I always worked insane hours."

"That asshole!" Isabella exclaims. "Why didn't you report him?"

I shrug sheepishly.

"You wanted to make sure you could still take care of your mom, didn't you?" Aria asks softly, brushing my forearm. "You were scared he'd fire you."

I nod, the knot in my throat tightening. "And look at where it got me. The second I told him I was done being his puppet, he did this."

"You need to report him, Sophia," Isabella says firmly.

I shake my head. "It doesn't matter anymore."

"So, this is it? You're just...leaving?" Isabella's voice wavers, and it shocks me, because Isabella isn't the type to show emotion.

I close the distance between us and pull her into a tight embrace. "You can always come visit. Now that you own a jet and all, *Mrs. Carter*," I joke.

"I have a feeling even if she *wasn't* Mrs. Carter, Matteo

would give her the world." Aria snickers. "God, I'll never get used to saying that." She crosses her arms, tapping her index finger against her cheek. "Isabella Carter," she says, testing the name like it's a foreign word on her tongue.

Isabella sniffs, stepping back and giving us a dry look.

After a beat of silence, Aria looks at me. "Is this what you really want?" she asks softly.

I let out a long sigh, nodding.

They exchange a quiet glance before looking back at me, understanding etched into their expressions. I open my arms, pulling them both into a tight hug, holding on to the comfort they bring.

Despite everything, I can tell my friends are sad. I can feel their unspoken worry, how much they don't want to see me go. And honestly, it breaks my heart a little.

But we don't talk about it for the rest of the night. Instead, they help me pack, keeping the conversation light, and for a few hours, they manage to help me forget, for the most part. I don't think there's enough will in this world that can help me forget about the man who simultaneously mended and broke my heart.

46

Lorenzo

I've fallen back into old habits. I practically live at Vortex now, gambling my money away like it's nothing and drinking whiskey like it's water. But none of it helps. The more I drink, hoping to forget her, the clearer she becomes—those blue eyes I fell for haunting me every time I close mine. The thrill of gambling, the hope that winning will bring some rush, brings me absolutely nothing. I can't even look at my damn Ace tattoo without thinking of her and that stupid nickname I learned to love a little too much. I don't even bother looking at other women. There's no point. None of them are her.

The article's still generating buzz, but I've tuned it all out. The board's pleased with the attention the club's gotten because of it, and they want me to do more interviews to gain even more exposure. Over my dead fucking body will I be doing any of that.

I haven't been in a kitchen since... Hell, I don't even know. Something that's usually my safe space and heaven is now hard to do.

I made a mistake. A colossal one, and I know it. I've had

plenty of time to sit with it. I'm still angry—hurt, really—that she wrote that article. But I've had to accept she was just doing her job.

It doesn't change anything, though. Even though it hurts to breathe knowing I'll never hold her again, never dance with her in the rain, never keep learning about and falling for her with every conversation, I made the right choice. Maybe now she'll find someone good. An honest man who doesn't carry all the burdens and scars I do. Someone who can love her the way she deserves.

But the thought of another man doing everything I wanted to do for her? It makes me want to put my fist through a wall. Still, I can't let myself think about it. I made my decision when I spoke to her the way I did. I've made my bed, and now I have to lie in it.

The elevator of my condo dings, but I barely register it, too lost in thought, staring at the untouched glass of whiskey in front of me. My finger traces the rim absent-mindedly as I stew in my misery. Self-pity is all I seem capable of these days.

Matteo strides into the kitchen, taking in the scene—me slumped against the island, staring at nothing. "Oh, so you're alive. Good."

"I should've told the concierge not to let anyone up here," I mutter, grabbing the glass and downing it in one go. I reach for the bottle to pour another but decide to skip the formality, drinking straight from it instead.

Matteo doesn't waste a second. He crosses the room and snatches the bottle from my hand. "When was the last time you ate? Or showered? You smell like a fucking distillery."

"None of your business. Leave me the hell alone." I lunge for the bottle, but he dodges me and dumps the liquid down the drain.

"What the hell, Carter? That bottle costs two hundred grand!"

Matteo tosses the empty bottle into the trash with a bored expression. "That's like a dollar in your world."

I groan, dragging my hands through my hair, fisting it in frustration. "Why are you here?"

"I've been trying to get ahold of you for..." Matteo pretends to ponder, tapping his chin. "Like a week now."

I shoot him a glare. "I didn't want to be found."

"I can see that."

I slump back in a chair, refusing to meet his gaze. There's a reason I've been staying away from everything—and everyone. I'm a complete pain in the ass right now, weighed down by every bad decision I've made. Not just this summer, but my whole damn life. That article put a lot of things into perspective for me, so I guess something good came out of it, after all.

He sighs, sitting next to me. "She didn't write the article, you know."

I shrug. "Doesn't matter anymore." It's the truth. I don't care. I just miss her so much it's unbearable.

"So, you're going to what? Feel sorry for yourself the rest of your life?"

"I really thought you'd become less of a pain in my ass now that you're married to a woman who hates your guts," I quip dryly, trying to deflect. It's still hard to wrap my head around the fact he and Isabella got hitched.

He ignores my jab and presses on. "Max wrote the article. Sophia threatened him—said she'd go to the VP with all the proof that she's been doing his job for the past few years." He pauses, waiting for me to react. When I don't, he keeps going. "I'm risking a lot by telling you this. If Isabella finds out, I'll never hear the end of it." He shakes his head. "But..."

I raise an eyebrow, unimpressed. "But what?"

"Sophia's moving back to Kentucky. She's leaving tomorrow."

My heart plummets like a stone dropping into cold water. Moving? No. She loves this city. She wouldn't do that.

"After what Max pulled, she handed in her resignation, and now she's packed and ready to leave." Matteo leans closer, his voice firm. "You need to get your shit together and figure out how you're going to get her back."

"I'm not," I rasp, the words barely leaving my mouth.

Matteo grips my shoulder, his expression hardening as he looks me dead in the eyes. "You're a lot of things, Mancini, but a coward isn't one of them. You need to get her back. Ivy was right, you know? You need to stop believing you're not worthy of anything. That's a lie. You know that, man."

His words hit me harder than I'd like to admit. When you grow up without guidance, without knowing what true love looks like, it's hard to feel like you're deserving of it. It's something my mind simply can't wrap around.

Matteo stands, shooting me a pointed glare. "This is in your hands now," he says, his voice firm and final before he walks away, leaving me alone in the quiet of my apartment.

I clench my jaw, fighting the war raging inside. My heart screams at me to go after her, to fix everything, but my head keeps reminding me I'm not enough. Not for her, not for anyone. I've always believed that. Maybe I've spent too long living in the shadow of who I think I should be, instead of letting myself be the man I want to be. I've spent all my life running without knowing where I'm going to end up.

But what if, after all the running, this is the destiny I never saw coming?

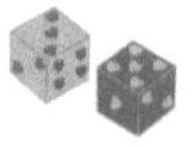

I've sat through board meetings that would break most men, made decisions that have altered people's life, but *nothing* compares to the anxiety gnawing at me as I stand outside Sophia's door. My hand hovers over the wood, my chest tight as I wrestle with whether or not I should even be here. What if she slams the door in my face?

What if she doesn't?

"Come on, Lorenzo," I mutter under my breath, urging myself to knock before my courage slips away. My fist makes contact with the door, and the longer the silence stretches, the more I regret everything. I didn't come with some grand plan, or even a good excuse. I just know I can't let her leave. Not like this. The thought of her disappearing from my life for good is unbearable.

She opens her door, and my breath catches at the sight of her. She looks...even more beautiful than I remember. Her hair is in a messy bun with the few loose strands that I know she hates but I think make her look devastatingly beautiful. She's wrapped in a cozy sweater, even though it's the middle of summer, and fuzzy socks peek out from beneath her sweatpants. It's so her—every detail, down to how she crosses her arms and lifts her chin as if trying to keep the world from seeing what she's feeling.

Everything I attempted—and miserably failed—to rehearse in my head vanishes, and all I can do is stand there, drinking in the sight of her. Just being near her brings me peace and a sort of comfort I haven't felt in God knows how long. But I know this calm is fragile. I'm standing on the edge of something, and I'm terrified of what comes next.

"Sophia," I finally manage, my voice low. "Can we talk?"

"We've already said everything we needed to say, Lorenzo." Her voice is steady as she reaches to close the door, but I stop it with my foot.

"Please." My voice cracks. "Give me five minutes."

She exhales, steps out, and crosses her arms. "Fine. Let's talk out here."

"Matteo told me the truth. About the article, and why Max did what he did."

"And?" she replies flatly.

"I came to..." I hesitate, rubbing the back of my neck, searching for the right words. "Apologize. I didn't let you explain. I shut you out, and you didn't deserve that."

"You're right. I didn't," she replies, her tone cold. Her walls are up, and I feel the distance between us like a physical barrier.

I nod, swallowing hard as I struggle to find the right words. "I messed up, Sophia. I was hurt, but that's no excuse. I should've listened to you, trusted you, instead of jumping to conclusions." My voice falters as I admit it out loud, the guilt heavy in my chest.

She raises an eyebrow, unimpressed. "So, now you want what? Forgiveness? Is that why you're here?"

"No," I blurt out, shaking my head quickly as desperation seeps into my voice. "I just—I couldn't let you leave without telling you." I grimace. "I know you're leaving tomorrow."

"Is that it?"

Her tone feels like a punch to the gut. *No, that's not it,* is what I want to say, but the words get stuck in my throat. I want to get on my knees, beg her to give me another chance. "I miss you, Blue," I manage to whisper.

For a moment, I think I see something in her eyes, a crack in her defenses, but then she shakes her head and steps back. "This doesn't change anything. I'm still leaving."

Panic claws at my chest, but I fight to keep calm. "I'm not asking you to stay, Sophia. I know you have responsibilities, your mom needs you. I'd never stand in the way of that."

She exhales slowly, her gaze drifting as though she's holding herself together. "I miss you, too," she says softly, her voice laced with exhaustion. "But you hurt me. You made me fall in love with you, only to take my heart and stomp on it, knowing full well there was a reason I never let anyone in." Her voice quivers at the end, and her words are like a sharp knife wounding my already fragile heart.

You made me fall in love with you.

Knowing this makes everything so much worse, and so much painful. Knowing we both fell hard, and fast, and I just...destroyed it all. The only good thing I had going for me.

Before I can reply, she turns and opens the door, and my body tenses, bracing for the blow I know is coming. "Have a nice life." She walks inside and shuts the door, leaving me standing in the hallway, heart in my hands, knowing I've lost the love of my life.

47

Lorenzo

4 weeks later...

"**A**re my eyes deceiving me?" Amos asks, amused. "You're blessing us with your presence?"

My jaw ticks at the tone of his smug voice, but I simply nod and take a seat without a word. These past few weeks, I've been really trying to get my life together, to fix everything before I go get my girl back.

Against all odds, Sophia Evans, the woman who completely flipped my world upside down, the one I've fallen deeply in love with, belongs with me. Even when I don't feel like a fraction of what she deserves yet, I'm working on it. It took a lot of self-reflection to realize all she needs is someone true to themself.

So here I am, taking the steps necessary to become the man she deserves.

The meeting goes by in a blur with more of the same talk—stricter acceptance guidelines and planning for the annual gala they throw for new members. Once we're finished, before they can call the meeting, I stand, clearing my throat. "Gentlemen, may I have a word?"

They exchange glances, frowning. Amos nods for me to continue.

"I've decided to resign as vice president, effective immediately," I say, keeping it direct. "I'm sure this comes as a surprise to some of you. You all worked with my father, and you know how proud he was of this place." I pause, swallowing the lump in my throat. "He trained me for this life from the moment I could walk. And I've tried to honor that. God knows I've tried." I let out a humorless laugh, shaking my head. "But I can't keep doing this. I can't keep pretending this is what I want. I'm not doing any of you a favor by sticking around."

I look around the room, meeting each of their gazes. "I know I've been a pain in the ass to work with, and that's because I never wanted this life. It was forced on me. I'll help with anything you need to make this transition as smooth as possible, but I'm done. This is it for me."

The room is silent for a long beat, and I feel the weight finally lift off my shoulders. This has been long overdue, walking away from the legacy, the name—it's time. Someone else can carry it forward. I've spent years chasing my father's approval, and I did my best, but the fact is he's gone, and it's time I start living my own life.

Amos finally speaks, nodding slowly, "I think I speak for everyone when I say we appreciate your honesty and knowing when to step down." He pauses, glancing around. "As you know, the guidelines state you can choose a successor, ideally from your family line. Do you have anyone in mind?"

I nod. "I believe you all know my cousin, Nico Mancini."

Amos raises his eyebrows, surprised. "Doesn't he live in New York?"

"He does," I confirm. "But he's got some business in

Chicago now, so he'll be going back and forth. And honestly, Nico would be a great addition to this place."

Nico Mancini is a force to be reckoned with. He's fought for everything he's got, and I know Vortex could use someone like him. He grew up under the shadow of impossible expectations from my uncle. The pressure has only made him stronger. Nico thrives in this cutthroat business world, in the ruthless tactics Vortex embodies. He's always belonged in a place like this.

Right now, he's in the middle of a battle for the CEO position of *Imperium Press*, competing with his older siblings. Landing a position here could tip the scales in his favor, proving to our uncle he's the right one to take over the largest newspaper company in the country. Nico knows how to maneuver through these circles better than anyone I've met, and that's exactly why I know he's the change Vortex needs.

He's also helped me achieve something only a man like him could pull off, so I owe him. But I was going to offer it to him anyway, even if he hadn't helped me.

Will this cause a war within the Mancini family? Most likely. But the position was rightfully mine from the start, so I get to decide who I want to pass it down to.

"I wish I could say it was a pleasure working with you all, but we both know it wasn't."

The room fills with knowing chuckles, and I find myself laughing along with them.

"I'll always remain a member here—this place is practically where I grew up," I add, glancing around one last time. "And I can't wait to see what's next from the sidelines."

I give them a curt nod as I stand, walking away from the table with a sense of lightness I haven't felt in years.

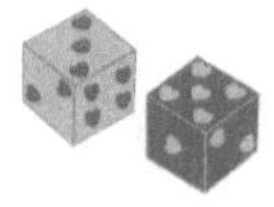

The conference room at *Vogue Elite* feels unnervingly calm as Nico and I sit at the head of the table, waiting for the guest of the hour to arrive. With Matteo's help—the tech genius he is—we uncovered some valuable information: the owner of *Vogue Elite* had made a string of poor investments, and the truth was, the company was hanging by a thread.

Luckily, *Imperium Press* specializes in buying struggling web media businesses and turning them around in no time. When I presented Nico with everything I had uncovered, he didn't hesitate to jump at the opportunity. This deal was as beneficial for him as it was for me. Bringing a company of such a high caliber as this one to the *Imperium Press* corporation is a huge win for Nico.

Mila, Nico's assistant, steps into the room. "He's here."

Nico gives a sharp nod. "Let him in."

Max strides in, surprise lacing his features when his eyes find mine. I really have no business being here, but I wasn't going to pass up the opportunity of seeing this asshole get what he deserves.

Nico stands, buttoning his suit. "Please, take a seat."

Max sits, looking around expectantly. "What's going on?"

"I'm Nico Mancini—"

Max interrupts, nodding eagerly. "Yeah, I know who you are. You're doing great things over at Imperium. It's an honor to meet you."

"Can't say the same," Nico deadpans. Pleasantries have never been his strong suit. He flicks his wrist, checking his watch with a bored expression. "I'll get straight to the point. *Vogue Elite* is under new management, and a few things were brought to our attention. After completing our investigations, we've discovered that not only were you abusing your position of power by making one of your employees do all of your work for you, but you also twisted an article to fit your narrative and published it under said employee's byline without her approval."

Max raises his hands in defense. "Everything I used for that article was taken from her notes."

"I don't give a fuck if you got those notes from Jesus himself. She had a complete, perfect article, and you twisted it because you felt threatened." Nico deadpans.

"Threatened?" Max sneers. "She was a good-for-nothing, mediocre journalist—"

"Mediocre?" I snap, unable to hold back. "The same mediocre journalist who has been doing your fucking job for years?"

Nico shoots me a withering glare, warning me to step back. We agreed I wouldn't intervene, but fuck it if I'm going to let him talk about Sophia like that.

Nico gives Max an enigmatic look. "I didn't call you here to have a debate. To be honest, I'm surprised you think I gave you the impression I care what you have to say. You're fired. And good luck finding a job as an editor in chief, because, as you know, Imperium owns about 90% of the media business. The other 10%? Well, I've made sure to inform them of your actions."

Max's face reddens, his eyes bulging as he stands abruptly. "You have no right, and no evidence—"

Nico interrupts without looking up, grabbing some paperwork from the table instead. "I assure you we have enough evidence." He looks up, tilting his head. "Did you think deleting all the emails from your employee's laptop was going to be enough? We have everything and more. So I suggest you leave, because I have very little patience for people who dare to question me."

Max is at a loss for words, the vein in his forehead so pronounced it gives me a sense of satisfaction like no other. The taste of victory is sweet, and knowing justice has been served has a sense of relief rushing through me. Without a word, Max walks out of the conference room with his head down, fume practically coming out of his ears.

"Good riddance," Nico mutters. "Honestly, he was probably going to get fired anyway. His qualifications are practically nonexistent. The only reason he got that position is because he's the nephew of the former owner." He shakes his head. "Fucking nepotism, man."

"Tell me about it." I laugh, scrubbing my face. "Thank you for this, man."

"No need to thank me. Taking over this company has been something my father always wanted, and the fact I got to secure this, well... I should be the one thanking you."

I salute. "Glad to be of service."

He laughs, shaking his head. "Listen, if your girl ever wants to come back and work here, we need an editor in chief. The position is hers if she wants it."

"I can tell her, but she's stubborn, I doubt she'll take the handout."

Nico gives me a confused look. "This is not a handout, trust me. I've been reading and researching the work Max passed as his. She's really talented, we need people like her here."

Pride fills my chest as I hear those words.

Now that everything's finally falling in line, there's only one thing left to do.

Sophia

4 weeks later...

"**M**om, that box is heavy. Let me do it," I say, grabbing the box labeled *POTS AND PANS* from her hands.

She scrunches her nose. "I think I liked it better when you were in Chicago."

I gasp dramatically. "I'm offended!"

Mom pulls me into a side-hug, laughing. "I'm lying. It's nice having you here."

I shake my head, feigning a pout as I carry the box out to the moving truck. It's been a little over two months since I came back home. I managed to land a waitressing job downtown about a month in. The hours are tough, but the tips make it worth it. It's not a forever thing—just temporary—but it's given me the chance to move us out of this house faster than I expected.

In between the chaos of packing and working, Mom and I have had some real conversations, the kind we didn't get to have when I was always busy in Chicago and always worrying about her. It feels good, like we're making up for lost time. While working at *Vogue Elite* wasn't the best experience, it helped me discover I actually enjoy the editing and proofing side of journalism. So once we're all settled in the new place, I'm going to start looking for a new job. There are a lot of remote opportunities, but even if a good one requires moving, Mom's on board with relocating. There's nothing for us here except bitter memories of my father, and now that we're moving out, that's all they will remain as—memories.

I've thought about going back to Chicago someday, but the idea of being in the same city as Lorenzo is still too painful. I don't hold a grudge for how he reacted when everything went down. I've come to understand Lorenzo has always been private for a reason, and when things got tough, his instinct was to assume the worst. That's all he's ever known. But the memories...they're still too fresh. Too raw for me to go back to the city.

I'd be lying if I said I don't think of him, because I do. Every day. And even though it's been so long since I last saw him, the feelings haven't faded. I'm still deeply, madly in love with Lorenzo. There's no denying I miss him—terribly.

But it doesn't change anything. We were doomed from the start. We were always going to end in heartbreak, because that's all *I've* ever known.

"Where do you want these boxes?" Matteo's voice calls out.

Somehow, the girls convinced the guys to help me move. Damian offered to pay for a moving company, but Aria and Isabella wanted to spend time with me, so they dragged the guys along. I'm still not sure how they managed it. I guess love really conquers all.

"Those are donations. Just put them in my car," I shout back.

Damian walks out with a couple of boxes, setting them down with a grunt. "I think that's the last of it."

"Thanks, guys. Dinner's on me tonight," I offer.

He shrugs casually. "No need. You know we'd do anything for you, right?" His pointed look throws me off guard.

I cross my arms, raising a brow. "And here I thought you hated me."

"He doesn't hate anyone," Matteo cuts in with a smirk. "He just looks like he's got a pole stuck up his ass."

Damian smacks Matteo on the back of the head. "Shut up."

Matteo rubs his head, wincing. "Hate it when you do that."

"Then stop talking nonsense."

"Hey." I lift my chin at Matteo, changing the subject. "How's it going with the missus?"

He scrubs his face and lets out a long sigh.

I wince. "That bad?"

He chuckles, shaking his head. "Not bad at all. Just an adjustment now that I've moved in."

"I can't believe she let you move in. Her place is like a personal temple."

He gives me a knowing look. "Exactly. The place is ridiculously small, but hey, whatever the wifey wants, she gets."

Damian fake coughs, muttering, "Pussy-whipped."

Matteo glares at him. "Like you're one to talk."

The girls and my mom come out of the house with the last few items. Aria walks straight into Damian's arms for a tight hug, while Isabella throws daggers at Matteo with her eyes as she heads toward my car. Whatever's going on between them, I don't get it. But hey, there's a fine line between love and hate, and I'm positive those two will be crossing it at any time.

"The guys are going to drop the stuff at the apartment, and we'll go to the hotel and have some fun. Yeah?" Aria says, linking our arms as we walk to my car.

"I'm going with the guys, too, want to get my room settled tonight," Mom says, waving her hand as she gets into the truck.

I look at Aria with a frown, shaking my head. "I have to be there to help them unload."

Aria waves her hand dismissively. "They can handle that. You are going to the hotel with us. You can't say no to a bride; it's bad luck!"

"How long are you going to keep using that excuse?" I ask, raising an eyebrow.

"You'd be happy to know we're getting married in December." Aria beams.

I stop dead in my tracks. "Wait. That's in like two months! How are we going to have time to plan?"

"Relax." She laughs. "We're having a small ceremony in Italy, only close friends and family. Turns out planning is too damn stressful."

I shriek with excitement and hug her tightly. "I can't believe you're officially becoming Mrs. Romano," I groan, overwhelmed. "I can't believe both of my best friends are married ladies!"

"You could be in the same boat..." she singsongs, teasing me.

"Yeah? Do you see any prospects lining up?" I rest a hand on my hip, feeling the familiar pang of disappointment. "Besides, you know me."

"Have you heard from him?" Aria's tone shifts, becoming more serious.

I shrug, avoiding her gaze. "No." Not that I expected anything from him, anyway. We said what we needed to say.

"I'm sure you'll hear from him." Aria shrugs, her tone laced with a conviction I wish I could believe. My best friend has always managed to see the good in everything, and while I'm all for that, I don't think that's the case. Sure, Lorenzo and I had a lot in common and a connection I've never had with anyone before, but that can only get you so far.

You just keep lying to yourself, even though you know if he were right in front of you, you would give him another chance.

I've thought about that a lot. I miss his friendship and the way he cared for me. I miss laughing every time he guessed the title of the show or movie I'm quoting. I miss our conversations and how everything flowed between us so easily, like we were always meant to find each other and pick up where we left off in a past life.

It's funny to think when I met him I didn't believe in destiny, thought it was a fairy tale. And in a way, it may still be. But now, after experiencing what it was like to fall in love with the last person I thought possible, destiny seems like a real possibility. Falling in love with him felt like discovering a piece of myself I didn't know was missing. And even though that piece was ripped out of me, I wouldn't change a thing. The memories will live in my head for the rest of my life, and I can't help but feel grateful for them.

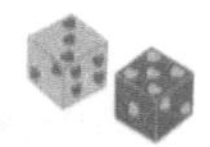

The last thing I wanted to do was go out, but the girls

insisted on making a whole day out of it. I'm talking spa, manicures and pedicures, the whole nine yards. I'm trying not to dwell on the fact that, once they leave, it'll just be Mom and me again. So, I'm soaking up every last moment with my best friends.

"Is curling my hair really necessary? It's only dinner, Aria."

"When was the last time we all got ready like this and actually had fun? When did you become such a buzzkill?" Aria teases.

"She misses Lorenzo, and it's making her miserable," Isabella adds, applying her lipstick.

I glare at her playfully. "Careful, *Mrs. Carter*, don't get on my bad side."

Isabella rolls her eyes, leaning against the sink. "That joke's getting old."

"How's married life treating you?" Aria wiggles her eyebrows.

Isabella presses her lips together and shrugs, still refusing to give us any details.

As we continue getting ready, music playing in the background, I have to admit I'm starting to enjoy myself. I used to love nights like these, laughing with my friends, getting all dressed up. I know it'll feel different once they leave, but little by little, I want to get out there again, start building a life outside of work.

When we're finally ready, we head downstairs and hop into an Uber. The ride is quick, and as I step out of the car, I pause when the girls don't follow me.

Instead, Isabella rolls the window down and smirks. "I want to point out this wasn't my idea."

"Why aren't you guys getting out?"

Aria's head pops out next to Isabella's. "Have fun! Love you!" she says before the car speeds off.

I groan in frustration, pulling my phone out to fire off a long, annoyed text to Aria, when a deep, raspy voice behind me stops me in my tracks.

"Hi, Blue."

There's only one person who calls me that. My heart catches in my throat, and I turn around to see Lorenzo standing there. He looks painfully handsome in a dark-gray suit that fits him in all the right places paired with a white dress shirt, a few buttons undone. He's grown a bit of a beard now, neatly trimmed, and the look suits him more than I care to admit. His hair is styled lazily, just how I like it.

I swallow hard, my pulse quickening as our eyes meet. "What are you doing here?"

He eats the distance between us, and with each step, I feel my heart beating harder and harder. Without a word, he hands me a small bouquet of purple Madagascar Periwinkles and a letter in my mom's handwriting.

"What's this?"

He rubs the back of his neck, shrugging with a shy smile. "Read it first."

With a frown, I open the letter.

Honey,

You've grown into a woman I'm incredibly proud of. You've always been the best daughter anyone could ask for—loyal, kind, and endlessly selfless, always putting others ahead of yourself.

But it's time for a change.

It's time to let yourself be loved, and I think Lorenzo might be exactly what you need. I'll be honest—he was an idiot, that much is clear. But it took real courage for him to come to me and ask for help. I know life hasn't been easy for you, and I didn't set the best example when it comes to love, but don't let that hold you back from the happiness you deserve.

I'm writing to tell you one thing: listen to him with an open heart and mind.

It's time to start putting yourself first.

Love,

Mom

I close the letter, my eyes locking with his. "You went to my mother?"

He shrugs, a knowing smile tugging at the corners of his lips. "If anyone could convince you to hear me out, it was her."

I cross my arms, silently urging him to keep talking. He's right, and it's moments like this that remind me why ending things with him hurt so much. No one knows me like he does.

He rubs a hand over his face, sighing deeply. "There's a reason I didn't come back for you these past two months. It wasn't because I didn't want to—it's because I knew, in order to deserve you, I had to become the kind of man worthy of you." He pauses for a moment, letting the weight of his words settle between us. "I was an idiot. I jumped to conclusions, because I was raised to believe people who get close to you always have an agenda."

My heart aches. Not for Lorenzo, the man standing before me, but for the boy he used to be—the one who was raised in a cold, ruthless world. The one who never knew a mother's love and had a father who only cared about one thing. It must have been lonely, and when you don't know what is like outside of that, it's easy to create a wall so tall, believing it's there to protect you, when instead it just makes you more lonely.

"In a messed-up way," he continues, his voice softer now, "I convinced myself you wrote that article because I needed a reason to push you away. I thought you were settling by being with me. You're strong, Sophia. You're fierce and capable, and you deserve someone who can take care of you, someone you can rely on." His breath catches, voice trembling slightly. "You are, without question, the most incredible person I've ever met. You deserve the world, and no words could ever fully explain just how much."

His words tighten something in my chest. I know he means every one of them, and that's what makes it so hard.

"Lorenzo," I say, struggling to keep my voice steady. "You broke my heart."

"I know." He steps closer, gently taking my hand in his. "And I want to spend the rest of my life making it up to you." His back straightens as he squares his shoulders, determination in his eyes. "I quit Vortex four weeks ago."

My eyes widen in surprise.

"And I took care of Max. I know you're going to say it wasn't my place, but it was. My job is to protect you, to take care of you. What he did was wrong. I have no regrets."

My breath catches slightly. I'm at a loss for words, my head spinning too fast as I try my best to catch up.

After a beat of silence, his voice lowers. "You asked me once if I'd ever been in love. Ask me again."

"Lorenzo—"

"Ask me again," he insists, his gaze never leaving mine.

I sigh, my shoulders slumping as I give in. "Have you ever been in love?"

His hand cups my cheek, thumb brushing lightly across my skin as he leans in, eyes full of emotion. "Yes," he whispers. "I see everything so clearly now. A part of me knew since the day you walked into my life that this was the only possible outcome. I'm in love with you, Sophia Annette Evans. I just didn't know how to see it or how to handle it. I didn't know how to let myself have something real. But there was never any question—my heart has always belonged to you."

The walls I've tried to build around my heart these past two months start to crumble at his confession, each word breaking through my defenses.

He absently licks his lips, his gaze never leaving mine. "I want to be the person you've always dreamed of. Build a life with you. Grow old together. I want it all—the kids, the house with the white picket fence, family dinners on Sundays." He takes a shaky breath. "I want the kind of normal that only exists with you."

He looks down for a moment, shaking his head before meeting my gaze again, his voice breaking, heavy with vulnerability. "You once said the idea of someone taking care of you felt strange, but that's where you're wrong. Because I'm here, Blue. I'm right here, with my heart and arms open, ready to take care of you." He pauses for a moment. "Just...please, stay. Don't walk away from me."

"I can't believe you remembered that," I say, my breath catching.

"I remember everything. Making you happy—that's my job." He smiles. "So, what do you say?"

"That's a lot of promises, Ace."

He gives me a small, knowing smirk. "Not promises. Guarantees," he replies confidently.

"I want to believe you, Lorenzo. I really do." I pause, my eyes flicking away as I press my lips together. "But words...they're just words."

"What if I show you instead?"

I let out a small, skeptical laugh. "How do you plan on doing that?"

"Do you trust me?"

Strangely, despite everything...I do. Deep down, I always have. I simply nod, and without another word, he grabs my hand.

"Where are we going?"

He looks at me with a knowing smile. "Back where you belong."

Sophia

The flight back to Chicago was quicker than I expected, but not quick enough to calm the storm brewing inside me. I asked Lorenzo a million questions, each one met with an amused smile and a gentle, "You'll see," until I finally gave up. Now, as we drive through the quiet streets, my nerves start to unravel.

This was such a bad idea. What was I thinking?

The car slows to a stop, and Lorenzo steps out without a word. He walks around to my side, opening the door with that same knowing look in his eyes. I take a deep breath and step out, my feet hitting the pavement, and when I finally look up, my breath catches in my throat.

We're standing in front of a gorgeous suburban house, with a sprawling front yard wrapped in a perfect white fence. The house itself is beautiful, modern yet warm, with large windows that reflect the evening light. The patio is wide, with a swing and a space that could easily fit a garden or a few kids running around.

Lorenzo stands beside me, his eyes tracing the same path mine are, and after a moment, he breaks the silence.

"This is our home, Sophia. Where we're going to build the life of our dreams." His voice is soft but certain, each word settling deeper in my chest.

I turn to look at him, my heart pounding erratically. "What do you mean, *our* home?"

He smiles, taking my hand in his. "Come inside."

We step through the front door, and my eyes widen in disbelief. The house is already furnished—elegant but cozy, with little touches that scream *us*. And then I see it. Familiar frames on the walls, a few of my favorite books stacked neatly on the shelves, a blanket I've had since I was a kid draped over the couch.

My things.

I whip around, eyes wide. "How...how did you?"

Lorenzo grins, pulling me closer. "Let's just say there was a reason the girls wanted to have one last night with you." He laughs softly. "To distract you while your mom and the guys flew back with your things to get everything ready."

I blink, completely overwhelmed. "But what about my mom? I don't want her living in Kentucky all by herself anymore. She needs—"

Before I can finish, he squeezes my hand, pulling me gently toward the back patio. My heart stutters when we step outside. Just past the big patio and pool, there's a charming guest house, small but beautiful, tucked neatly into the corner of the yard. The lights inside are already on, casting a welcoming glow.

"Your mom knew about this from the start, she's been helping me plan this for weeks," Lorenzo says softly. "She will be living in the guest house. It's already set up."

Tears prick my eyes as I stare at the guest house then back at Lorenzo. "You did all this for me?"

His thumb brushes against my cheek. "I did it for *us*. I

meant what I said, Blue. I want everything with you. And that means making sure the people we love are taken care of, too."

I can barely find the words. My chest is so full it hurts. "I don't know what to say."

He presses a soft kiss to my forehead. "Say you'll stay with me. That's all I want."

A tear escapes down my face, and before I can wipe it away, he does it for me. Like always. I let out a soft laugh, shaking my head. "For a girl who doesn't like showing emotion, I sure show a lot when it comes to you."

Lorenzo pulls me into his arms, pressing a tender kiss to the top of my head. "You never have to hide from me. I love you, no matter what."

I tilt my head back to look at him, taking in every inch of his face. His eyes, filled with so much adoration, find mine, and I get lost in them for a moment. How did I fall so deeply for this man? This man who sees me so completely and loves me anyway.

"Lorenzo?"

"Yes, Blue?"

"I love you, too."

The smile that spreads across his face is radiant and infectious, I can't help but match it.

"Ready to build a life with me?" he asks, his voice light but full of meaning.

I pretend to think it over for a moment then bite my lip with a nod, which earns me a soft laugh from him.

"This is crazy. What if I had said no?"

Lorenzo places both hands at the nape of my neck, his fingers threading through my hair as his lips capture mine in a way that makes my entire body melt. The kiss is slow, but it's deep and consuming, both of us pouring every ounce of love and promise into it.

When we pull back, he rests his forehead against mine, his breath warm against my skin. "There was never any question, baby. You and I were always destined for each other."

One year older, and how my life has changed.

For my birthday, we decided to go to Panamá. It seemed fitting.

It's funny how a year ago, I was celebrating my birthday feeling sad, empty, and overwhelmed by the life I had. That day had been one of the darkest moments in my life, yet it became the turning point I never knew I needed.

As I sit here, at the same beach where we told each other our deepest secrets, enjoying the warm breeze, I can't help but wonder, if I hadn't walked out of my restaurant that day to take a break from it all, would I have still met Sophia? If Aria hadn't insisted Sophia come to my birthday party, would fate have found another way to weave our lives together?

It's a strange thought, contemplating the butterfly effect of our choices. Every moment—every decision—has the power to alter the course of our lives. I think back to that day when I felt like I was drowning in expectations and responsibilities. How life pushed us to find each other and discover within each other what we needed, and what we deserved.

Sophia approaches, holding a small cake she worked on baking all day while FaceTiming Isabella for help. I love my girl, but she's a lousy cook and baker. I tried to help her, but she slapped my hand away and told me to get out, and I cherish my life, so I listened. The cake is round, with a simple white frosting and wobbly red handwriting that spells *HAPPY BIRTHDAY ACE*. As she sings "Happy Birthday" to me, I look at her with a smile, holding back the lump forming in my throat and the happy tears.

As I blow out the candles, I can't shake the feeling that I'm celebrating more than another year of life. I'm celebrating the serendipity of love, the twists and turns that brought Sophia into my world. I'm grateful for the chance encounters, the gentle nudges from fate that led us here. It's a reminder that sometimes, in the chaos of life, the universe has a way of guiding us to where we truly belong.

Without her, I wouldn't have realized the life I was living wasn't sustainable. Now, thanks to her, I'm pursuing what I love. While my restaurants are being managed by people I trust, I decided to start culinary school. To many, that seemed surprising and like a waste of time, given how much experience I already have. But it feels right. I'm working toward something, an achievement I can't wait to accomplish. I still have a year left, but in the meantime, the simplicity of it all makes me feel...complete.

Sophia has grown into her incredible career in no time, and it's nothing short of inspiring. After much back and forth, she had a meeting with Nico about six months ago, which led her to accept the editor-in-chief position where she worked until recently. She has been doing such a fantastic job, especially with *Vogue Elite* transitioning to new management. Because of her dedication and talent, she was offered the Executive Director of the Midwest Region, overseeing all the editor-in-chiefs in the area.

It's been amazing to witness her career blossom from what it was a mere year ago. She has finally started to receive the recognition she deserves for all the hard work she's put in.

"We should go back and cut the cake. I can't promise it's good, though." Sophia grimaces.

I kiss the side of her head, chuckling. "I'm sure it's great."

As we walk back into the villa, the same one that gave us the summer of our lives last year—which we own now—the nerves start to bubble up. Sophia busies herself cutting the cake, her laughter filling the space, while I glance at my phone. A text from Aria pops up, and I have to hold back a laugh at their impatience.

ARIA

Where are you?!

ME

Still at the house.

ARIA

Enzo, OMG!

ARIA

Lorenzo Mancini, I don't have all of my life, you know? Get to it. —Charlotte

ME

We'll arrive at the restaurant in thirty, max. I promise.

ARIA

I'm starting a timer. Hurry up!

The restaurant I opened in Panamá has quickly become

my favorite—not because of its success, but because of what it represents. I named it after Sophia's nickname—Blue—but in Spanish, Azúl. The whole place is imbued with soft, romantic vibes, with Madagascar periwinkles adorning the outside—all purple, of course. The restaurant feels like an extension of us, something we've built together, though she doesn't know just how much yet.

Aria even made a series of beautiful paintings that hang on the walls, and it's all been coming together piece by piece. Every time we visit, we add something new—something to give it that homey feel. Because that's what I want this restaurant to be for us—a place we can always come back to, filled with memories and reminders of the life we're building.

"Here, try," she says, lifting a forkful of cake to my mouth.

A satisfied groan escapes me as I savor the rich, chocolate goodness. "Baby, this is amazing."

Her blue eyes sparkle, stealing my breath away. "Yeah?"

I nod, wrapping my arm around her waist. She leans into me, her arms slipping around my shoulders as our lips meet in a slow, sweet kiss. It's crazy how each day I grow more addicted to her. Doesn't matter how much time has passed, the love I have for this woman consumes every bone in my body.

"We're going to be late," I say, reluctantly pulling back and grabbing her hand.

"Where are we going?" She frowns, letting go to slip on her sandals then trailing behind me.

"We have dinner reservations at Azúl."

She rolls her eyes, a playful grin on her lips. "You *own* the place. We don't need a reservation."

I shrug, trying to hide the grin threatening to break

through. "They've been booked." The lie is weak, and she knows it, but she simply shrugs, grabs my hand, and rests her head on my arm as we make our way out.

As we walk toward the restaurant, I guide her to the beach that's in front of it. The sun is beginning to set, and nerves have me on a chokehold, because I want it to be perfect. As we approach, her steps start to slow as she takes in the sight. Thousands and thousands of purple Madagascar periwinkles are arranged in a massive heart shape, each one glowing under the flicker of countless candles scattered around them, their soft light dancing in the golden hues of the sunset.

Her eyes find mine as she covers her mouth with her hands, at a loss for words.

With a shaky breath, I guide her to the center of the heart and step in front of her, taking her hand in mine as I drop to one knee. Her eyes widen more, tears already welling.

"Blue," I begin, my voice breaking as my heart pounds wildly in my chest. "A year ago today you came back into my life and changed me in ways I never thought possible. You challenged me in ways no one has ever done. After all the games." We both laugh. "After all the broken deals and the risks we took...there's only one deal left I want to make. A permanent one."

Tears start to fall down her face as I continue, and I rasp my throat, trying to hold back mine, but it's no use. My view becomes a bit hazy as I keep talking.

"I want to spend the rest of my life loving you, protecting you, and continue to build this life together with you. No more running, no more doubts. Just you and me, forever. That's the deal. What do you say? Care to make me the happiest man in the world and marry me?"

For a moment, time seems to freeze as she stares at me, her lips trembling before a soft smile breaks through. "Yes, Ace," she whispers, her voice full of emotion. "You got yourself a deal."

Relief and joy flood through me as I stand, pulling her into my arms. We laugh through our tears, and when our lips meet, the world fades away for the briefest moment. But then the sound of cheering and clapping brings us back to the moment. Sophia spins around, her eyes wide as she sees her mom and all of our closest friends running toward us, beaming with excitement.

"What did you do!?" she exclaims, her eyes wide with disbelief.

I gently lift her chin, locking her gaze with mine. "This is the start of our lives, and I couldn't think of a better way to begin it than with the people we love most here with us."

Her lip wobbles as her smile deepens, and she throws her arms around me. "I love you, Ace."

I tuck a loose strand of hair behind her ear and kiss the tip of her nose. "I love you way, way more, Blue."

She hums, teasing. "Doubtful."

I chuckle, scooping her up and spinning her around, her laughter ringing out as her head tilts back, carefree and full of happiness. "We have the rest of our lives to figure out who wins," I say, my heart swelling with the thought.

And in this moment, as her laughter fills the air, I know I get to be the one to make her laugh and smile for the rest of our lives—like it was always meant to be.

THE END.

Thank You!

If you enjoyed reading *Broken Deal*, consider leaving a review on Amazon. Reviews are like tips for authors, and it helps spread the word to other lovely readers like you!

Would you like to be the first to know what I'm working on, get some amazing book recs, and much more? Then join my newsletter, Yinn's Cove! PS. I always share extra, exclusive teasers over there. ;)

OTHER BOOKS BY YINN QUIRÓS

WINDY CITY BILLIONAIRES SERIES

BROKEN PIECES

CHICAGO STRIKERS SERIES

FALSE PLAY

Acknowledgements

Wow! What a rollercoaster of emotions writing this book was. Seriously, I can't tell if I'm sad or happy that it's over (I'm lying. I'm most definitely sad). This couple fought me A LOT, to the point where I was crying from frustration more often than not. But in the end... I fell in love with them HARD. These two hold such a special place in my heart, and I can't even begin to explain how much they mean to me.

After the release of *Broken Pieces*, writing this book was a real challenge. I wanted you all to love Sophia and Lorenzo as much as you loved Aria and Damian, so the pressure I put on myself was overwhelming. There were so many late nights writing until 3:00 AM, rewriting chapter after chapter and overthinking EVERY single word I wrote. These characters defied me every step of the way, but they also made me grow as both a person and an author. And for that, I will be eternally grateful.

I've heard authors say that writing a book takes a village and that it's always an adventure. To be honest, I never really understood that... until now. There are so many people I want to thank, but first, as always, I want to thank *you*—the reader. It's because of you that I get to write and bring these characters to life. Thank you for taking the time to read my books and for falling in love with my characters. I pour my heart and soul into every story, and I couldn't do this without your support.

Anthony—I don't think Lorenzo would exist if it weren't for you. You've been my partner for almost eight years now (and counting), and the support you've given me, the way you take care of me... well, I guess what I'm trying to say is that I'm thankful to have a book-boyfriend type of man in my life. Thank you for loving me and supporting me. I love you.

Ginger—You've become one of my closest friends throughout my career, and I'm so thankful for that. You understand how lonely being a writer can be, so I'm glad we have each other for this crazy ride. Thank you for supporting me, for always making me laugh when I needed it most, and for calling me out when I needed to get my shit together (lol).

Karla—Thank you for supporting me, for keeping my chaotic self organized, and for always listening when I needed someone to vent to. Your friendship means the world to me.

Aline—Thank you for being the ray of sunshine in our little group. You always make me laugh, and your perfect dose of crazy is exactly what I need in my life.

Andrea—I don't know how I got so lucky to find such an incredible editor, but I'm beyond grateful. Thank you for helping bring this story to life and for loving these characters as much as I do.

Ramona—Thank you for giving this book the love and care it needed and for helping me make it shine.

Street Team/ARC Team—You all are the BEST. Thank

you for supporting me, for fangirling over these characters, and for making my job so much fun. Being an author isn't easy, but your love and encouragement in my DMs make every challenge worth it. I wouldn't be here without you.

Until the next time!

Xoxo,
Yinn

Yinn Quirós is an indie romance author who loves writing epic love stories with laugh-out-loud banter, men who yearn like it physically hurts them, and plenty of spice. She loves all things sports (especially F1 and hockey), romance, and music.

When she's not writing, you can find her watching games or races, walking around the windy city with her rescued puppy, or listening to music and curating playlists for all the stories that live rent-free inside her head. You can find Yinn on all socials under **@yinnquirosauthor**.